SURRENDER

They snuggled down by the fire and pulled the blanket more closely around them. It was snowing steadily now, covering the earth with a white velvet blanket.

Summer felt warm and securely content. They lay like two spoons as he kissed the nape of her neck.

"Dearest," she whispered, "it wouldn't hurt anything if you only kissed me a little."

"No harm in that, Little One."

He leaned over and kissed her deeply. She felt her pulse quicken. She had not forgotten how his tender touch made her want him beyond reason. She breathed in his warm scent and kissed him back. The fire of desire burned hotter and brighter between them. She wanted more than kisses and caresses. She wanted all he had to give. . . .

TODAY'S HOTTEST READS
ARE TOMORROW'S SUPERSTARS

VICTORY'S WOMAN   (4484, $4.50)
by Gretchen Genet
Andrew—the carefree soldier who sought glory on the battlefield,
and returned a shattered man . . . Niall—the legendary frontiers-
man and a former Shawnee captive, tormented by his past . . .
Roger—the troubled youth, who would rise up to claim a shock-
ing legacy . . . and Clarice—the passionate beauty bound by one
man, and hopelessly in love with another. Set against the back-
drop of the American revolution, three men fight for their
heritage—and one woman is destined to change all their lives forever!

FORBIDDEN   (4488, $4.99)
by Jo Beverley
While fleeing from her brothers, who are attempting to sell her
into a loveless marriage, Serena Riverton accepts a carriage ride
from a stranger—who is the handsomest man she has ever seen.
Lord Middlethorpe, himself, is actually contemplating marriage
to a dull daughter of the aristocracy, when he encounters the
breathtaking Serena. She arouses him as no woman ever has. And
after a night of thrilling intimacy—a forbidden liaison—Serena
must choose between a lady's place and a woman's passion!

WINDS OF DESTINY   (4489, $4.99)
by Victoria Thompson
Becky Tate is a half-breed outcast—branded by her Comanche
heritage. Then she meets a rugged stranger who awakens her
heart to the magic and mystery of passion. Hiding a desperate
past, Texas Ranger Clint Masterson has ridden into cattle country
to bring peace to a divided land. But a greater battle rages inside
him when he dares to desire the beautiful Becky!

WILDEST HEART   (4456, $4.99)
by Virginia Brown
Maggie Malone had come to cattle country to forge her future as
a healer. Now she was faced by Devon Conrad, an outlaw
wounded body and soul by his shadowy past . . . whose eyes
blazed with fury even as his burning caress sent her spiraling with
desire. They came together in a Texas town about to explode in sin
and scandal. Danger was their destiny—and there was nothing
they wouldn't dare for love!

*Available wherever paperbacks are sold, or order direct from the
Publisher. Send cover price plus 50¢ per copy for mailing and
handling to Penguin USA, P.O. Box 999, c/o Dept. 17109,
~oenfield, NJ 07621. Residents of New York and Tennessee
᳘lude sales tax. DO NOT SEND CASH.*

GEORGINA GENTRY

CHEYENNE SPLENDOR

ZEBRA BOOKS
KENSINGTON PUBLISHING CORP.

ZEBRA BOOKS are published by

Kensington Publishing Corp.
850 Third Avenue
New York, NY 10022

Zebra and the Z logo Reg. U.S. Pat. & TM Off.

First Printing: November, 1994

Printed in the United States of America

For our only son, Sean, who is his father's pride, his mother's joy;
and
For Kris, the lovely Cajun beauty who became our third daughter through marrying him.

Chapter One

Late November, 1864

He wanted to make love to her. In the glow of their cozy tipi fire, the Cheyenne half-breed, Iron Knife, watched Summer curled asleep in the hollow of his big shoulder. He cuddled her closer and gently brushed a yellow lock of hair from her forehead, studying her heart-shaped face. Summer had grown even prettier and more precious to him in the six years that she had been his woman.

What an unlikely pair, he thought as he leaned over to kiss her lips. That long-ago day when the rich Boston debutante had been stolen from a stagecoach, Iron Knife had fought a fellow dog soldier, Angry Wolf, for possession of the beauty. First, Summer had been Iron Knife's captive, but gradually, he was the one who became a prisoner ... of desire.

Summer sighed and smiled in her sleep. Encouraged, he glanced around at their three small children snuggled down in their buffalo robes, safe and warm against the Colorado chill. All their little ones were asleep. The cold wind whipped around his lodge, and he pulled the fur robe up around Summer's shoulders, enjoying the feel of her soft body against his big one. They both liked the touch of fur against their bare flesh and sleeping naked in each other's arms. He wanted her, but he had not made love to her for months now. They must not have another child soon. Having her in his arms, yet not being able to possess her completely, made him think of nothing else.

He pulled her naked body against him and began to kiss her lips. They parted slightly, and he caressed them with his tongue, holding her against him so that he could feel her full breasts and the heat of her belly and long legs.

Summer stirred in her sleep, and he leaned over and kissed the tip of her nose. *"Ne-mehotatse,"* he whispered. Her pale blue eyes flickered open and she smiled up at him. "Shh! I love you, too, but you'll wake the children."

"They're all sound asleep." He held her even closer, thinking her eyes were the exact color of a summer sky. He caressed her with the tips of his fingers as he tangled his other hand in her long yellow hair and moved so that he was half on top of her. His pulse began to pound strongly, and he felt his manhood swell with urgency. He wanted her, and he felt her pulse quicken, knew from years of making love to her that she desired him, too. "They're asleep," he said more urgently, and kissed her, deeply, thoroughly.

She managed to pull her mouth away. "They won't be for long if we keep whispering." She threw one arm across him and laid her face against his brawny chest, feeling warm and safe in his powerful arms. He was a muscular, virile warrior who would kill any man who touched her or even looked at her with lust in his eyes. When Angry Wolf had tried to rape her by a secluded stream, Iron Knife had fought him to the death.

He was kissing her again. She knew she should protest and pull away, but it felt so right; so good to have his mouth tasting hers, his hard, calloused hands stroking her naked skin until she felt her pulse pound and her nipples harden. They used to make love a couple of times a night, she thought with regret, but they must not make another baby yet. It was the Cheyenne custom to nurse a child three years, and with Summer producing three children in four years, hers might have starved if Pretty Flower Woman had not helped. So this time, Summer was determined that until her baby girl, Garnet, was past two, they would not make love completely. To do without Iron Knife's skillful and gentle lovemaking was creating tremendous strain on both of them, and yet, Iron Knife had vowed he would not take a second wife as most of the Cheyenne warriors did.

More than six years had passed since that day she had been kidnapped from a stagecoach, then turning her back on the life of a prominent Boston society girl and becoming the dog soldier's woman. The fine white leather dress with the one thousand elks' teeth that she had worn in the ceremony was safely tucked away. She only wished they could be married in the custom of her people, too. She smiled up at him, not wanting to think about the stress their relationship had been placed under by the renewed trouble between the whites and Indians —and their abstaining from lovemaking.

"I am lucky to have you," he murmured and held her close against him.

She looked up at him in the glow of the tipi fire. Even with a broken nose and battle-scarred face, he was handsome. His raven black hair was pulled into a braid on the left side, and he wore a big brass button from a dead cavalry officer's uniform as an earring in his right ear. He was naked except for the eagle bone whistle he wore around his neck in the manner of all dog soldiers.

She felt the hardness of his manhood pressing against her body. Iron Knife was a virile man and needed a woman often. He was skillful with his lovemaking and had taught her passion that, as a staid Boston debutante, she had not realized she was capable of. That was part of the problem, she thought regretfully, as she ran her fingertips over the sun dance scars on his naked, sinewy chest and looked up into his handsome, scarred face. Iron Knife could make her forget that they shouldn't make love. When he took her in his arms and began to kiss her, she lost all resolve and all reason. Summer took a deep breath and managed to pull back. "Pretty Flower says you should take a second wife the way most other Cheyenne do."

"Would you like that? It would keep me from rubbing all over you like some aroused stallion, wouldn't it?"

"You know that's not what I meant." The thought of him touching another woman made her wince. Many Cheyenne warriors had a second wife for that reason. However, she and Iron Knife had too big a passion for each other not to lose control, so besides their oldest, Lance, there was his younger brother, Storm Gathering, and the baby, Garnet.

Each time, Pretty Flower Woman, cousin Two Arrows' wife, had helped Summer nurse the children when Summer's milk began to dry up. Garnet was almost two years old now, and the thought of doing without Iron Knife's lovemaking for another year was almost unbearable. More unbearable was the thought of him making love to another woman while Summer lay in the same lodge, pretending to sleep while he mated with a Cheyenne wife or a captive Indian girl. "Have you—have you been looking at some of those captives? I've seen the way they look at you."

"It won't happen," he reassured her. "I love only you, and you know it, Little One." He combed his fingers through her yellow hair; then his hand came down and cupped her breast.

He breathed heavier, and his palm felt like fire against her nipple. It didn't seem fair that he had taught her passion and now they must do without. It was the custom among his people to take the first wife's younger sister as a second, but of course, among the whites, that was a scandalous idea. Summer reached up and traced her finger across the hard planes of his dear, dark face. She knew every inch of his virile, muscular body from his whip-scarred back to the sun dance scars on his broad chest. He was powerful and dangerous, but with her, he was always tender and gentle.

"I want you," he whispered urgently against her ear.

"You can only kiss me," she whispered.

"I want more than that." His voice was husky with its urgency, and his hands shook as he pulled at the drawstrings of her doeskin bodice.

"We've been through this before and you know the answer." Was she almost angry with him because he was so insistent or was it only because she wanted him so much? She ought to turn over and stop this right now, and yet she actually ached for his touch. His big hands squeezed her breasts up to two points, and then his mouth claimed them, teasing her nipples with his tongue as his hand stroked its way down her belly. Her loins felt on fire, and she had never wanted him as badly as she wanted him at this moment. She must not let this go any further, and yet she had seen the way pretty Cheyenne girls and captives from other tribes had looked at him, running their tongues along their lips, thrusting out their bosoms so that he would notice. If she didn't satisfy him, some other woman might.

She let her thighs fall apart and reached to touch his big manhood. It was rigid and throbbing with unspent seed. He groaned at the touch of her hand.

"You hot little vixen," he said against her ear, "you

make me want to forget everything, fall on you and mate with you like a bitch in heat."

In her mind, she imagined him taking that passion to another woman, his lean hips driving deep as he mounted some willing girl. The thought of his taking a second wife and sharing his love drove her crazy with jealousy. She dug her nails into his wide shoulders and kissed his mouth, running her pink tongue deep into his throat, teasing him into sucking it still deeper. He kissed his way down between her breasts and concentrated on her belly, kissing and blowing his warm breath on her pale skin, running his tongue around her navel until she shook with the wanting of him. "Please. . . ."

"Please yes or please no?" He was trembling, his manhood hard as stone. She wanted him on her and in her, thrusting hard into her very core. She wanted to claw his back and lock him in her legs, pull him down on top of her for a passionate ride.

"We—we mustn't." Was she reminding him or herself?

She reached up to bite his nipples, and he gasped aloud. "Don't do that, Summer, you'll make me lose control. . . ."

She was frustrated and angry that she couldn't have him, that he could only tease her with his kisses and hands. She held her breath and felt his mouth warm and wet on her belly, then on her thighs. Was he going to kiss her there?

Almost in answer, he commanded, "Let your thighs fall apart, I'm going to pleasure you, Little One."

He was arrogant and confident, all male; yet he adored her now with his lips. It was the supreme compliment, she knew. His seeking mouth was hot, his tongue thrusting and wet. She tangled her fingers in his dark hair. "N—no, don't do that."

"You like it and you're mine."

Waves of white-hot ecstasy began to sweep over her as he loved her with his mouth. She pulled his dark face against her body, arched her back, breathed heavily through her mouth and convulsed with passion. "No, don't . . . don't stop!"

She didn't care about anything else as long as she could get his pulsating manhood in her. She was struggling to pull him on top of her when she climaxed from his deep kisses.

When she came to, he was looking down into her face intently, breathing hard. "How I want you!" He sounded frustrated and angry.

She lay there looking up into his passionate, dark eyes, feeling guilty because he had pleasured her and there were so many women he could use to satisfy his body in this camp. "I'm sorry, dearest."

"It isn't your fault, you little she-cat, that I want you so. You'd keep me drained of seed and your belly swollen continually if I loved you as much as I wanted."

She reached out and clasped his rigid manhood in her hand, and he gasped. His mouth covered hers again, and she tasted the essence of herself on his lips. "I—I'm only human, Little One, don't do that."

She stroked him instead.

He moaned. "I have to fight to keep from taking you every night when I am lying here with you in my arms, feeling your breasts all swollen with milk, your small body burning hot."

She rubbed her nipples against his chest, teased his big manhood with her fingertips. "Iron Knife; you're aptly named."

"Stop that or I'll lose control," he protested.

She didn't stop; she kept teasing him with her hand until he began to rut against her belly.

Iron Knife felt the rising surge as he rammed against her until he couldn't hold back any longer and wasted his virile seed against her abdomen. Then he lay next to her, shaking, a bit angry, his desire still not completely satisfied. For a split second, he had been tempted to grab her, thrust his manhood deep inside her where it belonged. He had struggled with that overpowering temptation and finally regained control at the last moment. Summer Sky was his woman and he wanted her a dozen times a day, but he must not dry up her milk again with little Garnet needing it.

Out on the war trail, they occasionally captured a pretty enemy Crow, Ute or Pawnee girl who knew she was expected to let the braves pleasure themselves with her ripe body. If she pleased one enough, she might be chosen as a second wife. Only a few suns ago, Iron Knife had watched a hunting party taking turns on a big-breasted Pawnee captive, and she had invited him with her dark eyes to lie between her thighs. Oh, he had been tempted. His manhood ached as he watched the other warriors rutting on the girl, and they urged him to enjoy her, too. He almost succumbed to the overpowering need and lust of mating, but he loved Summer Sky too much. Yet this abstinence kept him as short-tempered as a deprived buffalo bull.

He glanced down at the beautiful blonde in his arms. Summer was already asleep. He held her very close, pulled the buffalo robe over them both and kissed her cheek. She was his mate, and he would protect her and love her until the day he died. His once in a lifetime love. Summer had given up wealth and an aristocratic fiancé to share a half-breed's life of hardships. He wondered now if she regretted the choice she had made. Nothing, not torture, death or injury frightened him. He was a carrier of the *Hotamtsit,* the ceremonial rope carried by only four of the bravest dog soldiers; the ones expected to sacrifice their lives in a brave gesture if need be.

Only one thing terrified him: that someday he might lose Summer Sky; that someday she might regret the choice she had made and go away forever. No, he wouldn't lose her, even if it meant he had to hold her captive. She was his woman and he would never let her go.

Long after she was asleep, he lay staring into the darkness. There was growing trouble and tension between whites and Indians because all those gold seekers coming into Colorado were scaring off the game and digging mines on traditional Indian lands. It was as if the natives had no rights at all, and yet, he was himself half-white and not certain he could ever paint himself for war against them. Why, only a couple of weeks or so ago, he had rescued a blinded soldier, Cherokee Evans, and helped him get back to his little mining town in the mountains.

Lately, some of the young warriors had been sneaking off to attack whites, and the old chiefs were almost powerless to stop them. Black Kettle was attempting to make peace with the whites, return the captured white women and children, but the hot-headed young braves had been ranging all over Colorado Territory, Kansas and Nebraska, leaving death and destruction in their wake. It upset Summer Sky, he knew, to have these young braves riding in with a white scalp and boasting of burning a stage station or an isolated ranch. Those actions had caused increased tension between the couple, even though Iron Knife was not guilty of these attacks.

He frowned in the darkness. If things didn't change, might his beloved Summer Sky possibly take his children and return to her own people? Could he bear to make her unhappy, hold her against her will if she should make that decision?

He listened to the steady breathing of the three children. Their sturdy oldest son, Lance, would soon be five years old. The handsome boy looked white with his mother's pale blue eyes, but his hair was as black as a raven's wing. Storm Gathering, who was almost four, looked every inch the small, sturdy Cheyenne warrior. Their baby girl, Garnet, was a toddler, not yet two. She had hair as dark and skin as light as Lance's, but her eyes were like deep, dark pools.

Iron Knife saw the future and it troubled him. The whites were sweeping like a great tide across his people's hunting grounds. Iron Knife had been named for the weapon he carried, the broken blade of a cavalry officer's saber, whom he had killed in one of the earlier Cheyenne battles against the white soldiers. In the long run, the situation would only get worse; he knew that. This Civil War he'd heard about was slowing the white men's invasion, but that could not last forever. Then the whites would come to the West in ever-increasing numbers. The old way of life would have to change—unless the Cheyenne fought back. Would he lose Summer if he fought her people? He felt torn between two terrible choices, and there was no good answer.

It was almost morning when he finally dropped off to sleep. He was awakened by Summer stirring in his arms and getting up to nurse their baby. He liked to watch her with their children and know that each one had been a product of their love. That made him think of holding her, kissing her again, and he sighed with frustration.

He got up and walked to the creek to bring back water. The Cheyenne would not use water that had sat all night; it had to be dipped fresh from the creek each morning. This was considered woman's work, but the weight was heavy and the weather cold. Summer was small and delicate, and he could not watch her struggle under such a weight, so he did it for her. No man laughed at the big dog soldier behind his back, although he knew they might wonder why he did it. He loved Summer Sky enough to do anything to keep her with him always—make her happy. He had a good fire going outside by the time she came out and began to prepare food.

"The children are still asleep," she yawned.

"If you were back in Boston," he said, feeling guilty, "servants would be running to bring you anything you wanted, and all you would have to do with your day is decide which fine dress to wear."

She smiled and poked up the fire. "It was really a bother to wear those corsets and hoop skirts."

"Do you never miss your old life, Little One?"

"Not much; only when I think there's going to be fighting or the food runs a little short."

"I am the best hunter in the camp," he reminded her. "The soldiers and the miners are driving away the game."

She put her small hand on his arm. "I don't blame you, only sometimes. . . ." She sighed. "I wish we could live in peace with the whites and I didn't have to deny you. Sleeping in your arms every night reminds me of why I stayed."

"I wish I could promise that things will get better, but you know I can't."

Summer shrugged. "You are my forever love."

"Nothing is forever, maybe, but the mountains," Iron Knife said, looking toward the tall peaks to the West.

"Then you are mine for as long as it lasts or until you get tired of me and add a second woman to your lodge."

"Don't talk like that." He shook his head, watching the camp come to life in the cold dawn. Horses whinnied, dogs barked. Women passed among the tipis as they went about their chores. In the winter, there was not a lot to do except hunt a little, tell stories around the camp fires at night, and make love to one of your

women. He felt frustrated again, remembering last night
and wondering if their union could survive another year
with Summer sleeping in his arms and him unable to
mate with her.

He watched little Bear Cub cross the camp, picking
up sticks for his mother's fire. How old was he? Nine
winter counts? Maybe ten? Bear Cub was a favorite of
everyone because the child was a gifted artist and
painted scenes of hunting and warrior deeds.

Summer paused, and glanced over at him. "Why do
you frown, dearest?"

"I'm thinking about all the tension that has been
building between the tribes and those miners and settlers. The war among your people can't last forever.
What will happen when it is over?"

"Is there no end to our two people killing each
other?"

"I thought my people were your people?" He studied
her keenly.

"Remember that my people are also your people,"
she reminded him with a frown. "Was not your mother,
Texanna, stolen from a Texas wagon train by the great
chief War Bonnet?"

He conceded that with a nod. "I have been among the
Cheyenne so long, sometimes I forget I am half-white.
In my mind, I am only Cheyenne." Five years he had
lived among the whites after he and his expectant
mother had been captured by the whites and forced to
live among them. He thought again of his small sister,
Cimarron, left behind in the confusion of fleeing that
Texas town when he and his mother had been rescued
by War Bonnet and taken back to the Indians. His parents had both been dead for a long time, and it saddened
him that he didn't know the fate of his little sister. Cimarron; it meant "wild one." Cimarron would be grown
now—if his younger sister was still alive.

Summer dished up some cooked meat. "I worry about what is happening to us with this talk of my people and your people. Isn't there some way to stop this conflict?"

He snorted. "Easier to chase the water from the river. I told you when you decided to stay with me what you were facing." He thought, *She's regretting her rash action, regretting giving herself to a savage in a primitive land.*

"If the whites will only go away and leave us alone—"

"That's not going to happen," he snapped.

"Well, neither will the young warriors killing ranchers and their women and children solve anything."

"The whites kill ours, too," he reminded her pointedly.

"That's true. Sometimes I wish. . . ." Her voice trailed off, and he saw the regret in her pale blue eyes. What was it she wished? That she had never met him? That she had married Austin Shaw, the rich cavalry lieutenant she had been engaged to? That she and her children were safely away from here?

Dogs barking signaled someone coming. Children and old people gestured, heads turned. Iron Knife automatically reached for the big knife in his belt, the one that had given him his name. Now he relaxed and smiled as he recognized the rider. "It's one of the Bent boys."

Summer shaded her eyes with her hand. "William Bent's sons from the trading post?"

Iron Knife nodded as he rose. "I'll go see why he's here."

In a few minutes, he was back, face grim. "He says he's seen Jake Dallinger."

Her reaction was one of surprise and fear. "Jake Dallinger is out of prison?"

"Yes, and in Denver." Cold anger washed over him.

He had many reasons to hate the scout, not the least of which was the life-and-death fight they had had that spring day of 1859 when Dallinger had tried to abduct and rape Summer. Iron Knife had gelded the brute, and the army had taken Dallinger away to prison.

"What else did the Bent boy say?"

"There's talk around Denver that some of the whites are angry that we are trying to make peace before they can take revenge. Some of them won't be satisfied until there's much Indian blood shed." He looked up at the sun. "I have some things to do, but I could be there about dark."

"Be where?"

"I think I'll ride into Denver—"

"Iron Knife, no!" She caught his arm. "It might be dangerous!"

He patted her hand. "I've lived with danger all my life, Little One. Dog soldiers don't expect to die of old age, especially a carrier of the *Hotamtsit*. Besides, I told you about the ceremony of the badger that I went through as a young man."

"You don't believe that silly ceremony can really tell the future, that you aren't going to live to grow old?" She looked half-incredulous, half-scared.

"Yes, I do believe; it is a sacred ceremony of our people, not 'silly' as you think."

"I didn't mean that." She looked away.

"Sometimes people blurt out their true thoughts," he said. Maybe the bridge between their two cultures was too wide to be bridged even by love, he thought sadly, watching her. Maybe he should never have taken her as his woman. "Perhaps I can find out something from Cherokee Evans, that soldier I helped, or maybe your old family friend, Austin's brother."

"Yes, Todd Shaw would know what's happening since he works at the *Rocky Mountain News*." Summer shook her head. "But you shouldn't go to Denver. With all this trouble these past few months, the whites are so nervous, they might shoot you on sight."

"Or lynch me," Iron Knife said. "Raiding war parties have cut off Denver's supply lines for weeks. I hear there aren't any stages or wagons going in and out. There should be shortages of food soon."

Summer looked both saddened and a little angry. "So women and children go hungry while men fight!"

"War is always that way," he reminded her as he set his bowl to one side. "Remember, the whites are killing our women and children, too. I fear when this Civil War of theirs finally ends, they will again concentrate on wiping us out."

She didn't answer, but her eyes were filled with uncertainty. Instead, she played absently with the little gold locket around her neck, the last souvenir of her civilized life. Did she have regrets? Even now, she could probably return to Boston. There would be white men who would want her wealth; but they probably wouldn't want her three mixed-blood children.

He stood up. "I will go, see if I can find Cherokee Evans or Todd Shaw, find out whether the whites have made any plans."

"Be cautious." She put her small hand on his arm in the old familiar way, and he wanted to sweep her into his arms and kiss her until she was breathless; but such behavior was beneath the dignity of a dog soldier.

"I will be careful. I may be gone awhile; it is almost fifty or sixty miles to Denver." He shivered. It was cold and getting colder. Surely the soldiers would stay safely by their fires until their Christmas holidays were over. The Cheyenne and their allies, the Arapaho, were camped at one of their favorite camps on the Big Sandy Creek where there was water and good grazing for their many horses. In the spring, the tribe would be moving on to follow the buffalo herds which were fewer every year.

Iron Knife went to hug his children before he saddled up his big Appaloosa stallion, Spotted Blanket. He left his two warrior cousins, Two Arrows and Lance Bearer, with orders to look after his family.

His old aunt, Pony Woman, vowed she would see about them. His uncle, Clouds Above, was feeble with rheumatism in this cold, but still he enjoyed a pipe or two of tobacco with Black Kettle and old White Antelope. The three were sitting before Black Kettle's lodge where the American flag flapped in the cold dawn breeze when Iron Knife rode out, but he yelled that he would try to bring back some tobacco for them.

He paused and looked back at Summer, who watched him from a low rise. Never had she looked so beautiful to him with wisps of yellow hair blowing about her small face, her buffalo robe gathered about her slight form against the cold wind. She held up a hand in a gesture of farewell, but he could not bring himself to leave without riding back to her one more time. "I will return when I can," he said, looking down at her from his Appaloosa stallion. "If you need anything, ask my cousins."

She nodded, but her expression left no doubt as to her concern. "Please, be careful."

"I'll come back to you; I promise. A warrior's word is as good as his heart is strong."

Yet she stood there looking up at him with such intense yearning that he could not resist sliding from his horse to take her in his arms one more time. She laid her face against his wide chest, and he held her tightly, thinking how slight and vulnerable she was and how much she had given up for him. *"Ne-mehotatse,"* he whispered, "I love you, Summer, never forget that."

He kissed her, tasting all the sweetness of her lips as

she clung to him; remembering all the times they had made love and slept in each other's arms.

"I love you, too," she whispered, pressing her face against his, and her skin felt cold from the icy wind just as her lips had been warm. "Come back to me."

He nodded, his heart too full to speak. It was not seemly that a great warrior be so devoted to a woman that she meant more to him than anything on earth—even his own life. One more time, he hugged her to him; then reluctantly, he tore himself out of her embrace and swung up on Spotted Blanket. He nudged his mount into a walk. When he looked back, she still stood watching after him, her yellow hair blowing. Summer looked small against the vast prairie, and he did not want to leave her. Duty. He must think of his people and put them before his own needs and desires. Resolutely, he turned his back and nudged his stallion into a lope.

As he rode west toward Denver, Iron Knife made sure he stayed along gullies and in the edges of straggly brush so that he wouldn't be spotted by the white men he knew to be in the area.

It was dusk when Iron Knife rode into Denver. He stayed in the shadows, found his way to the newspaper office. Through the window, he could see Todd Shaw. When Todd looked up and saw him, he motioned Iron Knife inside and got up to pull the shades. "You're taking a chance coming here."

Iron Knife shrugged. "So Summer tells me. How goes the white man's Civil War?"

Todd brushed his brown hair away from his handsome face. "It rages on, but it appears certain now the South will lose, so Colorado is no longer worried about the Rebels invading, trying to capture the West for the gold and silver they need to pay for ammunition."

"When they invaded the West, they didn't do any good?" Iron Knife leaned against a desk.

"No, Colonel Chivington was a real hero, went off down to New Mexico, fought the Southerners at Glorietta Pass, whipped them and sent them running back to Texas."

"That means the soldiers can now turn their attention back to the Indians?"

Todd nodded. "Sorry, friend. I'm doing what I can."

Iron Knife paced up and down. "Some of us are trying to stop the young warriors from raiding, but the old chiefs like Black Kettle can't always control them."

Todd chewed the tip of his pen. "I know that. Your heart is true, my friend, and I realize the Cheyenne are trying to show good faith by returning the white prisoners they held."

"We've heard that Chivington and some of the others have been stirring up the whites with words, urging them to attack us."

"What can I say?" Todd turned his hands palms up in a gesture of helplessness. "The Third Volunteers haven't gotten much chance to fight, and since Chivington's a hero, everyone listens to him, even the newspaper. I only work here; I don't own it, you know."

"I know." Would the trouble between whites and Indians never end? He hadn't realized it could cause such a chasm of trouble between him and the woman he loved. "The Cheyenne and some of the Arapaho have moved out to the creek, not far from Fort Lyon, so they will be under the army's protection should a mob decide to take things into their own hands."

Todd's hazel eyes grew serious. "The way some of the rabble rousers are whipping locals into a frenzy, there's no telling what's liable to happen."

Iron Knife considered. "I would also like to talk to a man called Cherokee Evans."

Todd jerked his head toward the door. "Cherokee? I know him. He's in town, over at the Essex Hotel. I'll give you directions, but you be careful. No telling what would happen if some of these men spot a Cheyenne on the streets, especially with the holidays upon us; there's a lot of drinking going on."

Iron Knife listened, thanked Todd, and went to find Cherokee's hotel. Looking around to make sure no one saw him enter the building, Iron Knife found the right door and knocked.

"Silver?" A man's voice from inside.

"No, it's me, Iron Knife."

"Iron Knife! Good God!"

He heard footsteps, and Cherokee Evans threw open the door and let him in. They hugged each other.

Iron Knife said, "Any improvement in your eyes?"

"Some. I can see a little now." Cherokee led him over by the fireplace. "What are you doing in Denver? The way folks feel about your people right now, this isn't a very safe place to be."

"One of the Bent boys came out to our camp." Very quickly, he told Cherokee what the half-breed boy had said and how he had sneaked into town under darkness to see Todd Shaw.

"He's a fair and honest man. Is that how you found me, through Todd?"

Iron Knife nodded. "He's a friend. Todd tells me he's afraid there's going to be more trouble. He says Colonel Chivington is out in eastern Colorado now, looking for Indians to attack."

"If that's the case, you're needed by your people. You ought to go back."

Iron Knife told Cherokee about Jake Dallinger and how he had come to Denver intending to kill him if he found him. "The Cheyenne will always be in danger as long as that scout lives; he hates Indians."

Cherokee stood up. "I owe him justice myself, if my

vision ever improves enough; so please don't do me out of the pleasure of killing him."

"Since you put it that way. . . ." Iron Knife stared into the fireplace. "I'll go back to camp now and warn my people that we may be attacked."

He must have looked as uncertain as he felt because Cherokee asked, "What's the matter?"

"I'm not sure my people will believe me." Iron Knife sighed. "We've been promised protection by the officer at Fort Lyon. I'm afraid Black Kettle and the others will think I'm fearful and suspicious for no good reason."

Cherokee walked him to the door. "Believe me, I think it's wise to be cautious. I heard Dallinger in a mob the other day. He said something about helping the colonel find the Indian camp."

Iron Knife turned with his hand on the doorknob. "That would be bad news. Dallinger is a skilled scout who knows this country. The troops would be lost without him."

"Maybe I can keep him from joining up with Chivington's forces, if he's a mind to. I owe your people that; you, especially, for finding me and saving my life when I was lost and helpless."

They exchanged a few more words; then Iron Knife held out his hand. "Goodbye, my friend. Someday, maybe we'll meet again. I will ride out and tell my people what you and Todd Shaw have said. Maybe I can convince them they are not safe and that we should move our camp, even though it would be a lot of trouble to move right now, and my people feel safe with the fort close by."

They shook hands solemnly, and Iron Knife started to leave, then remembered. "Do you have any tobacco? I promised three old chiefs I'd bring some back."

"Sure, anything for a friend." Cherokee felt through his coat and came up with a package.

"Hahoo," Iron Knife said, which was the word all tribes used and understood as "thank you."

"Eventually, if things work out for me," Cherokee said, "I'd like to go back up into the Rockies, build a cabin; you know the area."

Iron Knife nodded after he listened to Cherokee describe it. "Perhaps we will meet again someday, friend."

"You and yours are always welcome under my roof," Cherokee said solemnly, and they shook hands again.

Then Iron Knife slipped out the door and was gone, as swift and quiet as a shadow. He only hoped Cherokee was up to dealing with the evil white scout. Without Jake Dallinger to lead them, the army might have trouble finding the Indian camp. Iron Knife made a mental vow to pass the word that Cherokee Evans was a friend of the Cheyenne. That way, the big man could travel or dig for gold without any of the Cheyenne or their allies attacking him.

Summer and his children waited back at the creek. He worried now that his people would be complacent where they were, not wishing to move their camp in this bitter cold. He could rescue his own family if he got there in time, but the rest of his people might be hesitant to move if they weren't totally convinced of the danger. Frost crunched beneath his stallion's hooves as he rode toward the stream the whites called Sand Creek.

Chapter Two

Iron Knife had wasted precious time before he could slip out of Denver. Because of the white man's approaching holidays, there were many drunks on the streets, even though it was late. At last, quiet as a *seoto,* a ghost, he had crept out of town, run to where he had hidden his big stallion and galloped east toward Sand Creek. The night wind now blew bitter cold against his face. The moon shone as big and bright as a twenty-dollar gold piece, throwing shadows on the frozen crust of buffalo grass that crunched beneath Spotted Blanket's pounding hooves.

Iron Knife had only one thought in mind; he must reach the camp before the soldiers did. His intuition told him the attack would come soon. The Third Regiment of volunteers would be marching from Fort Lyon on the Arkansas River to the Indian camp which lay to the northeast of the fort. There were others who could guide the army, if Cherokee could stop Jake Dallinger from being their scout, but looking for one might delay them a few hours. Iron Knife must travel many miles in white man's measurements to reach the Indian camp, a long way to go before dawn without an extra horse.

The Appaloosa stallion had a mighty heart, but even

it had its limitations. Every few miles, Iron Knife was forced to stop and cool his mount when it became lathered and blowing. A horse ridden too hard would collapse and die, leaving its rider afoot. Years ago, a Nez Percé chief had given him the fine stallion out of gratitude for saving his small son's life, and there was a strong bond of trust between Iron Knife and his horse.

Time. He feared he didn't have enough. Time was something that no man, however rich, could buy and sell. The moon moved relentlessly across the black, cold sky, mockingly reminding him that precious minutes were ticking by. Iron Knife despaired of making it to the camp before dawn. He'd heard that the Pony Express riders rode their horses at a gallop and changed them every ten to fifteen miles, but he had maybe five times that to cover and only his beloved stallion.

Summer Sky. His heart seemed to almost burst when he thought of her and his children sleeping in that unsuspecting camp. If she was wearing a buffalo robe pulled around her light hair, the soldiers wouldn't know she was white until it was too late. From what Todd and Cherokee had told him, the mood of the Third Volunteers was ugly, and they were out for blood. He would not think of what would happen should he fail to arrive in time to warn the Cheyenne; he would only concentrate on his riding. In the moonlight as he rode, his breath was visible in the cold air, and each time he inhaled, it was like small daggers of ice inside his lungs.

It was bound to come to this, he thought with bitter resignation as he galloped across the frozen buffalo grass. Always the whites crowded the tribes a little farther west; but soon there would be no more places to push the Indians, and they knew it. In self-defense, the Cheyenne and their allies had been attacking across the plains and into the Rockies, taking white hostages, hitting lonely outposts. Denver had been isolated and cut off for weeks, and the mood among the people there was becoming vengeful as food supplies ran low. Even though the wise old men of the tribes were now attempting to bring about a truce, the whites were angry and craving blood because of the latest killing of that Hungate family on Running Creek near Denver.

Spotted Blanket stumbled, and Iron Knife reined in, dismounting to check the stallion. Anxiously, he examined the foreleg while patting the big stallion's velvet nose. "Good boy . . . good boy."

It wasn't broken, but the horse was lame and limping. Waves of frustration mixed with relief. The horse would be all right with some rest, but now Iron Knife was afoot.

"Good boy." He patted the stallion's nose again, trying to decide what to do. If only he had another horse. He thought wistfully of Summer Sky's dainty chestnut mare, Starfire, but she and their other horses were with the Cheyenne. There was only one answer: travel the rest of the way on foot.

With regret, he took the bridle off his horse and turned the animal loose. "Find your own way back to camp, Spotted Blanket; maybe by then, this trouble will be over."

The stallion nickered and limped toward him, but Iron Knife shook his head. "Sorry, boy, I can't walk you there. I haven't time to wait."

Iron Knife took a deep breath and began to run, his long, muscular legs eating up the ground. He felt the frozen crust of grass beneath his soft moccasins as he crossed the flat prairie. The cold air hurt his lungs, and the wind cut across his face. He wasn't sure he could cover the rest of the distance in time; but in his mind, he saw his woman's pale blue eyes looking up at him so trustingly, and he knew he had to try.

Every Cheyenne boy had been trained to endure hardship and run for many miles. But he was no longer a boy; he was thirty-one years old, scarred and cut from many battles that had taken a toll on his lean body. Every muscle now seemed to ache with pain as he ran. He was expendable. Only his tribe, his woman and his children were important; they must survive. A dog soldier expected to sacrifice himself and die young against the tribe's enemies.

What was it Summer had once called the four carriers of the sacred Dog Rope? A suicide squad. Yet he had never loved life so much as he did now with his heart pounding as though it might falter and breath coming in gasps of cold air as his long legs crossed the miles of ground. He stumbled. Like a horse, he would have to rest a moment or risk dying before he could complete his task. Iron Knife collapsed on the icy terrain, his legs aching, his great heart pounding like a war drum. The hard ground was covered with frost and remnants of snow, yet it felt good against his sweating body. He staggered to his feet, ran another mile, fell again. He was tempted not to get up, to lie there and sleep, but he knew to do so would mean freezing to death.

Somewhere, a coyote howled, and the sound echoed and reechoed across the frozen, lonely land. If he lay here until he slipped into unconsciousness, coyotes or wolves might find him and begin to eat him alive before he was completely dead. Slowly, painfully, he forced himself to his feet and began to move forward again at a slow trot. His legs were without feeling except that they ached. His own shadow loomed large on the snowy landscape as the full moon moved slowly and relentlessly across a black winter sky. His breathing sounded like a roar in his own ears in the echoing silence. He must get to the camp in time. He must.

Iron Knife's powerful legs followed his lead as he forced his feet to move one ahead of the other. He felt sweat on his dark face, and when the wind blew, it was as if he were being kissed by Death. Again, he tripped over a rock, stumbled and fell. The snow soothed his sweating body. He lay there with his eyes closed, half-delirious from his ordeal. In his mind, he and Summer swam in a cold, sparkling stream. It was the time of Hemotseesehe, the breeding moon the whites called August. They cavorted like two playful otters in the heat, naked and alone, just the two of them, and he lifted her and kissed her bare full breasts. Then he carried her to the shallows and made love to her with the cold water lapping around them. Her body was warm and soft under him. It was so peaceful lying here. When he looked up at the moon, he saw the gold of her hair as she leaned over him and put her mouth on his. He did not want to move.

Then he realized through a vague haze that it was not Summer who embraced him, but the lady Death. She wanted to wrap her voluptuous, chilled length around him, pull him down deep inside her, press her icy breasts against him. *Stay with me,* she seemed to whisper, *just lie on my soft, cool belly and let me take you to a long, dark climax that will last forever . . . forever. . . .*

He raised up and shook his head to clear it. Summer Sky and his children depended on him. The tribe needed him. If he could just make it to the outskirts of the camp before he died, maybe he could blow his eagle bone whistle hard enough to be heard; whisper a warning to those who found him. Almost by sheer willpower, he staggered to his feet. Lady Death seemed to call to him not to leave her embrace. She had such delights, such a release for the pain in his aching body. All he had to do

was surrender to her and stay spread on the snowy
ground in the moonlight.

Instead, he focused on his memories of Summer Sky,
the warmth of her lips and breasts, the slow, sizzling
days of the season making love to his woman under the
shade of a tree. Summer was hot and willing in his
arms. Flesh was warm; she was warm. His once in a
lifetime love. He had been so lucky to have her; most
men lived a whole lifetime without ever finding such
eternal devotion. The thought of her encouraged him to
put one foot in front of the other and start off again at
an uncertain trot. He would get back to his woman even
if he died in her arms.

He ran now on sheer heart, past feeling any pain in
his laboring lungs and legs while the gold moon moved
slowly across the sky. His moccasins had worn through
in places from the jagged rocks and hard ice of all these
many miles. When he glanced down, he saw faint scarlet smears in the snow from his tortured feet. He had
lost all track of time and distance, and only sheer, dog-
ged determination kept him moving.

Iron Knife was within sight of the camp now and
barely stumbling ahead. In the darkness, he saw a few
small camp fires, the silhouette of tipis against the sky.
In the distance, the horse herd grazed on frozen grass,
and one dog barked. So close and yet so far. He brought
the whistle to his lips, but the sound was lost on the
wind. He tried to call out, but his voice was a dry,
crackled whisper. Then he passed out.

He did not know how long he lay there, but he was
roused by a camp dog sniffing his face curiously. Iron
Knife looked around. The moon had disappeared, and in
the east, the faintest gray light of dawn hovered on the
flat horizon. He cursed as he staggered to his feet. Had
he lost hours or minutes? It couldn't have been too long

or he would have frozen to death out there within sight
of the camp. He ran to his tipi.

Summer came up out of her fur robes as he entered
and fell. "Iron Knife? Dearest, what's happened? You're
half-frozen!"

For a split-second, he let her hold him; her warmth
against his chilled flesh felt so wonderful. "Little One,"
he gasped, "wake the camp! Soldiers are coming!"

"What? How do you know—?"

"No time to talk!" He caught her small, heart-shaped
face between his two big hands. "Tell Black Kettle;
alert my cousins! Get horses so you can escape!"

"But—"

"Do as I tell you!" He caught her by the arm, struggled to stand. The first pink light shone on her sleepy,
troubled face. "Soldiers on their way!" He staggered
outside, dragging her with him. "Get your horse and
take the children out of here!"

Abruptly, cannon echoed on the cold air, and he knew
it was too late. With supreme effort, he ran through the
camp, shouting, "Soldiers! Soldiers!"

Sleepy faces peeked out of lodge openings; dogs
barked even as the cannon echoed again. He heard the
sound of thunder and the rattle of metal. Then he turned
toward Fort Lyon and realized it wasn't thunder at all,
but the drumming of hundreds of horses' hooves as the
Colorado Third Regiment rode to the attack. He ran
back to his tipi, grabbed his *howan,* his dream shield,
and a rifle. Summer looked up at him and then at the
horizon as if she couldn't believe she wasn't dreaming.
He grabbed her arm and shook her into reality. "Get the
children, Summer, I'll try to catch your horse!"

He could hear his three precious little ones awake and
whimpering, but there was no time to comfort them.
Around him, total confusion and chaos reigned as the

camp came alive, everyone shouting and running. Why
hadn't the chiefs posted a sentry who could warn them
when the soldiers first appeared? No doubt they had felt
they were safely under the protection of the commander
at Fort Lyon.

Iron Knife paused to get his bearings, saw the hundreds of soldiers and galloping horses, dark against the
snowy landscape. One soldier's horse had run away
with him. Even as the others reined in to take positions,
that luckless man's horse galloped straight for the camp
with the man yanking in vain on the bridle. Iron Knife
would always remember the stark terror in the bluecoat's eyes as his horse carried him right into the middle
of the Indian encampment. Iron Knife shot him from his
saddle. It was ironic, he thought with a mirthless smile,
that the first death at Sand Creek should be a white
man.

All around him now was total chaos as women
screamed, babies cried and guns echoed. He coughed at
the acrid scent of gunpowder as he ran through the
camp, nodded to his cousin, Two Arrows, who appeared
half-dressed from his lodge.

"What's happened?"

"Soldiers from Fort Lyon!" Iron Knife shouted.
"Make them pay for this attack!"

All around him women scrambled to protect screaming children; warriors recovered from their sleepy confusion as they rallied. Dogs barked, and frightened
horses thundered through the camp. Gunfire echoed,
drowned out by the booming cannon; women shrieked.
Somewhere he heard a baby crying and wondered if it
was one of his own children.

The first rays of sunlight caught the colors of the
American flag flapping in the wind before old Black
Kettle's lodge. Bluecoats, white snow, red blood. How

ironic that the flag colors were being reflected all around him. Warriors fought hard, attempting to provide a defense, or at least a delaying return fire. Women ran hysterically, trying to find lost children. A small toddler wandered about crying, but there was no time to help it because the soldiers galloped through the camp, firing at anything that moved.

Iron Knife raised his weapon and fired, knocking another soldier from his running horse. He hurried past the body of a woman clutching a baby. The baby was dead, too. He had known this young girl, had ridden many times with her husband. There was no time now for pity; he must help save the living.

He heard a shout of warning from Lance Bearer and looked up just as his cousin thrust his lance through a soldier who had been galloping straight toward Iron Knife. The soldier's blue eyes widened with surprise almost as if he couldn't believe the blade impaling him and jutting from his back. He dropped his weapon, grasped the lance in a vain attempt to dislodge it, then fell from his bay gelding. Iron Knife grabbed its bridle, and the mount, terrified at the roar of guns and scent of blood, whinnied and reared. Iron Knife hung on, even though it lifted him off the ground. "Lance Bearer!" he shouted. "We've got to save the women and children! Catch some horses!"

All around him, men were fighting hand to hand; loose horses galloped through the camp, trampling tipis and children who ran about in confusion. A number of lodges were aflame, whether deliberately torched or from gunfire, there was no way to know. Blue sky. Red flames. White faces of the dead. The flag still flapped in the wind, making a strange sound, but it was ragged and torn now.

Black Kettle was attempting to rally the warriors.

Iron Knife ran over and gave him the reins of the soldier's bay gelding. "Flee! The people must have a chief to guide them later! We will protect the retreat!"

The chief looked as if he might protest, then seemed to realize Iron Knife's logic and accepted the horse.

Iron Knife turned back toward the fighting. In the smoke of gunfire and burning lodges, people were only shadows, and it was difficult to know who was friend and who was foe. His ears rang with the screams, curses and echo of cannon. When he breathed, he smelled the acrid scent of smoke, blood and burning powder, but his mind was calm and logical now. Old White Antelope stood before his lodge, arms crossed as he stubbornly sang his death song. The soldiers shot him down.

Iron Knife was a dog soldier, the elite fighting troops of the Cheyenne. More than that, he was a holder of the *Hotamtsit,* the Dog Rope, one of the four bravest of the brave. Only a few times had he been forced to use it, the gallant symbol of his willingness to sacrifice himself to save the tribe. Iron Knife reached now to touch the sacred badge of honor looped over his shoulder. The dog soldiers by tradition brought up the rear of the column when the tribe was on the move to protect the retreat at the cost of their own lives. Those who had won the honor of the *Hotamtsit* were expected to stake themselves to the ground and fight from that spot, not retreating until they either won the battle and pressed forward or were killed by the advancing enemy.

Iron Knife was prepared to do that, but this was no place to stake his rope, his badge of defiance, not with the enemy all around and behind him. He could not protect the retreat this way. Lance Bearer also carried the honored band. He must find him. Together they could provide a line behind which the scattered and confused Cheyenne might retreat. He and his cousins, Two Arrows and Lance Bearer, were prepared to die to protect the withdrawal. He ran through the smoke and fire, then saw his cousins' handsome, set faces as they loaded and fired their old weapons.

He did not mind dying. He had known all these years that he would die young; the honor of being a dog soldier did not allow one to grow old. He had been through the ceremony of the badger and had come away knowing the signs said he would die young. Was today that day? If so, he was first determined to save his family and his woman. This was no place to make a stand, here in the flat, sandy soil without even a rock the size of a man's hand to provide shelter. Except for a small bank that ran along one side of the little creek, there was no shelter from the withering gunfire. Among the handful of straggly, small cottonwoods by the water, people were attempting to hide or dig pits to protect themselves from the merciless rifle fire.

"We must regroup in a more defensible spot!" he shouted. "This is no place to make a stand."

People heeded his call, and around him, the few people who had caught horses were trying to mount up to escape the deadly hail of bullets.

He coughed and choked on the acrid scent of gunpowder and smoke. The sweetish scent of blood gagged him. The dead lay tangled in the wreckage of their tipis and trampled by terrified horses that milled through the camp. Here and there lay a dead soldier. He craned his neck, searching for his woman. How long had this hell been going on? Ten minutes? Ten hours? Was it real? Time had no meaning, and he wondered for a split-second if he had actually died out there on the prairie trying to make it back to camp to warn his people. Maybe he was really dead and in the white man's hell and didn't know it yet. Then he heard Summer scream his name, and no matter what, he had to reach her side.

As he ran through the camp, he saw little Bear Cub, the gentle boy who wanted to be an artist. The child was running across the camp, a mounted soldier in hot pursuit. The bluecoat fired and the boy fell, then struggled to get up, his leg and foot all bloody. He tried to limp away, but the soldier grinned as he reached for his sword and took off in pursuit as if he were chasing an injured rabbit.

Iron Knife's rifle was empty. He ran at the soldier, swinging the gun. The butt of it caught the white man across the chest. He fell and landed on his own sword. Iron Knife caught the lathered horse. Bear Cub hobbled toward him, and Iron Knife realized with a sinking heart that the child would always be crippled even if he managed to survive this attack. Maybe he should give the horse to a healthy warrior who had more to give than this crippled child. Who was he to make that decision?

"Bear Cub, get out of here fast!" He half helped, half lifted the boy to the horse, slapped it across the rump, and watched it gallop out of the camp to safety.

Summer. Where was she? The scattered herd of Cheyenne horses thundered past him, churning up a spray of sand. Summer's beautiful mare, Starfire, was in that bunch. He grabbed the rope that trailed from the animal's neck, then looked around. Through the dust and smoke and noise, he saw Summer Sky clutching their daughter, the two boys at her feet. The morning sun reflected off her golden hair, and she had never been more beautiful to him.

"Little One!" He struggled through the confusion toward her. Pretty Flower Woman held her own baby on a dancing pinto and waited. Old Pony Woman, his aunt, had mounted a ragged gray gelding and was reaching for Summer's children. Summer turned when she heard his shout, and the relieved look on her face told him how much she depended on him. Leading the skittish mare, he ran to them.

"Here, Lance! Get up behind Pretty Flower!" He lifted his oldest boy to the back of the pinto, grabbed Storm Gathering, and handed him up to old Pony Woman.

He heard his aunt shouting questions, but he couldn't understand her words in the hellish noise. However, he knew by the looks on their anxious faces that they were asking about their men. "Get out of here while you still can!" he yelled. "We'll regroup at that place in the willows!"

Everyone knew that camping spot miles from here. The two women thundered out of camp. Now he reached for Summer and the baby.

"Are you going with us?" she cried.

He shook his head as he lifted her onto the mare's back. Little Garnet shrieked at the top of her lungs. He had to protect the retreat, even if it cost him his life. Iron Knife peered through the smoke. Many of the Cheyenne had caught horses and were fighting their way out of the camp. He looked toward the direction they would have to ride to make it to the camp of the willows. There were soldiers between the women and the escape route. Even as he watched, a woman was shot from her rearing horse.

"Iron Knife! I—I don't think I can make it!" Summer tried to cling to him as he lifted her to her mare.

There was a good chance she was right. He grabbed a pistol from a fallen soldier and checked to make sure it was loaded. "I'll get you and the baby through the line of fire; then I'll come back to fight!"

He swung up behind her, slipped his arms around her and the sobbing baby, and put his face against Summer's yellow hair. "You'll be all right, Little One. I won't let anything happen to you!"

He felt her relax in his arms as he guided the mare through the smoke and shooting. She trusted him with her life, and he would not let her down. If nothing else, his big body partially protected her small one as they threaded their way across the camp. Up ahead of them, three soldiers were picking off riders as they passed. Iron Knife urged the mare into a gallop, rode one of the soldiers down before the man realized what he intended. He would always remember the bearded man's startled face as he whirled with his rifle even as the mare's hooves caught him in the throat and chest. Behind him, he heard Two Arrows' shouts of encouragement and turned his head to see his cousin attempting to catch a horse. The warriors were abandoning the camp, determined to cover the women and old ones' retreat.

A soldier grinned drunkenly as he aimed at Iron Knife, but the big dog soldier was a better shot. Even on the dancing mare, he took aim, then pulled the trigger. The shot cracked out and caught the man in the heart. "Now, Summer!"

He dug his heels into the mare's sides, putting it into a gallop as he thundered past the other soldier. That one held a rifle. All Iron Knife could do was throw his jammed pistol at him as they galloped by. The man dodged away. *We've made it,* Iron Knife thought almost unbelieving, *we've made it out of hell!*

He wrapped his arms around Summer Sky and their crying baby, feeling her warm and trembling, sheltered against his great chest. She was his woman—his to protect and cherish—and no man would ever hurt her while he lived. Behind him, Two Arrows shouted a warning. Iron Knife half turned to see the soldier taking aim.

He heard the thunder of the shot at the instant a point of fire burned into his side. He was hit! He clung to Summer and urged the horse onward as he felt his blood trickle warm and sticky sweet down his buckskin shirt. Maybe he had no chance to live, but he could provide cover for his woman until he could get her safely away from here. He gripped her with one arm and reined the horse forward, urging it onward.

Summer looked back at him, smiling with relief, her beautiful face pale. "We're going to make it!"

"Yes, we'll make it," he whispered through gritted teeth, "keep going!" He dared not tell her he'd been hit; she'd want to stop and staunch the flow of blood, thus endangering her and his child. Even if he bled to death, he thought he could last a couple of miles before he fell from the saddle. That would be long enough to get her away from danger, save her life, and that was all that mattered to him now.

It felt as if he had had a glowing poker thrust into his side. His buckskins were wet with blood. He bit his lip to hold back a cry of pain as the horse galloped across uneven ground, jarring him as it ran. Every jolt of its hooves against the frozen dirt hurt deep inside as if he were jabbed and jabbed again with a burning blade. The crisp morning air blew icy cold against his sweating face. He swore that no one would ever hurt Summer Sky, not as long as he had the strength to raise a hand to protect her. The baby hushed as the noise of the fighting faded in the background. The mare jumped over a small gully, and the sudden pain was more than he could take. He gasped aloud.

"Iron Knife"—Summer tried to look over her shoulder at his sweating face—"is something wrong? Talk to me! Are you hurt?"

"No," he lied, "keep riding! Two Arrows and Lance Bearer are coming behind us; we'll make it to the willows. Don't talk, just ride!"

He promised himself that he would not die until they

reached refuge from the soldiers and the cold wind. If he died now, he might fall from the bare-backed horse and take her with him. After they made it to the willows, his cousins would look after his woman and children.

It seemed a million miles that the horse jolted him as it ran. He tried not to think of the pain and concentrated on staying conscious, staying on that horse. He had endured pain before from many battle wounds, from the time he had taken part in the Sun Dance ceremony, from his boyhood when Jake Dallinger had strung him up and whipped him almost to death in a Texas town square.

The passage of time was a blur of pain and the sweet scent of Summer's hair against his face. He kissed her hair and said a mental goodbye to her. Behind them, the noise of the battle seemed to be fading on the cold winter wind. Either they were putting distance between them and Sand Creek or most of the Indians had been slaughtered, maybe both.

The baby girl whimpered, and Summer shushed her as they rode. "Hush, sweet, we're going to make it, aren't we, dearest?"

He bit his lip hard to control a groan, burying his face deeper in her yellow hair. It always smelled so good, and he loved to tangle his fingers in it when he made love to her. "I—I— Didn't I promise you, Little One, that I would always protect you, look after you?"

"And you always have," she murmured. "Look, there's the willows up ahead."

He had gotten her to safety, he thought dimly. He heard the frost crunching beneath the mare's hooves as they rode into the windbreak of the slope. Nothing mattered to him but protecting her, he loved her so. As Summer reined in the horse, Iron Knife relaxed. She was safe; he could die now. He said one final thing in Cheyenne. *"Ne-mehotatse."* I love you.

With a sigh, he unclenched his hands from around her small waist. As blackness began to engulf him, he toppled from the horse, and the frozen ground rushed up to meet him.

Chapter Three

Summer reacted with horror as she felt his hands relax and he slid from the horse to the ground. "Iron Knife! Two Arrows, come quick!"

She dismounted, then handed the sleepy baby over to old Pony Woman. Kneeling by her fallen man, Summer reached out and touched the wet, scarlet stain. "Oh, dear God, he's hit!"

His two cousins ran immediately to his side.

Lance Bearer's handsome face was stern. "I saw it happen; I got that soldier with my lance."

She put her hand on Iron Knife's pulse. It felt weak and thready. "Are you telling me he was shot as we left the camp?"

The other nodded. "He has ridden all this way with his life running down his shirt, but what else could he do? Safety lay in escaping Sand Creek!"

All around them, women were weeping as they tried to aid the wounded, running to each new straggler, asking for details of loved ones.

"Help me get him to shelter," Summer said. Keeping her hand on his arm for reassurance, she directed his cousins in picking her man up and carrying him to a brush arbor out of the wind. "Are there any matches?"

Two Arrows nodded. "Only a few, but if we dare build a fire, the soldiers might see or smell the smoke."

Summer looked up at the mid-morning sun. "It'll be a cold night. Some of these people will freeze to death if we don't get help."

Plump old Pony Woman hugged Summer's baby to her. "My husband has sent a runner to the Arapaho for help. In the meantime, we do the best we can; no one knows for sure how many are dead or so badly hurt they will die later."

"What about the old chiefs?" Two Arrows asked.

"Some are dead. Black Kettle and his wife made it out, but I think they may be hurt," Pony Woman answered.

For a long moment, Summer put her face in her hands and shook. If she were back in Boston, she'd have the best of doctors at her disposal. She'd have a big warm bed for Iron Knife, and all the warm broth and medicine she needed.

She looked at the flow of blood from Iron Knife's side, but Two Arrows shook his head. "He's too far gone, Summer. Let us work on the ones we know we can save."

"No!" She looked from her love's wan face to his cousin's sad one. "No, I won't give up on him, not when he's made this sacrifice to save me!"

She grabbed the big knife from Iron Knife's belt and cut the deerskin away from the wound. He was still losing blood. His cousins were right; if she couldn't stop the bleeding, he didn't have a chance. She remembered then what he had done long ago when she had been wounded. "Two Arrows, stake him down so he can't move and build me a little fire."

The two handsome Cheyenne brothers looked at each other a long moment. Lance Bearer said, "What you've got in mind may take more nerve than a white girl has."

"I'm not a white girl any longer; I'm Summer Sky of the *Hevataniu* band of Cheyenne, and I intend to save my man! Now help tie him down."

It seemed warmer in the little shelter once Two Arrows had a tiny fire burning. Iron Knife's clothes were wet and bloody. Summer took a deep breath and began to cut them away. His cousins had spread-eagled the unconscious man and staked his hands and feet down securely. She examined the wound; it appeared the bullet had gone clear through and left a clean wound that might not have hit any vital organs. If only she could stop the bleeding, he might have a chance.

She put the knife blade in the fire and took a deep breath. Could she do this? He was staked down securely, so he couldn't fight her if he came to while she was attempting to cauterize the wound. Summer swallowed hard. "Now you clear out," she whispered to his cousins, "and see if the women can take care of my children for me the next few hours."

"Consider it done." Lance Bearer, the older one of the two cousins, looked at her a long moment. Among the Cheyenne, should a warrior die, one of his brothers usually added the widow to his own family as another wife so the dead man's woman and children would be cared for. If Iron Knife didn't pull through this, she would have to take one of his cousins as her man. It was the way of things, but she couldn't even imagine another man touching her but the one lying so pale and still before her. She wouldn't think about that now. She motioned them both to leave.

Iron Knife lay there staked down and unconscious. She picked up the big knife that glowed red in the coals. Oh, God, she wasn't sure she could do this, but if she didn't, he would bleed to death. For an instant, she almost went outside and called to Two Arrows and Lance Bearer, but they had other responsibilities with wounded still straggling in and the possibility that the soldiers might trail them here. To ask for help would show that she was only a weak white girl after all, unworthy of the warrior who had made her his woman.

Iron Knife's dark eyes flickered open. He looked almost delirious as he glanced around, as if he were not certain where he was or what had happened. His gaze centered on the glowing knife in her hand and then went to her set face.

"No!" He pulled at his restraints. "No! Don't torture me!"

"Stop that, you'll hurt yourself more!"

Oh, if only he had remained unconscious! His magnificent naked body strained against his bounds as he tried to break free. "This is going to hurt, but there is no other way, dearest."

He was protesting and struggling. When he opened his mouth to cry out, she gagged him with a strip of leather. He would need something to bite down on when she put that glowing blade on the wound. He bucked like a trussed stallion as she knelt over him with the knife. He didn't seem to recognize her in his delirium. Did he think she was going to kill him, torture him or geld him? Summer couldn't know; she only hoped that Two Arrows had driven the stakes deep so that the virile warrior couldn't move. He tried to protest, but now she had him securely gagged and bound.

"Close your eyes," she ordered, "and it won't hurt so much."

Instead his dark eyes glared into her blue ones as she slowly brought the glowing blade down. At the last moment, her hand hesitated, trembling. She couldn't do this; she must do this. He strained against his bindings like a wild stallion. Summer swallowed hard and laid the glowing hot knife against the wound. He cried out against the leather gag. Sweat broke out all over his face

and muscular dark body as he tried to wrench free.
Then, mercifully, he fainted.

In his mind, he was a thirteen-year-old boy in a Texas
town again who had been invited up to a pretty red-
haired whore's bedroom. He didn't know Jake Dallinger
was her pimp who hired her out to soldiers and took her
money. When Jake walked in unexpectedly, he beat the
boy unmercifully, then strung him up by his wrists in
the town square and took his bull whip to the boy's bare
back. Only the half-breed boy's brave mother, Texanna,
had saved his life when she held the crowd off with a
shotgun and ordered Dallinger to untie him. At that very
moment, his father, the great chief War Bonnet, had ridden in just in time to put them on galloping horses and
race out of town ahead of the mob. There was no way
to get the sick baby sister, Cimarron, who had been left
behind with a kindly minister and his wife. His mind
was a swirl of nightmare and bloody pain. If his back
was being whipped, why did his side feel on fire?
    Maybe he was again taking part in the medicine lodge
ceremony: the Sun Dance. In that, the bravest of the
Cheyenne warriors ran leather thongs through their
chest muscles and hung from the pole chanting sacred
songs for hours or days until the men finally managed
to pull hard enough to tear the thongs out, leaving scars
that attested to their bravery. No, he couldn't be in the
Sun Dance; the agony was in his side.
    He opened his eyes slowly, looked around. He was
naked and staked out on the ground. There was a fire
and a pretty, yellow-haired white girl just putting down
a glowing knife and taking a gag from his mouth. Was
she torturing him? Gelding him? She looked familiar
somehow. Then she leaned over him, looking at him
anxiously, and he knew her and smiled. His woman—

his once in a lifetime love—Summer Sky. He knew every inch of that beautiful body. He had thrust into her and come away stained with her virginity. And that full, soft mouth had kissed his lips and kissed his manhood. He had tangled his fingers in that yellow hair the color of ripe wheat and ridden her hard, putting his babies in her lean belly. They had lain in each other's arms warm against the elements and secure against the world. She was his, and he would protect and cherish her always. "Little One?"

"Iron Knife, do you know me?" Her lip trembled and she began to cry.

Everything came back to him. He wasn't dead after all. It was not his day to die. "Yes, I know you, my Summer Sky. You have just done a very brave thing."

"I did what any Cheyenne woman would have done." She untied his hands and legs.

He felt weak. "If I don't make it, Lance Bearer has no wife."

She wiped tears from her eyes and gave him a weak smile. "I'll have you know, I don't intend to warm his bed, so you'd just better get well, do you hear?"

He nodded. So tired . . . so very tired. But she was safe; it had been worth the sacrifice. "The children . . . ?"

"The children are all right. All our family got out, but there's many dead and hurt among the people."

"I—I must help." He tried to sit up.

Summer restrained him. "There's nothing you can do that's not already being done. Just lie there and let your cousins do what they can."

It was good to finally pass the responsibility on. He wasn't sure he could sit up anyway. "Cold," he whispered, "cold."

"I'll take care of you." He felt her small hand on his

face, and he took a deep, comforting breath and dropped off to sleep.

Summer looked at his clothes. They were wet with blood, and cut to pieces, so she couldn't put those back on him. There was part of an old buffalo robe in the shelter, and she had her body heat. She stripped off her deerskin shift and lay her naked body down the length of him. His skin was cold and he trembled. If she couldn't warm him, he might freeze to death. She pulled the scrap of buffalo robe around their naked bodies and pressed against him, praying her body heat would permeate his skin and warm him. After a while, he stopped trembling. She lay with him all afternoon, afraid to leave him, but her milk-filled breasts grew swollen and painful. She slipped on her shift as the sky darkened and went outside. The day had warmed some.

Young Pretty Flower came to her, carrying Garnet. "How is he?"

"I can't be sure." Summer sighed, and took the baby. "How bad is it with the others?"

"Bad. Many women and children dead in their blankets, not realizing we were being attacked. We are sharing what little food there is. Maybe by tomorrow, we can count on some help from our friends among the Arapaho."

They found a place out of the wind, and Summer nursed her baby. "Is there not even food for the wounded?" If he didn't get nourishment, he would die.

Pretty Flower shook her head. "Not much. I'll boil a scrap of meat, see if I can make some broth for him. There's only a little pemmican until the Arapaho come."

"I—I'm not hungry," Summer said, "give my share to Iron Knife and the young and wounded." Summer checked on her sons, then handed little Garnet back to Pretty Flower. "Look after her, will you?"

The Indian girl nodded as she handed Summer a small gourd of broth. "I'm sorry there isn't more."

Summer inhaled the scent. The tantalizing aroma made her mouth water, but she must not eat it herself; her man needed it too badly. It was almost dark now as she crawled back in beside the big dog soldier.

Iron Knife's eyes opened. "Food?" he whispered.

"Yes, there's broth." She raised his head and held the gourd to his lips.

He started to sip it, then looked at her. "Have you—have you had some?"

"Of course," she lied, "now eat so you can regain your strength; we need strong warriors to go hunting as soon as you can." She must not let him know how little food there was or he would refuse this bit of broth, insisting that Summer drink it or share it between the children and the old ones.

He sipped it, and it brought tears to her eyes to see how weak this mighty warrior was now. "Are our children all right?"

"Yes, our family is fine; others are hurt." She must not tell him how many were dead or badly wounded. He needed rest to get well, and if he knew how dangerous their situation was, he would struggle to his feet and try to help. She managed to get the little bowl of steaming broth into him, and he sighed and closed his eyes again.

He was shivering in the winter night, and she was cold, too. She knew an injured person must be kept warm to survive at all. Quickly, she stripped off her doeskin shift and snuggled down against him under the scrap of cover. Immediately, her body heat began to radiate through his big one, and after a moment, he stopped shaking. She was growing warm also as she held her beloved close. Summer was still hungry; but he had been fed, and her naked body was keeping him warm, holding the breath of life in him. That was all that mattered at this moment and all she could do anything about.

Somewhere out there in the cold, other wounded were freezing to death, scattered and alone after the attack. She could only hope and pray that they could make it until morning so that the able-bodied Cheyenne could return to find the injured and the lost children.

All during the night, Summer shared her warmth and willed him to live. By morning, when the Arapaho rode into the little camp to bring food and buffalo robes, Iron Knife was conscious and growing stronger.

In early December, the month the Cheyenne called Mahkhekonini, the big freezing moon, the people remained hidden while the wounded improved, and the able-bodied warriors talked of painting their faces for war. Iron Knife grew stronger every day once he had meat to eat, but for a few days, Summer had not been certain her beloved would live. She worked tirelessly as she looked after him, stopping only to see after her three children, but for the most part, Pretty Flower and old Pony Woman cared for them.

Old Pony Woman scolded, "Take better care of your own health. If you get sick and die, who will take care of him and your children?"

The old woman was right, she knew, but still she would not let anyone else touch him or take care of him. Time lost all meaning, and sometimes she collapsed in a sleep of sheer exhaustion.

Gradually, as the days passed, Iron Knife began to improve, although she knew the wound would have killed a lesser man. His uncle, old Clouds Above, looked at the weak, wounded Iron Knife and said to Summer, "It may be a long time before he carries a lance or bow again, and the survivors are cautious as wild horses about staying where the soldiers might attack them."

She looked back over her shoulder at Iron Knife asleep on his blankets. "He is better, but in no shape to ride hard and far."

"Exactly." The old chief fingered the bear claw necklace he wore as he asked, "Did his stallion ever come in?"

Summer shook her head. "He loved that horse like a brother. It may have found its way back to Sand Creek, but by then, we were all gone."

"We have all been on the watch for it, but it may be that a soldier rides it now." He considered. "We must move far from here, away from the soldiers, so we can make plans."

She knew by the set look of his lined old face, but she hoped against it. "Will there—will there be war?"

"The soldiers have brought it to us, and now we must fight them or be tracked down and killed like rabbits in their burrows."

"But Iron Knife has always tried to live in peace with the whites."

"And where did it get my nephew?" His lined face looked grim. "The whole Cheyenne tribe is punished for what a few hot-blooded young warriors do. No, there will be raids, and women and babies on both sides will die."

Summer put her hands over her ears at his words and winced. "No. My man is half-white himself and—"

"His heart is Cheyenne," his uncle snapped, "and you will have to decide where your loyalties lie. Are you white or are you Cheyenne?"

"I am human," she wept, "and we will not get caught up in this bloody war!"

"A woman does not speak for a Cheyenne warrior, especially one of the carriers of the Dog Rope. I know my brother's son better than you. When he is well, he will put on the war paint, dance the ceremonial dances and ride against our enemies, no matter what their color."

Summer turned and walked away. How had she gotten herself and her children into this hellish mess? All she wanted was to be allowed to live and raise her children in peace. She looked about her and imagined that the other Cheyenne glared at her with suspicion and anger because of her white skin. Where did her loyalties lie? Once, a long time ago, she had been called upon to make that decision when she turned her back on her rich, white civilization because of her love for a half-breed warrior. Things had been fairly peaceful between red and white since that spring day in 1859 when she had handed back the fine diamond and sapphire engagement ring to her fiancé and ridden away with Iron Knife. What would she do now if she had to decide? And what would Iron Knife choose to do when he was well enough to ride again? She didn't ever want to think about it.

Days passed, and across the Rockies and the Colorado plains, icy winds blew as the tribes huddled around their fires and stayed put. Gradually, the stories drifted back to them of the half-breed Cheyenne, Robert Bent, being forced at gunpoint to lead the soldiers to the Sand Creek camp, and how, after the massacre, the drunken victors had paraded scalps and captured Indian children through the streets of Denver. Over a hundred Indians had been killed, mostly women and children, and at least three chiefs. No one, even the Indians, would ever be sure of those figures; it was probably much higher. Only eight or ten soldiers had been killed.

When Iron Knife heard these stories, he tried to get up, vowing with anger in his voice to join the other braves in riding the war trail.

Summer restrained him. "If you aren't careful, you'll tear that wound open and you won't be any help to anyone."

He glared at her. "You're white down to the bone. Of course you don't want me attacking them, do you?"

She saw the look on his face, and tears came to her eyes. "What's happening to us? You never thought the color of my skin was important before."

He looked troubled and turned his face away. "That is the first thing I think of now when I look at you. Sometimes I wonder if love can really bridge the gap between two warring cultures. Sometimes I think I should not have taken you as my woman. Don't you ever have doubts?"

Indeed, was love enough? She didn't answer him because often now, late at night, she lay sleepless, listening to the wind moan like the dead at Sand Creek, like the dying cries of white settlers, and wondered if she should have stayed in Boston where no one knew about terror, starvation and death.

"You have answered me with your silence," he said.

"I don't know—"

"That is what bothers me, Summer Sky, that you don't know, that you are no longer sure. Well, I am sure of only one thing; I must fight to preserve my way of life."

"Oh, please, no!" She caught his arm, but he shrugged it off.

"What else can I do? You know I am one of those who has always counseled for peace, but now I see it has brought only death and pain to my people. When I am well, I will join the other braves in riding the war trail."

"Against my people?"

He laughed without humor. "So the truth comes out; you still think of yourself as white!"

"I think of myself as a human being!" she lashed out, "and I don't want to see women and children of any color tortured and killed!"

"Remember," he said grimly, "the whites started this."

Had they? She no longer remembered who had started it or where, and to her, it didn't matter. However, she knew how it would all end: with death and destruction. "The tribes cannot win against the whites."

Iron Knife shrugged and looked at her as coldly as if she were a stranger. "Maybe not, but I would rather be a dead lion than a live dog."

She couldn't believe they were arguing like this. Their love had been enough to bridge any chasm—until now. "What's that supposed to mean?"

"Just what you think it means, my white captive. When the old chiefs call for who will smoke the pipe, I will paint my face for war and ride to attack the whites who box us in, attack us. I will not be herded to a reservation while I can fight and die breathing free air."

"So what happens to me and my children if you are killed?"

He shrugged. "You know the answer. If you were really part of our culture, you would be satisfied to mutilate yourself in mourning, then let Two Arrows or Lance Bearer take you as a wife."

"I will not be treated as chattel or a mere captive."

"You are mine and I do not intend to lose you over this."

"As a possession or your woman?"

"That's your choice." His face was troubled.

"I don't seem to be getting any choice at all . . . master." She got up and stalked out.

She thought she heard him call her name as she walked away, but she didn't look back. The Indian wars had changed many things, including their relationship.

Summer was in a Cheyenne encampment with three small children sired by a warrior who might be spilling blood next week. She didn't even want to think about what the future would bring or what she would do next.

Later, she overheard Iron Knife's cousins and uncle come into the makeshift lodge to talk with him.

Two Arrows said, "The old ones want to have the Ceremony of the Arrows before they go into any full-scale war against the whites."

Old Clouds Above grunted. "That will have to wait several months, of course, because as you know, all ten bands of our people will have to gather for the ceremony, and with this bad weather, that is impossible."

"The Ceremony of the Sacred Arrows?" Iron Knife sounded hesitant.

For the first time in years, Summer remembered Angry Wolf and what had happened to him; that secret between she and Iron Knife. Murder among the Cheyenne was a terrible taboo, and she was guilty of it. She knew the ceremony was only done once in a great while; certainly it had not been done all the years she had been Iron Knife's woman. She shuddered, thinking about it. It was said that if murder had been committed among the people, when the bundle of Sacred Medicine Arrows was opened, they would be covered with blood. Then everyone would know there had been a murder for which no justice had been done.

Blood. She put her head in her hands and thought of that crisp autumn day in 1858. She had been a new captive among the Cheyenne and had tried to escape. There was a pretty Arapaho girl with the Cheyenne back then, Gray Dove, who was jealous of Summer because the Indian girl loved Iron Knife. Gray Dove had plotted to send Angry Wolf after Summer to kill her so there would be no chance she would ever be recaptured and returned to the Cheyenne and Iron Knife.

That long-ago day, Angry Wolf had captured Summer near a fast-moving creek where she had stopped to drink.

"So, white bitch, we meet again," he hissed as he pulled her to him. "Only this time, there is no half-breed bastard to save you or even my own men to share you with!"

"Let go of me!" she shrieked, clawing at him.

"Scream all you wish!" he said, laughing, twisting her arm behind her painfully as he pulled her up against him. "There is no one to hear you!"

She could smell the reek of his sweat, and she recoiled from his clammy skin.

"You will not mind the smell of me when I am through with you, Yellow Hair! You will beg to be allowed to kiss my sweat away if only I will stop hurting you!"

"If you hurt me, you will regret it," Summer challenged as she turned her direct, stubborn gaze upon him. "Even now, a soldier patrol from the fort might cross this area and find us."

"Not likely!" Then he proceeded to tell her with relish that Gray Dove had purposely given the white girl wrong directions so she would never find the way to the fort and to make sure she would never come back to the Indian camp; Gray Dove had sent Angry Wolf to kill her.

Angry Wolf had his hot mouth on hers now, forcing her lips open. She freed one hand and clawed his face.

He swore a white man's oath and struck her, knocking her half-conscious to the ground.

"This time," he promised, "you are going to pay for that, and Iron Knife will not be here to stop me! Because of you both, me and my followers have been whipped through the camp like misbehaving puppies. You have brought disgrace on me, and now you will pay

for that. I only wish that son of a white whore could be
here to see what I do to his woman!"

He staked her out, spread-eagled, and cut the deerskin
shift from her ripe body. Then he taunted her with how
he intended to rape her repeatedly, then smear her naked
body with wild honey and cover her with thousands of
big, red ants.

When he went off to a bee tree down the trail to get
the honey, Summer lay there, tied down and shaking
with terror. She closed her eyes at the sound of a step,
not wanting to look into his ugly, grinning face as he returned.

But a big hand touched her face ever so gently. She
would have known that touch anywhere. Her eyes
blinked open to look up into Iron Knife's angry face.
She saw his dark eyes glitter in hate at the bruises and
teeth marks on her fair skin.

"Whoever did this will not live to see the sun set!" he
muttered as his blade flashed and he cut her ankles and
one wrist free, but then Angry Wolf sneaked up behind
him and attacked Iron Knife. The squat, heavier brave
caught Iron Knife off balance, and her rescuer hit his
head on a rock as he fell. The two rolled over and over.
Then they stumbled to their feet, facing each other warily.

Iron Knife gestured toward Summer, still pinned by
one wrist. "You have tried to violate my woman, you
whelp of a coyote! For this, you will surely die!"

"Brave talk for one who stands before me empty-
handed; no knife, no quirt," the other sneered, pulling
his quirt slowly from his belt, hefting his knife in his
other hand.

Summer saw her big brave glance toward his horse.
His quirt hung from the saddle; his knife lay on the
ground just out of Summer's reach. Angry Wolf

crouched between him and the weapons and now smiled slowly.

"We shall see who will die! I have been whipped through the camp by the leaders of the seven warrior groups! Never have I felt such humiliation! I want you to know the taste of my lash!"

He whipped his quirt against the ground. "Always I have lived in your shadow before the Council of Chiefs. Always the people follow you, listen to your words so you will be chosen next time they pick a chief. My friends and I will go off to join the outlaw dog soldier band. When the people see our bravery, they will sing songs of us around the camp fires, and Gray Dove will look at me with new eyes."

Iron Knife did not answer as he backed slowly toward the swollen creek. He moved as if injured, and Summer saw the blood well up scarlet over one eye where he had struck a rock when he fell. He wiped the blood from his brown face and gestured. "Let us talk of this, fellow dog soldier."

"Talk! You are as bad as your woman about wanting to talk!" He gestured disdainfully. "Sing your death chant, Iron Knife, son of a white whore! And then with your dying eyes you will see me mount your woman. Because of you, I have been spurned by mine!"

The big warrior backed slowly into the swirling water as Angry Wolf advanced on him with knife and quirt.

Summer reached for the knife on the ground that lay just out of her reach. She tried to pull the last stake out of the soil to free her wrist, but she was too weak. The rope would have to be cut. She clawed the dirt ... reaching ... reaching.

Iron Knife glanced at her in wordless appeal, the scarlet blood running down his bronze face and into the water. She couldn't do it, but she must do it! Again, she clawed the dirt, straining toward the knife. The rawhide thong bit into her wrist as she struggled toward the weapon. Blood seeped under the rope as she reached and threw her weight against the rawhide.

Once more she strained, and then she had the knife by the tip of the blade! For a long, heart-stopping moment, it almost tumbled away from her, but she had it! Quickly, she cut the remaining rope from her wrist. Now she crouched, knife in hand, watching the two in the knee-deep, swirling water. So intent was Angry Wolf on his injured quarry that he never turned to look behind him. He quirted his enemy across the face, and Iron Knife grabbed the lash. But it dropped into the swift water and was swept away.

The other laughed in triumph. "So now, it is only we two with no council or tribe to back you up. I have dreamed of this moment. Your heart is about to take my blade, and then I will finish off your woman; and no one will ever know what happened to either of you!"

"You know it is a terrible taboo of the Cheyenne to commit murder among our own. You would be exiled for four years, and my cousins would seek revenge."

Angry Wolf shrugged. "As I said, they will never know. Since you will both be missing, they may think you have dishonored your people and returned to the white civilization to live with your woman."

Behind him, on the bank, Summer hesitated with the dagger in her hand and looked toward the Appaloosa stallion grazing nearby. Why should she care what happened to either of the men? All she had to do was let them fight it out to the death while she took the swiftest horse and fled. She knew which direction to take now, and she did not think either man could catch her if she rode the fine stallion. What did it matter which man was killed? Why should she care about the wounded dog soldier? And yet. . . .

Even as she turned toward the horse, she stopped and

looked back to the battle in the water. Iron Knife would surely lose. He was at a clear disadvantage, wounded and weaponless, as the other moved in for the kill.

In that moment, the squat Indian lunged, cutting the other a glancing blow across the shoulder. They meshed, struggling in the racing water, churning it to bloody foam like two great stags in an age-old battle. Iron Knife hung on valiantly, but his opponent, using his heavier weight, took him to his knees in the boiling current.

As she watched in growing horror, Angry Wolf dropped the knife, but lifted a rock from the bottom and struck Iron Knife a glancing blow. Iron Knife staggered, seemed to slip on the slick bottom. He went down in the foaming water, and the squat dog soldier had him by the throat holding him under, drowning him.

This was her last chance to run for the horses; she knew that. In another minute or so, her attacker would be finished with his murder and coming after her. Still, she hesitated. Her head told her to run, but her heart told her something else. Without even realizing it, she ran toward the water, her hand still clutching the dagger.

Angry Wolf had his back to her, intent on murder. She was almost upon him, running lightly and unencumbered by clothes across the sand. Summer was in the water before he seemed to hear her. His hands let go of Iron Knife's throat as he turned abruptly to face her.

He made a futile grab, but her anger made her swift. As he lunged, she dodged his arm and plunged the knife deep into his chest, then jerked it free.

His mouth opened in disbelief, and fear spread across his face. He gave a weak cry as he staggered, the scarlet stain spreading down his chest into the water. He made a threatening gesture, then clutched at his fatal wound as he fell backward into the current and was swept away.

Summer stared in shock, the bloody knife hanging limply from her numb fingers. She had killed a man!

Iron Knife staggered to her side, still choking and coughing from the water. Together, they watched a long moment as the body washed down the stream and on over the rapids.

She looked up at him and then at the bloody knife in her hand, suddenly feeling very faint. "I—I owed you that," she said simply and swayed on her feet. But deep in her heart, she knew she lied. That wasn't the reason she had done it.

Quickly, he caught her in his arms and lifted her as she collapsed, carrying her to the shore. The sun came out from behind the clouds in sudden brilliance as the warrior stood on the sand and cradled her gently in his powerful arms, looking down at her.

Summer stared at the bloody knife in her limp fingers that now draped across his broad shoulders. It occurred to her that it was still not too late for her to stab him in the back and run away, freeing herself from the Indians forever. She need only take his horse and head for the fort. No one ever need know what had happened here. She could keep the secret.

For a long moment, he looked deep into her eyes as the sun warmed them. Finally he spoke. "Will you now kill me with my own knife, Summer Sky?"

Her mouth dropped open at his question and at the realization that he made no move to protect himself. Her fingers unclenched, and the dagger clattered harmlessly to the ground behind him.

"I might have killed you!" she whispered.

He still held her naked, wet body swinging lightly from his strong arms. "I was willing to bet my life that you wouldn't."

"You're a reckless fool!" she challenged. "Why were

you so sure? I didn't know for a moment what I would do."

"I knew, my Summer Sky. I knew the moment you came into the water to save me instead of running for the horses."

She could only look dumbly up into his eyes, her emotions a tangle. He bent his head, and his lips brushed hers, as light as a butterfly's wing caressing a flower. It was a hesitant kiss. He seemed almost to be awaiting her command to pull back. He seemed to expect her rejection which would be swiftly followed by the sting of her hand across his scarred face.

She was surprised by his hesitancy, this bold savage who had tasted her lips with such assurance in the past. And this, perhaps, triggered her own reaction. She seemed to have almost no control over her own body as she felt her arms reach around his sinewy neck. Her soft hands pulled his bronzed, bleeding face down to hers, and she kissed him in a way that she did not know she knew.

He started in surprise as instinctively, her mouth explored his deeply, thoroughly. Then, he was all man, crushing her to him as she still swung in his embrace.

That long-ago day, they had made love the very first time, lying naked on the creek bank after Angry Wolf's death. For the very first time, she had experienced the splendor of sharing her Cheyenne warrior's passion. 1858. A long time ago, Summer thought with a sigh as she came out of her memories and looked around at the cold. Now the Cheyenne were scattered from the attack on Sand Creek, she and her once in a lifetime love were tense and short with each other, and sometime soon, the Medicine Arrow bundle would be opened. Would there be blood on them or was that only a superstition? One thing was certain, if the arrows were bloody, her secret would be out. Had her actions that long-ago day brought this bad luck to Iron Knife's people? And what could be done about it now?

Chapter Four

Summer waited until old Clouds Above and the cousins had left the makeshift lodge, and then she went to sit by Iron Knife's pallet. "I have been thinking about Angry Wolf."

He didn't look at her. "I have, too."

She felt almost a wall between them. "You are thinking that all this bad luck to your people might have been brought about by his death?"

"The thought occurs to me now and again."

She put her hand on his arm. "Don't blame yourself; after all, I was the one who killed him, not you."

He shook her hand off. "Yes, but I helped keep the deed a secret instead of going to the council. You are my woman, so I am responsible for your actions."

She was angry that she felt so defensive. "He was killing you; what else could I do?"

"I know; I owe you my life." His dark eyes softened. "But covering up the deed was cowardly of me; not worthy of a carrier of the Dog Rope."

"The council might have ordered my death," she reminded him.

He reached out and caught a lock of her pale hair and fingered it as his fingers followed it down her throat to where he touched the swell of her full breast. "I know, and I would have done anything, no matter how dishonorable, to protect you. It is not good that a warrior should be so obsessed by a woman. Men think of females as a convenience to warm their beds and bear their sons."

"You arrogant savage! Is that all I am to you?" She started to get up, but he caught her hand, turned it over, kissed her palm.

"Would you be more than that in your white civilization?"

She thought of the women she knew in Boston with their tight corsets and few legal rights. "I will not settle for that."

He kissed her palm again. "Little One, at times I can think of nothing else except lying on your white belly, pumping my seed into you while you offer me your breasts and claw my back. There, I have lowered myself by admitting what an obsession you are. Does that satisfy you?"

His expression was grim, almost as if he resented the power she held over him. He had spoken of lust and coupling, not love. What she had wanted to hear was that he loved her, but the gentleness of him was gone as if he could not close the door on the horrors his eyes had seen the soldiers inflict at Sand Creek. It was almost as if he had just noticed the color of her skin.

"Are you afraid your people will now no longer accept me?" She wished she could read the emotion in his dark eyes.

"I have given up a chance to be a chief in my father's place because I was determined to keep you by my side."

"But it looks bad for a dog soldier to have a white wife?"

"Many braves across the plains keep a white captive to warm their beds." His voice was cold.

"A wife has a place of honor, while a captive is a slave. Do you think to replace me with a Cheyenne girl and keep me to pleasure yourself with?"

"Let us talk of this no more; you talk foolishness," he snapped.

What she wanted was reassurance and she was not getting it. He lusted after her, he had admitted that, but did he no longer love her? She had given him children: sons. Surely no warrior would throw away a woman who had given him such fine sons. Could he be thinking of taking a second wife to share his tipi so that he would be better thought of among the Cheyenne warriors? *No one really knows what another is thinking,* she thought sadly as she watched his face. She wanted nothing more than his happiness, even if it meant going away so that he could take a Cheyenne wife.

"The people will be moving out," he said. "They fear the army will track them here if they stay too long."

He struggled to sit up, and she cried out, "Be careful; you'll hurt yourself!"

"I am useless to the warriors until I heal," he said bitterly. "My cousins tell me they have found Cherokee Evans and his woman in a cabin in the mountains. They have offered to give me shelter for a few days until I am fit to ride."

Was that the only reason he had been so short-tempered?

"It will be good for you to rest a little longer without worrying that the soldiers may run across us."

"And you, do you look forward to living among whites again, having a roof over your head instead of a tipi?"

She took his big, rough hand in hers and kissed his knuckles. "I am happy to be where ever you are, my love, you know that."

He looked deep into her eyes. "What is happening to

us, Summer Sky? Once I never thought we could argue or say bitter words."

"We must try not to let the trouble between our two people become trouble between us."

He still seemed distant. "You are right. Perhaps it is only because I was so used to coupling with you several times a day, and now, I look at you and cannot have you. I think about it constantly. That is why the other warriors have been urging me to take a second woman, or at least a captive. It is not meant for a virile warrior to live like the black-robed priests who come to tell us of their virgin and their God."

Summer winced. "I am not Cheyenne, my warrior; I can't live with the thought of you touching another woman."

"Neither can I," he admitted, "yet seeing you, touching you, yet not being able to possess you is driving me loco." He seemed to clench his fists for a long moment.

What was she going to do? Summer blinked back unshed tears. He needed the pleasure and relief her body could give him, yet she dared not risk having another baby now with so little food. Little Garnet might starve as Summer's milk dried up, even though she was now trying to wean the toddler.

Summer Sky sighed and began preparations to bathe her man. Iron Knife was still too weak to desire a woman; but as she washed him, his manhood swelled and throbbed, and he pulled her to him, kissed her. She forgot caution then and answered in kind, rubbing her swollen breasts against his hard chest, putting her tongue deep in his mouth. Only when he pushed up her doeskin shift and put his hand on her mound did she force herself to pull away.

"Please . . ."

She saw the hunger and the naked desire in his eyes as she forced herself to take a deep breath, fight for control. "We—we must not surrender to this again." Summer didn't know whether she was reminding him or herself. Cheyenne splendor—a passionate climax like nothing she had ever experienced.

Now she saw the heat of anger and repressed passion in his smoldering gaze. He had reduced himself to begging and thus humbled himself while she had found herself in the role of a nagging wife, denying him the pleasure of her body.

"All right," he snapped, "I keep forgetting, but I suppose I can always count on you to remind me."

"Iron Knife, please!"

Now it was his turn to pull away, turn over and ignore her entreaties.

What was she to do with this impossible situation? With a shuddering sigh, Summer rose and went outside. In the camp, children laughed and ran about. She watched her own strong sons chasing each other, a mongrel puppy barking at their heels.

Little Garnet played in the dirt next to Pretty Flower, Two Arrows' wife, who sat rocking her baby in its cradleboard. "Summer Sky, is something wrong?"

Summer didn't answer for a long moment as she sat down by the fire and picked up her own fat toddler. What was wrong was the difference and the clash of two cultures. Most of the other warriors had two wives. Two Arrows had also married Pretty Flower's younger sister, and her belly was beginning to swell with child. Summer asked Pretty Flower, "Doesn't it bother you to think of your man taking another girl in his blankets, even if she is your sister?"

The other girl gently rocked her baby's cradleboard. "It is the way of things," she answered softly. "If he gets me with child before my little boy is big enough to eat meat, my son will starve. A man can not be expected to do without a woman in his bed, so they take a second wife."

"Iron Knife will never do that."

"Won't he?" The lovely Indian girl looked at her. "It means nothing if he should select a captive for his pleasure; you would still be first wife."

"I want to be his only woman."

"He is very unusual if he will do without."

Summer felt defensive. "White men only have one woman."

Pretty Flower shrugged. "Do not many of them keep a second woman that maybe the wife doesn't know about?"

A mistress, Summer thought as she held her pretty little girl and stroked her black hair. She wondered if her father had one? Certainly there was no passion between her parents. "Iron Knife will never do that; he loves me too much. Besides, I suppose in that way, I am white, not Cheyenne. If he took a second wife, I would leave him."

As the days passed, Iron Knife improved rapidly, and the elders of the tribe had sent out calls to all the ten bands of the Tsistsistas to come in for the Renewal of the Sacred Arrows. They feared to ready an attack against the whites without the good luck of the ceremony.

Although they did not speak of it, Summer felt a wall between them now built of both sexual tension and misunderstanding. When they spoke, each seemed careful to judge every word. She began to wonder if they would find the old feelings for each other once Iron Knife's wound had healed? Neither mentioned the bitter dispute over whether Iron Knife would fight against the whites.

Perhaps, Summer thought, *if I don't bring it up, the problem will resolve itself.*

Now they all waited for the tribes to gather. It was a great hardship to bring the people together in the cold weather when it was difficult to travel, but the old chiefs thought it important enough to send out camp criers to carry word from camp to camp. Summer told herself again and again that it was all ignorant superstition, that when the bundle was finally opened, all they would find would be four ancient arrows. But Iron Knife believed in the arrows with all his heart.

He sat in front of the fire, staring into the flames while Summer nursed her baby. "When they open the bundle and the arrows are bloody, how can I keep quiet? I fear to bring bad luck to my people."

She watched him, her heart aching with his anxiety. "Maybe they won't be bloody."

He scowled. "You think it is all nonsense, don't you?"

She didn't know herself. "I see no reason to fear and worry until the bundle is opened. I want to see these sacred objects for myself."

He shook his head. "Women are not allowed to see these. Two are painted red and two black, and our people have had them many, many years. The hated Pawnee stole them once, and we only managed to get two of them returned. The substitutes we have made for the others don't seem to have the same magic."

"You really believe that the Cheyenne will not regain their position of power until the originals are recovered?"

He nodded. "That may seem ridiculous to you, but it makes sense to us. We see that our people have been in a gradual decline ever since it happened."

"That's silly," she burst out before she thought. "Maybe all the things that have happened would have happened anyway. Maybe part of it is the power of suggestion."

He turned away from her. "In other words, Summer Sky, what you are saying is that we are only simple savages who don't understand civilization. I cannot help but worry about the arrows being covered with blood when they are opened and what I will do then."

She didn't answer. Perhaps there was a greater gap between the two civilizations than she had ever realized.

The ten bands of the Cheyenne gathered in over the next several weeks for the renewal. Iron Knife was healing rapidly and able to get around; but he wasn't resting well, and he seemed as tense as a bow string. He didn't touch Summer, although he played with their children. It was almost, it seemed to her, that the sight of her reminded him of the recent slaughter of his people.

She began to have nightmares about the bloody arrows and what would happen if the council found out she had killed Angry Wolf. The penalty for murder was exile for four years. If she were exiled, would they let her take her children and would Iron Knife be willing to go with her? If not, in four years, the children would no longer remember her, and her beloved would find another woman.

Some nights as she lay staring into the darkness, it almost seemed as though the wind cried with her. She tried to keep her anxiety a secret from Iron Knife because she knew he worried, too, and he needed to rest and let his wound heal. She began to wonder if she should solve everyone's problem by returning to her own family, or at least, leaving the Cheyenne. However, she was certain Iron Knife would not let her take his adored children away, and she couldn't bear to leave without them. She wasn't sure she could live without

him, either, but conscious of the tension, her fear of
pregnancy and his injury, she did not make any affec-
tionate overtures to him. What unnerved her even more
was that while they still shared a blanket, he no longer
wanted to hold her and caress her as he had done continually before the massacre at Sand Creek. Was she
now more a white person than as his little love?

Finally, several weeks later, came the cold winter day
they had waited for and dreaded. The Cheyenne had arrived from all over the plains, some of them wading
deep snow or dodging soldiers to attend the meeting.
The usual custom was to have the renewal in the summer. The men of the tribe had gone through elaborate
ceremonies and finally today would unwrap the arrows
in the lodge with the warriors looking on.

Summer waited in her tipi, holding her breath while
her small children played around her feet. Little Lance,
blue-eyed and black-haired with skin as fair as Summer's. The baby girl, Garnet, looked like Lance except
for her beautiful dark velvet eyes. It was the middle
child, the husky boy who looked more Indian than his
father, that she wondered about. Lance and Garnet could
blend in back in Boston, but Storm Gathering could
have passed for a full-blood Cheyenne.

The time seemed to be dragging, and Summer was
ready to scream, wishing it would all be over. She
looked toward the big lodge where the warriors were
performing their arrow ceremony. It was all nonsense,
Summer assured herself, primitive superstition. Surely
when they opened the bundle and nothing happened,
Iron Knife would realize that. Otherwise, to take the bad
luck away from the tribe, she would have to exile herself.

Abruptly, shouts and confusion echoed across the
camp. What had happened? Men were running about,
shouting and gesturing. Were there soldiers attacking the

camp again? Summer gathered up her baby and the two little boys, ready to run if need be. She started out into the cold morning. Then Iron Knife was striding toward her, face set and white.

"What has happened?"

He brushed past her, and she followed him into the lodge where he slumped down by the small fire, face taut and pale.

"What has happened?" she asked again.

"Don't you know?" His mouth was set in a grim line.

It couldn't be. She wouldn't think about it. She shook her head.

"The arrows," he muttered and put his head in his hands, "we bring my people bad luck. The Medicine Arrows were gleaming with fresh blood!"

She put the sleeping baby down on a blanket, then shooed the little boys outside to play. "I—I don't believe it!"

He grabbed her arm. "Believe it, woman, believe this bit of savage superstition. It is our fault; we have brought this bad luck down upon my people!"

The shouting and cries of dismay still echoed across the camp outside. "What—what shall we do? Did you tell them?"

He stared into the fire and shook his head. "May our God, Heammawihio, help me, I cannot bear to see you stoned from this camp; so I have told no one. Admitted nothing."

She knelt and put her arm around his wide shoulders, but he remained stiff in her embrace. "What shall we do?"

He seemed to be speaking to himself. "We must take ourselves away from this camp; far away, where we will bring my people no more bad luck."

"But they're your people," she protested, "and they

need you! I stabbed him; I will own up and let them exile me."

"And how long would you last out there in the wilderness with no one to help you kill or cook food, fight off wild animals or enemies?" He looked at her. "You would be in some enemy warrior's blankets before a week was out, whether you liked it or not."

What he said was true, but she would make this sacrifice for him; she loved him so. "I will go before the council, admit my guilt. You and the children will not be made to suffer because of me."

"Listen to me, Summer." He caught her arm and jerked her down to where he could look into her face. "You are my woman, and I am held responsible for what you do. I have made my decision."

The old spunkiness flared up, and she pulled out of his grasp. "*You* decided? I forget how arrogant and typically male you are. What about consulting me?"

"You are mine to protect and care for," he snapped, "and my children need their mother."

She waited for him to say he needed her, too, but his face was set and drawn as if he mulled over the great problems of the universe.

"Here is what I have decided," he said. "Cherokee Evans has offered me his hospitality any time I am near his cabin because I once saved his life. We will go stay with his family until I decide what to do; at least, during that time, I won't have any more massacres on my conscience."

"So now what happened at Sand Creek is our fault because we kept quiet about defending ourselves? Why don't you just throw me to the mob and let them kill me since I'm an outsider anyway!" She was raging and hurt.

He pulled her to him, looked down into her face. "Once I thought you might someday become one of us, now I wonder if you will ever be anything but a rich society girl who has made a bad choice that she regrets more and more!"

"I didn't say that! You are the one having regrets and seeing me as white!" She tried to twist from his hands, but he held her.

"You are my woman, Summer Sky, and God help me, I would turn my back on my whole tribe to keep you in my arms, even though I am no longer sure that we can overcome the gulf between our two civilizations. We will go to Cherokee for the time being."

"And what will you tell your people?"

He tangled his fingers in her hair, turning her small, heart-shaped face up to his. "The tribes are ready to move out, but everyone knows my wounds are not yet completely healed and I will only slow the march."

He was looking down into her face with an intensity that frightened her. She took a deep gulp of air and ran the tip of her tongue across her bottom lip. "You—you promised you would never hurt me."

His grip on her relaxed and his eyes grew moist. "You fear me? I don't know what's gotten into me. The only thing that could make me hurt you is if I caught you with another man; for that I would kill you and you know it."

He was so very troubled, and she realized it when she saw his shoulders shaking. "I will go with you, dearest, no matter where you go or whatever it is you want us to do."

He slipped his arm around her and held her against his wide chest as he gently stroked her hair. "I am sorry, Little One; it is the stress of all this, of having lost Spotted Blanket, the unknown future, the horrors that may be awaiting my people. Most of all, maybe it is the stress of doing without your beautiful body when I was so used to making love to you often."

That abstinence was stressing her, too. Summer couldn't even kiss him or feel him stroke her without wanting to make hot, passionate love to him. "I'll go tell Pretty Flower and the others," she murmured. "Maybe the tribe's luck will change while we are self-exiled."

His cousins seemed puzzled; but they assumed it was something his white woman wanted to do, so they helped them gather a few things, a horse or two. Once, Iron Knife had been rich in horses, but the soldiers at Sand Creek had rounded up most of the good ones for themselves. No one had dared venture back to the massacre site to see if Spotted Blanket had turned up there; they were all afraid soldiers might see them. Next time, the warriors said as they gathered around the big fire in the snowy winter cold and talked, next time, they would choose the place of battle, and the outcome would be very different. So Summer Sky, Iron Knife and their children rode away from the Cheyenne camp with vague words about when they would rejoin the tribe as it roamed the frozen plains and hills.

Iron Knife felt his spirits rise as the pair rode through the crusty snow toward that isolated little cabin in the Rockies where Cherokee, his woman, the former dance hall girl, Silver, and their two adopted children, Wannie and Keso, did a little gold panning and lived at peace with the Indians.

Maybe things would get better now, Summer thought as they hailed the cosy cabin and a tall half-breed and a pretty blonde with hair even lighter than her own came out to greet them. Summer carried her baby, Garnet, in a cradleboard, but handsome young Lance and the sturdy, solemn Storm Gathering pressed forward on their little paint ponies to stare with curious eyes at the

foursome coming out on the cabin porch. Summer
waved with a big smile, and said as an aside to Iron
Knife, "They have children? I thought they had just
married?"

Iron Knife dismounted carefully, still cautious about
his healing wound. He held up his arms to assist her
down. "I had forgotten about them. Keso, the boy who
looks to be ten or twelve winter counts old is Ute, but
he thinks he's Cheyenne, and—"

"Why would—?"

"Never mind," he said. "Keso spent the first years of
his life among the Cheyenne, so Cherokee, Silver and
the little girl have probably learned enough language
from him to be able to talk to our children."

"Good," Summer said, "although I have been teaching our children a little English." She knew that sooner
or later, they might need it; especially if the unthinkable
happened and she ever returned to white civilization.

They smiled and waited for the couple to cross the
snowy ground to them.

Summer couldn't stop looking at the pretty little girl
with her black hair done up in braids on her head. Summer thought she must be about five years old. "What an
adorable child! Why, she looks like a half-breed herself!"

A shadow crossed Iron Knife's face and Summer
wondered about it, but then the couple joined them. The
two men shook hands.

"Iron Knife, we've been worried about you!" Cherokee drawled in a deep Southern accent. "I've got your
stallion in my barn."

"Spotted Blanket? How—?"

"Todd Shaw bought the stallion from some soldier
who had caught it just outside Sand Creek. Spotted
Blanket wouldn't let anyone on his back, so he was use-

less to them. Todd brought us word about what happened. I'm sorry."

"Thank you, my friend." Iron Knife seemed to sigh
with relief over his horse. "This is my woman, Summer
Sky, and my children."

Summer smiled awkwardly and held out her hand.
For the first time, she noticed the slight smallpox scars
on the other girl's lovely face. "You must be Silver. You
certainly have a beautiful daughter."

"Oh, she's not mine, she's, well—" The silver-haired
girl looked down at the inquisitive child. "Here, Wannie, why don't you and Keso take these two boys and
show them around?"

The strapping Indian boy called Keso was eyeing
Lance's pony. "Is that yours?"

Lance nodded. "I will someday be a dog soldier like
my father so I must have a mount."

His brother Storm said, "No, me be the dog soldier."

Keso squared his thin shoulders. "I am Cheyenne myself."

The grown-ups exchanged glances.

Lance said, "In that case, Keso, you may ride my
pony."

Garnet pointed. "Pony—ride pony."

"No," Lance objected grandly, "you are a girl and
can't ride a war pony."

The beautiful little girl, Wannie, reached up to touch
the baby's hand. "Never mind, Silvery and me have
pretty clothes and things, we'll play dress-up."

The adults headed to the porch.

"I want to see my horse," Iron Knife said, and
walked with the three boys and the ponies across the
pasture toward the barn.

Little Wannie led Summer's toddler girl into the
cabin, leaving the three grown-ups smiling after them.

Summer watched them disappear into the house. "She's darling, unusual name, Wannie."

"It's really Waanibe," Silver said, "it's Arapaho, means 'Singing Wind.' Come in, I've got some coffee made."

Summer nodded and followed her. In a moment, they were joined by a smiling Iron Knife. "Spotted Blanket is fine and glad to see me."

While the men talked about horses and whether it would be a bad winter, Summer watched Wannie. Something about the child troubled Summer, but she couldn't be sure what it was. She had noticed an unusual birthmark on Wannie's chubby hand as the little girl had reached to take Garnet's. Funny, it stirred a memory; what was it?

Silver put her arm around Summer's shoulders and smiled. "You've come a long way and must be exhausted. I've got a Christmas cake, too."

"Christmas?" Abruptly Summer saw a picture in her mind of the big tree all decorated back in her parents' home, the food and music, and felt terribly homesick. She sighed, and when she glanced at Iron Knife, he was watching her as if he realized her thoughts. "Had we better check on the boys?"

Cherokee lit his pipe and laughed. "Keso will take care of them."

"But they're all so young," Summer protested.

"Except Keso," Cherokee laughed, "he's a street kid who looked after himself for years until I found him, and now that he's got a little sister, he seems bent on looking after Wannie, too. She's spoiled rotten, and loves pretty clothes and jewelry, unusual for a kid. Keso adores her even though he pretends to be annoyed to have her following him around."

They went inside by the roaring fire of the cozy log cabin. It had been a long time since Summer had had a real roof over her head. Maybe this time with the Evans would be good for them; certainly Iron Knife needed time to heal, and Summer was looking forward to visiting with Silver and getting the news of civilization. Maybe she had missed it more than she had realized. She didn't even want to think about the broken taboo and the bloody Medicine Arrows. What if they could never return to the Cheyenne?

Chapter Five

Angry Wolf lay in his deserted forest camp, his head aching from the cheap whiskey. In fact, he hurt all over. He sat up slowly, thinking he hadn't felt so bad since that long-ago time he had fought the dog soldier, Iron Knife, for possession of that white girl, Summer Sky. That yellow-haired bitch! He reached to touch the old scar on his chest where she had stabbed him as he had attempted to drown Iron Knife.

How long had it been? With his head aching, it was hard to think; more than six winter counts ago. Yes, it had been a long time, but even now, he could remember the thrill of holding the big dog soldier under the rushing water of that creek.

Iron Knife was almost dead when Angry Wolf heard a slight noise and whirled around to face the naked beauty just as the white girl buried the blade in his chest. After that, he remembered only falling and the cold water sweeping him off his feet. He must have lapsed into unconsciousness, and the current grabbed him, washing him away. He remembered vaguely struggling to keep his head above water as the flooded creek swept him along. So this was what it felt like to die. He didn't want to die, not without killing Iron Knife and raping that white beauty, but he was slipping into blackness and couldn't fight the current anymore.

When he finally awakened, he was lying on a sand bank at a bend in the creek, half in, half out of the water. Angry Wolf was too weak to even move, and there was no way to know how far he had floated or how long he had been lying here except that it was almost dark. The only way Angry Wolf could be certain he wasn't dead was that he was in pain and very hungry. Somewhere far in the distance, he smelled the scent of burning wood, and when he managed to raise his head, he saw a wisp of smoke on the horizon. Had there been a great forest fire somewhere? If so, he hoped Iron Knife and Summer Sky had burned to death, trapped in the inferno.

Angry Wolf tried to crawl up the creek bank, but the pain in his chest was more than he could bear. Had Heammawihio spared his life only so he could die by inches here by this creek? He managed to turn his head to take a few sips from the rushing water. He was wet, wounded, shivering and he had no food. In the water, he could see small fish swimming just a few inches away as if they mocked him, but he hadn't the strength to rise up and try to catch them. Besides, Cheyenne might eat turtles, but seldom fish.

He heard sounds of voices, a woman's laughter coming toward him. Iron Knife and Summer coming to make sure they had finished the job? He couldn't defend himself if they did. Maybe if he pretended to be dead. . . .

He heard the creak of wagon wheels and a man's voice. "What on earth? Honey, look at this!"

And the girl's soft voice, "Oh, Ethan, it's an Indian, and he looks dead."

"You stay right there, honey, let me see about him."

The creak of the wagon as the young farmer stepped down, the shadow thrown across Angry Wolf's body as he bent over him.

"Ethan, is he dead?"

"I'm not sure, if he ain't, he oughta be; you should see this wound."

"Maybe I can help." The girl's voice as she jumped down from the wagon. "Oh, my, he's an ugly one, ain't he? Poor thing, what do you reckon happened?"

Their pity was his only chance for life, Angry Wolf knew. He opened his eyes and looked up at them, more dead than alive. The young man wore overalls, and his skin was weathered and tanned. A poor dirt farmer, Angry Wolf thought with contempt, glancing past the man toward the ragged old wagon and the straggly mule.

"Stay back, honey, he's moving!"

"Mercy! He's so near dead, he can't hurt anyone." She leaned over him and he noticed that she was dark-eyed with long brown hair. She wore a faded gingham dress, a sunbonnet, and a gold band on her work-worn left hand. She bent over Angry Wolf and he saw that the swell of her breasts tightened the faded calico.

Angry Wolf smiled evilly now as he remembered the young couple from all those long years ago. They had taken him to their cabin and nursed him back to health. Then they had put him to work around their little farm, hoeing and chopping wood. Angry Wolf had waited until late one night when the couple slept to attack Ethan with the axe. With the young farmer lying dead and bloody across the bed, Angry Wolf had raped the girl, despite her pleas for mercy. Then he had stolen anything of value on the place, taken the one old mule and ridden out. He hadn't even bothered to look back at the sobbing, naked girl.

Six long years ago. Now Angry Wolf groaned aloud as he sat with his aching head in his hands and thought of those past events. He wondered what had ever happened to the young farmer's woman or to Summer, that pretty yellow-haired girl who belonged to Iron Knife. He reached to touch the old scar on his brown chest. Only the strongest survived, and women were meant to be used to bear a man's sons or pleasure him. Summer. If he ever got his hands on her again, he'd find ways to torture her she'd never even thought of.

Where was he? Angry Wolf lifted his throbbing head and looked around. His mouth tasted sour of old cheap whiskey. Yes, now he remembered. Some days ago, he and two other renegades had raided a wagon load of whiskey bound for Denver. The teamster still hung tied to his wagon wheel over the ashes of a dead fire. Angry Wolf grinned now and rubbed his pock-marked face as he stared at what was left of the wagon driver, remembering how he and his partners had laughed and passed the bottle around as the man screamed. That was what he got for sneaking whiskey into Indian country with a war going on. The white man had hoped for big profits. What he got was slow death roasting alive while the renegades laughed and drank his whiskey.

By the time the three had drunk gallons of the firewater, they had been quarreling among themselves. Angry Wolf looked around. Where were the other two braves? Among the wreckage and broken bottles, he dug around and found Horse Stealer, his throat cut with a broken whiskey bottle.

Now it all came back to Angry Wolf: the quarrel, the fight. Deer Slayer, the third Cheyenne, had run for his horse as the two fought, riding out just as Angry Wolf cut Horse Stealer's throat. Deer Slayer's eyes had been big with horror at the broken taboo. Angry Wolf had yelled at him and tried to stop him from leaving, but the Cheyenne brave had fled.

Angry Wolf had committed the worst crime, murder, and there was a witness. He considered whether he could ride Deer Slayer down and kill him before he could get to any Cheyenne encampment with the news. No, this had happened some days ago, from what he vaguely remembered. What to do? If word got out, he would not be welcome in any Cheyenne camp, and when the Sacred Arrows were opened, there would be blood on them. He staggered to his feet, then retrieved his knife and lance. It wasn't the first time Angry Wolf had killed a fellow Cheyenne. He didn't much believe in the superstition of the bloody arrows, but a live witness was something else.

He looked around the littered camp site, trying to decide where he was and what he should do? Mountains. He could see peaks around him that he knew the whites called the Rockies. For six years now, he had survived riding with the outlaw dog soldiers or raiding lonely settlers' cabins. However, now he had killed a brother Cheyenne, and that was serious, especially since there was a witness.

Angry Wolf needed a place to hole up, maybe one with good food, a warm fire and a pretty woman. He gathered up his things. There was only one old horse grazing in the deserted camp. Either Deer Slayer had taken the others or they had strayed away in the week or so Angry Wolf had been drunk. He looked around, trying to decide where to go, what to do. The winter wind blew cold against his pock-marked face. Somewhere in the distance, his keen nose detected just the slightest scent of smoke. That might mean some isolated settler or miner.

Angry Wolf grinned with yellow teeth, remembering how trusting the young farmer and his woman had been.

He would follow the scent of that smoke. With any
luck, it would lead him to some lonely cabin where
there would be food, a stupid, trusting white man to kill,
and a pretty woman to warm his loins until he tired of
her and cut her throat. As soon as he could steal a good
horse and more supplies, he would be on his way again.

Angry Wolf's head didn't ache so much now except
when the old horse stumbled on the trail. "Buzzard
food," he swore and whacked the horse with his bow.
He hoped he would run into a field of fat ponies at that
cabin he was searching for in the hills ahead of him.
The wind blew cold, and who knew when it might decide to snow again?

At least he was better off than the Cheyenne who had
been camped at Sand Creek weeks ago. He and Horse
Stealer and Deer Slayer had heard rumors about a massacre there. When they had tortured that fat white
wagon driver, he had told them more. *Vehoes.* No wonder the Cheyenne word for "spider" and "white man"
were the same. How he hated them! Many years ago,
the whites had brought disease among the Indian tribes,
and his whole family had died. Angry Wolf reached to
touch the ugly pockmarks on his dark face. Whatever he
did in revenge against all white people was not enough
to bring his family back to life.

He wondered as he rode whatever had become of
Gray Dove, the sultry Arapaho beauty he had hoped
would become his woman. She, too, had turned away
from his ugly face, wanting Iron Knife, the handsome,
tall dog soldier instead. He hated Iron Knife for that.
Angry Wolf touched the scar where Iron Knife's yellow-
haired woman had stabbed him. He hoped something
terrible had happened to them both.

Licking his yellow teeth, he reined in the old nag and

sniffed the morning air. Again he smelled the faintest
scent of smoke. He kept riding, thinking he would have
to be careful; the smoke might be coming from a camp
of Ute, Crow, or Pawnee all traditional enemies of the
Cheyenne. If the odds weren't in his favor, he would
skirt the area and keep riding until he found easier prey.
The scent of smoke was stronger now. Angry Wolf dismounted and tied a strip of rawhide around the old gelding's muzzle to keep it from nickering at other horses.

He climbed up on a little rise in the forest of spruce
and pine, then peered at the small cabin in the clearing,
smoke drifting lazily from the rock chimney. Even from
this distance, he saw children playing out front.

"Good!" he grunted. Children meant a woman, a
young woman. He licked his lips with anticipation.
He'd kill the man, ransack the place, steal the best
horses, rape the woman. Children he could probably sell
to the Comancheros along the border—if he decided it
was worth the bother to deal with taking them there.
With all the Indian troubles going on, who would notice
one more burned cabin and murdered settlers? The soldiers might even blame it on the band of Cheyenne Iron
Knife had belonged to, which suited Angry Wolf just
fine.

He scouted the area, as cautious as a lynx that's been
caught in a trap before. The settlers might be on their
guard right now with what had happened at Sand Creek.
Angry Wolf hoped the whole band had been wiped
out, including Iron Knife if that dog soldier was still
alive. Angry Wolf hadn't been near that band in all
these years since he'd tried to kill the big dog soldier
and take his woman.

He rode closer, staying in the shadow of towering
trees so that he would not be seen from the distant
cabin. There were horses in the corral and two small
pinto ponies. Angry Wolf narrowed his eyes as he

looked them over from the shadow of the trees. Fine horses. This would be a very good raid! Why, that Appaloosa sticking its head over the barn door looked almost as fine as the one Iron Knife used to ride. His heart beat a little faster with anticipation. If the settler's woman and whiskey were as good as his horses, Angry Wolf was about to be very lucky indeed.

He dismounted and tied the old nag to a tree, watching the corral all the while. Absently, he ran his hand across his pock-marked cheek and studied the Appaloosa. It couldn't be Spotted Blanket, could it? Maybe his memory was faulty; he hadn't seen that stallion since that autumn day in the forest when he had fought Iron Knife for the yellow-haired girl and lost. Maybe it was a colt sired by Iron Knife's horse. As he considered, a small boy came out of the cabin, a boy about four or five years old. He was light-skinned and handsome with very black hair. Angry Wolf watched the little boy with interest. There were places along the border where men with strange appetites would pay big money for such a handsome child.

From inside, a woman's voice called, "Lance, wait and someone will come out and help you!"

The boy strode toward the ponies in the corral. "I can feed them myself, Mother."

So there was a woman, and from the age of the son, she must be young. Angry Wolf grinned and felt his groin swell and ache with anticipation. But he reminded himself that her man might not be as trusting and easily fooled as Ethan had been. Most of these frontiersmen were good with a rifle.

He watched the little boy lead the ponies into the barn. Then as silent as a sneaking coyote, Angry Wolf crept around the barn and went in. The scent of hay was sweet on the dim, dusty air. The little boy was strug-

gling to throw some hay into the stall where he had put
the ponies.

He should just snap the boy's neck, but if the child
put up a fight or managed to cry out, people in the
house would be alerted. Besides, he needed the boy to
lure the woman out.

He sneaked up behind him. The boy might have Indian blood, because he whirled at the sound of Angry
Wolf's moccasin in the soft straw of the barn floor. His
blue eyes widened as Angry Wolf hit him in the jaw,
and the boy crumpled. Grinning, Angry Wolf threw him
over his shoulder and carried him away from the barn,
out to where he had tied the old horse in the trees.

He really needed to know how many people were in
the house. If the woman was alone, this would be easy.
If she wasn't, he needed to know how many adults
might be in the cabin.

He took another look at the big Appaloosa standing
in the corral. If it wasn't Spotted Blanket, it had to be
one of his grown colts.

Inside, Summer looked around as she helped Silver
set the table. The men were sharing a pipe and conversation at the other end of the room before the fire, talking about Sand Creek and the Indian outbreak. Storm
Gathering sat near them, listening to the men talk.
Wannie and little Garnet were playing on the floor with
a doll. "Did Lance ever come back in?"

Silver shrugged, busy ladling gravy over a haunch of
roast venison she had just pulled from the fire. "If he
got his pony put away, he may have followed Keso off
down to the stream to get a bucket of water."

"Oh, of course." Summer returned to slicing hot
bread. Keso was a big boy, maybe ten or twelve years
old, by the look of him. He'd take care of Lance. Still,

Summer had the most uneasy feeling she couldn't shake as she stood there by the window with the bread pan, almost as if someone were watching her. *Don't be silly,* she scolded herself, *you've been jumpy ever since the ambush at Sand Creek.*

Keso came in just then carrying a bucket of water. He was a handsome, tall Indian boy, Summer thought, and getting broad-shouldered.

He put the bucket on the table. "Hey, Mom, dinner looks good."

Silver turned and put her arm around him affectionately. "Drat! You rascal! You know how to make sure you get a big piece of cake, don't you?"

Summer paused. "Keso, did Lance come in with you?"

Keso gave her a blank look. "I ain't seen him, ma'am."

"He went out to see about the ponies."

The boy shrugged. "I was up by the creek, not down at the corral, ma'am."

"Would you mind—? Oh, never mind, I'll call him in for supper." Summer grabbed a coat and headed out the door. She didn't want anyone to think she was being a nervous mother hen. Ever since Sand Creek, Iron Knife had complained she was being overprotective. If Lance had gone very far from the cabin, she wanted Iron Knife to caution his son. It wouldn't be that difficult to get lost up here on this mountain with all these thick forests of pine and spruce.

She looked around. "Lance?" No answer. Of course he had gone into the barn. She walked across the pasture. "Lance?"

Spotted Blanket nickered a welcome as she went inside the semidarkness, and the two ponies stuck their heads toward her, looking for hay. Strange, here was the pitchfork lying on the barn floor. It wasn't like either of

Iron Knife's sons to neglect a horse. Had he gone off somewhere? She came back outside and looked all the way around the clearing toward the woods. Was that a reflection off something metal? Of course! She almost smiled with relief as she walked toward the woods. For some reason, Lance was out in the woods this chilly late afternoon. Was she being overly protective? His father would probably think so. "Lance? Lance, where are you?"

With shocked disbelief, Angry Wolf stared at the woman crossing the clearing. It couldn't be! His eyes must be playing tricks. Yet as she drew closer, he recognized the walk, the swell of her breasts, the light hair and pretty face. Iron Knife's woman. No, it couldn't be. If it were Summer, she would be with the Cheyenne— unless Iron Knife had been killed or she had left him and taken up with a white man.

Angry Wolf looked down at the unconscious child in his arms. Could this be Iron Knife's son? If he thought it was, Angry Wolf would slam the child's head against a rock and splatter his brains. No, it didn't make any sense that Iron Knife's woman, son and horse would be at a settler's cabin up in the Rockies. A happy thought occurred to the renegade Cheyenne. Suppose Iron Knife had been killed, and his woman had taken his possessions and found herself another man?

"Lance? Where are you?" Summer looked all around her, but nothing moved and no one answered her call. "Lance? Lance?"

The echo came back mockingly: Lance . . . Lance . . . Lance. . . .

The little rascal, if he had gotten very far away, he

was in for a good scolding. Maybe she should go back and get the others to help her look. If she didn't find him in the next few minutes, that was exactly what she would do, even if it did embarrass him for everyone to be out searching as if for a stray colt.

Where had she seen that flash of reflection? Uncertainly, she looked over her shoulder toward the cabin. Maybe she ought to go back and get Iron Knife to help; but he and his friend Cherokee were having such a good time talking, and Silver was busy with dinner. She came to the edge of the wood. "Lance? Where are you?"

Angry Wolf watched her and grinned. The gods must like him to send her right into his trap. He lay the unconscious, trussed-up child across the path and stepped back behind a tree. He made a small sound in his throat like a whimper.

"Lance?" She ran toward the woods, taking no caution now. "Lance, are you hurt? Where are you?"

He stayed in the shadow of the trees as Iron Knife's woman ran toward him. She was concerned now only with the safety of her child. The yellow-haired girl seemed to see the little boy lying across the path ahead. She cried out in fear and ran into the woods, past Angry Wolf hiding in the shadows.

"Lance? What's happened?" Her whole attention was centered on the child. Silent as a snake, Angry Wolf stepped out behind her. Before she had any warning, he slipped one arm around her trim waist while he clapped his other hand over her mouth. She struggled and fought him, but Angry Wolf was strong. Her waist was narrow, her flesh warm. His arm slid up under her breasts as she fought to get away from him.

"So we meet again, white bitch!"

Terrified and confused, Summer attempted to turn her head, break her captor's grip. She couldn't see who had stepped out of the shadows and grabbed her. There was something vaguely familiar about the voice, but she couldn't quite place it. One thing she did know for sure was that he was strong, and from the tone of his voice, he meant to harm her. Every woman's nightmare, being grabbed by a faceless evil who leaves no doubt as to his intentions. Her first thought was for her child as she struggled. Had Lance been hurt? If she could just break free enough to scream, Iron Knife would come running, and woe to the man who had touched his woman! Her heart seemed to pound against her ribs so hard, she was sure her assailant could feel it. Who was he? What did he want? A million thoughts and terrors ran through her mind as she fought, but her captor held tight.

He laughed against her ear. "I'm taking you, and when I finish, bitch, you'll pray to die! I'll ambush your man as he hunts for you!"

He whirled her around, his dirty hand still clamped tightly over her mouth. Summer looked up at him, eyes wide with disbelief. No, it couldn't be!

He grinned with yellow teeth. "You thought me dead? I lived, but I carry the scar still. Now it's my turn to see what I can do with a knife!"

At that, he clipped her across the jaw, and she collapsed, unconscious. Quickly, he tied her hands behind her, tore a strip off her skirt and stuffed it in her mouth. She was as beautiful and desirable as he remembered, Angry Wolf thought as he ripped away the front of her dress. Such full, soft breasts. Before he carved marks on them with his knife, he intended to spread her out and rape her until he got enough of her ripe body. By then, her man would be looking for her, and if Angry Wolf was clever enough, he would kill him, too.

Angry Wolf ran his hands across her breasts, his manhood swelling and aching with urgency. He wished he had time to throw her down and take her right here, all bound and gagged, but he dared not take the chance. He knew of a cave not far from here, an old mining tunnel. That would be a good place to enjoy Iron Knife's woman. Her screams as he tortured her might lure Iron Knife to the spot where Angry Wolf would be lying in wait to kill him. Then he would geld Iron Knife and cut his throat. Maybe he shouldn't kill Iron Knife's woman; maybe he should sell her to the Comancheros. He grinned as he picked her up and ran his hands up and down her smooth thighs, across her breasts. It pleased him to think of her being forced to service brutal rene- gades or outlaws. But that wasn't a decision he had to make right now. First he had to escape from here, set up the trap and then enjoy his capture.

He lifted her up on the horse before him and held her against his male hardness. It had been a long time since he had wanted a woman this bad. He looked down at the little boy. The child was awake now and stared up at him with wide blue eyes. Trussed and gagged, the lit- tle boy could not scream for help. Was this Iron Knife's son? If so, he'd enjoy the pleasure of cutting the child's throat; but he'd have to dismount to do so, and it would be difficult with the limp woman in his arms.

In that split second, as he considered, he heard a door slam, and a woman with even paler hair came out on the porch, calling, "Summer? Did you find him? Drat it all! You men come help me look!"

Damn that other woman! If she sounded the alarm, he wasn't going to have much time to get away. Digging sharp spurs into his horse, he took off through the woods, the girl soft and limp in his arms. Angry Wolf licked his lips with anticipation, remembered how close he'd come to enjoying her many years ago by that creek. The white scar on his chest seemed to burn. He would make her pay for that; oh, he would make her pay!

It was late afternoon, and the night would be cold if

he didn't get out of the wind. He grinned to himself. Now he had something to keep him warm. Stripped naked, Summer would be soft and hot in his arms as he enjoyed her body. His heart beat a little faster just thinking about how she would feel under him.

They traveled for miles to reach the old abandoned mine, and it was dark when they got there. The ground Angry Wolf had just covered was hard and becoming flinty with frost, making it almost impossible to track a horse. Once he had enjoyed Summer's ripe body for an hour, he could drop back, then pick off any pursuers one at a time along the trail, if any were loco enough to attempt to trail him in the darkness. Most warriors hesitated to fight at night; they thought a man killed in the night would have a hard time finding his way up the *Ekutsihimmiyo,* the Hanging Road to the Sky.

Roughly, he dumped the half-conscious girl inside the mouth of the mine on thick, dead leaves that had piled up over the autumn months. Then he led his horse away and tied it by a creek a few hundred yards from the mine. If anything caused that horse to nicker, he wanted to have plenty of warning. Now to enjoy some food and the woman!

Chapter Six

Angry Wolf grinned as he dug in the horse's saddlebags. He'd been smart to steal supplies from the teamster's wagon. The meat and coffee would taste twice as good knowing white settlers in Denver or soldiers at Fort Lyon might be going hungry because of that waylaid wagon. He'd also helped himself to whiskey and tobacco. After he filled his belly and enjoyed a smoke, he'd turn his attention to the woman. He had decided he was in no big hurry; he had all night to rape and torture the yellow-haired girl. His pursuers would no doubt wait until dawn to begin tracking.

Summer gradually came awake, looking about in confusion. What had happened and where was she? Images came back along with the pain in her swollen jaw. Angry Wolf. Just like in a nightmare, he had returned to haunt her, only he was no ghost. She couldn't even begin to wonder how he had survived in that creek or where he had been all this time, but she had no doubt what his plans were for her. Summer raised her head and looked around. Way off by the creek, she could hear him tying the horse, digging through the saddlebags. Could she possibly escape in the dark?

Taking a deep breath for courage, Summer managed
to stagger to her feet. For a long moment, she felt dizzy,
as if she might crumple to the mine floor. Then she
thought about what he would be planning for her tonight, and she knew she had to escape. It took everything in her to do it, but she slipped out of the mine,
running lightly through the frosty leaves.

"Who's there?" He whirled around at the sound.

Summer's heart almost stopped breathing, and she
crouched behind a bush. Her jacket wasn't warm
enough for this cold winter night, and she began to
shiver. *Oh, please, God, don't let him find me. . . .*

Poised to run again, she waited as he gathered up
supplies and headed back to the mine entry. Could she
get to the horse? There was too wide an open space between the bush and where the horse was tied; she
couldn't make it before he saw her. Summer watched
him go to the mouth of the mine, throw down his supplies and begin to curse as he realized she was gone. He
wheeled, looking out into the night.

He wasn't looking in her direction, she thought, and
crept from one bush to the next. Maybe she could work
her way around that open space and come up on the
horse from the far side. But how was she going to
mount it with her hands tied?

Angry Wolf furiously shouted, "Where are you?
White bitch, I play no games with you, do you hear
me?"

She didn't answer, but as cold as she was, she could
feel perspiration breaking out all over and wondered if
the renegade could hear the crazy drumming of her
heart that seemed to echo in her own ears.

"All right," he yelled, "come in now and I won't hurt
you! If I have to hunt you down, you will wish you had
not played this game!"

She wasn't about to surrender. If he were going to

rape and torture her, he'd have to make a real effort to catch her. Summer shuddered, remembering that the day she had stabbed him, he had tied her down, spread-eagled and naked, and was just about to pour wild honey over her so a big hill of nearby red ants could feast on her delicate flesh. Again, she looked longingly toward the horse.

Almost as if he read her mind, even though he didn't know her hiding place, he strode out, untied the horse and brought it back to tie in front of the mine opening. "You see?" he yelled. "I have the horse; you cannot escape, white girl, unless you walk out of here and get lost in the forest. Maybe a hungry wolf or pack of coyotes is out there waiting for you; maybe a big bear."

She almost smiled, knowing bears were in hibernation at this time of the year, but he wouldn't think she'd know that. Summer had been among the Cheyenne long enough that she knew a lot about wild animals and nature. She'd try to retrace the trail the horse had followed on the way up here. It would be difficult in the dark, and she might not make it; but anything was better than having that dirty beast rape her!

However, he was evidently listening carefully now, because when she took a step in the frozen leaves, he cocked his head. "I hear you! Do you really think you can hide out there? Come in now and I won't hurt you—much."

She tried to tiptoe quietly away from him, but the dry leaves were frozen and crackled at her step. She paused again as Angry Wolf came out into the darkness.

"I hear you," he shouted. "I know exactly where you are!"

He was bluffing, Summer thought, because he wasn't looking straight at her, but off to one side. If she could just tiptoe a few hundred feet, she might be far enough away that he couldn't hear the crunching leaves, and she could take off running. "Okay, white bitch, I am tired of humoring you! Now I'll make you sorry you didn't surrender!"

The fury in his voice scared her out of her caution, and Summer took off at a run through the woods. Behind her, she heard the squat, powerful man crashing through the brush. He had picked up her trail by the sounds of her feet. She collided with a tree branch and fell, got up, staggered on. Behind her, the ugly Cheyenne sounded like a bull buffalo charging.

Oh, please, God, I have three babies to raise. . . . She ran on, tripped over a tree root and fell. This time as she got to her feet, Angry Wolf tore through the brush and grabbed her. "Aha, white bitch! Now you'd better make it worth all the trouble!"

"My man will give you more trouble than you bargained for!" She tried to twist out of his hands.

He slapped her hard. Stunned, her head snapped back, and she tasted blood from her cut lip.

"No, white whore, you will entertain me, and I will make you pay for this extra trouble." Her shirt was torn, and he ran his hands across her breasts familiarly and grunted with satisfaction at what he felt. "The Comanchero will pay me well for you!"

She was too stunned and exhausted to do anything but stare up at him, gasping for breath, knowing her full breasts moved as she breathed in a way that made his eyes glow with lust. He picked her up, threw her across his powerful shoulder like a sack of grain, his dirty hand across her hips, fondling there as he carried her back to the mine, and dumped her on the leaves by the fire. "There'll be no more tricks from you, slut."

So saying, he looped her tied hands above her head over an outcrop of rock in a way that made her wince, but Summer would not give him the satisfaction of crying out in pain. With her hands tied, her full breasts swelled out of her torn shift.

He grunted and smiled. "After I have had my fill of meat and whiskey, I'll have my fill of those, girl."

Summer didn't answer; she was too busy thinking of a way to escape. Right now, she saw none. Angry Wolf seemed very pleased with himself as he poked up the little fire and sat down close to it, warming himself by its flames while he roasted meat on a stick and drank whiskey. The meat smelled good, and she felt her mouth water, remembering that it had been a long time since she had eaten. She and Silver had been fixing dinner when she was kidnapped. At least her child was all right.

He took a big drink of whiskey, letting it run from both sides of his mouth, sighed, smiled and wiped his lips with the back of his hand. "Ahh! Tastes good! You behave yourself, please me, and I might give you a little food."

In answer, she spat at him and he slapped her again. Her head snapped back, and her face stung where he had struck her. She felt the scarlet blood dripping from the corner of her mouth, dripping onto her naked breast. "You carrion, we thought you were dead."

He only laughed, tore off a haunch of the meat and began to pull it off the bone with his yellow teeth. "Knowing Iron Knife, his conscience has been bothering him all these years while he worried about the stupid Medicine Arrows—"

"But they were covered with blood. How—?"

"Because I murdered a fellow Cheyenne only a few days ago, probably just before the Renewal of the Sacred Arrows; it wasn't the first time."

She took a deep breath of relief, glad for her man. Even if she were raped and killed, Iron Knife could stop worrying about putting a taboo on the arrows. Summer stared at the scar on Angry Wolf's chest.

He looked down to see what she was looking at, shrugged. "I did not die; no thanks to you."

"Then how—?"

"I was swept down the creek for many miles by the current, washed up nearly dead on a creek bank far away." He stuffed more food in his mouth, then took another swig of whiskey. "The woman who tried to help me was as pretty as you only brown-haired."

She felt the hair rise on the back of her neck. "What—what did you do to her?"

Angry Wolf grinned, evidently remembering with pleasure. "I scalped her man and raped her; just as I'm going to do tonight."

She tried not to let her horror show in her eyes, knowing he enjoyed terrorizing her.

"Are you hungry, Summer Sky?" He waved a piece of the meat under her nose where she could smell the succulent juices, but she did not answer.

"I might feed you if you lie down like an obedient cow and let me mate you."

"I'd rather starve!" She spat the words at him.

He laughed and put the meat down, picked up the bottle again and took a big drink. "It'll go easier on you if you have a drink."

She turned her face away, but he tangled his fingers in her hair and turned her face toward him, twisting her neck cruelly so that she cried out.

When her mouth opened, he rammed the neck of the bottle between her teeth and tilted it up so that whiskey poured into her throat. She choked and coughed, and tried not to swallow, but he was holding her face so that she was forced to.

"When I get through with you," he whispered, "we have some unfinished business. I don't have any honey

or ants this time, but I wonder if I can smear meat
grease on your naked body, leave you bound and
gagged for the wolves?" He cupped her bare breast with
his hand. "A shame for varmints to finally feast on
these."

Summer tried to pull out of his groping hand; but the
wall of the mine was against her back, and she could do
nothing but close her eyes so she wouldn't have to see
him running his hands all over her naked breasts. She
had never known such terror. Here she was a captive of
a crazy, cruel warrior she had thought was dead, and she
was once more at his mercy. Perhaps this wasn't happening; perhaps she was having a nightmare. *Oh, Iron
Knife, dearest, where are you?* With any nightmare she
had ever had in the last half-dozen years, she had awakened to curl up in her lover's strong arms while he held
her close against him and murmured that she was safe
and protected. No one would ever hurt her as long as
she was in his arms. What in God's name would she do?
She'd rather be dead than submit to this loco beast.

"Maybe I won't leave you for the wolves." He
grinned at her, stroking her breasts. "The Comancheros
would pay big money for a beauty like you. You could
end up in Mexico City or San Francisco as a white
slave, pleasing fifty men a night and earning money for
your owners."

She tried to keep from shuddering at the thought because she knew it pleased him to scare her, but she
couldn't stop trembling. Maybe it wasn't the thought of
being a sex slave in a bordello, but the idea that this
beast was about to vent his lust on her body. Ironic,
Summer thought, that she had denied Iron Knife her
body because they were both worried about getting her
with child again. What in God's name would she do if
Angry Wolf put his whelp in her belly?

He pawed her bare breast and took another drink,

then laid a gleaming big knife by his side on a rock. "You submit, white bitch, and pleasure me, or I will carve my sign across the white map of your flesh." He picked up the knife and ran it lightly across her breast, leaving a thin trickle of blood. He was going to have her, she thought, pulling at her bonds and realizing the rawhide thongs were strong and tight. It was only a matter of if he cut her up before or after he raped her. Would it do any good to stall him? Was Iron Knife on his way here right now through the darkness, or fearing an ambush, would he wait for dawn? By first light, Angry Wolf would have raped her half a dozen times and might have her thrown across his horse, headed south to sell her. If only this were a nightmare and she could wake up scared but safe in Iron Knife's strong arms.

Iron Knife and Cherokee had been enjoying their pipes and steaming coffee before the roaring fire of the cabin while the little girls played on the floor near them and the women fixed food in the kitchen. Then Iron Knife had paused and looked out at the sunlit pasture. "I think I hear your woman calling, Cherokee."

Cherokee paused to listen, then looked toward the tall Indian boy pouring water from the bucket in the kitchen. "Keso, where'd the women go?"

The boy shrugged. "Outside. I can hear Silver calling; maybe the other lady wandered off."

Cherokee frowned. "What do you suppose those women are up to? Hope the cow isn't out again."

Iron Knife looked around. "Where's Lance?"

Storm Warning looked up at his father, his dark little face solemn. "Went to feed ponies."

An uneasy feeling borne of years of surviving in hostile country went through him, and Iron Knife stood up.

"Let us go take a look; this isn't like Summer Sky at all."

Cherokee gestured to the older boy. "Keso, look after these three little ones a moment."

Storm Warning shook his head proudly. "I big boy, not need."

"Then, son, you help Keso look after the little girls," Iron Knife ordered. "We'll go out and see what is going on."

They grabbed their coats off the peg and went out on the porch, leaving the two little girls playing dress-up before the fireplace while the two boys sneered at "girl things."

Iron Knife's keen eyes took in the landscape at a glance and saw Cherokee's wife down by the corral. "Where's Summer?" he yelled.

She shook her head as they walked toward her. "Drat it all! I—I don't know. Lance is gone, too."

Now Iron Knife was worried. "This isn't like her to get very far from me or her baby."

Cherokee made a dismissing gesture. "Oh, Lance's pony may have gotten out and they're both looking for it."

Silver's pretty face paled and she bit her lip. "The pony's in a stall inside the barn."

Iron Knife had a sudden premonition that ran a chill up his back. "It'll be dusk soon. It isn't like Summer to venture far from her own camp fire when there are children to be looked after."

Now the other man seemed to pick up his alarm. "If there was trouble, we would have heard her scream or shout for help—"

"Maybe not," Iron Knife's keen dark eyes searched the horizon. "I've killed men before without them even being aware I was there so they never got out a whimper."

Even in the dusk, he saw Silver's face tense. "Oh, God, you don't think Indians—?"

"Not Cheyenne or any of our allies"—Iron Knife shook his head—"they all know my woman and that I'd kill the man who touched her. Any Utes been seen in this area lately?"

"I don't know," Cherokee said, "we haven't seen much of anyone since we got here."

Iron Knife crossed to the corral with long strides. "I'm saddling up."

"It's almost dark," Cherokee protested. "You can't track in the dark."

"I can try." He kept walking, and the other man matched his long strides to the corral. "If they're just lost in the woods, Summer would have sense enough to stay in one place, try to keep warm until daylight."

Cherokee said, "We'll spread out and see if we can find anything before dark."

Silver agreed with a nod, "Go with me, Cherokee." She ran toward the woods. "I thought I heard something . . ."

Iron Knife saddled Spotted Blanket and watched the two searching the ground in the clearing between the cabin and the woods. Then he mounted up and rode out to them. He was getting frantic, but he reminded himself he must stay calm. Women and children had been lost in forests before, and Summer had gotten as good as any Cheyenne about survival skills. Then he remembered she wasn't carrying a weapon or any matches to build a fire. It didn't seem logical to him that she and Lance would both have gotten lost or disappeared without a trace. Besides, if there was a war party of hostiles out there, they would have run off the livestock, fired the barn and attacked the house.

Somewhere in the cold twilight, a wolf howled and it echoed and reechoed through the snowy mountain peaks. He imagined Summer fallen and helpless, at the mercy of a starving wolf pack that would eat her alive as she screamed his name. Wolves wouldn't attack people, he thought, but if they were starving and she was hurt or unconscious. . . . He didn't even want to think about it. Summer Sky was his to protect and cherish, and he would find her if he had to stay out all night in the cold.

Cherokee's woman ran toward the woods. Now she waved her hands frantically. "Come quick, I've found them!"

Iron Knife breathed a sigh of relief as he nudged the big stallion into a trot. Thank Heammawihio they were all right! Why hadn't they answered everyone's calls? He was going to scold his woman and son for scaring him like that.

But when he rode up, there was only little Lance, all bound and gagged; his blue eyes were bright with excitement and horror.

Iron Knife dismounted before the stallion had even stopped as Silver jerked the gag from his mouth. "What happened here, my son? Who did this? Where is your mother?"

"The—the man took her." Lance was attempting manfully not to cry as Iron Knife untied him.

"Man? What man?"

The little boy shook his head and scrambled to his feet. "Don't know."

Iron Knife hugged him to his chest, thinking how precious his family was to him. "You're all right now, son. Was the man white or Indian?"

"He—he spoke Cheyenne. Ugly," Lance gulped, "yellow teeth; scars all over face."

"Scars?" Recognition hit Iron Knife. No, it couldn't be; the warrior Lance was describing was dead. Was it *mistai,* magic? Could a ghost have come back for revenge?

He looked around at the growing darkness and the chill descending on the mountains. His belly felt like it was full of molten lead. "He'll hurt her."

Cherokee blinked. "You know this man?"

Iron Knife nodded. "It can't be the man I remember."

Yet when he urged Lance to describe his assailant again, he was even more puzzled. It couldn't be Angry Wolf; Iron Knife had seen him die and be swept away by rushing water more than six years ago. Perhaps there was someone who looked like the bad dog soldier. Smallpox scars were common enough among the lucky ones who survived the deadly scourge the white settlers and scouts had spread so carelessly among the native population.

The dusk had deepened to a cool lavender sunset. "I'll trail them."

Cherokee said, "It's almost dark. You can't do any good now, wait until morning to start."

It made sense. Yet when he pictured his woman, frightened and at the mercy of a brutal rapist, he shook his head. "I have to start now. I'm a good tracker."

"There's dozens of old abandoned mines and hunter's cabins where he could hide out," Cherokee argued. "They could be anywhere."

Iron Knife felt impotent fury as he unsheathed his big dagger, checking the blade for sharpness. It would take a man's head off with one hard lunge. "Wherever they are, I'll find them. Will you look after my children?"

Silver nodded. "You know we will. Let me get you some supplies." She turned and hurried toward the cabin.

"Friend," Cherokee said, "you want me to go with you?"

Iron Knife shook his head. "Look after my children.

Suppose you went with me and then the rotten snake doubled back to the cabin?" He nodded to Lance. "Go with Cherokee, son, and look out for your sister and brother. I'm going after your mother."

"Want to go with you." The child wiped chubby fists against his blue eyes.

Iron Knife shook his head. "Go with Cherokee, son."

Cherokee took Lance's hand. "Silver will take care of the children; I hope Garnet will drink cow's milk."

"She won't like it, but she will drink it. Take care of them all, Cherokee, if I don't come back. . . ." He wasn't sure what to tell his friend. He didn't know if Summer's elegant family in Boston would want the children or not.

"You'll come back," Cherokee said firmly. "We'll be waiting to hear from you."

Silver came running from the cabin now with a small bundle, two canteens, and a blanket. "Good thing I had dinner almost ready; there's hot coffee in one of the canteens."

"Hahoo," Iron Knife said, using the intertribal word for thanks. He took the supplies with a nod, turned and rode out at a lope, following the tracks in the soft dirt and the fresh horse droppings. It was a fool's mission to be wandering around out there in the dark, making himself a target if he got against the moon. Why did he think he might be able to find them? A thought came to him that he didn't want to admit. If a woman screamed in this desolate wilderness, the sound would carry for a long, long way. The image of Summer Sky in that renegade's arms made him ride a little faster, even though it was already getting difficult to see any signs.

The faint tracks soon were lost in the growing darkness, but they seemed to be heading toward an old trail through the hills that he remembered from his boyhood. He knew that now the area was dotted with newly abandoned mines. For the last half-dozen years, ever since the first big gold strike on Cherry Creek where Denver was now established, white men had poured into the Rockies to dig for precious metals, causing even more trouble with the Indians who claimed those hunting grounds.

Angry Wolf's horse would have to have water, and there were only a couple of places where the cold clear stream crossed that trail. Hours passed. He rode as quiet as a ghost, pausing now and then to listen, dismount and try to see any track or sign by moonlight. The air was frosty, and here in the mountains, it could begin to snow without much notice. Iron Knife's body grew cramped and cold. He paused occasionally to sip the hot coffee, grateful to Silver for packing some crusty fresh bread and meat. Good sense told him he should have waited until daylight. No warrior liked to fight at night; they feared dying in the darkness when the soul, the *tasoom,* couldn't find its way up the *Ekutsihimmiyo,* the Hanging Road to the Sky, to join the dead warriors who now rode forever through the clouds.

Every once in a while, he would pause and listen, not sure what he listened for: the nicker of a horse, maybe, the sound of a metal horseshoe against a rock—or maybe a woman's terrified crying. No, Summer wouldn't cry. His woman was brave for a white girl. Maybe in her heart she really was Cheyenne. He had begun to doubt that she fitted in among the Indians and their harsh lifestyle. Her yellow hair drew lusty men like a magnet and they all wanted her. The wind picked up and blew cold against his face. It was going to be a long, miserable night. At least when dawn finally came, he'd be able to look for the broken branch, horses' droppings, anything that would tell him which way the kidnapper had gone.

He tried not to think of what might be happening to his Summer Sky right now. He comforted himself with the thought that Angry Wolf would be too worried about Iron Knife being on his trail to stop and enjoy the delicate blonde girl's body. He reined in again, patted his stallion's neck, and listened. Abruptly, an owl hooted and flew out of a tree near the trail, startling him. Iron Knife felt sweat break out between his shoulders even though the night was cold. The hoot of an owl meant death; the question was whose?

Chapter Seven

On the wind, Iron Knife smelled just the slightest scent. He turned his face and breathed deep, not sure. Yes, it was wood smoke. Could it be from Cherokee's cabin? No, he was up wind from that. It was just the slightest whiff of smoke; maybe from a tiny camp fire. His heart beat a little faster with hope. Iron Knife rode cautiously now for the next several miles after tying a scrap of rawhide around Spotted Blanket's muzzle to keep it from whinnying should it smell another horse. He faced the fact that it might not be Angry Wolf ahead. He would have to be cautious approaching that camp; it could be a half-dozen well-armed white hunters, scouts, or enemy warriors.

His mouth tasted dry with tension, but his palms were wet as he smelled the breeze and tried to judge where that camp fire was located. The scent was stronger now. He rode a little farther, dismounted, and tied his horse to a tree, moving through the woods as quiet as a shadow. The moon had disappeared behind a bank of clouds, and the night was spitting snow. He'd be lucky if he didn't get caught in a bad storm.

Following the scent of smoke, he crept through the forest, watching and listening. In the mouth of an abandoned mine, a woman and a man sat before a tiny fire that threw giant, grotesque shadows of them against the rocks. The woman was trussed up, her hands tied above her, the front of her shift torn so that her full, soft breasts were visible. Long blond hair hung loose like spilled gold down her creamy shoulders. Around her neck, a little gold locket gleamed in the firelight. Summer Sky! He had to force himself not to run to her. The Indian who sat cross-legged had his head half turned, guzzling whiskey from a bottle. As Iron Knife watched, the man put the bottle down, wiped his mouth with the back of his hand and leered at the helpless captive.

Iron Knife leaned forward, peering closely at the ugly, pock-marked face. It couldn't be, but it was Angry Wolf. How had the man survived when Iron Knife had seen Summer stab him? In the light, the white, jagged scar contrasted sharply with his dark chest. Somehow, Angry Wolf had survived that wound and recovered. Now he had crossed his enemy's path again and planned revenge on a helpless girl.

Iron Knife gritted his teeth with rage. He would seek vengeance, even though it violated tribe taboo to kill one of their own.

As he watched, Angry Wolf reached for Summer. "Now that I have filled my belly, I have time for you, white bitch, before I set up an ambush for your man!"

Summer struggled to pull free while the drunken warrior laughed and pawed at her, tangling his hands in her hair. "It does you no good to fight me; I will take you anyway."

Angry Wolf put one hand on Summer's bare breast; the other jerked her mouth against his as he kissed her brutally.

Iron Knife shook with anger as he unsheathed his big blade. Angry Wolf wore a knife, too, but Iron Knife didn't intend to give him a chance to use it. The drunken brave's attention stayed focused on the half-naked woman as he pawed and kissed her. Iron Knife stepped out of the woods, moving as silent as a shadow while he crept closer.

But even as he crept up behind Angry Wolf, Summer seemed to see him for the first time, and her eyes widened in relief. Angry Wolf froze, realized she was looking at something behind him, and whirled even as he grabbed for his own blade.

"Iron Knife!" she cried out, trying to scramble to her feet, but she was tied.

"So you come!" Angry Wolf stood feet wide apart, dagger in hand. "Now we settle this at last, and then I rape your woman!"

"We've talked enough!" Iron Knife thundered. "Prepare to die!" He attacked, knife flashing brightly in the firelight. For a drunk, Angry Wolf was as agile as a rattlesnake. He dodged away, and Iron Knife's blade sliced empty air.

Angry Wolf threw back his head and laughed. "Your worry for your woman affects your judgment, dog soldier!"

He was right. Iron Knife struggled to get a grip on his raging emotions. If he was going to kill Angry Wolf, he would have to be as cold and emotionless as if he were killing any predator. Certainly both had survived enough life and death battles against enemies of the Cheyenne to go at killing each other coldly and methodically. All these years, Iron Knife had worried about breaking that taboo, and yet here he was prepared, no, eager, to do it again.

Angry Wolf lunged at him, but Iron Knife sidestepped the move deftly, threw back his head and chided, "You're drunk; you run on liquid courage!"

"Big talk for a warrior whose woman saved him the last time we fought!"

Summer lay there, watching helplessly. With her hands tied, there was nothing she could do to aid her man, and she didn't think Iron Knife had completely recovered from his Sand Creek wound. She struggled to break free, but she was tied tightly. Her heart hammered, for she knew that if Angry Wolf won, he would scalp Iron Knife, throw the bloody trophy across her naked body and rape her. There seemed to be no way to help her man.

The men parried and clashed, steel blade ringing against steel blade.

Angry Wolf laughed as the two circled each other warily. "Are you not worried about the taboo of the Medicine Arrows if you kill me, dog soldier?"

"They already run with blood—" Iron Knife drew great gulps of air into his mighty chest—"but it is not my doing."

"I killed Horse Stealer," Angry Wolf snarled, "and now I will kill you, too!" He lunged toward Iron Knife, but the big man was as graceful as a mountain lion. He stepped to one side, and the drunken savage tripped, lost his balance, staggered and fell as he thrust with his knife. He screamed out as he landed on his own dagger.

"Angry Wolf?" Iron Knife ran to him and turned him over. The other lay with his own blade buried to the hilt in his chest at almost exactly the location where Summer had stabbed him all those long years ago.

The dying man grimaced and looked down at the knife stuck in his flesh almost as if he could not believe what had happened. "Strange ... so strange ..." he muttered, "the great god, Heammawihio, takes revenge for my killing Horse Stealer. . . ."

Summer stared, stunned at the scarlet stream running down the man's chest. Even from here, she smelled the sweet, hot scent of his blood. He gasped one more time and died.

Iron Knife stood up, swayed for a moment as he got his breath, and came over to pull her to her feet. "Little One, are you all right?"

"I—he had Lance. . . ." Summer lost control and began to cry as he slipped his big arms around her and started untying her hands.

"Don't cry, Little One, you're all right. I'm here."

When he got her hands untied, she threw her arms around him, burying her face against the protection of his muscular chest while he held her tightly, stroking her hair. "He—he was going to force me—"

"It's all right, Summer," he whispered. "I won't ever let anyone hurt you; you're mine."

A sudden thought came to her, and she looked up at him. "The children?"

"All right." He tilted her small, heart-shaped face up to his and kissed her gently. "Silver's looking after them."

She was shaking with cold and exhaustion. It was snowing in earnest now. "Did you hear? He killed a Cheyenne warrior. He's the reason there was blood on the Medicine Arrows!"

"I heard." He cradled her in his arms, soothing her, murmuring to her while he held her close.

She buried her face in the hollow of his wide shoulder and clung to him, shaking with sobs while he comforted her. It felt so good to have his powerful arms around her. She was his in the most primitive definition of the word, and for the moment, nothing else mattered. He picked her up like a fragile doll, carried her into the cave, then stood her on her feet gently.

Iron Knife said, "The snow's getting worse; we'd better make plans to wait out the night here."

"But the children—"

"Silver can deal with the children until morning," he said firmly. "I'll drag the body away, get the horses in out of the wind. You build up the fire and see how much food there is. I can use some coffee; it's in the canteen."

She was so shaken, she didn't want to let him out of her sight, but there were things that had to be done, she knew. He was back in a few minutes and grunted with satisfaction to see she had built the fire into a warm blaze. "Good. I've also got a blanket."

They wrapped up in the blanket together before the fire.

"I'm still cold." She shivered, and he handed her the whiskey.

"Here, this should warm us both up."

They snuggled down by the blaze, pulled the blanket more tightly around them, ate the meat and bread Silver had sent, and drank strong coffee laced with whiskey. It was snowing steadily now, covering the earth with a white velvet blanket.

With her belly full of meat and whiskey, she felt warm and securely content curled up in her man's arms under the blanket by the blazing fire, watching the snow fall. They lay like two spoons, his body around hers, kissing the nape of her neck, his big hand on her bare breast. His hand slipped down to her belly.

"I—I wish. . . ." He let the words trail off, but she felt his maleness big and urgent against her hips.

She wanted him, too. It didn't seem fair that he had taught her passion and now they must continually deny that need.

"Dearest," she whispered, and realized she was a bit drunk, "it wouldn't hurt anything if you only kissed me a little." She turned on her back and laid her golden head in the hollow of his powerful dark shoulder and felt his fingers trace the aura of her nipple.

"No harm in that, Little One." He leaned over and kissed her, running his tongue deep into her mouth. She could taste the warm whiskey on it as he teased around the edges of her lips. Without meaning to, her body went tense and molded itself against his. His manhood was pulsating hard as he pressed against her. She felt her pulse quicken, felt his heart beat harder against her breast.

"Just a few kisses," she murmured against his mouth, "to keep us warm."

"No more than that," he warned and touched the tip of his tongue in her ear, sucking the lobe as he caressed her breast.

She had not forgotten how his tender touch made her want him beyond any reason. Without meaning to, she arched against him and locked her hands behind his dark head so he couldn't move away from kissing her deeper and with mounting passion.

His big hand went down to cup her small bottom, bringing it up against him. "Just keeping you warm," he said.

"Keep me warm; I like it." They were both a little drunk, she thought, but it didn't matter. They were safe and snug, and there was a long, cold night ahead of them. What did it hurt if they just teased each other's bodies a little as long as they didn't complete the act?

She reached down and clasped him with her hand. He was rock hard and wet with seed. He groaned aloud when she did that and kissed both her breasts, teasing her soft skin with his lips as they brushed across her body. She closed her eyes and concentrated on the feelings, giddy with whiskey and exhaustion, yet cosy and safe in his arms.

"I want you," he said insistently. "I want to put myself deep in you so men can smell the scent of me on you, know you belong to me."

"We don't dare," she reminded him, "but you can touch me a little if you want."

"Touch you?" he snorted, "how about possess you?"

In her mind, she saw herself as it had been between them in times past with her thighs spread wide and his lean hips pumping hard into her depths while she writhed under him, clawing his back and hips, kissing his lips while he urged her into ecstasy.

He kissed her again, breathing his whiskey-sweet breath deep into her mouth. "Do you know how a warrior makes a horse his obedient possession?"

She knew. A warrior blew his life's breath into a horse's lungs. It also worked with a woman, she thought dimly as she breathed in his warm scent and kissed his lips.

His hands were stroking down her belly to her thighs. He ran his thumb gently over the rosebud of her femininity. It felt like a bolt of lightning striking her. She protested, "I—I don't think you'd better . . ."

"I just want to touch you . . . stroke you." His voice was full of urgency, and he didn't stop his caressing and kissing.

Yes, that's all they were doing, she told herself as she spread her thighs wider, unable to resist his touch as he kissed her again. His breath was coming in gasps, and she felt the pulse beating in his big manhood as he pressed it against her. She wanted more than kisses and touches; what she really hungered for was his big manhood throbbing deep in her inner core. She yearned to feel him stiffen as he released his seed into her waiting vessel. It had been a long time since they had mated.

He wasn't going to do it, she told herself vaguely; he was pleasuring himself with the feel of her soft, warm flesh. She was glad he had willpower, because as drunk and comfortable as she was in his embrace, she wasn't sure she could make herself stop if he left it up to her. He leaned over her, and she bit his nipple so that he groaned and pressed it against her mouth while his hand gently massaged her full breasts.

They kissed longer and deeper and more urgently each time. "We should stop," she whispered, but he only kissed her harder in a way that excited her.

He was stroking her thighs, and she spread her legs so he could stroke where she most wanted his touch. The fire of desire seemed to burn hotter and brighter between them. He had moved so he was half on her, kissing her breasts, rubbing himself against her belly.

"Oh, Little One, I want you so . . . please. . . ."

It wasn't fair; they needed each other, and their passion was flaming as hot as the fire they lay before. She dug her nails into his muscular shoulders as he kissed her eyes, her lips, her throat.

"Please," he gasped.

We shouldn't, her mind cried out, but she couldn't stop herself from pressing her body against his insistent manhood.

"Summer, let me . . . please let me . . . I want you so. . . ."

She had lost all judgment and worry about tomorrow. She only knew that her whole insides seemed to be an aching void that needed to be filled with something iron hard and pulsating, throbbing down to her very core. When he reached to put himself against the velvet of her womanliness, they were both silky wet. He lay half on her, pressing against her, throbbing. Summer knew she should push him away, but the truth was she wanted him every bit as badly as he wanted her. She kissed him wildly, reaching down to dig her nails into his hard hips. She surrendered by letting her thighs fall apart, arching her pelvis up to meet him.

With a groan, he buried himself in her.

It felt so good, being pinned against the soft blanket by his steel maleness throbbing deep inside her while his warm insistent mouth caressed her tongue, drew it deep into his mouth.

His fingers tangled in her hair, he began to ride her body, hard and deep and sure. She arched her back so that her pelvis came up and met his thrust for thrust. He had the power to play her body until her nerves were as taut as wires, wanting the release that only he could give. Summer locked her legs around his lean, dark body. "You know what I want," she demanded, "give it to me! Please . . . !"

He pulled back his long length and came into her hard, pulled back and then came down on her again. Summer arched up to meet him, encouraged him to ride her with hard, relentless thrusts. His big hands covered her breasts, squeezing them in a gentle caress while his tongue went deep in her throat. She was his woman, his to possess and mate—his alone.

She had forgotten how much she loved him, how satisfying it felt to have him inside her. Summer dug her nails into his shoulders, urging him deeper still. "More!" she gasped. "Give me everything you've got!"

"Little vixen, you can't take everything I've got!"

"Try me!" she challenged, and spread her thighs farther, arching up to meet him stroke for stroke. She had forgotten just how big he was. And she was small. Every time he slammed down into her, he seemed to rub against her very womb. The sensation excited her to new heights of passion. "Don't stop!" she whispered, frantic with her own need. "Oh, God, please don't stop!"

"Not until I satisfy you," he promised, and began to ride her with an intensity she hadn't experienced in a long time. Her rising ecstasy seemed to excite him to even greater passion. It was wild, beautiful, and savage.

"My once in a lifetime love," she whispered against his lips as he gasped and began to climax. She felt him shudder all the way into her depths as he gave up his seed. It had been a long time since they had mated, and it seemed it was taking a long time to release all that he had saved. Then she couldn't think of anything else because her body began to react to his, locking onto his manhood as if to squeeze every precious drop from him deep into her womb where it belonged. They trembled thus a long moment, giving and getting from each other. Then, with exhausted sighs, the splendor faded, and they clung to each other.

"Oh, Summer . . ." he sighed again, "what have we done?"

What had they done? Now, as their passion cooled, she realized the chance they had taken. "We—we shouldn't have." She was apprehensive and a little annoyed with both him and herself. But when she had been in the throes of rising heat, she had wanted him enough to throw caution to the wind.

He brushed her damp blond hair out of her eyes and kissed her forehead. "I've had to fight to keep my hands off you all these months while the other braves were telling me to take a second woman."

She closed her eyes and pictured sharing the tipi with a dark and beautiful Cheyenne girl, listening to her man panting and mating with his other woman. How could a civilized person deal with the reality of the Indian culture? "I hate their primitive custom!"

"I know, Little One, I know; but I'm only a man after all." He kissed her gently. "What do white men do?"

"Well, they don't do that." She didn't know the answer; yes, she did. White men went to whores or kept a mistress. Did her father keep a mistress? Somehow she couldn't imagine proper and stern Silas Van Schuyler in the throes of passion with any woman. "Maybe I'll never really be part of your culture," she admitted. "I'm the jealous type. I don't know what I would do if I ever found out that you had been unfaithful to me with another woman."

Iron Knife looked down at her, his mind troubled. If only. . . . If only he could go back and erase the past. Once, in a rage of passion when he had thought Summer had betrayed him, run away back to her people, he had been angry and hurt. A lusty Indian girl had seduced him in a quick coupling that was not love, but nothing more than a frenzied, mindless mating. He regretted it bitterly, and only hoped his beloved never discovered his secret. He didn't want to lose Summer Sky, and if she ever found out, he would. Iron Knife prayed that Summer would never learn about the time when he had mated with that Arapaho tramp, Gray Dove.

Chapter Eight

The snow had drifted by dawn when Iron Knife and Summer started out to return to Cherokee Evans' cabin. They left Angry Wolf's body in a ravine, covered with snow. At one time, their old enemy had been an honored dog soldier, and it was not uncommon to leave the body of a dead warrior on the field where he had fallen.

"They'll be worried to death about us," Summer said, as he carried her out to Angry Wolf's horse and tenderly lifted her to the saddle. They rode out, the horses' hooves crunching through the thin crust of ice on the snow.

"They'll know we couldn't get back in the dark, Little One. Besides"—he smiled at her—"spending the night with you in that mine was worth it; I had almost forgotten what it's like to make love."

Had he been feeling that deprived? She felt stung, but said nothing as they rode along. After all, it was his civilization that presumed women would nurse children for three years. Summer knew they shouldn't have taken the chance last night, but it had been so long since they had made love totally and completely. She wouldn't let it happen again, she vowed, but how could she deny him without expecting that he, like the other Cheyenne warriors, would take a second wife? Lost in her own thoughts, she said little as they rode back to Cherokee Evans' cabin.

Everyone came out to meet them as they rode in and dismounted. The three children ran into their arms, chattering and delighted.

Cherokee looked relieved as they handed their reins to Keso to put the horses away. "I didn't know whether to follow you or see if I could get soldiers to come."

"I'll tell you all about it later, my friend." Iron Knife clapped him on the shoulder and nodded toward the listening children.

Silver sighed as they all trooped up the porch and into the cabin. "Thank God you're all right."

Cherokee motioned the pair to sit close to the fire while Silver busied herself bringing hot coffee. "Want to talk about it?"

Summer hugged her baby to her as somber little Storm Gathering, Lance and Wannie hung on the arms of the chairs to listen. She didn't even want to think about Angry Wolf ever again.

Iron Knife started to speak, then glanced around at all the curious children. "Let's just say the enemy is not a threat anymore."

Storm leaned forward eagerly. "Father, you kill him?"

"Of course not," Iron Knife said, "it is taboo to kill a fellow Cheyenne." His eyes met and locked on Summer's. "He fell on his own knife as we fought; but he confessed he killed another Cheyenne warrior named Horse Stealer a few days ago, so now we know why there was blood on the sacred Medicine Arrows."

Summer smiled at her love, feeling tremendous relief. The weight of guilt from the killing she'd thought she had committed was finally lifted.

Summer hugged her baby again and reached to kiss the two little boys, but they both made noises about mothers kissing warriors, and wiped the kisses from their little brown faces. However, they stayed close to her knee.

"How did Garnet take to cow's milk?" she asked Silver.

"Fine," the other answered, "I think she's weaned."

"Oh, really?" Summer sneaked a look at Iron Knife and smiled.

He grinned and looked back at her with a secret message in his dark, smoldering eyes.

Summer thought of the passion she had experienced in his arms so many times. With the baby weaned, there was no reason that tonight and every night they couldn't enjoy endless ecstasy in each other's arms.

The scent of baking filled the air, and Silver said, "I've made some cookies; it's Christmas, you know."

Christmas. Summer had forgotten about the holiday out here with the Indians.

Lance's serious, handsome face furrowed. "What's Christmas?"

"It's a holiday, son"—she patted his head—"with gifts and special food." She was suddenly homesick for the extravagant Victorian holidays in Boston. At the wealthy Van Schuylers', there would be a decorated tree, lavish food and many gifts. She looked up and realized Iron Knife was watching her. Could he tell by her expression what she was thinking?

Wannie said, "Does that mean lots of presents?"

The big Indian boy, Keso, had come inside just then. "Girls!" he snorted. "All Wannie thinks about is dressin' up like a grown lady when she's nothin' but a baby!"

"Am not!"

"Are too!"

"Children!" Silver moved in to stop the fuss. "We've got some gifts to hand out and some cookies, too."

The children set up a chorus of excitement.

Summer looked at her questioningly.

Cherokee shrugged. "It's not much; I carved some wooden toys, and Silver stayed up late a few nights after the kids were in bed to make rag dolls."

With shouts of delight, the children gathered around the tree to receive their simple toys, then trooped off to the kitchen for warm cookies and milk. Baby Garnet had dropped off to sleep in Summer's arms.

Summer smiled at Iron Knife, content to be here in a setting that was more familiar to her than the Cheyenne's nomad life-style.

Iron Knife sipped his coffee. "Cherokee, you've got two nice children."

Cherokee nodded. "Aren't they something, though? Never thought I'd end up raisin' two orphan children, but I love them like they were our own."

"I thought they were sister and brother?" Summer said as she looked toward the kitchen where shouts of delight echoed.

Cherokee shook his head. "Keso's a street kid that I picked up in Denver; thinks he's full-blood Cheyenne—"

"But he's not," Iron Knife said. "I've heard about him. He's Ute, but raised Cheyenne; kidnapped years ago, I think. The two tribes are enemies. It was not my band, so I really don't know much about it."

Silver came in just then, leaving the children in the kitchen eating cookies. "And Wannie is half Arapaho; I was her governess when I worked for the duchess in Denver."

Summer was curious. "There was a real duchess in Denver?"

"Not hardly!" Cherokee laughed. "Just an Indian girl named Gray Dove trying to pass herself off as Spanish royalty."

"Gray Dove?" Iron Knife said, and there was something strained about his face that made Summer uneasy.

"She's dead," Silver said, "died in the fire trying to rescue her money when her saloon burned."

"So who's Wannie's father?" Summer asked. Knowing the promiscuous Gray Dove as she did, it could be anyone.

"A horrible man named Jake Dallinger who's dead now." Silver shuddered as she remembered that horrible night just weeks ago when she'd been forced to kill the Army scout to save Cherokee's life. "We know because of the birthmark on her hand like Jake had, but almost to the end Gray Dove thought it was—" She paused, exchanged looks with her husband, turned red, and cleared her throat uncertainly. "Well, enough of that; who'd like some more coffee?"

But Summer had seen that warning glance Cherokee gave Silver. Sweat broke out on Iron Knife's face.

"I'd like another cup," Iron Knife said a little too quickly. "Do you think it might snow again tonight?"

There was something here that made Summer uneasy, something she couldn't put her finger on. She had a feeling that the other three knew something that she did not. "Gray Dove thought it was who?"

"Yes, it might snow at that," Cherokee drawled. "I do believe Iron Knife's right. I'd like some more coffee."

"Good," Silver said a little too brightly and hopped up, "I'll get it!" She fled the room.

Cherokee rolled a cigarette. "Yes, it may snow some more after all."

"Haven't seen such miserable weather for a couple of winters," Iron Knife said. "Deep snow makes it hard for ponies to find grass."

What was going on here? All this talk of weather and coffee. She didn't say anything else, mystified as she watched the two men, who seemed as nervous and tense as rattlesnakes on a hot griddle. The mood had changed the moment the question of Wannie's father had come up. Was there something she wasn't supposed to know?

The silence almost seemed to shout. Except for the noise of the children laughing in the kitchen and the wind blowing outside, it was quiet enough in the room to hear her rocker creak as she shifted the sleeping child from one arm to the other.

Iron Knife cleared his throat and avoided looking at her. "So how goes the white man's war? Are the blue-coats and the gray-clad ones still fighting each other?"

Cherokee shrugged and stared into the fire, not looking at her, either. "I don't know much more than you do, except what little news we managed to get while I was in Denver."

"Well, here I am, everyone." Silver came into the room, smiling with a wide, nervous grin. "Here's fresh coffee all around!"

Summer watched her pour, puzzled over the things that had been said—and left unsaid—in the past few minutes. There was something secretive here, what was it? Wannie looked to be about five years old. That meant the pretty little girl was conceived somewhere late in 1858, the year Summer became Iron Knife's woman. Gray Dove had been in love with Iron Knife. Could it be . . . ? No, of course not. She must not even think about it. Summer managed a weak smile. "Cherokee, were you a soldier?"

He nodded. "As you can tell by my accent, no doubt, I fought for the South, but ended up a prisoner in a Yankee hellhole. To get out, I volunteered to put on the blue uniform and go west to fight Indians; that's how I met Iron Knife."

"Our hunting party found him on a riverbank many miles from here, half-blind and lost."

"I got my sight back and, with Iron Knife's help, made it to civilization. I was luckier than many Southerners." Cherokee sighed. "Lord only knows what happened to my old colonel. Shawn O'Bannion may be dead for all I know."

That name sounded familiar somehow, but Summer didn't know why. "Shawn O'Bannion?"

"He owns a big Tennessee plantation called Shannon Place. I don't know if he's even still alive, but invading Yankees have probably burned Shannon Place to the ground by now."

She remembered then where she had heard the name. "I—I suppose it's a common enough name, but the one I'm thinking of was a poor immigrant gardener."

Cherokee sipped his coffee. "He's an Irish immigrant, all right, can tell by his accent. Don't know much about his past except that he went west as a young man and struck pay dirt in the California gold rush. He's one of the richest men in Tennessee—or was before the war."

Shawn O'Bannion. Could it be the same one? Hardly likely. What difference did it make? She realized the other three were staring at her curiously. Summer held her coffee cup up. "Well, Merry Christmas and here's to a happy New Year for us all!"

"Hear! Hear!" They held their coffee cups high in a toast while the sounds of laughing, playing children drifted from the kitchen.

Summer lay staring at the ceiling long after the last lamp had been blown out for the night and all the children were asleep. The couple was in bed in the spare room of the cabin.

Iron Knife pulled her against him. "Tomorrow, we'll rejoin the Cheyenne." She stayed stiff in his arms as he kissed her cheek. "Little One, is something wrong?"

"Should there be?" It came out more tersely than she had planned.

He chuckled. "When a woman answers a question with a question, a man knows he's in big trouble."

"Now, unless you've done something you wouldn't want me to know about, why would you think that?"

A long pause. "What kind of question is that?"

"You tell me." She didn't know herself why she was upset; it was just a vague suspicion that kept gnawing at her vitals like a mouse chewing away. It was discomforting enough that she couldn't sleep.

"Summer, I don't know what the hell you're talking about!"

"Then there's nothing to discuss!" She rolled over in bed, her back to him. She wasn't sure whether she was angry or hurt. She yearned to blurt out her suspicions and have her lover laugh them off because, of course, he loved her more than life itself.

Instead, he sighed heavily and punched up his pillow. "Fine, we won't talk about it. After this thing with Angry Wolf, I suppose you're tired and—"

"You're saying I'm a hysterical female!" She rolled toward him, raised up on one elbow, seething.

"I didn't say that—"

"You all but did! What a typical male reaction!"

"This is a typical male reaction!" Before she could move, he reached up, pulled her down to him, and kissed her deeply, passionately while she tried to break away.

She must not let him wear her down, get her mind off the subject with his kisses that had always melted her so.

She pulled out of his powerful arms and made a big show of wiping her mouth with the back of her hand. "Men always think that's the answer to everything."

He smiled up at her. "Last night, you thought it was a pretty good answer."

She gritted her teeth, wanting to smack him for pointing out how vulnerable she was to his charms. Instead, she lay down, turned her back on him and tried not to weep, but the tears came, making the mattress shake ever so slightly.

"Summer?"

She didn't manage to stifle a sob, although she tried.

"Little One, what is it? What's happened?" He put his arms around her, holding her close, murmuring to her, stroking her hair.

She wanted to melt against him, cry against his chest. Instead, all she could do was hold herself rigid and fight to stop her tears. She wanted to ask but was terrified to hear the truth. "I—I guess I am more tired than I thought."

"That's what I said." She hated the smug tone of his voice, yet what had always attracted her to him was his almost swaggering masculinity, his protective savagery, his primitive arrogance. But, oh, he could be such a gentle and sensitive lover. He kissed her forehead. "Let's get some sleep then; we've got a long way to go tomorrow."

They lay together, with her head in the hollow of his shoulder. She still didn't have the answer to her unasked question, and she couldn't bear to bring it up again because he might tell her what she most dreaded to hear. "We're going back tomorrow?"

"Umm." He sounded distant, sleepy. "I'm feeling stronger, and I want to report to the council about Angry Wolf."

She stared up at the ceiling. *"Ne-mehotatse,* dearest," she said finally. *I love you.*

She waited for him to say he loved her, too, but what she got was the gentle sound of his breathing. He had dropped off to sleep. Damn him! She had wanted him to lie awake and hold her awhile, kiss her tenderly, say sweet things, tell her over and over how much he loved her, but he had drifted off to sleep. *My marriage to a warrior is, after all, much like any marriage,* she thought, disappointed and disillusioned. *Once you become a wife, they take you for granted except when they get aroused. The rest of the time, they expect you to behave in a non-hysterical way, be "sensible," and go to sleep.* Maybe things would look different to her tomorrow. However, tonight, while he slept, she lay looking at the ceiling, her soul in turmoil while she tried not to cry.

Things didn't look much different to her in the morning, but Summer said nothing as she gathered up her things and thanked Silver for her hospitality. She thought she could never draw an easy breath again until she knew for certain whether her man had ever betrayed her with Gray Dove, that easy slut of an Arapaho.

Silver hugged her as they went out to the horses. "We loved having you, come back any time."

"We enjoyed it," Summer said.

Cherokee pushed his hat back. "Will you two be in any danger because of this Indian war?"

"No more than any of the other Cheyenne." Iron Knife lifted Lance and Storm up on their little pinto ponies. "You're the ones who ought to be worried, my friend, up here in the wilderness. I've hung a medicine object on your gate post that will tell warriors you are friends and should be left in peace."

"Thanks," Silver said. "If you two ever need anything, you know where to find us."

"And, Cherokee, if you ever need to get a message to us," Iron Knife said, "that medicine object will give you safe passage among our warriors across the plains."

Summer put little Garnet in a cradleboard, then hung it from Starfire's saddle. "I've got another old friend in Denver, Todd Shaw."

"I know him." Cherokee nodded and put his big arm around Silver's shoulders.

Summer hesitated, looking at little Wannie. The pretty, dark little girl was playing dress-up in Silver's old clothes and teasing Keso, who kept muttering that if she didn't stop, he'd dunk her in the horse trough, high-heeled shoes and all. Yes, Wannie looked like her Indian mother, all right, and someday, she'd be a great beauty. Her big brother and Cherokee would have a difficult time keeping suitors away from her then. *Gray Dove.* Summer tried not to imagine the lusty Arapaho beauty in Iron Knife's arms.

"Summer?" Iron Knife said.

"What?" She came out of her thoughts with a start. The others were looking at her strangely.

"I said, we're ready to go."

"Oh, of course." They said their goodbyes again, turned and rode out, Lance and Storm loping their ponies ahead down the snowy trail. When she turned to look back and wave, Keso was giving Wannie a piggy-back ride to the cabin. Summer waved at the little family as the Evans turned and went up the steps.

Iron Knife smiled. "Did you see the way that Wannie torments Keso?"

"He's a half-grown boy"—Summer shrugged—"she's a little girl. Bratty sisters have always made life miserable for brothers."

"It'll be interesting to see how they get along in ten years or so."

Summer didn't answer. She didn't want to discuss the Evans' adopted daughter; it made her think about Wannie's mother, even though she knew she should push all this from her mind and forget it. It was a Pandora's box that she might not be able to close the lid on if she ever opened it. Right now, she wished she didn't even have her suspicions because they tormented her.

She tried to tell herself that even if it were true, it was over and done a long time ago, and that it didn't matter. Then why hadn't he told her about it?

"Little One"—Iron Knife rode alongside her—"you are very quiet and thoughtful this morning."

She looked at the long shadow she was throwing on the shimmering, crusty snow instead of looking at him. "I—I'm just tired, that's all."

"I love you, Summer Sky."

She looked up sharply, wondering if he knew, deep in his heart, what was troubling her. Usually, she would have said, "I love you, too," but now, she said nothing, merely returned to staring at their silhouettes dark against the snow. Could anyone ever really know what another human being was thinking? She had thought she had known him so well; that there were no secrets between them. Now she wondered if there were other things she didn't know?

They returned to their Cheyenne band. Old Pony Woman and Pretty Flower came out to meet her, and she realized she was glad to see them—except that Summer soon learned the warriors were planning a revenge raid on Fort Sedgewick, near the town of Julesburg. That knowledge made Summer sad. She couldn't even think about what would happen a few days from now when the warriors attacked. Added to that was the terrible suspicion that at the Evans' cabin, the other three adults had tried so hard to end any discussion of Wannie's parentage. Her suspicions deepened as the day wore on, and she lay sleepless that night in their tipi after the children were asleep.

"Summer Sky," Iron Knife murmured, "you are angry with me for making love to you in the mine?"

"I lost control; now I wish we hadn't."

He turned over and looked at her in the glow of the fire. "Is that what has been bothering you? You have been so silent and moody."

"Is there any reason you should be so suspicious?"

A long silence. "All right, my little love, let's get this out in the open, shall we?"

"There's nothing to discuss, unless you know something I don't."

"I have a feeling I'm being accused of something. I wish I at least knew what it is."

"You should know that better than I!" Her voice rose in spite of all she could do.

He clapped his hand over her mouth. "Summer," he said, his tone cold, "I am not sure what this is about, but a woman does not embarrass her man by screaming at him loud enough that others in the camp might hear."

She did the first thing that came into her mind; she bit his hand.

He gave a low cry of indignant pain and shook the injured fingers. "If you were anyone else, I'd break you in half for that and you know it."

"Go ahead, hit me; you're bigger than I am, hit me!"

"You have tempted me too far this time!" Before she could react, he grabbed her, flipped her over his lap, jerked her buckskin shift up and paddled her bare bottom thoroughly while she fought and kicked, trying not to wake her children.

"You arrogant bastard! How dare you do that! How dare you use violence against me!"

He yanked her up, then pulled her skirt down. "You hurt me first," he reminded her, "and what's sauce for the goose, as the white man says, is sauce for a gander!"

She was in a fury as she pulled away from him. "I didn't think you'd do it!"

"May I remind you," he said with cool logic, "that you dared me to do it."

"But I didn't think you would!" She was crying from sheer anger now, and the more she cried, the angrier she got.

He reached out to her, and she slapped his hand away. "Don't ever dare me, Little One. You are my woman and I will not be pushed around or led around by the nose like some damn fool white man."

"I don't know what I ever saw in you," she sobbed in fury. "I hate you!"

"And I love you," he said softly. "I love you more than anything in this world. Can't you stop all this?" He slipped his arms around her, pulled her to him.

She tried to fight him, but he was so much bigger and stronger than she was. "No, I—" and his lips blocked her angry words. She tried to pull away from him to voice her indignation again, and he slipped his tongue between her lips. She tried to bite his tongue, but his hand reached up to hold her chin so he could ravage her mouth with his. One of his big arms held her against him while the other then stroked her hair, her back, her breasts.

He was too strong to pull away from, so there was nothing she could do but let him kiss her and paw her until he grew tired of his sport. Then she would escape his embrace and continue her tirade. She managed to pull her lips from his. "I—I resent you treating me like nothing but a woman—"

"You are a woman, Summer Sky," he murmured against her lips, "my woman to protect and please and pleasure."

"That's not what I want right now." She tried to keep her body rigid in his embrace, but his hand was playing with her nipples.

"Isn't it?" he whispered against her ear, and his hot breath sent a shiver through her as he nibbled and sucked on her ear lobe. "It's what I want; would you settle for that?"

"No . . ." When she opened her lips to deny it, he put his tongue in her mouth again, teasing and caressing. She would not let him arouse her and get her mind off the subject at hand, she decided.

"Let me do that to the rest of you," he murmured, "run my tongue all over you, in you. I want to taste every bit of you, caress every inch of you with my mouth."

"No . . ." She shook her head, but already his mouth was working its way down her neck. His fingers were stroking between her thighs.

He was whispering to her now, whispering of how much his body wanted hers, how much he knew she wanted him. "Tell me you want me, too, Summer Sky."

She was trembling with desire, with banked passion. "No!" She shook her blond mane violently. "I—I can't take the chance of another baby."

"Then consider me your slave," he murmured. "I'll please you any way I can."

She knew she should object, but she wanted to feel his mouth sucking her breasts, and she let him open the lacings of her doeskin bodice.

"Such a beautiful pair of breasts and all mine," he said and cupped his big hands around her creamy white mounds, squeezed them up into two peaks of desire which he explored thoroughly with his lips and teeth.

"Don't," she began, but she could not keep her hands from pulling his dark head against her nipple so he would suck and caress and bite while she breathed heavier, gasping through open lips.

"You mean, 'don't stop,' " he said, and he didn't.

He was driving her wild with desire, Summer thought, and did not try to stop him as his mouth moved down between her breasts and worked its way down to where the tip of his tongue flicked in and out of her navel. Her whole body felt aflame with fiery passion. She reached out and took his throbbing maleness in her hand. God, how she wanted that! It wasn't fair that her man was so virile he could get her with child just by getting close to her. She'd be lucky if he hadn't already bred her that other night in that abandoned mine. She didn't even want to consider that possibility.

"I am your slave—your savage," he whispered against her skin, "tell me what it is you want me to do to you."

"N-Nothing, just let me up."

"You lie! I know what you want. . . ."

She could feel his tongue licking and caressing its way down her belly to her thigh. Her whole lower body felt as if it would burst into flame at any second. He was her savage, her stallion slave for the moment, ready and eager to do whatever it took to satisfy her body. She let her legs fall apart, and his mouth trailed and teased the inside of her thigh.

"Ask for it, Summer." She could feel the heat of his breath on the tender bud of her femininity.

She was almost too modest to voice it, but he was hers to satisfy her desires for the moment. "Kiss me there in a way that drives me wild."

At that he pulled her thighs wide apart and wrapped his arms around them before his mouth came down on her, hot and wet and searching.

"Ahh!" She arched her back and let his mouth ravage her while she tangled her fingers in his black hair, holding him against her. Oh, it felt so good. His tongue was caressing and exploring deep and thoroughly.

"You like that, Little One? You like that? Tell me. Tell me you like it . . . you want it."

Her passion had risen to the point that she was clawing his shoulders as she held him against her. He had turned so that he lay almost with her head in his lap. His maleness was hard and pulsating; she could feel it against her cheek and she began to convulse. She knew he would be unfulfilled this way and there was something she could do for him. She kissed him there and felt him throb hard and big. She did for him what he was doing for her. They began to convulse at the same time, and she couldn't get enough of him, wanting him, wanting the taste of him as he was tasting her. He was the ultimate lover, she thought as they rode a blazing sky rocket of mutual need and desire into the darkness together. For a timeless moment, they were caught in an eternity of mutual passion, a black sky full of exploding fireworks. In his arms and only in his arms did she experience this ultimate of fulfillment, this Cheyenne splendor.

Iron Knife pleased her and teased her all night long until she was too wrung out to do anything but admit she was his woman and that she wanted nothing more than to drift off to sleep against his big chest, safe and secure against anyone or anything that might hurt her.

Yet the images of him in another woman's arms came again to haunt her, and she couldn't stop herself from asking. "You—you have avoided my questions the last several days."

"About what?" He sounded sleepy but on guard.

"You know what it is I want to know; don't pretend you don't."

Another long pause. "You're tired, Little One. Why don't we forget all this happened and go to sleep? You'll feel differently tomorrow."

Was he evading her unspoken questions? He was treating her like a hysterical, jealous woman. Hot tears came to her eyes, and she blinked them back. "I don't want to forget about anything; I want the truth."

"About what?"

"You know about what!"

He sighed loudly. "Oh, Summer, are you sure you want to take this any farther? I love you; I've never loved another woman like I love you. Can't we leave it at that?"

Her common sense told her he was right, but she was jealous, hurt and suspicious. "I want to talk about it."

"You're like a small dog with a bone," he said in the darkness. "When you get hold of a subject, you don't let go of it, do you?"

"Obviously there's a big bone here to chew on." She didn't know whether the tears in her eyes were from jealousy or fury.

"All right!" He sounded angry himself. "We will talk, but I think maybe in the long run, I will wish I had refused."

"Just tell me what I need to know."

"Does it matter that I love you, Little One?" His voice was so soft, he was whispering.

She should drop it, she knew. She was delving into something she was going to regret knowing; she was certain of it or he wouldn't be so evasive. Yet she was too stubborn to kiss him, roll over and go to sleep. She blurted it out before she could think about it, throwing caution to the winds. "Did you sleep with Gray Dove?"

A long hesitation. "Long ago, before I ever knew you, I slept with her a time or two; all the warriors did. She was free and easy with her favors."

She took a deep breath. "What—what I want to know is did you ever sleep with her after we became lovers?"

A silence so long, she could hear the wind whining around the snug tipi.

"Did you?" she asked again.

"No."

"I don't believe you!"

"Then, damn it, why did you ask, since you know already?" He sat up suddenly, his tone and body tense and angry.

So now she knew.

Chapter Nine

For a moment, she felt no emotion. It was as if she'd been hit hard in the stomach; all the breath had gone out of her. Then the pain came deep in her soul, and it hurt worse than anything she had experienced—hurt worse than birthing a baby. She bit her lip to keep from crying out and tasted blood. Oh, God, why had she hung on to the subject? This was something she didn't want to know.

"I—I'm sorry, Summer." He sounded like a beaten man, so different from the proud, arrogant one of only moments ago. "It meant nothing to me. You had returned to Boston. I thought you had betrayed me, gone of your own free will. I didn't think you were ever coming back."

She was so hurt, she was struggling not to weep, and yet she was so angry, if she had had a weapon, at that moment, she would have killed him. "How like a man!" she said wryly, "can't do without a woman to top, doesn't matter who she is!"

He made a dismissing gesture in the moonlight streaming through the lodge opening. "That's not true and you know it. I thought you were gone forever."

"Was she good?"

"Why do we have to get into all this now that I've admitted it?"

"I just want to know; was she good?"

"Not like you; never like you. She was there, I hadn't had a woman in weeks, she threw herself at me."

She turned over and began to cry, angry with him for admitting it. "Why in God's name did you tell me? Why didn't you deny it?"

"I tried. You insisted on the truth." He attempted to put his arms around her, but she pushed him away.

"You cheating, cheating bastard!"

"It doesn't matter that I thought you didn't love me? That I believed you were never coming back?"

"Excuses! Why is it men always make excuses?"

"I don't see any point in dragging this out any longer with questions that you obviously don't intend for me to answer." His voice was grim. "I told you it didn't have any love in it, only lust. What happened in the late fall of '58 while you were in Boston is history; that's a long time ago."

"Not long enough."

"Little One, I am sorry; I never meant to hurt you. I love you like I have never loved another woman." Again he tried to put his arms around her, and she slapped him.

"Get your hands off me, you cheating, rotten bastard."

"If you were a man, I'd kill you for that!"

"And if I were a man, I'd kill you for hurting me!" She got up, sat down near the fire, put her arms around herself and rocked back and forth. The baby in her cradleboard began to cry. "Now see what you've done, you woke up Garnet."

"I—" He started to say something, cursed under his breath, and turned his back to her.

The two little boys stirred restlessly in their sleep, and Summer picked up the baby, shushing her quietly as she soothed her and offered the child her breast. Garnet sucked hungrily, and Summer closed her eyes. At least it was relaxing to nurse her baby. Her Cheyenne warrior had given her three of the most handsome and endearing children. They meant more than anything in the world to her—except him.

She both hated him and loved him at the same time, but he had hurt her in a way she had never experienced before. *No one can hurt you like someone you love,* she thought dully. What to do now? She was wounded and she was angry. She listened for Iron Knife to sit up, reach for her, take her, baby and all, back to his buffalo robes to cuddle and kiss. Once long ago when they had argued and she had taken her blanket and gone to the other side of the tipi, he had come across that tipi, swept her up in his arms, and taken her back to his blankets to make love to all night long.

He didn't move now, and she couldn't be sure whether he slept or not. She sat there until almost dawn, holding her baby. She couldn't sleep anyway. When she closed her eyes, she tortured herself with mental images of Iron Knife and Gray Dove together, him lying between the Arapaho girl's brown thighs, his mouth on her big breasts. Had she been more exciting, a better lover than Summer? Did he ever think of the girl's body wistfully and compare her lovemaking to Summer's?

Stop it! she thought, but it was difficult to force it from her mind. More than that, what was Summer going to do in the future? She couldn't think at all right now; all she could do was hurt inside. She felt betrayed. His reasoning that he thought Summer had left him forever was a weak excuse. Of course, some might point out that when she'd gone back to Boston, she'd gotten herself engaged to Austin Shaw, her old childhood sweet-

heart, but she hadn't let him take any liberties, like
sleeping with him. Not that a very proper Boston gentleman would have taken advantage of a lady.

What was she going to do now that she knew? She
might ask Cherokee and Silver for refuge, but Cherokee was a friend of Iron Knife's, and Silver struck her
as a no-nonsense type who would probably tell her to
forgive and forget. How could Summer forgive when
she could think of nothing else right now? She might
contact her rich father; but he would enjoy saying "I
told you so," and Summer was too proud to ask for his
charity. Silas Van Schuyler had not built his fortune by
being soft and merciful; he was a hard, unforgiving
man.

If she took her children and went to Denver, what
kind of a job could she get? At Miss Priddy's Female
Academy, they had taught her to speak French and
play the harp. No one expected a wealthy, aristocrat
girl to ever support herself, be anything but decora-
tive. Todd Shaw, her old fiancé's younger brother,
might try to get her a job at the newspaper; but she
had no journalism skills, and she was too proud to accept Todd's charity. The longer she thought about it,
the more Summer faced the fact that she probably had
no alternatives but to stay with her man. How many
women over the centuries had been stuck in this very
same predicament? *Millions,* she thought, *but that
doesn't make me feel any better.*

In the morning, the atmosphere between her and Iron
Knife was cool, distant. They avoided looking into each
other's eyes. Summer wished now she had never found
out about Gray Dove. He was evidently angry that she
had forced him to admit his transgression and then became furious with him for behaving like most men
would. Summer couldn't think rationally anymore. She

might be behaving like a jealous, hysterical bitch, but the image of her man in the arms of an enemy girl who had once plotted to kill Summer infuriated her. If it had been anyone else but the Arapaho slut, perhaps she could have pushed it out of her mind.

She loved and hated him at the same time. She wanted to throw herself in his arms and listen to him tell her he loved her, and she wanted to attack him with both fists because of the anger that burned within her.

He came to her that night, tried to take her in his arms, but she remained as stiff as a ramrod. "I'm sorry I hurt you."

He started to kiss her, but she turned her face away so that his lips only brushed her cheek. "I—I just never thought that you would ever touch another woman."

"You left me; what was I supposed to do?"

She whirled on him, her fists clenched. "I was kidnapped, I didn't leave of my own free will. You could have at least trusted me enough to wait and find out the truth."

"Maybe I should have, but I'm a man—"

"And men do their thinking with what hangs between their legs!" She was working herself into a fresh rage.

He half-raised his hands as if he would embrace her, seemed to think better of it, then dropped them to his sides. "If I could go back and change that, I would, Summer; it tears me up to see you so hurt. The past is set in stone; I can't change it. You were and are and always will be my once in a lifetime love, and I don't want to lose you."

"You won't lose me"—she kept her voice glacier cold as she turned away from him—"I don't seem to have many alternatives except to stay."

"And we're going to live like this from now on; you turning away from me when I touch you?"

"What do you expect me to do, say 'it doesn't matter, sleep around anytime you want'?"

He sighed. "I'll do anything I can to make it up to you. What is it you expect me to do?"

She didn't know. He had apologized, but that didn't change the fact that he had lain with another woman after he had been making love to her. She clenched her small fists, resisting the urge to strike out at him, beat him in the face and on the chest until she fell panting with exhaustion. That wouldn't change what had happened; that was what was making her so sad and so angry. The past was set in stone, and it couldn't be changed, no matter how sorry he was. In her mind, she saw him between Gray Dove's thighs, thrusting hard into the Indian girl, putting his mouth on her big breasts. It seemed she could think of nothing else.

"I love you," he said again. "Will you stay and give me a chance to make it up to you?"

She shrugged, her voice cold. "I don't seem to have a great many options with no income, no place to go and three little children."

"I am sorry I have no money to send you wherever you want to go," he said with great dignity, "but you knew that when you chose me. And if you think I would let you take my children from me to be raised by another man, you know me better than that." He twisted his fingers in her pale hair, turned her face up to his. "You are mine, Summer Sky, and I will not give you up. I love you too much."

"Don't speak to me of love; all you feel for me is lust." She pulled away from him. "All right, I am here for your convenience, to cook and warm your bed. You can trade me off for a rifle or a good horse, just like other warriors have done with their captive women."

"If that's the way you want it." He glared down at her. "I'm a proud man, Summer Sky, and I am not used to begging. If you won't forgive me and I won't give you up, we'll run this relationship on your terms."

"As master and captive?"

He swore under his breath. "If you say so."

"Then you can take a second wife, an Indian wife," she snapped curtly, flinging her head so that her hair fell across her shoulders in a golden swirl. "I will have to lie there at night and pretend to be asleep as you enjoy her—unless you feel an urge for me that night."

His dark eyes were cold and hard with anger. "I may just do that—white slave girl."

It was cold that first week of January that the Cheyenne called Okseyeshihis. The Cheyenne, Arapaho and Sioux gathered in the northeast corner of that vast area that was already being called Colorado to plan their revenge raids.

Summer and Iron Knife had been like two strangers sharing the same lodge the past few days. Now, when she knew that the warriors were to ride out to attack the stage station and the town of Julesburg, Summer felt she must protest, at least in the privacy of their tipi. "Can't this be solved in any other way without killing people?"

Iron Knife's expression was cold and remote. "You answer that, *veho* squaw; your people spilled much blood at Sand Creek."

She winced at the hardness in his eyes, but her hurt and anger had not faded. "I forget I am only a captive and not permitted to speak without knowing my master may beat me."

For just a moment, she saw his eyes soften, and his hand trembled, almost seemed to reach toward her; then he squared his broad shoulders. "Even now, the soldiers are no doubt plotting to attack us again, treacherous as rattlesnakes. What will happen next is out of my hands."

"And you expect me just to sit and wait while the warriors of this band kill other whites?"

"You are a captive, remember? You said so yourself, with no standing in this tribe. Neither of us could stop this should I want to, and at this moment, my heart is filled with bitterness at the whites. We will attack that place called Fort Sedgewick."

"But there's a town there, Julesburg, with a stage station. There'll probably be women and children."

He frowned at her. "There were women and children at Sand Creek, remember? Have you seen little Bear Cub? Remember that young, gentle boy who only wanted to be an artist and draw pictures? With that leg injury, he will limp the rest of his life."

She looked at his stony face as he turned and left their lodge, realizing he no longer listened to her and his heart had gone hard. She blinked back tears as she soothed her baby. What had happened to the once in a lifetime love that had been meant to last forever? Deep in her heart, she knew she had had a hand in killing it with her jealousy, her screeching accusations. She had moved her blankets and buffalo robes away from his so that she no longer slept in his arms at night. Once, a long time ago, when she had insisted on sleeping alone, he had come after her, forced her back into his bed where he could kiss her and hold her close. Now she slept alone with her children clustered around her, and Iron Knife didn't seem to care.

Little Garnet looked up at her and took her thumb from her red rosebud mouth. "Mama sad?"

"I—I'm all right." The realization hit Summer. Her
child spoke Cheyenne. Unless she began to teach them
immediately, her children would never speak English.
She was rearing white savages to live in tipis and skin
buffalos while her friends' children back in Boston
would be learning to curtsey and dance the waltz. If the
Indian wars didn't end, someday her sons would be riding the war trail with their faces painted; her daughter
would be scraping hides and begging around forts for
scraps of food.

She heard noise outside and went to the entry of her
tipi to watch Storm Gathering galloping past on his
pony with the other little boys, pretending to be a dog
soldier raiding party. He was darker, more like the
Cheyenne in temperament than his older brother. When
he grew up, her son would kill white people and eat raw
buffalo liver—if there were any buffalo left by then.
She had loved Iron Knife with all her heart, and nothing
else had mattered to her; but since they had grown apart
these last few days, life among the Indians seemed like
a hopeless prison sentence. She was indeed nothing
more than a white captive.

Iron Knife strode to the camp circle where the honored warriors met in council. As a dog soldier, and a
carrier of the Dog Rope, he was one of those who sat in
the circle inside the big lodge. Outside, he saw the half-
grown Bent sons, half-breeds who had fled their father's
trading post and rejoined their mother's Cheyenne people.

Iron Knife, his uncle and his two cousins sat cross-
legged in the circle. He waited respectfully as the pipe
was lit and offered solemnly to the earth, sky and all
four directions before being passed around the warriors.
Spotted Tail and Pawnee Killer of the Sioux were in
that circle, as where chiefs who had survived Sand

Creek. A young leader of the Oglala Sioux, Sitting Bull, impressed Iron Knife with his thoughts on battle strategy. After much talk, it was decided that yes, they would attack Fort Sedgewick which guarded both the buffalo plains and the stagecoach and wagon routes along the South Platte River.

Iron Knife stood to speak. "You know me and my deeds of war."

"We know you have a white wife," a very young and scornful dog soldier snorted.

Everyone glared at the young one. It was not proper to interrupt a warrior who had stood to speak. Iron Knife glared at the offender. "Coyote pups make much noise," he said gravely, "but men fear the silent adult grizzly."

The others smiled and nodded at the retort, and the outspoken one slumped down in his place, humiliated.

"Once I was in favor of peace," Iron Knife said, "but it seems we cannot count on even the whites' flag flying over us to keep our women and children safe. Some of those here have lost loved ones at Sand Creek, and some of us will carry scars of that attack forever."

Again there was a murmuring of assent among the warriors. Iron Knife's and his cousins' valor were well known. "I say to you that if we hit the fort, remember they have the talking wires, the telegraph that will need to be cut so they won't be able to sound the alarm."

Scalp Taker looked at him gravely. "Now that Deer Slayer has told us why the Medicine Arrows were bloody, and we've done the cleansing ritual, I no longer fear to fight. Can we take this fort?"

Iron Knife nodded. "If we plan our ambush carefully. Remember, too, that we can use the food and supplies we will find at the sutler's stores there in the town.

There may also be good horses since Ben Holladay's stagecoaches stop there."

Pawnee Killer listened for a long moment. "The Cheyenne dog soldier has the advantage of the white thinking. The Sioux would like him to help plan the ambush."

Iron Knife hesitated. Once he would not have ridden against white settlers; but now his body was scarred from the attack of Sand Creek, and he no longer thought of himself as white. He was Cheyenne, son of War Bonnet, with many coups to his credit. Summer Sky would be sad if he helped kill whites, but he had hardened his heart because she had spurned him and his apologies. A proud man could only humiliate himself so much before rebelling. "I would be honored to help plan this raid. We will be sending a message to all whites that we will retaliate when attacked!"

A murmur of approval went around the circle, and the pipe was passed to him. He did not hesitate as he asked the great god, Heammawihio, for guidance and took a puff before passing it gravely to his cousins. His old uncle, Chief Clouds Above, fingered the bear claw necklace that hung around his wrinkled throat and pulled his Pendelton blanket around his bent shoulders against the January cold. His grave smile and nod told Iron Knife how proud he was of his nephew.

His mind was troubled when the meeting broke up, so Iron Knife did not talk much to his cousins, Two Arrows and Lance Bearer. Clouds Above was having trouble again with the clogging of the lungs that cold weather sometimes brought to the old. He did not think the old man would survive the harsh winter, but then, he had already lived a long time for a Cheyenne warrior. Most of them died young in battle, and he expected that it would be the same for him. If old Clouds Above died, that would make Iron Knife the oldest of the warriors of his family, with his cousins looking to him for wisdom. And he was not even a respected master of his own lodge.

Iron Knife went out on a rise and offered prayers. He also sacrificed small pieces of skin cut from his body in hopes of a successful raid. This custom was the inspiration for the Cheyenne name in sign language, a cutting motion of the right forefinger across the left. Their Sioux allies had given them the name Shahiyena—strange-talking people—when they had first met, and the name remained.

It was cold, a sharp wind blowing this first week of the new year, 1865. What it would bring, he was afraid to contemplate, but he sat before his own fire late that night, long after the chanting and drumming of war parties around the big camp fire had ceased.

Summer watched him from her blankets, but pretended to sleep. He had been staring into the flames for hours. Finally she could stand it no more. She sat up and looked around at her children sleeping soundly in the glow of the fire. "You ride in the morning?"

He only nodded.

She didn't know what to say. She loved him still, and the idea that he would ride out to battle with this silence between them upset her. Then she thought of the old white people, the women and children who might die on the morrow, and her heart hardened. "Is there no way to stop this?"

He turned and looked at her. "If you think to ride and warn the settlers, you would never get out of this camp."

"You trust me so little, then, that I might plot in ways that would get you killed tomorrow?"

"I don't know what to think anymore. I look at you and see a yellow-haired stranger, not my woman."

She didn't know what to say. The gulf between them

had started as a crack and now seemed to be a canyon. "You've been treating me like a stranger, a captive."

He only grunted and, wrapping himself in his blankets, turned his back to her and slept.

Summer did not sleep all that night. She was not sure he slept much, either. She lay there waiting for the cold, gray dawn, knowing that he might be killed today as might some white people. There was no good answer.

With the dawn, Iron Knife and the other warriors began to make their preparations to ride out.

Summer watched him gather his things in silence, the dream shield, called a *howan,* the Dog Rope, his buffalo robe and his weapons. As was the custom, he stripped to a small breechcloth and moccasins. The eagle bone whistle that marked him as a dog soldier hung from his sinewy neck, and in his right ear gleamed the brass button earring taken from the uniform of a dead cavalry officer. His hair shone as black as obsidian as he combed it with a porcupine tail brush and drew it into a braid over his left ear. Hammered silver coins and otter fur decorated his braided hair.

They did not speak as he began to apply his war paint in the mirror of a shiny brass pot. From a burned tree struck by lightning, he had made ebony paint and now drew black, jagged lightning streaks on his face. With yellow clay, he painted hail marks of the mighty storm on his brawny chest. At last, he put on his father's fine eagle feather war bonnet. In the past, he had worn the usual dog soldier raven feather bonnet, but he had won enough war honors now to wear his father's. Each eagle feather advertised a coup, an act of bravery. The band was decorated with dragonflies, and in the center of the band was painted one tiny bluebonnet flower, to represent Tejas, that place called Texas, where War Bonnet had stolen Iron Knife's mother from a wagon train, the white girl with eyes as deep blue as the prairie flower.

Now Summer Sky reached for his *howan,* the dream shield he had inherited from his father, and took it from its tripod. Made from the tough hide of a buffalo bull, it would deflect lance and arrow, even some bullets. A dream shield came with its own taboos. Its owner must not eat an animal's heart or eat from a kettle in which such had been cooked before he went into battle; to do so would bring him bad luck, possibly even death. It was a beautiful, savage thing, she thought, fringed around the edge with the feathers of gray eagles and sandhill cranes with bear claws sewn to the four cardinal points of the circle. In the middle was a large painting of a dragonfly because this insect was a predator, a warrior among insects, difficult to see and difficult to catch. She handed it to him, and he hung it over his mighty arm.

"You are taking the *Hotamtsit,* too?"

"You know I am. Why do you ask?" He took the red, long leather band, richly decorated with porcupine quills, and hung it over his shoulder.

Then he went out to ready his bay Appaloosa stallion. With white clay, he painted jagged lightning bolts down Spotted Blanket's forelegs to make him swift. Along his flanks, Iron Knife painted magic dragonflies to make the steed dart fast and sure. On the horse's shoulders, he put red and black handprints to show the owner had fought and killed other men in hand-to-hand combat. Now he tied up his stallion's tail as was the custom. Finally, he sprinkled the magic gray powder, *sihyainoeis-seeo,* on all four hooves and blew it between the horse's ears to make it invulnerable to wounds.

He turned to his children. "Take care of your mother, my sons, until I return."

Storm smiled. "You will kill many enemies, Father. I wish I could go with you!"

Summer winced. Back in Boston, her friends' children would be learning how to handle a fork and proper diction. Hers would be learning how to cut a man's throat so swiftly he could not cry out a warning and how to take a scalp.

"Summer?" He waited.

She blinked back her tears, looking up at his tall frame. With the war paint, his handsome face seemed almost a grotesque mask. *A stranger,* she thought, *the father of my children is a savage stranger.* Then she saw the longing in his eyes. He wanted her to give some sign that she cared for him, and she almost weakened. Abruptly, she saw an image in her mind of him lying on the ripe body of the Arapaho girl, Gray Dove, and thought of the whites who would die today. Instead, she held out his buffalo robe and his weapons. "You will need these."

He took them from her, and his face hardened. "If that is the way you want it."

Was it? She was so torn by emotion, she wasn't sure how she felt about him anymore, so she did not answer.

With a sigh, he turned from her and began the final preparation. He rubbed the magic gray powder all over his body to protect himself from bullets. Now no woman might touch him until he returned from battle; to do so would nullify the magic.

Taking his weapons, his buffalo robe and his dream shield, he mounted his horse. Spotted Blanket seemed to know they were riding into battle because the stallion stamped its feet and danced with excitement. The Pawnee scalps hanging from the decorated war bridle swung with the motion. The long tails of Iron Knife's war bonnet trailed almost to the ground, and the wind blew the feathers as Iron Knife looked at her.

She wanted to run to him; but he had already applied the magic powder, so she dared not. Instead, she took her two sons by the hand. "Go with God," she said.

He nodded, put his heels to his stallion's flanks and loped out to join the others.

Chapter Ten

The Cheyenne, Sioux and Arapaho rode to attack Fort Sedgewick, that small fort that protected the stagecoach and wagon train crossing on the South Platte River in northeastern Colorado Territory. There was a telegraph there, too, so Iron Knife cautioned men to cut the wires as soon as the attack began so the fort could not call for reinforcements. The young half-breed, George Bent, had been away to a white military academy, so he helped plan the strategy to lure the soldiers from their fort.

Big Crow, a leader of the Crooked Lance society, rode out with a small force of ten men to lure the soldiers from the fort and ambush them while twelve hundred warriors waited hidden behind low hills near the arroyo called Devil's Dive.

However, the very young warriors, those eager for their first coup, broke ranks prematurely as the soldiers rode out to chase Big Crow's decoy. The soldiers seemed to realize an ambush awaited them and reined their horses around. Iron Knife cursed and put his heels to his stallion even as the forewarned soldiers turned and raced back toward the fort. Now the battle began across the plains and low hills, the vastly outnumbered soldiers bringing their cannon into play with great casualties among the warriors.

In the midst of the fighting, a stagecoach approached down the road, realizing too late the fort was under attack. There was nothing the driver could do but whip up his horses and make a run for the safety of the fort with warriors in hot pursuit. He made it inside, but there were arrows sticking out all over the dusty coach as he slammed his lathered horses to a halt.

From dawn until midafternoon, the fight raged, but finally the townspeople abandoned their stores and fled into the fort. Now the braves could help themselves to the food and supplies there. Pandemonium reigned. Young warriors laughed and yelped as they scattered and burned things they could not use. Bright bolts of calico were tied behind horses and unrolled like colorful banners as the horses ran. Too late, Iron Knife and George Bent arrived to stop the braves who had found a chest full of green paper and were throwing it to the wind and burning it.

Iron Knife shouted for them to stop, but the young warriors had already destroyed most of it, throwing the rest to the wind. He sat his horse now and watched them wreak havoc, thinking of the weapons and supplies the tribes could have bought from Comancheros and gun runners with that money. A civilization that was so primitive it did not understand money could never win in the long run. *My way of life will not last my lifetime,* he sighed, and he motioned the young warriors to make ready to ride out with their loot.

Summer heard the drumming of a thousand hooves like thunder coming into the Indian encampment, and ran to meet the returning war party. Anxiously, she watched them riding in, silent and shoulders drooping, their faces not painted completely black as was the custom when there had been a great victory without loss of warriors. Some had been killed; was her man among the dead? The victorious trilling of the women faded as they noticed some were missing and soon gave way to shrieks and mourning chants as women searched for faces among the riders and realized their loved ones were among the lost.

Summer ran among the riders, heart hammering. Suppose Iron Knife had been killed when she had allowed him to ride away in anger. Suppose—? And then she saw him, riding proud and tall among the warriors, the fine war bonnet trailing almost to the ground. "Are you all right?"

He nodded and dismounted, face grim. She gave a great sigh of relief even as she heard the mourning cries around her. She looked at him questioningly, and he nodded. "There will be shorn hair and women mutilating themselves in sorrow tonight," he said, and handed her the reins of his Appaloosa and his war shield.

With mixed feelings, she walked ahead of him, carrying his shield and leading his painted war pony. White people had died today so that her man could have new war honors. But he was alive. Over at Julesburg and Fort Sedgewick, women with skin as fair as her own were weeping tonight for dead husbands and sons.

She put his shield on the tripod outside the tipi, then turned to face him as she tied up his horse. Only then did she realize that fresh scalps hung from his belt. Hesitantly, he held out his arms to her, making visible the red stains on his hands. Blood. His own? No, she thought with growing horror, white soldiers' blood. She began to shake her head and back away. "You come to me with blood on your hands?"

"I come to you as a mighty warrior who has added two coups to his honors today. You may paint new coup marks in your hair to show your pride."

Outside, the wives of the victors were shouting their

men's triumphs, and it mingled with the shrieks of the bereaved. Every brave deed, every coup, counted toward an eagle feather, Summer knew; and Iron Knife was well qualified to wear the many feathered bonnet of his dead father.

When he had been fighting Pawnees, Crows or Utes, that was one thing, but killing whites was something else. "I—I think perhaps I do not know you at all."

"I killed no women and children," he retorted. "My kills were seasoned soldiers who were trying to kill me. Is it so different from this white war between the blue-clad soldiers and the ones dressed in gray?"

Was it? If he had been in the Union army as Austin Shaw was and had killed opposing Rebels, Iron Knife would be awarded medals for bravery. "You expect me to attend the feasting and dancing with you?"

"There is much feasting on the supplies taken from the stores in Julesburg, cloth and ribbons we brought back, even a captive."

"A captive?" She looked toward the big camp circle.

"Just a Crow girl"—he shrugged—"one of those loose women of that cowardly tribe that hang around the fort and whore for the soldiers."

"What will the warriors do with her?"

"You know the answer to that. If she can whore for the soldiers, she can also pleasure any warrior who wants her."

"I suppose you'll be first in line," Summer snapped.

The light reflected on his brass earring as he glared at her. "I might. She may at least give me a warmer welcome than I've been getting around here!" With that, he turned on his heel and left, stopping to greet his small, proud sons. The three of them walked toward the big bonfire lighting up the deepening twilight of the camp circle.

The drums were starting, calling the warriors to dance

around the scalps that were now stretched over small wooden hoops and hung up on lances near the fire for the people to admire. Was it her imagination, or in walking back from greeting her man, had the bereaved women glared at her as if she were an enemy with her pale skin, even though she now spoke Cheyenne almost as well as any of them?

No, she would not go to the dancing and feasting and have to stare at those white scalps. If the warriors had raided settlers' stores, no doubt there was whiskey in the camp, too. She nursed Garnet and put the toddler down to sleep.

It was dark and chilly outside now except the glow coming from the big camp fire. Ignoring Iron Knife, she strode to the celebration, grabbed each of her sons by the arm and brought them back to sleep. Storm Gathering protested loudly that he wanted to stay awake for the entire victory dance. She would not hear of it; later in the evening, it might get very violent and rough with the drinking and the celebrating.

She put the protesting boys in their blankets and walked down to the river to get a skin of water. That was when a young Sioux warrior stepped out of the shadows. The way he swayed on his feet told her he'd been celebrating the victory. "You are a white captive?"

She didn't like the way he was looking at her in the moonlight. The young man was handsome, Summer thought, but quite drunk. "You're blocking my path; let me pass. Take your passion to the captive Crow girl."

He made a dismissing gesture. "Too many wait for their chance at mounting the enemy chit." He threw up his arm, blocking her path.

"Let me pass," she said with quiet dignity, "or I will tell my man."

"You bluff, white woman," he sneered, "you are only

a captive meant to pleasure the victors; so pleasure me."
His hand snaked out and caught her wrist.

"I am Summer Sky. I belong to Iron Knife."

"The big Cheyenne who carries the honored Dog
Rope?"

She nodded and he turned loose of her arm. "I meant
no harm," he said humbly. "Among the Lakota, we also
have such an honor, the scarlet sash. Someday, I hope to
earn one. Your man was brave on the field of battle today. I meant no disrespect to him." The young warrior
turned and fled.

Summer sighed. She forgot sometimes how honored
and feared Iron Knife was. Yet tonight he was dancing
around the scalps of white people. That she could not
celebrate. Her once in a lifetime love. What had happened to the feeling they once had shared for each
other? Sadly, she returned to her lodge, pulled a blanket
over her ears to shut out the chanting and drums, and
tried to sleep, but she could not. What was she going to
do? She could think of nothing but Iron Knife in the
arms of Gray Dove. When she tried to erase that from
her mind, she saw instead Iron Knife with the soldiers'
scalps hanging from his belt, his hands smeared with
blood. She lay and listened to the victory dancing, the
drums echoing through the cold January night. Finally,
from sheer exhaustion, she slept.

Iron Knife joined in the dancing, humiliated that his
woman was not here with the others to celebrate the
men's victories.

Over on a blanket in the shadows, any of the warriors
who wanted her were pleasuring themselves with the
girl of the Crow tribe. He felt his groin tighten at the
thought. He was a virile man and Summer Sky was a
passionate woman. Before the children came, they had
pleasured each other often. He strode over to watch.

She was pretty and young with big breasts and shiny

black hair. No wonder the soldiers kept her around the
fort. Lance Bearer, his unmarried cousin, was between
her thighs, his mouth on her breasts. She was pleasuring
him as a skilled whore knew how to do, wrapping her
long legs around him, clawing his shoulders while he
rutted on her, offering her breasts up to his eager mouth.

Other men laughed and encouraged Lance Bearer to
hurry so they could have their turn. As Iron Knife
watched, his cousin finished and rolled off her, then
looked up at him. "You, Iron Knife, I have kept her
warm for you. Do you want her?"

Iron Knife felt his groin ache with lust. The girl
smiled archly at him and held out her arms. "I know a
good man when I see one; come play the stallion and
show these fumbling boys how a man does it!"

She was there to be enjoyed by the victors and she
seemed to know it. From what he had heard, she had
been a toy of the white officers, and now nothing had
changed but the color of the men's skin who mounted
her. Perhaps she didn't care what man mated with her as
long as they gave her pretties and ribbons and maybe
some whiskey.

How many had had her already tonight? Ten?
Twenty? What was one more, and he needed a woman.
She was staring boldly at the bulge in his breechcloth as
she ran the tip of her pink tongue over her lips. "I
please you, I become your woman, yes?"

It was tempting with Summer acting so cold to him
lately. It was his right to take a second woman, and this
one was pretty. The enemy Crow girl arched her back,
displaying her breasts even though the night was cold.
"Come warm me!" she said.

And yet, for him there would always be only one
woman, his Little One. If Summer wouldn't make love
to him, what was he to do? Would she punish him forever for his sins? He shook his head. "I already have

my own captive," he said. "I don't need another slave."

As the next man moved to lie on her supple body, Iron Knife turned and went to his own lodge. He'd had a little too much whiskey, he knew, but his blood was pounding hard in his groin. He had a captive of his own to warm his bed; why should he do without?

Summer stirred and turned toward him as he lay down beside her. Her bodice was half-open, revealing a creamy expanse of breast, her long, golden hair tumbling down her bare shoulder. She opened her eyes and looked at him in the firelight.

He needed a woman and she was here. In other lodges tonight, warriors were reaffirming their maleness, leaving their seed in their women. Summer was, after all, his to enjoy. "I want you."

She looked disconcerted. "But we discussed this and—"

"You are mine and I want you tonight." Maybe he was more than a little drunk, he realized as he reached out, caught her shoulder, and dragged her to him. He was past tenderness, past caring about next week or even tomorrow. He put his mouth over hers and forced her lips open.

"You're drunk!" she managed to say, and her annoyance angered him. She struggled, but he was stronger than she was.

"You are mine and you will pleasure me!" He jerked open the front of her bodice as she struggled and cupped her full breasts, ramming his tongue deep in her throat. The taste and scent of her fired his blood, and he was determined to quench this fire. His hunger for her made him rough, not her usual sensitive, caring lover. She had rejected him, kept him from mating with her for months and then had chided him for taking another woman years ago. The whiskey in his blood built a roaring fire of his indignation. Iron Knife pinned her wrists above her head and began to run his tongue across her breasts as he lay half on top of her soft body. He smiled at her sharp intake of breath. "Despite your denial, you like that."

Summer didn't answer. She would not have admitted it if he had tortured her. His touch fired her passion, but her feelings were deeply hurt at his rough, drunken behavior. She felt his mouth insistent on her breasts again. She must pull away from him. She couldn't take the chance that he might breed her again. Summer arched her body, struggling to break free, but her fighting only seemed to excite him more. He held her hands pinned over her head with his great strength as his mouth tasted her breast. "Lie still and let me enjoy you!" he ordered, and she tasted the whiskey on his lips as he kissed her.

"And if I don't?"

"Then I'll stake you out like a captive and enjoy you anyway; then you'll have no excuse to resist me."

She started to deny that she needed an excuse, but his mouth was ravaging hers again. Summer breathed heavily, her chest heaving as he ran his free hand up and down her body. He was awakening feelings in her that she didn't want to succumb to. She tried to buck out from under him; but he kept her tightly pinned, and his mouth tasted and teased hers. "You little vixen," he whispered urgently, "you drive me wild and then deny me your body! No woman ever made me hunger for her the way you do!"

"Let go of me! I don't want you!"

He tangled his fingers in her hair, brought her mouth to his. "You lie! Even now, I feel your body trembling under mine. You want me all right; and even if you don't, you said yourself that you are only a white slave and you know captive women are used to give a warrior pleasure!"

With that, he proceeded to devour her mouth, sucking

her tongue deep into his throat. He massaged her breasts and nipples until she was shaking with desire, all the while denying it with her mind and voice. He kept her wrists pinned above her head while he kissed his way down her belly very slowly. His tongue caressed her navel, causing her to shudder with the sensation. He laughed. "No, you don't want me much, do you?"

"I hate you for your arrogance! You didn't ask me if I wanted to make love and—"

"From now on, I take, I don't ask." He tangled his fingers in her hair, stroking and caressing her.

"I don't need another baby—"

"Then pleasure me in other ways—or would you rather I went out to that Crow girl who begged me to take her?"

She thought of Gray Dove. "Like some buffalo bull, you'll probably take her anyway!"

"You don't think much of me, do you?" His voice was full of hot desire and anger. "Very well, satisfy me, slave, in a way that won't make a baby!" He pulled her face to his groin. He was so rigid, he throbbed, and he could feel her warm breath against his flesh. He moaned aloud as he felt her lips hot, wet and seeking, and he arched up and let her please him.

Summer tasted him. He was rock hard and throbbing. His desperate need excited her, even though she tried to deny it. If she didn't pleasure him, he might go out to that sultry, dark Crow girl, and the thought drove her wild with jealousy. She rubbed her bare, swollen breasts against his thighs as she kissed his groin.

He tangled both hands in her hair, holding her against him and moaning with ecstasy. "That's it . . . you know how to please me!"

The scent and taste of this big man excited her. She knew she must satisfy him or submit to being mated. But she could pleasure him in other ways. She ran her tongue around the head of it, down the full length of his hard rod. Then she relaxed her throat and urged him to give her his full length. She gripped his muscular thighs and pulled him against her face as he grunted with pleasure. The ultimate conquest, she thought, but who was the conquered? He was the one writhing under her and begging.

Iron Knife felt her mouth on him, hot and wet and demanding. He arched his back, tangled his fingers in her silken hair and gave her his full length. He had forgotten how she could heat his blood, make him want her as no woman ever had or ever could. In the glow of the fire, he could see her beautiful face, her long blond hair spread out across his muscular dark belly as she loved him with her soft lips. He felt her hot, swollen breasts against his bare thighs. "Take it!" he begged, "take it all!"

Her insistent little mouth teased him, then demanded what he had to give. He wasn't finished enjoying her ripe body, but her mouth demanded that he give up and surrender to her. He tried to hold back, make it last a little longer, but she was insistent. He quit fighting it, relaxed and let her take everything he had to give until he was writhing under her greedy mouth. "Enough! I—I can't take any more of this!"

She wouldn't stop. By sheer strength, he finally dragged her up his body to lie in his arms while he held her and shuddered.

Her eyes were as cold and blue as frozen lakes. "Is that what you wanted from your captive? Did I satisfy you, my master, or do you intend to hand me over to be passed around to the warriors as you would any captured enemy woman?" She began to weep.

"Summer. . . ." He didn't know what to say. He wanted to strike her and shout at her. He wanted to murmur apologies, kiss her and hold her tenderly; tell her he was ashamed to make her cry. But he was a proud, arrogant man and a bold warrior. Warriors were not supposed to apologize to females for doing what came naturally to a male. Yet, because he was more white than he realized, he brushed her hair away from her face with a tender gesture and muttered, "I—I was drunk; I didn't mean. . . ."

He rolled over, but he himself did not sleep. He longed to take her in his arms, let her fall asleep in the hollow of his shoulder where she had always belonged, safe in his strong embrace. More than that, he wanted to kiss her breathless, stroke her, make her cry out with pleasure and dig her nails in his back as she tried to pull him deep into her body. Instead, he didn't do any of that, but lay there for hours, angry and ashamed. Perhaps things would never again be the same between them. Well, there were warriors living with captives who had never experienced the ecstasy he had shared with Summer Sky, men who knew and expected nothing more than cooking, warming a man's blankets and allowing him to rut on her when he felt the urge. He and his captive had had something special, but he was not sure they would ever be able to recapture that. He turned his back and stared into the darkness for a long time before he finally dropped off to sleep.

Summer lay there feeling furious and betrayed. Once she had been the center of his heart. Tonight, he had treated her like a cheap whore. Why had she been such a fool as to choose this man? She belonged back in Boston with her own kind. Summer lay there awake until the cold, gray dawn, bitter and angry.

The tribes split up the next day, knowing the soldiers would be bringing in reinforcements, combing the area looking for the attackers of Fort Sedgewick. The Cheyenne were moving back toward the protection of the Rockies.

Summer had already decided what to do. After last night, she couldn't stay with Iron Knife anymore. If she could get in contact with Silver or Todd Shaw, she was going to find a way to leave the Cheyenne forever!

Chapter Eleven

She didn't have to make the decision to search out her friends. As they camped in the lee of some trees in the shadow of the Rockies, Cherokee came riding out to meet them. He had Todd Shaw with him.

A sentry started to fit an arrow to his bow, but Iron Knife held up a hand and cried out, "Stop! These are friends! They warned me of the attack on Sand Creek!"

The other Cheyenne looked the white men over, but no one challenged them as they rode down through the tipis and reined in before Iron Knife's lodge. Curious children ran through the crusty snow to gather around, and mongrel dogs barked at the strangers.

Iron Knife beckoned. "Get down, friends, we will smoke and talk."

"It is good to see you," Cherokee said. The men shook hands solemnly, went into Iron Knife's lodge, and sat down cross-legged before the fire.

Todd looked around at the wide-eyed little boys, Storm and Lance. "Where's Summer?"

Iron Knife shooed the little boys outside. "Go find your mother; she's over at Pretty Flower Woman's lodge. Tell her we have company."

Todd offered tobacco, and Iron Knife took it with a nod of thanks. "Are you here to council? My people have not forgotten that you both tried to warn us about Sand Creek."

He filled the pipe, lit it, then passed it around.

Todd said, "I suppose we should have seen that coming sooner. The people of Denver were angry about all the outbreaks. Across the frontier, the newspapers say many whites have been killed."

"And did they also tell how many Indians have died?" Iron Knife asked wryly.

"Good question," Cherokee agreed.

Todd shook his head. "The singing wires have brought news of the attack on Julesburg. Stagecoaches even stopped running for a while again."

"Good," Iron Knife grunted with satisfaction, "perhaps if whites think the great buffalo plains are too dangerous, they will not come out West."

Cherokee smoked and considered. "I wish it was that simple, friend, but you know it isn't. The war between the states will end any time now. That fight between the white men is all that has slowed immigration temporarily. Soon there will be a flood of whites looking for opportunity they can't find in Europe or the slums of the eastern cities."

"Yes," Todd said, "and the end of the war will make lots of soldiers available to fight Indians."

"I know all this, my friends," Iron Knife sighed. "Remember I spent time living among whites as a youth. The tribes only buy ourselves a little extra time."

Cherokee pushed his western hat back. "It happened to my people before it did yours," he reminded them. "Eventually, your people will be herded to reservations as the Cherokee were when they were forced to walk that bloody path called the Trail of Tears to Indian Territory. All native people will finally be forced onto reservations."

Iron Knife smoked in silence for a long moment. "Will they not be satisfied until they have all the land, then?"

"I'm afraid not," Todd answered, "although I do what little I can at the newspaper. I think your way of life will not last your lifetime."

Iron Knife sighed. "Then perhaps I should be glad that my medicine tells me I will not live to be an old man." He thought of Summer Sky. He was both angry with her and in love with her. He did not fear death, but he did not want to leave her behind in a hostile world where she would be afraid and alone.

Todd cleared his throat. "We came with a purpose, my friend."

Iron Knife held up his hand to keep him from speaking further. "Let us eat and visit awhile before you tell it. It must be important for you to risk death riding through this cold, hostile country to find us."

Summer came in just then, her baby in a cradleboard, Lance peeking more shyly at the visitors from behind her skirt. Storm Gathering strode in boldly and sat down cross-legged next to his father, a miniature copy of a brave warrior. Iron Knife smiled at the little son's serious demeanor as if sitting down in a tribal council.

Summer held out both hands. "Todd! Cherokee! I'm so glad to see you!"

She was glad, Iron Knife thought—too glad.

"You're looking well, Summer," Todd said as both visitors scrambled to their feet.

She was abruptly keenly aware of the differences in civilization. Indian men did not hop up like jumping frogs when a woman came into their presence. She realized with self-conscious awkwardness how she must look to Todd; hair braided, no corset, dressed in beaded buckskin and moccasins with a baby in a cradleboard like any squaw that white men saw near trading posts and sneered at. She was aware of his keen stare and a trifle disconcerted. "I—I will get food for you. I roasted a buffalo hump this morning."

"Sounds good!" Cherokee said, but Todd looked a little queasy. Buffalo hump wasn't usually on the menu back in Boston, she thought, retreating in confusion. Todd Shaw had known her when she was the belle of the debutante's ball, a wealthy, privileged girl moving in the highest social circles. She wished she had know he was coming so that she could have made herself more presentable.

Summer dished up the food for the men and left them to eat alone as was the custom. However, she hovered near the lodge, knowing the two must have come on some errand of importance or they would not have risked such a dangerous trip through snow and hostile Indian lands.

Finally, Iron Knife called her in to join them by the fire. His face was grave. Something was terribly wrong. "They have come to bring you a message."

"Me?" She touched her chest in surprise. "What is it?"

Todd cleared his throat again. "Summer, I've gotten a telegram from your father. He sent it to me on the off chance I might know how to track you down, and Cherokee helped me get here."

"My brother!" She breathed in sharply. "My brother David's been killed in the war, and—"

"No, no one's dead," Todd put in hastily, "at least not yet." He held out the wire.

She read it, then read it again, her brain refusing to comprehend what her eyes told her. *"Your mother dying. Stop. She begs to see you and your children. Stop. Please come. Stop. Father."*

Priscilla. She saw her in her mind's eye the pretty, bitter woman who had made the wrong choices in life and now lived on liquor and laudanum rather than deal with the painful realities of it all. But she was Summer's mother, and she loved her. "How—how old is this telegram?"

"I got it a few days ago," Todd said. "The minute it came, I dropped everything and set out to find you."

How could she not go? Yet she shrugged in helpless embarrassment. "I—I have no money for travel."

"Your father told me to advance it to you," Todd said, "and he'd reimburse me."

She looked down at her deerskin shift. How could she walk into the big Boston train station in a deerskin shift and moccasins? She pictured entering her father's grand mansion with her children. While her deerskin was the softest and most heavily beaded among the Cheyenne, denoting her man's prestige and wealth in many ponies, her father and friends would pity her or scorn her.

Cherokee said, "I know you don't have time to have clothes made, but Silver is about your size and said she will lend you anything you need."

Summer looked at Iron Knife. He sat there, his face grave and impassive, saying nothing. Before she had found out about Gray Dove, she wouldn't even have considered the trip; after all, her mother might already be dead by now, and she was on strained terms with her father. However, now she looked forward to getting away for a while to sort things out in her own mind. Perhaps Iron Knife needed time alone, too. She fumbled with the little gold locket that hung around her neck. "What do you think?"

He hesitated. "This is not my decision to make. Always do what your heart tells you to do, Little One."

Her mother had said something like that to her once,

Summer remembered. *When you find a once in a life-time love, run after him, don't look back and damn the consequences!* Maybe that hadn't been such good advice after all, or maybe the big half-breed wasn't really her true love. "I think I should go," she said, "someone needs to be there."

"Then go," Iron Knife said without expression, so she couldn't tell what he was feeling. "I will escort you to the stagecoach myself so that you need not fear any attacks. It will take you to where you can link up with the train."

Mother. She blinked back tears and clasped the little gold locket in her hand. Inside was a delicate miniature of Priscilla in her younger days. Even though Priscilla did not seem to want to live, she was a fairly young woman, and Summer could not believe she was really dying. "Is there any chance this is a trick of my father's to get me home?"

Todd ran his hand through his hair. "I don't think so because I also heard from my mother, who urged that I find you, because your mother wanted to see you one last time."

One last time. *When people die,* Summer thought dully, *we usually don't get a chance to say goodbye, that one last opportunity to say those little things we always meant to say and somehow never did. Then one day, the person is gone like a candle flame in the wind, and it's too late; forever too late.*

"I will go," she said.

Iron Knife watched her, listened to her words and managed to keep his face impassive. His woman. His children. If he let them go far away, would they return? If you love something, set it free. If it loves you, it will return to you. A butterfly can be crushed by holding on to it too tightly. Was his love enough to bring her back to him, especially with the strain between them?

How—how long will you be gone?" he asked.

It seemed like an eternity before she answered. "I have no way of knowing." Her face was a mask that gave no hint of her true feelings. Was she thinking that once she got to Boston, she might never return?

The two men had been waiting silently. "Do you want me to wait and escort you?"

Summer Sky shook her head. "Iron Knife will bring me to Cherokee's, and then I'll come to Denver, Todd. Maybe by then you'll have more news."

Todd seemed to notice Iron Knife's expression. "She may be gone for weeks, friend, especially with the war winding down. Who knows how crowded trains will be or what the weather will be like in the north. If you will contact me every few weeks, I will let you know if there has been any news."

Summer brightened. "That's right; we can used Todd to pass messages and letters back and forth."

Iron Knife breathed a sigh of relief. "You will write me, then, Little One?"

"Yes, and you let me know how things go here."

Cherokee smiled. "It's settled, then."

Summer chewed her lip a moment.

"What is it?" Iron Knife said.

"Cherokee, didn't I hear you say one time that you knew Shawn O'Bannion?"

"Why, yes. He's an old friend and I served under Colonel O'Bannion in the Army of the Confederacy." He took off his hat and scratched his head, looking puzzled.

"It has to be the same one," she murmured as if to herself, "it just has to be. Cherokee, could you contact him for me?"

"I reckon so, but I don't see—"

"He's an old ... friend of my mother's," she said. "They haven't seen each other for a very long time. It's important that they get a chance to see each other one more time."

"You realize," Cherokee said, "that Shawn may be dead in the war? I haven't seen him since that night at Shiloh when I was captured."

"Well," Summer said, and her eyes beseeched him, "all we can do is try. Tell him a woman named Priscilla Blackledge Van Schuyler in Boston may be dying. Ask if a song, "The Last Rose of Summer," means anything at all to him. His answers will tell me whether I've got the wrong Shawn."

Todd's handsome face frowned. "Remember, with the war still going on," he cautioned, "a letter may not get through, or even a wire, but I'll help in any way I can."

Was she doing something foolish and romantic? If this were the same Shawn, it would make her father furious to have her mother's old sweetheart come to the house. Would an old love still care enough to come all that way to see Priscilla one last time? Summer reached up to touch the little locket hanging around her neck with the miniature of her mother inside. Was Priscilla dying of some disease or did she just not want to live any longer?

Cherokee and Todd rode out with an escort of warriors sent by Iron Knife to make sure they got back safely. Summer went about getting things together. Garnet was too young to realize what was happening, but little Lance and Storm ran about telling the other boys, "We ride the Iron Horse to the white man's many lodges place!"

Her children were beautiful and smart, Summer thought as she hugged them, and any man, even Silas Van Schuyler, should be proud to call them his grandchildren—but would he? She couldn't worry about that now. It was sad telling everyone goodbye, as if she were seeing some of them for the very last time. It was dark now, and they would leave at dawn. She put her children to bed. They were asleep when she settled herself next to Iron Knife, who stared morosely into the fire. "I am sorry about your mother."

"I don't think she really cares about living anymore. If I had been there. . . ."

He waited a long moment. "You feel guilty because you are here?"

"No . . . yes, I suppose I do." She folded her arms across her knees, laid her chin on them and stared into the fire. "Mother and my little sister never got along, and my brother, David, has been away, Todd says, helping with the wounded in the war."

"What about your father?"

She sighed and shook her head. "There is nothing between them."

He watched the firelight play on her golden hair. *Almost like us,* he thought, and felt a terrible need to slip his arm around her shoulders, but afraid of rejection, leaned on it instead. "Was there ever?"

"A bad bargain all around," Summer said. "Silas Van Schuyler had money, and her blue-blooded family had lost everything. She was in love with another man."

"The one called Shawn?"

Summer nodded. "She made a bad choice and has lived to regret it."

He wanted to ask, "Like you?" But he dared not. He was afraid he would hear a truth that he did not want to face. He wanted to ask her not to leave or to beg that if she must, would she give her promise to return? He couldn't hold her with words. If she didn't love him anymore and love wouldn't bring her back, then empty words wouldn't either. *Like the butterfly,* he thought, *love is like a butterfly; you can't hold on to it by force without crushing it.* "It is late," he said, "and we've a long way to go tomorrow."

"Yes, we'd better get some sleep." She went automatically to her blankets on the other side of the fire; he went to his.

She lay there listening to him turn over, knew he was not asleep. Things had changed between them since that night he had come in drunk, insisting she pleasure him. While she was gone, would he take that captured Crow girl or another into his lodge as a second wife? Summer had thought she had known him so well, and the foundations of her trust had been shaken; she wasn't certain she knew him at all anymore. Now she had new worries with her mother. What Summer yearned to do was crawl over into Iron Knife's blankets, try to work this out; but she had as much pride as he did, and she was also afraid that perhaps he didn't care anymore. She lay there sleepless a long time before she finally dropped off into a troubled sleep.

Iron Knife lay awake and listened to Summer moving restlessly. He had an urge to reach out, pull her into his bed, and make love to her; but he was a proud man, and he had been rejected as much as he could take lately. He knew she had once been engaged to Todd Shaw's older brother. Had Austin Shaw ever married or would he be waiting in Boston, hoping to take up where he had left off with Summer? Austin had seemed like a kind, decent man. He might even want to adopt and raise the three children. At that thought, Iron Knife was tortured. No, she wouldn't do that—stay in Boston, let another man raise Iron Knife's sons as his own—would she? He was tempted not to allow her to take the children, but the dying mother wanted to see them. No, he could not deny Summer this one last request. Finally he, too, dropped off to a troubled sleep.

The next day, they made the trip. Silver dressed Summer Sky in some of her clothes, and Todd had bought some children's clothes in the stores in Denver. Iron Knife escorted Summer and the children to the stage stop. He was glad that Todd and Cherokee had come along because the driver and the man at the station looked at him with hostility. He didn't care; he only cared about telling his woman goodbye. "You have everything you need?"

She nodded and laid the sleeping baby on the stagecoach seat, and Iron Knife lifted her aboard. "We'll be fine; don't worry about us."

In the moment that his hands encircled her slim waist, he almost pulled her to him and kissed her, but he wasn't sure how she would react if he did. Besides, he was a very private person, and there were people watching the stage that was about to depart. With all the Indian trouble, many whites were afraid to take the stage, but this one would be safe. War drums had carried the message across many miles that Iron Knife's family was aboard and to let it pass in peace.

Lance bounced on the opposite seat and punched Storm, who promptly took his older brother to the floor and pummeled him. Iron Knife laughed as Summer rushed to stop the sibling tug of war. "I'm not sure Boston is ready for that pair. You'll have a hard time traveling with them."

"Oh, I'll manage somehow."

The waiting was awkward. There was so much to say and yet so little to say as they waited for the guard to

climb up on the stage. Iron Knife slammed the door, and
Summer leaned on the window ledge, looking out.

Iron Knife said, "Well, I suppose this is goodbye."

"Yes, I suppose it is. Tell Pretty Flower I'll be fine."

"I'll do that. Lance and Storm, you take care of your
mother."

The little boys nodded, too excited to do anything but
hang out the stage window.

The driver cracked his whip, and the stage lurched
and pulled away, harness jingling. Summer waved and
he merely nodded; waving was not dignified for a warrior. He wanted to run after her, kiss her one last time,
but he was shy about displays of affection in front of
others; it was not seemly. He watched as the stage began to pick up speed. *"Ne-mehotatse,"* he whispered in
Cheyenne. *I love you.*

Summer looked back and watched him until he was
only a lonely, small figure on the cold, sparse prairie behind her. She had waited for him to hold her or ask her
not to go, tell her he loved her, anything besides putting
her on the stage as he would some stranger. Maybe that
was what they had grown to be. The gentle rocking of
the coach soon put the exhausted children to sleep. On
this long trip to Boston, she would work on teaching
them English.

Summer leaned back and closed her eyes, listening to
the stage creak and the cold wind blow. Winter, 1865.
She hoped she wasn't coming down with something;
she didn't feel very well, but she'd been afraid that Iron
Knife would keep her from leaving if she told him. Every winter, people died of grippe, pneumonia, smallpox,
diphtheria and a host of other maladies. If she were
about to get sick, she hoped it wasn't anything conta-
gious that the children might catch.

She wondered if her mother was still alive. She
wanted to see her one more time, tell her how much she

loved her, that her life hadn't been a total waste when she had produced children who cared about her. Tears came to her eyes, and Summer blinked them away, remembering that New Year's Eve, 1858, when after the costume ball where Summer had announced her engagement to Austin Shaw, her mother had asked her to come to her bedroom to talk. It had been only weeks after Summer's return from the Cheyenne.

She and her mother had never been close, so she had wondered what it was that Mother wanted as she went down the hall to Mother's room.

The light shone from under the door. Summer rapped softly, then opened it.

Mother's large room was done in faded pinks and burgundies with big cabbage roses on the yellowing walls and fabrics; immensely dark Victorian furniture stood here and there. It looked like the sanctuary of a woman who did not care about the present, had no hope for the future, and preferred to live in the past.

"Come in," Priscilla said from where she stood before the fire. She wore a dressing gown of pale pink velvet, and Summer looked at her and knew she was seeing almost the ghost of a great beauty.

There was an open crystal box of potpourri on the table, and Summer took a deep breath of the scent of old rose petals saved from her mother's garden. It hadn't occurred to her before, but the whole house seemed to have that faint scent, that ghost of dead roses, about it.

"You wanted to see me?"

"I thought, just once," Mother said uncertainly, moving to stare out the window, "I thought we might try to carry on a conversation."

Summer bit her lip, deciding not to make a bitter comment about how impossible it was to communicate with someone who was in an eternal narcotic haze. Incredibly, Mother seemed sober at the moment.

Mother stood staring out at the rose garden that lay below her window. "I hate winter," she whispered so low that Summer strained to hear her. "It's very dreary and lonely and my roses die. Summer is my favorite season, that time that roses bloom and warmth and love flourish."

She wasn't sure if Priscilla expected a reply. Mother seemed to have forgotten anyone else was in the room and was talking to herself.

The music box sat on the table where it had always been since Summer could remember. She ran a finger over it, really looking at it for the first time. It was a cheap, small music box, and Summer wondered idly about it as she opened the lid. Father's pride would never have allowed him to give such an inexpensive gift.

As she opened the lid, the music tinkled out: *'Tis the last rose of summer left blooming alone . . . all her lovely companions are faded and gone. . . .*

"Don't touch that!" Priscilla said so sharply as she whirled around that Summer snapped the lid down with a startled motion. Now the only sound was the crackle of the fire and her mother's sigh as she turned to stare into the flames. "You're really going to marry Austin Shaw?"

"Yes, in late June."

Priscilla whirled and laughed, but her eyes didn't laugh. "That should make Silas very happy; he always hoped to use you to connect his fortune to the Shaws'. But then, Silas has bought everything he ever wanted with his damned money, including me! Although those who make a bargain with the devil shouldn't be bitter when their note is called!"

Summer stared at her, startled at the rare show of energy and courage from a woman she had come to regard as a rather pathetic, helpless dove. Once, she thought, her mother had had all the passion and spirit of Summer. Was she seeing herself as she would be twenty years from now?

The thought was disconcerting and troublesome. "You're behaving very strangely tonight, Mother. Are you telling me you do not approve of my marrying Austin?"

Priscilla looked her directly in the eyes. "Do you love him?"

Uneasily, Summer avoided the direct look and question. "After all these years, it's interesting that you are suddenly terribly worried about my future."

"New Year's Eve has a way of making people reflect on their past and future, making old ghosts come back to haunt them. I know I haven't done right by any of my children, and I'm attempting now to rectify my mistakes by stopping you from going down the path I took."

There was so much Summer wanted to ask, yet dared not.

In the silence, the old house creaked and groaned in the cold wind.

Mother said, "I keep seeing something in your eyes that tells me you are in love with another man, someone your father wouldn't approve of."

The scarred, bronzed face of Iron Knife came to her mind. "You're right, of course."

"Then I want you to go back to that man." Priscilla came over to Summer. "I have a little money hidden, not much, but certainly enough for a train ticket one way."

Tears came to Summer's eyes. "How could you guess about the other man? And why tonight, are you deciding to go up against Father?"

Mother paused almost wistfully. "Because tonight, as you announced your engagement to a rich man, I saw myself as I was twenty years ago, and I don't want you to make the same mistake I did. Not every woman gets a chance at a once in a lifetime love, and if you're lucky enough to find it, run after him, damn the consequences and don't look back! Do you hear me? Don't look back!"

The realization dawned slowly on Summer. "Who was he, Mother?"

A very soft, gentle look came over her mother's face as she remembered. "His name was Shawn O'Bannion, and he was very poor and Irish Catholic. He had very black wavy hair and eyes green as shamrocks. Shawn was strong and sensitive and had a way with the soil. You should have seen the roses he grew. That's my only link to him now, my roses."

She tried to imagine her mother wrapped passionately in a man's arms as Priscilla stared regretfully into the past. It occurred to Summer that she had never seen her parents in a loving embrace, not even once.

"Did Shawn not want to marry you, Mother?"

"He did. But I was already engaged to Silas Van Schuyler, and my parents were pressuring me to marry Silas. Shawn and I had only that one summer, and then with winter, I had to make a decision, a choice."

"And you chose Silas Van Schuyler instead?"

Priscilla tried to laugh, and her voice became a ragged sob. "I know you can't understand that, can you? Now that I look back, neither can I! But you have to understand Shawn was so poor and all I could think of was how terrible it would be to have no money and how Boston society would laugh when they heard about it. I couldn't see any other way out since my parents had lost their fortune."

"Was Shawn so terribly unsuitable?"

The deep silence was broken only by the crackling of the fireplace logs. Summer heard the big grandfather clock downstairs chiming as she waited.

"Shawn was my father's gardener," Priscilla said finally. She went back to the window and stared out at the falling snow as Summer regarded her in stunned silence.

"It was snowing that night, too," Priscilla said as if speaking to herself. "I was supposed to meet Shawn under the street lamp across from my parents' home and we would run away together. I remember standing at the upstairs window with my luggage, looking down on him as he waited patiently for me."

Summer stared in horror at her. "You—you didn't go?"

Priscilla shook her head as she stared unseeing into the night, and her shoulders trembled slightly. "No, I let the man I loved turn and walk out of my life because I was afraid and weak. Now, with each long, lonely night, I think of what might have been and would give anything to change the past."

Tears came to Summer's eyes. "Do you not know where this Shawn O'Bannion is? Have you never heard from him?"

"No. Does that surprise you? Can you imagine how he must have felt that night as he walked away through the snow?" Priscilla's voice was tinged with regret and bitterness. "I let Silas purchase me like a fine-blooded brood mare, and so, I've cheated him, too, you see. I wanted luxury and money; he wanted a beautiful, blue-blooded wife. Now we have nothing to share but bitterness and regrets."

"Oh, Mother. . . ." Summer choked back her tears.

Priscilla went to her desk and tried to press money into Summer's hand, but at that time, Summer thought Iron Knife was dead. "So now you understand why I'm going to marry Austin Shaw next June."

"I don't blame you, then." Mother poured herself a glass of sherry, then gulped it. "I don't blame anyone for trying to escape from this house, from the wreckage your father and I have made of our lives."

Priscilla lifted the lid of the music box. As the sad little tune tinkled out, she took her drink and went back over to stare out the window at the falling snow. "I hate winter," she said in a whisper. "Summer is the time for roses and love, and the cold brings only sad memories and regrets. . . ."

Summer watched her mother drain her goblet and stare out the window at the snow, as if forgetting her daughter was even in the room. Then, very quietly, Summer walked out and her mother never turned around. Even with the door closed behind her, she could hear the faint music from Shawn's little music box. She lay sleepless and weeping on her bed the rest of that night, listening to the chimes of the grandfather clock echoing through the big, gloomy house as the hours passed.

However, that spring, in 1859, before she and Austin could wed, Summer and Austin had been sent to Colorado to track down his younger brother, Todd, and she had found Iron Knife again. He wasn't dead after all. At that moment, faced with a choice between the two, Summer had heeded her mother's advice and had turned her back on everything she knew to run away with the Cheyenne dog soldier.

The stagecoach jolted her awake, and Summer blinked, looking around at her sleeping children. Where was she? Oh, yes, almost six years had passed since she had chosen between the two men, and now she wasn't quite sure she had made the right choice after all. Now she knew that while she'd been in Boston, Iron Knife had slept with Gray Dove and had never told Summer. So now her mother was dying and Summer was headed back to Boston to be at Priscilla's bedside. She could only hope she got there in time. And Shawn O'Bannion? If the one Cherokee knew was the right man, Summer prayed that he cared enough to come and arrived before her mother died. Father would be furious, but Priscilla deserved one last chance to see the man she had loved so long!

Chapter Twelve

Summer had second thoughts about having asked Todd to contact Shawn O'Bannion as she took her children from the stagecoach to a Boston bound train. Suppose with Cherokee's help, Todd did reach the man? Summer's father would be furious! Who would want his wife's old love showing up on the scene as she lay dying? However, it would be worth weathering Father's anger if she could find a way to bring a little happiness to her mother.

She hadn't repeated her mother's mistake, although it had taken courage to turn her back on everything she knew and go with her half-breed lover. But was their love strong enough to weather this storm of hurt feelings, anger and betrayal? Could it stand the test of a separation? She wasn't even sure any more how she felt about Iron Knife or if he would still be waiting for her when she returned west.

Summer had forgotten how cold and grim the weather could be in Boston. She shivered and waited in the station, holding her whimpering toddler. Her two little boys were so astounded by all the crowds and noise that they stood staring big-eyed and silent at the hurrying people and commotion. Would Father meet her himself?

The question was answered as she saw her mother's

personal maid, Mrs. O'Malley, puffing toward her. The plump Irish woman had become a little heavier, a little grayer, in the ensuing years. "Miss Summer, lamb, I've been looking all about for ye!" She threw her arms around Summer and hugged her. "And are these the little bairns? Ah, such little loves they are now!" She bent to hug them, and the children stared up at the jolly white woman with suspicious eyes.

"Did Father come?" She craned her neck looking.

"The mister sends his regrets, lamb." The widow looked a bit embarrassed. "He really meant to, but there was business to take care of; you understand."

"Of course." Had she expected him to change? Nothing mattered to Silas Van Schuyler except making money. With it, he was still attempting to prove he was worthy to be called one of the leaders of Boston. No doubt he hoped the blue-blooded nabobs would forget or overlook his past as a New Yorker whose family fortune had been built on "blackbirding"—running illegal but highly profitable slaves past federal blockades—before he branched out into more respectable enterprises.

"I've got Flannigan looking for the luggage, love. You remember Flannigan?"

Did she? Oh, yes, the bulbous-nosed coachman. Summer wouldn't ask about her mother yet. If Priscilla had died before she arrived, she didn't want to hear the news in the middle of bustling crowds and noisy trains. "I'm afraid there isn't much luggage," Summer said. "One doesn't accumulate a lot when you're on the move all the time, dragging everything on a travois. It's a simple life."

"Come then." Mrs. O'Malley gathered up Garnet, and took Lance's hand. "Now we'll all go home and have a bit of food and meet everyone."

"Food?" Baby Garnet lisped out one of the few English words she knew, then asked for her father in Cheyenne.

"Praise the saints! What is the little love saying?" Mrs. O'Malley asked as she hustled them toward the carriage.

Summer took Storm's hand. "It's Cheyenne; she's wanting her daddy."

She didn't want to think about Iron Knife at this minute. He seemed like a part of another life, perhaps as in a novel or a dream. "Let's get out of this noise and cold so we can talk."

On the drive home, she bounced her daughter on her knee while the two little boys stared out the window. Finally she had the nerve to ask about Priscilla.

Mrs. O'Malley reached for the bag of knitting she always carried. "Aye, she's still alive. Dr. Morgan says he doesn't know what's keeping the poor lass's heart beating; it's as if she's waiting for something."

Summer breathed a sigh of relief. "Is there no hope? Perhaps another doctor—"

"And do ye not think Silas Van Schuyler's money hasn't brought all the best doctors in the country to her bedside? No one can find anything special wrong with the poor lamb; it just seems as if she's tired of living."

Summer remembered Priscilla as she had been that New Year's Eve, so very sad and weary. How old was her mother? Surely not more than forty-five or six? "What has been happening in all these years while I've been gone?"

"Things don't change much at that house year in and year out except the calendars." Mrs. O'Malley's knitting needles clicked over her blue yarn. "Same servants, mostly, although there's been a few part-time scrub women added with the missus so ill. Mr. Van Schuyler has a special hate for the Irish, always has had. My poor countrymen are pouring in here by the millions; starving back in the old country, they are." She crossed herself.

"I'm sorry," Summer said, embarrassed for her father. Was his hatred for the Irish merely economic or did he know about Shawn O'Bannion?

The maid's needles clicked busily. "Nice lady and her daughter had been working for us cleaning now and then, Maureen Malone and her daughter, Sassy. Now the mother's died, and your father won't let me give any of the Malones full-time employment; and they're desperately poor. If the master would, we could certainly use that Mike Malone, Maureen's husband. Now there's a fine, big man with some construction background."

Summer only half-listened and held Garnet to her. She wasn't feeling too well herself. Perhaps she had gotten hold of some spoiled food on the trip.

The plump Irish servant peered at her critically. "You don't look too pert, love. That West is a barbaric place for a gently raised lady like yourself. The servants will be wanting to spoil these bairns and fatten you up a bit."

"Have you heard from David?"

"Aye, he's been here, got called back. They do say the war is winding down, but there's still bloodshed aplenty. He's toiling night and day with the Sanitary Commission, trying to help the wounded on the battlefields. They say more men are dying from infection and disease than wounds. Your father's grumbling that your brother might get some loathsome disease and bring it home."

"Father always was so kind and compassionate," Summer said wryly.

The servant pursed her lips and didn't say anything for a long moment. When she did speak, it was almost a whisper. "He's a strange one, is Silas Van Schuyler, and there's a thin line, they do say, between love and hate; and I sometimes wonder which it is he feels for my poor lady." She paused to wipe her eyes and crossed herself.

She wondered if Mrs. O'Malley knew about Shawn O'Bannion? Summer didn't even want to contemplate the wreckage of her parents' life when she seemed to be making such a disaster of her own. "And the Osgoode sisters and my friend Maude?"

"The Osgoode girls are as prim and proper as always and desperately looking to make good marriages since their family money is gone. They invested in some company that made uniforms for the soldiers."

"That seems like it would be a good investment," Summer said absently.

"Ah, but there's gossip the company owner, Albert Huntington, of Philadelphia, was spending company funds on women and gambling. He's been murdered, they do say under very mysterious circumstances, and anyone who invested is losing everything."

She had forgotten how much small gossip interested women in civilization. They didn't, after all, have very much to entertain them. She didn't know any Huntington family and certainly wasn't interested in their finances. "Didn't the Osgoode girls have a brother, Carter?"

The maid nodded. "Aye, and in the service, too, because he didn't have the money to send a substitute like some of the other rich boys of fine families did. It don't seem fair that the poor and the Irish are mostly the ones being sent to die, does it?"

"No, but the young and the poor are always the ones killed in war." She thought about Sand Creek. "And sometimes women and children."

"There's been draft riots in New York," Mrs. O'Malley said as her needles clicked busily. "They say President Lincoln's weary and heartsick, but it does

look like the war should be ending this spring; least-
wise, everyone thinks so."

She thought about her former fiancé, Austin Shaw,
who had hoped to serve with his fellow West Point
classmate, George Armstrong Custer. She thought of the
plump, rich girl who had a taste for garish dresses and
big words she didn't understand. "What about Austin
and my friend Maude Peabody?"

Mrs. O'Malley chuckled as the carriage clopped
along the street. "They say Miss Priddy's Female Academy will never be the same after you and Miss Maude
led that march to the capitol for women's rights and got
some lady students thrown in jail."

Summer smiled in spite of herself. It seemed like
such a long, long time ago. "Maude wasn't thrown in
jail."

"Aye"—the maid shook her finger under Summer's
nose—"but the only reason she wasn't was that she had
chained herself to the state house door and forgot to
bring a key."

"So where is she?" Summer asked again. "I hope to
see her and—"

"Nobody knows." Mrs. O'Malley crossed herself
again. "Bless the saints, she was determined to be a
nurse in this fight. No one knows where she is, although
there's rumors she might have gotten dressed up like a
man and gone along with the troops. There's even talk
she might be in Andersonville."

"Andersonville?" Summer shuddered. On the train,
she had heard talk of that infamous Southern prison.
The Rebels didn't have enough food or medicine to feed
their own people, much less hundreds of Yankee prisoners. "They say thousands are dying in that prison."

"Aye, let's hope the poor lass is not there."

They passed the big Shaw mansion with its white pillars, and Summer looked at it, remembering. The Shaws

were well-known for their lavish balls. She thought
about Austin Shaw. If she decided not to go back to
Colorado, would he help her to cope? Her brother's best
friend had loved her since they were children, and everyone had expected her to marry him.

Now the carriage pulled through the ornate iron gates
of the Van Schuyler estate next door and stopped at the
entry. She sighed, thinking it really was the most ornate,
ugly Victorian house in Boston. Silas Van Schuyler had
wanted to flaunt his success to showcase the society
blue-blood he had married. Priscilla Blackledge Van
Schuyler was a prisoner princess in a garish castle.

Flannigan reined in, then got down to help them out.
Evans, the arrogant British butler, opened the door to
greet them. "Welcome home, Miss Summer, I'm sorry
it's such a sad occasion."

"Thank you, Evans." She noted he was looking over
the children curiously. She would have to get used to
that staring, she knew; however, dressed in regular
clothing, their Indian blood wasn't that apparent.

A thought crossed her mind. "Are you related to a
Southerner I met called Cherokee Evans?"

"I doubt it, miss." His nose wrinkled at the thought.

Summer went into the front hall and sighed. The
house never changed, perhaps because the head of
the household spent most of his time at his office and
the lady of the house had never taken any interest or
pride in the mansion. The interior smelled musty and
decayed, with just the slightest scent of ancient roses,
almost the ghost of dead blossoms. Gloom descended
on Summer as she looked about the entry, remembering
the dark, ornate furnishings throughout, the murky oil
paintings and lots of bric-a-brac. Expensive Oriental
rugs lay on dark walnut floors. In the front hall, the big
grandfather clock ticked ponderously as it had ever
since Summer could remember. Father took an enor-

mous amount of satisfaction in it. One of her earliest memories was it booming out the hour of six and her scurrying down the stairs to dinner. Silas reigned at dinner, and he expected everyone to be there punctually. "Mrs. O'Malley, would you settle the children and I'll go to my mother."

She left the servants fussing over three tired, listless children and went up the stairs to Priscilla's room, hesitating a long moment before opening the door. She was torn with wanting to hurry inside or turn and run down the hall. Remembering that New Year's Eve, Summer took a deep breath and went in.

The room had not changed one bit in six years. A young, red-haired servant girl was bent over a carpetbag next to her mother's bed. What was she packing? Then Summer realized the girl wasn't packing, but unpacking it.

"Hello," Summer said, "I'm Summer Van Schuyler and you are—?"

"Sassy, ma'am," the pretty Irish girl said, "Sassy Malone. I'm sorry about your mother, miss."

"Thank you." Summer looked around. A fire blazed in the fireplace, and outside the window, snow had begun to fall on this February afternoon. The scent of roses now mingled with the scent of medicines. "How is she?"

"Sometimes she knows everyone and sometimes she doesn't," Sassy said. "So sad!"

Summer looked at the luggage again. What was going on here? "Isn't that my mother's?"

The girl nodded. "Aye, ma'am. The missus keeps packing when she can drag herself from her bed. The master likes things neat and tidy."

Summer looked at the contents curiously. The old carpetbag contained one shoe, an old corset, a crocheted antimacassar from the back of a chair, a maid's apron, a few hairpins, some faded ribbons, and old clothes that a self-respecting beggar couldn't use. "What is all this stuff? It makes no sense."

"It must to her, miss, she repacks whatever she finds, whenever she can drag herself out of bed. But by the saints, the poor thing couldn't get out of the room unassisted."

Summer looked toward the bed. "Does it seem to put her mind at ease to see that luggage?"

"Yes, miss, but the master says—"

"Then just leave it packed, Sassy," Summer said, "no matter that its contents don't make any sense."

"But Mr. Van Schuyler told me—"

"I will deal with Father." She must be growing up; she wasn't as terrified of him as she had once been. "Just repack it and leave the luggage out where she can see it when she looks around the room."

"All right, ma'am." The girl began to repack.

Summer came to the bed and stood looking down at the slight form beneath the down comforters. The woman seemed almost lost among the pillows, her hair spread out like a gray-tinged yellow fan on the white sheets. "Mother?"

She looked so very old, Summer thought with horror, and so very, very tired. Fine lines etched the beautiful face, and she breathed so shallowly, the covers barely moved. "Mother, it's me, Summer."

For a long moment, she was certain her mother was asleep or in a coma, but when she leaned closer and put her hand over Priscilla's thin one, the eyes as pale blue as her own flickered open. Priscilla stared up at Summer, her brow furrowing as if she was not quite certain of the identity of the girl who leaned over her. "Mother, it's Summer, I've come home to visit."

"Summer?" It seemed almost like the echo of her own voice. Then recognition seemed to come to the pale eyes, and the wan lips smiled ever so slightly. "Summer?"

"Yes, I'm here." She blinked rapidly as she leaned over and kissed Priscilla's cheek, not wanting to have a hot tear drip on her. "You're looking well," Summer lied. "Now that I'm here, you'll have to get well so we can take the children to the park and out for drives when the weather warms."

Her gaze seemed to fasten on the falling snow. "Cold . . . tell little Summer, David and Angela to wear their mittens."

"Mother, *I'm* Summer."

Priscilla looked at her blankly a long moment. "All grown up?" she whispered. "How can that be?"

"It—it just happens."

Priscilla stared at her, then shook her head as if to clear it. "I remember now; you had a lover in the West."

Summer nodded. "That's right. I ran away with him."

Priscilla smiled feebly. "I'm glad. You're happy?"

She must not disturb her mother with her own problems. Summer stared out at the falling snow. How many years had Priscilla sat by this very window as the seasons came and went, remembering and regretting? "We're very happy. I have children; I'll bring them up to see you."

"Children?" Priscilla again stared at her blankly. "Who are you?"

She had never felt such inner pain. "Mother, I'm Summer, your daughter, remember?"

Priscilla closed her eyes and shook her head. "I want the other Summer."

"What other Summer?"

"My little girl."

The Irish servant gave Summer a warning shake of her head and touched her own temple. At that, Summer squeezed the frail hand. "Yes, Priscilla, I'll see about

Summer. She must be out playing in the snow." Priscilla smiled without opening her eyes and seemed to drift off to sleep.

Tears blinded Summer as she stumbled out of the room, and she was sobbing as she closed the door and bumped into Dr. Morgan, who was just coming up the stairs. "Why didn't anyone warn me she was so bad?"

The old doctor patted her arm. "It comes and goes. She has her good days and bad days. Years of laudanum and sherry have done their damage, I suppose; but I couldn't stop her, and neither could your father, Miss Summer."

"Is that what's wrong with her?" Summer wiped her eyes.

He hooked his thumbs in the vest across his portly chest. "Not entirely. Sometimes I think she's just very weary of life and has willed herself to stop going through the motions."

"Then why doesn't she die?" Summer almost screamed it at him. "She's so frail and thin. She looks like an old woman already!"

"I can't answer that, either." Dr. Morgan chewed the end of his mustache. "I told Silas she would be gone before the New Year, but something is holding her; it's as if she's waiting for something or someone."

"Me? I'm here and she doesn't even know me." Summer began to cry again.

"Who knows? Maybe you, maybe to see your brother again, maybe just a change in the weather. As I recall, your mother spent a lot of time in her garden with her roses. Maybe she wants to smell the new blossoms one more time before she goes."

"Is she in any pain?"

"I don't think so; at least not physically. Something seems to keep replaying itself in her mind over and over because she keeps staring out at the snow; we've had quite a lot of it lately."

Abruptly, she felt sick and weary and so very sorry for her mother. "You're telling me Priscilla could go on like this for months?"

"Only God knows." Dr. Morgan shook his head. "If I could look in her mind and tell you what she waits for, what's keeping her here, I could tell you when it all will end. At least everyone now has a chance to say goodbye to her."

She began to weep again. "What good does it do to say goodbye to a mother who doesn't even recognize me?"

"Summer, do it for yourself, not for any good it does her." He peered at her a long moment, stroking his white mustache. "You don't look too well; is there something wrong in your own life?"

"Of course not! I have a wonderful man and three healthy children."

He regarded her thoughtfully. "You seem to be under a terrible strain."

"My mother is dying; I'd call that strain enough! Now if you'll excuse me, I need to see about my children." She lifted her skirts and swept down the hall to the old nursery. She didn't want to discuss the doubts and problems she was having, and she was upset that maybe it was so very obvious.

All three of the children had been fed and tucked in to bed. Summer kissed each one and went down the stairs. It was growing dark outside, and father's carriage was arriving home. She was too weary to face him tonight. She asked Mrs. O'Malley to send a tray up to her room, pleaded illness, and retired, leaving a message she would breakfast with him in the morning. That was soon enough to face him.

Her own bedroom hadn't changed, either. It still had

its light colors of blues and yellows and a window seat full of cushions on the south side of the house where when she was small, she used to sit on sunny days and read for hours. Tonight, she sat there for hours after the big mansion had grown dark and silent, watching the snow fall past the window and listening to the big grandfather clock boom the time all night, echoing throughout the big mansion. Silas was extremely proud of it, and often used it to set the gold pocket watch he carried.

Summer slept late the next morning, and when she awakened, the snow was still falling outside the window. She stared at it a long moment, trying to figure out where she was. Boston. She almost groaned aloud. She was back in Boston in this prison of a house because Mother was dying. Her love was many miles away, and she wouldn't be able to rush back to him, try to straighten out their problems, until her mother died. She could be here for weeks. Or even months.

Summer got up and went through her wardrobe, looking for something to put on. No, she shook her head, she didn't intend to stay for weeks. Iron Knife needed her, and she loved him; they would work all their problems out. Her first priority was her man.

Summer sat down at her desk and wrote Iron Knife a hurried note telling him so. Then she addressed it to Todd with instructions to pass it on and went downstairs just in time to bump into Father, who was putting on his hat and overcoat.

"So there you are"—he frowned—"we missed you at breakfast."

If just once, he would say, "daughter I love you so much and I'm so glad to see you," or hug her. He was such a distant, cold man.

"I—I'm sorry, Father, I wasn't feeling well."

"Humph! No wonder! Living in the wilderness away from civilization is enough to kill anyone!" He fixed cold, blue eyes upon her, and his beaked nose made him seem like a bird of prey. "I did meet little Lance at breakfast, smart tyke and looks white, too."

"He is three-quarters white, if you'll recall," she reminded him. "And of course, there's Storm."

Father frowned. "Oh, yes, the dark one. Now that Lance, spunky little fellow." Silas smiled. "He's a Van Schuyler, all right!"

"He's inquisitive and not at all shy."

"Certainly different from your brother, David." Silas frowned. "Don't know how I ended up with such a mollycoddle for a son; no interest in my business at all."

"Father, David is sensitive and talented; he wants to be an artist," she rushed to defend her twin.

"An artist!" Silas snorted. "No money in that. Angela has more interest in my business than your brother does."

There was no point in going through this old argument again. "I'm glad you approve of my sons; maybe sometime you can take them to the office. I'm sure they'll find this house dull with no other little boys around."

"You mean, take that dark one, too?"

"Well, yes, they are brothers, you know."

Silas said, "What's that in your hand?"

"A letter to Todd Shaw to get to Iron Knife. I was hoping maybe Flannigan might be up in town on an errand today and could mail it."

"Flannigan will be lucky to get me to my office in the sleigh with this snow. Here, give it to me, I'll mail it on the way."

She was touched by his kindness. "Why, thank you,

Father." She handed it over, and he tucked it in his overcoat pocket.

"It's not any extra trouble—" he cleared his throat—
"I can at least do that for you."

"I appreciate that." She favored him with a tender
smile and he beamed, then nodded. Could her father be
softening after all these years? Perhaps the fact that her
mother was dying had brought him face-to-face with the
bankruptcy of his personal relationships.

He acted as if her gratitude embarrassed him as he
turned toward the door. "I don't suppose you're considering staying on?"

She looked at him blankly. "You mean, permanently?"

"Ye Gods, of course I mean permanently!" He was
back to his old self, snappy and irritable. "There's a
Plains war going on that you and your children might
not survive, your brother is off playing nursemaid to a
bunch of dying soldiers and your mother will not make
it 'til spring. It seems only sensible that you might want
to stay, either permanently or at least for a few months."

He was lonely, and his life and children hadn't turned
out as he would have wished. Her heart went out to
him, and she put her hand on his sleeve. "Perhaps I'll
stay awhile and get you through this difficult time until
. . . well, you know. But then. . . ."

Disappointment crossed his flinty face as the pompous butler hurried to hand him his briefcase, then stood
waiting by the front door.

"Well, I'll mail your letter," Father said again. "We'll
talk more tonight. Dinner is at six, remember?"

How could she forget? The whole house was a slave
to the big grandfather clock. At precisely six every
night, day in, day out, week in, week out, year in, year
out, the big clock chimed, and everyone showed up to

sit down at the ornate dining table set with the fine china painted with pink and burgundy roses.

"Thank you, Father." She turned and went into the kitchen where the servants would be having a crusty bit of homemade scones thick with butter, marmalade, and a cup of strong tea for breakfast. She was looking forward to it.

Silas stood watching her a long moment as she disappeared toward the kitchen. Then he turned to the butler, who was opening the door. "Evans," he whispered, "any mail or message that comes or goes to or from Miss Summer, I want to see first, you understand?"

"Yes sir, perfectly."

A fine employee; always did exactly as he was told with no questions asked. Silas smiled as he went out into the cold where Flannigan waited to help him into the sleigh. He stared at the letter in his hand as Flannigan cracked the whip and the fine bay horse pulled away, the bells on its harness jingling merrily.

Silas had not realized how much he had missed having Summer in the house; she reminded him of Priscilla when she was a young woman. That made him feel young, too, as if he could roll back the years.

He hadn't expected to like Summer's children; he had expected them to be dark little savages dressed in buckskin, and that Storm was. But Lance and little Garnet were light-skinned. He could show those two grandchildren off in any crowd of his peers without being embarrassed. Lance was just the kind of little boy Silas had always wanted; the son he had dreamed of who might be sharp and ruthless, ready to take the empire Silas had built and carry on, build it even bigger. Silas was resigned to losing his wife; he had come to accept that long ago. In fact, he had never really had her. Priscilla had only been the beautiful princess imprisoned in the castle he had built her and had always acted as if someday, a prince would arrive on a white horse and carry her away.

Silas frowned. A prince. A damned Irish dirt grubber was what he'd been. He'd always had to compete with that ghost from her past. The Irish—how he hated them! He smiled, thinking how he'd just given the butler orders to fire all the Irish except Mrs. O'Malley. Well, at least he had Summer and her children back in his empty big mansion, but unless something drastic happened, Summer intended to return to the West, leaving him again desolate and alone.

Summer's letter in his hand brought him back to the present. What was he to do? He didn't have any trouble deciding that. When he got to his office, he read the letter. Then he tore it up and threw it in the trash.

Chapter Thirteen

Iron Knife braved the raw wind to ride to the rendezvous point that night where Todd Shaw waited.

Todd hailed him. "You're loco to want to meet me this close to Denver! With all the trouble, if any of the miners or cowboys spotted you, you'd get lynched!"

"I've lived my whole life on the edge of danger." Iron Knife shook hands warmly. "I don't worry about little things anymore."

Tomorrow was the first day of March, and it was cold tonight, sleet driving against his face now like small knives. "I thought you might have heard something from Summer."

Todd shook his head. "Not a word." Then he seemed to see Iron Knife's expression. "But that isn't anything to worry about; with all the Indian trouble, half the time the mail isn't getting through, nor the telegrams either."

"Of course"—Iron Knife nodded—"she's no doubt sent me messages and they aren't getting here."

"And remember, the war's still going on; that may have a little to do with the mail mix-up." Todd seemed almost pathetically eager to offer excuses.

"Is no mail getting through?"

Todd looked away, and the wind ruffled his brown hair. "Well, yes," he admitted.

"I am not even sure Summer arrived in Boston," Iron Knife said, "suppose—"

"Oh, she arrived safe and sound," Todd blurted, "the note I got from Mother. . . ."

"Yes?"

Todd shrugged as if it were of no consequence. "Mother's letter merely said Summer's mother was still hanging on, although no one could understand what kept her alive, and that Silas is quite taken with the children, particularly Lance."

"I see," Iron Knife said glumly. Then he brightened. "Of course she can't return, she is caring for her mother."

"Yes"—Todd smiled—"Summer was always a dutiful daughter; she'll feel she has to stay until her mother dies."

Iron Knife frowned and pulled his buffalo robe closer around his broad shoulders. "When the war between blue and gray is over, the long knives will give full attention to fighting Indians. It will be a bad time for my people."

"I know. I wish I could help, but emotions are running high in Denver and the mining camps."

Iron Knife's Appaloosa stallion stomped its hooves and shifted its weight, eager to be out of the cold wind and sleet. "You're a good friend to the Indians, Todd Shaw. Would you do me a favor?"

"Certainly, friend, anything."

He thought about her, pictured her heart-shaped face and big blue eyes in his mind. "Would you send my Summer Sky a message over the singing wires, telling her I miss her and want her back?"

Todd nodded. "That I will do."

"I will check with you in several weeks to get her answer. In the meantime, if there's a letter or wire, you'll send word?"

"You know I will."

"Until then." They shook hands, and Iron Knife turned his horse and sadly headed back to where some of his tribe was camped, hidden away in a valley, hoping the soldiers would not find them until the spring when the ponies were fat and strong on new grass. Chivington may have thought he was solving the Indian problem with his attack at Sand Creek; instead, he had fanned a small flame that now blazed across the frontier as a full-fledged Indian war.

It was unusually cold for the first day of March, Summer thought, staring out at the sleet hitting like pebbles against the windows. The only comfort in this dreary house was that her twin brother, David, had managed to get home yesterday for a short leave. Now, as she went down to join him for breakfast, she wasn't feeling too well, but she was so glad he had come.

Joining them at the table was her sister, Angela, and little Lance. The other two children were having their breakfast in the nursery with their adoring nurse, Mrs. O'Malley.

They looked up as she entered, sensitive, blond David half-rising from his chair. "We were wondering where you were."

"Don't get up." She motioned him back down. "I almost didn't come at all; I'm not feeling very well, I'm afraid."

David frowned. "A lot of grippe and pneumonia going around. Hope I haven't brought you some terrible disease from the hospitals."

"How is it going?" Summer picked up her fine linen napkin and spread it across the lap of her blue dress. Angela was feeding that elderly black cat from the table, but Summer pretended not to notice. How old was

Angela now? Fifteen? Sixteen? She was going to be a breathtaking beauty.

"I don't even want to talk about it." David shook his head.

"That bad?"

"There's a poet, Walt Whitman, helping in the wards; he's a very compassionate man. Sis, we're losing more men to disease and infection than killed on the battlefield." David looked weary and stressed.

Summer picked up her ornate silver fork and looked around. "Where's Father?"

"Already gone to the office, something about selling supplies to the army," Angela said. "I wish he had waited, now I'll have to wait for Flannigan to bring the sleigh back to get me to school."

Just looking at the omelet made Summer queasy. She reached to butter Lance's toast. "The war, the war. We never hear of anything else. Will it never end?"

"It's all but over," David assured her, "another month or two at the most."

Summer watched her son eat. It was amazing how easily Lance had fallen into the roll of privileged child. She noticed he was watching the way David handled a fork, attempted to emulate him. "Have you heard from Austin?"

"He's somewhere deep in the South, serving with his friend, Custer. Remember meeting him?"

Summer searched her memory. "Oh, yes, that brash, handsome cadet from West Point who came to the Shaws' costume ball before the war."

David sipped his coffee. "Custer is the youngest general in the army and extremely ambitious. For that reason, you can expect him to be in the thick of the final battles and Austin right along with him."

"So, David, what are your plans when this war ends?"

David toyed with his food. "I don't know; maybe go west. The army will always need medical personnel and orderlies. Maybe I can do a little to ease pain and suffering."

"Father will be so upset; he expects you to take over his empire."

"I don't want his damned empire!" David threw his napkin down.

"Well, I do!" Angela said. "Why does no one even consider me?"

"You?" Summer looked at her, surprised. David also stared.

"Yes, me!" Angela snapped. "Everyone overlooks me because I'm a girl, but I've been watching and listening when Father talks business. I'm bored to death with Miss Priddy's Academy where the girls prattle of clothes and needlepoint. I think I could someday take over his empire and run it as well as he does!"

Summer took a really good look at her younger sister. It was amazing that Angela had Priscilla's beauty but none of her softness. The cold blue of her eyes and the grim line of her mouth were very much like Silas'. "Perhaps you can, dear; after all, neither of us want it, and there will come a time when women will come into their own and maybe even vote."

In the silence, the cat meowed, and the sleet beat against the windowpane. Lance looked from one to another.

"I wish I could go back west," Summer said, feeling suddenly lonely for her man. She pushed her plate away and stared at the pink and burgundy roses that bloomed eternally around the rim of the china. "If only we knew how long Mother was going to last—"

"I know," Angela said, and stroked the black cat.

"Don't be silly," Summer said, "how could you know? No one knows—not even Dr. Morgan."

Angela's pale eyes stared out the window. "She will last until the first week of April."

A shiver went up Summer's back at the certainty in her sister's tone. "How can you possibly know that?"

"I just know; that's all." Angela got up from her chair, picked up the cat and left the dining room.

Summer and David stared at each other wordlessly. Generations ago, a Blackledge had been hanged in the Salem witch trials, and Summer was not all that sure about that ancestor's innocence. There was a secret about their younger sister that even Angela couldn't know, a secret David had kept since he was a small boy, a secret he had finally told Summer that night of the Shaws' 1858 New Year's Eve ball.

Even as she looked into David's eyes, she remembered that time in the carriage when he had told Summer what he had witnessed one long-ago night when he was only nine years old and everyone else in the house was asleep.

David had said the noise, the screams and cursing, had awakened him as Silas tore Priscilla's door down. David had run into Mother's room to see Silas brutally raping Priscilla in a fit of whitehot rage. Angela had been the result of that terrible night. Had the violence of her conception affected their strange younger sister's personality, or was it only the Blackledge blood coming through?

Even now as she sat at the table, remembering, Summer wondered what had happened to have sent Silas into such a murderous rage that long-ago night? She supposed they would never know; Summer could only wonder. . . .

"Sis, are you all right?"

She blinked, and realized she sat at the breakfast table with little Lance and her brother looking at her anxiously. "I—I'm all right, just not feeling very well; that's all."

"You go on up and lie down, then," David said gently as he got up and helped her from her chair. "Lance and I will find something to do; maybe go sledding."

"Thank you." She was feeling so nauseated, she was afraid she was going to lose what little breakfast she had eaten. The quibbling at the table had upset her more than she wanted to admit. Summer had a secret of her own, yet she dared not tell it yet until she decided what to do.

She heard the front door open and close as she went down the hall. The pompous butler came from the door. "Was that the mail, Evans?"

"Yes, mum."

She hardly dared hope. "Was there—was there something for me?"

"Now, Miss Summer, if there had been, wouldn't I have told you?" His tone was coldly polite.

She felt like a fool. "Of course. I'm sorry; I didn't mean that you weren't efficient and doing your job."

His nose went a bit higher in the air. "In England, the gentry never apologizes to the servants, mum."

Was she being chided by this pompous butler who always seemed to be reminding her he knew how Father had made his money? She felt an angry flush rise to her cheeks.

The nausea was growing. Lifting her skirts, Summer raced up the stairs and barely made it in time. Afterward, she was so weak, she could hardly wet a cloth with cold water and lie down on her bed, staring out at the raw weather. What was she going to do? Even if Priscilla died, or got well, Summer wasn't in any shape to begin a long journey back to the West.

Besides that, she had to face the facts that she had heard nothing from Iron Knife, no answer to her letters.

We've got your authors!

If you seek out the latest historical romances by today's bestselling authors, our new reader's service, KENSINGTON CHOICE, is the club for you.

KENSINGTON CHOICE is the only club where you can find authors like Janelle Taylor, Shannon Drake, Rosanne Bittner, Sylvie Sommerfield, Penelope Neri and Phoebe Conn all in one place…

…and the only service that will deliver their romances direct to your home as soon as they are published—even before they reach the bookstores.

KENSINGTON CHOICE is also the only service that will give you a substantial guaranteed discount off the publisher's prices on every one of those romances.

That's right: Every month, the Editors at Zebra and Pinnacle select four of the newest novels by our bestselling authors and rush them straight to you, usually *before they reach the bookstores*. The publisher's prices for these romances range from $4.99 to $5.99—but they are always yours for the guaranteed low price of just *$3.95!*

That means you'll always save over $1.00…often as much as *$2.00*…off the publisher's prices on every new novel you get from KENSINGTON CHOICE!

All books are sent on a 10-day free examination basis, and there is no minimum number of books to buy. (A postage and handling charge of $1.50 is added to each shipment.)

As your introduction to the convenience and value of this new service, we invite you to accept

4 BOOKS FREE

The 4 books, worth up to $23.96, are our welcoming gift. You pay only $1 to help cover postage and handling.

To start your subscription to KENSINGTON CHOICE and receive your introductory package of 4 FREE romances, detach and mail the postpaid card at right *today*.

We have 4 FREE BOOKS for you
as your introduction to
KENSINGTON CHOICE
To get your FREE BOOKS, worth
up to $23.96, mail the card below.

FREE BOOK CERTIFICATE

As my introduction to your new KENSINGTON CHOICE reader's service, please send me 4 FREE historical romances (worth up to $23.96), billing me just $1 to help cover postage and handling. As a KENSINGTON CHOICE subscriber, I will then receive 4 brand-new romances to preview each month for 10 days FREE. I can return any books I decide not to keep and owe nothing. The publisher's prices for the KENSINGTON CHOICE romances range from $4.99 to $5.99, but as a subscriber I will be entitled to get them for just $3.95 per book or $15.80 for all four titles. There is no minimum number of books to buy, and I can cancel my subscription at any time. A $1.50 postage and handling charge is added to each shipment.

KC1194

Name _____

Address _____ Apt. _____

City _____ State _____ Zip _____

Telephone (____) _____

Signature _____
(If under 18, parent or guardian must sign)

Subscription subject to acceptance. Terms and prices subject to change.

We have
4
FREE
Historical
Romances
for you!

(worth up
to $23.96!)

Details inside!

Could he be dead in all this Indian war? Or had he decided that their union was a mistake and didn't want her back?

What to do? She stared out the window, trying to make some plans. Perhaps she could send a letter or wire to Todd and ask him if he'd heard anything, ask him to inquire after Iron Knife's health and whereabouts. Yes, that's what she would do.

Summer rested awhile, wrote the wire, and went downstairs. She'd give the telegram to David, let him take care of it if he was going to town this morning. She would tell her brother her secret; but she wasn't sure what he could do to help. "Where's David?"

Evans said, "He took Master Lance and Storm sledding."

"Oh, yes, of course. And the baby?"

"I believe Mrs. O'Malley and the servants have her in the kitchen playing with her." His tone gave her to know he did not approve of such camaraderie between servants and employers. "If you don't mind, miss, I was just on my way up to town to pick up supplies."

"Oh, good. I won't be putting you to any trouble, then, if I ask you to send this wire?"

"A wire? Of course not, miss, I am employed to serve."

She gave it to him, then went back upstairs to her mother's room.

The little music box tinkled out its melody as Summer went in.

The new little maid, Nancy, said, "I'm sorry for playing it, miss, but it's the only thing that seems to quiet her."

"That's all right." She wondered what had happened to that last maid; what was her name? Oh, yes, Sassy.

The room seemed so cheerless and gloomy. "I wish we had some roses; it would make it seem more like spring."

"Hard to come by in this weather." The maid moved the suitcase as she dusted around the lamp table.

Priscilla's eyes opened, but she didn't seem to see anyone. Her gaze fastened on the suitcase, and she smiled ever so slightly and dropped back off to sleep.

What was it about a piece of luggage that triggered her mother's emotions, even when the woman's mind was so far gone that she packed it with an odd collection of miscellaneous junk? Summer was suddenly very weary of this vigil and wished it were all over so everyone could get on with their lives. Immediately, she felt guilty for wanting her mother dead, this long ordeal ended. What was it that was holding Priscilla here? Perhaps she might be waiting for spring, to sit in her garden and smell the roses one more time.

Summer went to the window and looked at her mother's dead garden with its fountains and ornate benches buried under ice. She remembered now there was a particular bush that her mother favored, a bush of yellow roses. How many times as a child had she seen her mother sitting on the grass by that bush, an armful of the yellow blossoms in her arms, her face buried in them to inhale their slightest scent? Once, when she had looked up at the sound of her daughter's step, little Summer had noticed that Priscilla was weeping. Perhaps her mother had pricked her finger on a thorn; what other reason could there be?

Now the skeleton of that bush stood out stark against the winter snow below the window. . . .

"Miss Summer, I'm havin' a bit of tea and muffin, would you care for some?"

Summer turned away from the window and the sight of the dead garden below. The tea looked inviting, but then she got a whiff of the cheese and jam on the plate with the muffin. She swallowed hard, feeling ill again. "I—I think not, Nancy, but thanks for asking."

Her nausea returned. The scent of the food seemed almost overpowering. Summer turned and fled the room, headed for her bathroom. There was nothing to throw up, but she retched anyway for a long moment.

She got another cold cloth and collapsed on her bed. That gave her a little relief, but only a little. She was so weak from not being able to keep anything down, yet she moaned aloud at the thought of food and mopped her perspiring face again. Oh, Lord, how could she deal with this added complication? What was she going to do now?

Silas reread the message the butler had just brought to his office, then tore it up. So now Summer was trying to reach that damned redskin by sending wires to Todd in Denver. Silas smiled and drummed his fingers on his desk. She would get an answer, all right, supposedly from Todd telling her he'd had no contact with that half-breed. Maybe after a few months, Summer would decide that damned Indian didn't care about her, get sensible and decide to stay in Boston where she belonged. Silas was getting quite attached to Summer's children, Lance and little Garnet. He had been teaching them English, and the other things civilized children needed to know. He didn't want them raised as savages.

Silas got up and walked around the polished desk, looking about his big office. He owned shipping and manufacturing, importing, telegraph and even some petroleum shares that might someday be worth something if anyone could figure out some use for that oil; certainly greasing buggy wheels wasn't much of a market. What good did it do to build an empire if he was going to lose his two oldest children and have no one to pass his money and power to? There was always Angela; but of course, she was just a girl, and women had no power and no business sense. He'd rather leave it all to a male heir.

What he needed to do was figure out a way to keep Summer in Boston permanently so he could raise little Lance. Summer wasn't feeling well lately, and in this cold, she seldom went uptown. So far, every message coming and going to Colorado had been intercepted, and he meant to keep it that way. Silas also might send fake letters and telegrams. After all, he had friends in high places.

If she didn't hear from that damned redskin, she'd forget about him or decide he was dead or didn't want her back. Besides, she wasn't really married to that half-breed, not by white, legal standards. Could he marry her off to someone else? Silas paused by the window, tucked his hands behind him and stared out at Boston Harbor with his ships riding at anchor on the cold, gray water. Austin Shaw had loved Summer since she was a little girl, but she seemed to have no interest in him. Well, if not Austin, who else might appeal to her? It needed to be someone rich, from a fine family and with good business connections. What other man did he know he might introduce to his daughter? What about Beau St. Claire?

Silas smiled, pleased with himself. Now there was a blond, handsome man in his late thirties, from the St. Claire plantation family of Georgia. Beau had no loyalties or interest in the Civil War or who won it; he was only interested in what profits could be made from it. A man after Silas Van Schuyler's own heart. Beau should be back in town soon, and Silas would invite him over to talk business so Summer could meet him. Smiling at

his own cleverness, Silas sat down to write the fake
message he would send.

Summer was resting when she heard the door chimes
and the pompous butler's step on the stairs. Perhaps it
was a wire from Iron Knife! She opened her bedroom
door. "Yes?"

"Mr. Austin Shaw is waiting in the music room, Miss
Summer."

"Oh." She felt mixed emotions about her old fiancé.
"Tell him I'll be down in a minute, and you may serve
tea there, Evans."

He nodded and left while she hurriedly splashed water on her face, then pinched her cheeks to make them
rosy before descending the stairs.

Austin. He was her brother's best friend and much
like a big brother to her. Everyone had expected her to
marry the boy next door. Good, dependable Austin from
a background exactly like her own.

Taking a deep breath, she went into the music room
holding out both hands. "Austin! So good to see you!"

"Summer, I've missed you." He stood there before
the fire in his blue lieutenant's uniform, smoking his
pipe. Now he took her hands in both of his, and his hazel eyes betrayed the fact that his feelings for her hadn't
changed.

"Sit down. Evans is bringing tea." She gestured toward the sofa and sat down herself, looking around. The
music room was her favorite with its pastel Chinese
rugs, grand piano and the big harp near the fireplace.
"You're looking well; so fit and trim."

"It's a hard life in the army; in the saddle a lot." He
knocked the ashes from his pipe into the fireplace,
slipped it in his pocket and joined her on the sofa as the
snooty butler carried in the ornate silver service.

"Shall I pour, miss?"

"No"—Summer waved him away—"thank you, Evans."

The butler left, and she poured and served, genuinely glad to see her old boyfriend.

"Are you all right, Summer?"

She didn't look at him as she sipped the strong tea and nibbled a delicate scone. "It's very difficult, waiting for Mother . . . well, you know."

"I'm so sorry. Is there anything I can do?" His voice and expression were so warm, so genuine. Austin Shaw was a thoroughly decent, civilized human being.

Summer shook her head. "There's nothing anyone can do." It occurred to her that she didn't know if she was speaking of her mother or about her personal life. She looked around the rich furnishings, remembering happier times, parties here in this room. Once she had thought it worth while to throw it all away for a big, virile half-breed; now she wasn't so sure. "Will you be in town long?"

He shook his head and put his cup down. "Unfortunately, I had to use Father's considerable influence, move heaven and earth to make this quick trip."

The war; always the war. "Will it ever end?"

He nodded. "The South is in its death throes now. Of course, Custer is in the thick of it; means to be there for the kill; great publicity, you know."

She finished her tea, then set it down with a sigh.

"I'm sorry I won't be here for you when your mother. . . ."

The door opened slowly, and three small heads peeked around it.

Austin grinned with genuine warmth. "Hello! And who's this?"

Summer waved them in. "Children, come meet my old friend; this is Mr. Shaw."

Storm and little Garnet advanced slowly, staring at him.

"Bluecoat!" Storm's dark face frowned with disapproval, but Lance walked right up and held out his hand.

"How do you do, sir, I'm happy to make your acquaintance."

Austin shook hands with him, then looked at Summer questioningly.

"Father's been coaching him," she said, "turning him into a regular little Boston gentleman. The others, well, we were at Sand Creek; the blue uniforms, you know."

Instantly, his kind face showed concern, and he smiled at the children. "I'm your mother's good friend," he said, "and I will always be yours, too."

The three of them looked at him gravely. Summer translated his words into Cheyenne.

Storm said, "Does the white soldier speak true, Mother?"

Summer nodded. "You can always trust him; I promise."

Now the three turned their attention to the cookies and scones on the ornate silver tray.

Lance said, "May we please have a cookie?"

"You may," Summer said, and held out the ornate tray.

The three took cookies, then started to leave.

Lance turned, came back, and held out a small hand. "Thank you for coming, sir. It was nice to meet you."

"Nice to meet you, too," Austin said, and shook it gravely.

Summer watched her three children leave the room, her heart bursting with love and pride.

"They're fine children," Austin murmured, "you and Iron Knife must be very proud. I wish. . . ." He didn't finish.

She looked down at her hands in her lap.

"Are you happy, Summer? You don't look at all well."

Why had he asked? They had known each other since childhood. He knew her so well; did he sense something was wrong? She longed to pour out her heartbreak at discovering about the other woman, about how difficult and dangerous life was on the frontier, how she had heard nothing from Iron Knife. But it did not seem loyal to her man, and besides, she was proud. "Yes, I—I'm happy."

The big clock in the hall began to boom the hour, and Austin pulled out his pocket watch, looked at it, and sighed. "I've got a train to catch. How I wish I could stay." He stood up.

"Must you go so soon?" She stood up and took both his hands in hers. "Frankly, it's been lonely here."

"I don't know when I'll be in town again," he said, looking down at her, "you may be gone before I return."

"Perhaps not."

"If you should ever need anything. . . ." He paused, and she knew he was fighting an urge to kiss her.

She made it easy for him by letting go of his hands, stepping away from him. He was so decent, so ethical. "I know I can always count on you, Austin."

He cleared his throat as he ran his hand through his brown hair. "Iron Knife is a lucky man; tell him I said so."

"Thank you, Austin; I'll pray for your safety."

He nodded and blinked rapidly. "Goodbye now." He turned and hurried from the music room.

Summer stood looking after him long after she had heard the front door close. Austin Shaw would marry her in a minute and help raise her children. It would be a safe, respectable and predictable union.

She had traded that future for the wild passion of a virile dog soldier's arms. Had she made the right choice? She didn't know herself.

Chapter Fourteen

The days were passing slowly for Summer at the Van Schuyler mansion. Perhaps it was the bad weather, she thought, staring out the window of her mother's bedroom, or was it only that the whole family was so very weary of waiting for Priscilla to die so they could all get on with their lives?

She felt guilty as the thought crossed her mind. Summer turned from staring out at the falling snow and went to her mother's bedside. Priscilla stirred restlessly, opened her eyes and looked up at her vacantly.

"Mother?" Summer forced herself into a cheery exterior. "How are you this morning?"

Priscilla looked at her blankly, then turned her head so that she could see the carpetbag that stood packed by the door. She seemed to sigh with relief, and Summer wondered again what it was about the packed luggage that pleased her. Where could she be thinking she might be going when Priscilla was so frail, she couldn't even get out of bed? Nothing had been heard of Shawn O'Bannion, and maybe it was just as well, Summer thought. It had been a romantic impulse on her part to try to reach him. Maybe he hadn't gotten the message or maybe he was dead. Or perhaps after more than a quarter of a century, he had gone on with his life and didn't remember or care about Priscilla Blackledge Van Schuyler.

Now Priscilla turned her wan face to stare out the window. "Snow," she whispered so softly that Summer had to strain to hear her, "we'll be cold walking in the snow."

Summer started to say that Priscilla was so weak, she wasn't even going downstairs, much less out into the snow, but there was no point in upsetting this pale, dying wraith. Who on earth was she planning to walk through the snow with?

"Mother," Summer whispered and patted her thin shoulder, "it won't be cold, we'll bundle you up in furs so you can walk in the snow all you want."

Once again, Priscilla stared at her blankly. It was obvious she had no idea who Summer was. ". . . can't go yet," she whispered with just a faint shake of her head, "can't go yet . . . waiting. . . ."

"For what?" Summer said, a bit out of sorts, but Priscilla had already closed her eyes and drifted back off to sleep. Summer collapsed on a chair. It was difficult enough dealing with a mother who no longer recognized her most of the time, but the fact that she'd had no reply to her letters to Iron Knife kept her sleepless with worry night after night. The wire she'd gotten from Todd hinted that maybe Iron Knife seemed no longer interested in whether she returned or not. The stress of that and this dreary existence here in Boston was no doubt the reason Summer felt so poorly. She didn't want to even think about, much less face, the real reason.

Tonight, she had promised Father she would join him for dinner with some business associate, Beauregard St. Claire. She had tried to beg off, claiming weariness, but Silas Van Schuyler was used to getting what he wanted.

Well, she could be nice for a couple of hours to some pompous old goat if it was that important to Father. After all, he had pointed out, she owed him some respect and obligation.

Priscilla moved restlessly, and without thinking, Summer reached to wind up the little music box, then opened it on the pillow by Priscilla's head.

... *'Tis the last rose of summer left blooming alone, all her lovely companions are faded and gone....*

Priscilla smiled in her sleep, and Summer wondered what her mother dreamt of? There was an open book lying on the nightstand. Summer picked it up. The book wasn't that old, but it was well-worn. It must be one of Priscilla's favorites. Poetry. Summer's gaze swept over the print. Yes, she knew this poem: *Maude Muller,* by John Greenleaf Whittier. It was a sad tale about a girl and a man who met, then went their separate ways. Many years later, when they were both married to other people, the two still daydreamed vainly about the other.

... *God pity them both and pity us all who vainly the days of youth recall; for of all the words of tongue or pen, the saddest are these: it might have been....*

Summer closed the book, then laid it on the nightstand again. The music box had slowly tinkled to a stop. She put it next to the book, blinking back tears, then went to the window again, stared out at the snow and wondered what was happening in Colorado right now.

"Miss Summer?" Mrs. O'Malley's familiar voice jarred Summer out of her thoughts as the maid opened the door. "Are you in here?"

"Yes, I—I was seeing about Mother." She turned to face the plump Irish maid. "Are the children all right?"

The gray head nodded. "Aye, lamb, they're napping. You don't look so good; maybe next time the doctor comes, he should look at you."

"Don't be silly," Summer sighed and crossed the room, almost falling over the suitcase standing by the door. She wasn't ready to deal with Dr. Morgan yet. "Mother doesn't have anything catching; at least, Dr. Morgan doesn't seem to think so."

The plump maid looked toward the bed. "Has the poor lass changed any?"

Summer shook her head. "She doesn't get better, she doesn't die; she just waits."

Mrs. O'Malley crossed herself and wiped a tear from her eye. "Aye, I know. I've been her maid many a year, and even I don't know what it is she waits for."

Summer felt very sad and very tired. "Was there—was there any mail for me?"

The maid shook her head. "Suppose not; at least Evans didn't give me anything to bring up to you." She seemed to notice the bereft expression on Summer's face. "Now, it would be hard indeed for your Indian to get a letter out with all the trouble in the West."

"Of course; I only hoped. . . ." Summer's voice trailed off. Another day without any word from Iron Knife. "I—I think I will lie down a few minutes."

"Remember, love, your father expects you at dinner."

She wanted to go home to her man, not entertain some dull old customer of Father's, but there was nothing she could do tonight except be pleasant. "Of course. I'll rest awhile and you can help me dress later." With that, Summer brushed past Mrs. O'Malley and went to her room.

* * *

Summer had planned to wear a deep blue dress to dinner, but Mrs. O'Malley couldn't get the hooks fastened. "I didn't realize with all the rich food I've been eating these last fews weeks that I must have put on a little weight," she confessed as she took it off and the maid selected another from the big wardrobe.

"Aye, possibly ye never took it off after the last wee one," plump Mrs. O'Malley suggested. "After all, you haven't worn this dress since before you ran off to the Indians, and you were thin as a rail then."

"I was never thin as a rail," Summer said.

The Irish maid smiled. "Now, lamb, compared to some of us, ye was thin as a shadow. You'll take it off gradually, never you mind. Some women, it just takes longer than others."

Had the dear woman guessed? If she had, she was waiting for Summer to announce it. Summer looked through her vast wardrobe, finally settling on a low-cut, plum-colored velvet that had been a trifle big for her several years ago. Now it fit like a glove. Summer studied herself in the mirror with satisfaction. "Doesn't look half bad, does it?"

The maid put her hands on her own ample hips and nodded. "You'll entertain your father's business client, all right. Just the sight of you in that dress would interest any man. Now let me do up your hair, Miss Summer."

Summer felt a little better looking at her reflection in the mirror. Yes, the dress did look good on her with the swell of her breasts visible above the bodice. Maybe attempting to be an entertaining dinner partner would be interesting after all; at least it would be better than the dull evening meals with Father and Angela night after night. "Just how old is old Mr. St. Clair?"

"Older than you are." Mrs. O'Malley sat down in a

chair and picked up her knitting. "But he's hardly an old man."

Of course the maid would say that. At her age, if he were less than sixty, Mrs. O'Malley would think him young and handsome.

The maid got out the curling irons, heating them over the glass chimney of a lamp before applying them to Summer's long, blond locks which she now put up in a cascade of curls with plum and pink ribbons.

Summer twirled in a circle. "Are you sure I look all right to entertain guests?"

"My, yes, now you go on down and let me knit in peace. I've promised your babes some mittens for the winter snow."

Summer took one final look. "I'll check on the children on my way downstairs."

"No need; they're probably asleep by now."

Still Summer looked in on them before she went downstairs to join Father in the library. "Has your guest not arrived yet?"

Silas started as he looked at his daughter. It was almost like seeing Priscilla for the very first time, all those long years ago. He had loved her so very much then. He took the cigar from between his teeth and shook his head. "Not yet."

"Is something the matter?"

He blinked to clear his eyes. Silas Van Schuyler had a reputation as a cold, shrewd man, and in many ways, he had earned that. In business, no one could outmaneuver him, and he delighted in besting another, humiliating and destroying men. "I was just thinking how much you look like your mother."

"Hardly. Mother was a great beauty in her day, wasn't she?"

"The most beautiful in Boston; maybe in the world."

And she had been his; at least, he had owned her body. Some things money would buy.

"I spent most of the afternoon in her room."

He did not want to ask, but he couldn't stop himself. "Did she—did she ask for me?"

"No." Then she seemed to add as a merciful afterthought, "She isn't asking for anyone, Father; mostly, she doesn't seem to recognize people."

He leaned back in his chair and sighed. "I went into her room last night to look in on her; fell over that damned suitcase. I thought I gave servants orders to unpack it."

"I countermanded that order." Summer's chin came up, and her tone sharpened. Obviously the girl had more of his own temperament than he realized. "Besides"— Summer stared into the fire—"when we unpack it, she stumbles out of bed and attempts to repack it."

Silas swore softly under his breath. "I don't know where in the hell she thinks she's going!"

"Does it matter? She's dying, Father, and if it makes her happy, let it stay packed; she's had little happiness in this house."

"Are you reprimanding me, young lady?" His voice rose, although he tried to control it.

"No, Father, I'm sure you tried."

He stared at the glowing tip of his cigar in silence. Silas Van Schuyler had loved Priscilla madly—or maybe he had only loved what she had represented; blue-blooded, respectable Boston society. He had suspected she was in love with another man when she wed him, but Silas found out soon enough. Gradually, his love had turned to hatred because she wouldn't love him in return, so in his frustration, he had humiliated her and driven her to drink. The very last time he had been in her bed was the night he had raped her because he'd seen that Shawn O'Bannion lurking in front of the house. With her belly big with Angela, Priscilla couldn't leave him for that other man. Would she have? They had never discussed that cursed Irish gardener, not once in all these years. Maybe she didn't even know he knew about Shawn.

"Father," Summer said, "I've been meaning to speak to you about Lance. I hope you won't get too attached to him; remember we're going back when Mother— well, you know."

"And is it a crime to be fond of my grandson?" He puffed his cigar. "Reminds me of myself; could be a real empire builder. Your weak brother certainly will never do anything with the Van Schuyler fortune."

"There's other things besides building empires." She sounded defensive, and he noted her lovely face was pale. He hoped she wasn't coming down with anything. Yellow fever wasn't around during the cold weather, but there was always typhoid, diphtheria, smallpox. "Father, would you mind putting out that cigar? The smoke is making me quite ill."

She did look sick. He snuffed out the cigar. "It does seem a shame to take the children back to live as savages when I could give them so much." Silas decided to try both guilt and logic.

Her face reddened. "Money isn't everything. The West is wonderful; big and free. Lance could build his own empire out there with all those opportunities."

"He'd do even better with my money behind him."

She whirled on him. "Father, he's only a little boy; let's let him plan his own future, shall we?"

"I only thought he could go on to great heights with some education and all the other advantages I could give him." He had botched the raising of David some- how, but with Lance he'd have another chance to mold the kind of son he'd always wanted. "Don't decide now, Summer," he said gently. "You have a while to think about it. Perhaps you could leave him with me awhile and then come back for him in a year or two."

"His father wouldn't like that."

Silas managed to control his temper and his tongue. Iron Knife. The big virile savage was not the kind of son-in-law he had wanted at all. He almost said something to Summer about the scandal she had caused when she'd run away with that Indian, then decided against it. The first thing was to persuade her to leave the child with him and maybe little Garnet, too. He sipped his brandy and thought. Storm, no, he didn't think he wanted that Injun-looking one, but he'd like to raise the other two. By the time she came back to retrieve them, Silas would have his firm of lawyers ready to prove she was not fit to have custody. No civilized court in the land would return them to her. Long ago, he had bought himself the wife he wanted, and now he was prepared to buy the grandchildren.

He cleared his throat and tried to smile kindly. "Just think on it, Summer; it would be a wonderful opportunity for Lance. Think how lonely I will be when your mother is gone and you go back west. I doubt that David will ever return to Boston."

"You have Angela."

Angela. The child of rape. There was something evil about that daughter; perhaps because of the violence of her conception. "Yes, but a man needs sons. No woman can manage an empire."

"I could." Angela stuck her head around the door, and Coaldust, the black cat, preceded her.

Silas frowned. "It isn't polite to eavesdrop. Go to your room, young lady."

The blond beauty picked up her cat. "I could manage all the Van Schuyler holdings; much better than anyone," she snapped. "I'm more like you than either Summer or David."

"She's right, Father," Summer said. "Someday, women will take an active part in the business world. You underestimate us."

"As I recall," Silas said acidly, "all this women's equality thing is what created the scandal that got you sent away west to begin with."

"Don't change the subject," Angela snapped. "I'm old enough to be invited to have dinner with guests; I'm almost sixteen."

"Go to your room," Silas ordered. "Mr. St. Claire is coming to meet your sister."

With an angry sob, Angela turned and, still carrying her cat, ran from the room.

Summer eyed him strangely. "Coming to meet me? I thought he was here on business?"

Ye Gods! Why had he let the words slip out? "I merely meant he had said he was looking forward to talking to anyone who'd been in the West; he's wondering about business opportunities out there."

"Oh." She appeared somewhat mollified.

He heard the doorbell chime and Evans going to answer it. "That's probably our guest, Summer. I'm thinking of turning a tidy profit doing business with him, so please be polite."

Summer smiled. "I can be nice to the old codger, Father."

Where had she gotten the idea that Beau was old? Silas gave her his warmest, most innocent smile. "Thank you, my dear."

Summer was not expecting Beau St. Claire to be so handsome and polished—not as young as he was. He was probably in his late thirties. She managed to recover from her surprise as they were introduced and the handsome, suave Southerner bent to kiss her hand. "Charmed, I'm sure, Miss Summer. Your father's description doesn't do you justice."

She felt herself redden at the compliment. "You are certainly a charmer, Mr. St. Claire."

"No, ma'am, *you* are the charmer." He smiled at her, and a lock of curly light hair fell down across his patrician forehead. "Ma'am, please call me Beau."

He had the most wonderful Southern accent and soulful brown eyes, Summer realized.

"As in Beau Brummel, the famous lover?"

"As in Beauregard, one of the best known names among Southern aristocracy, ma'am."

She felt like a fool. Why had she flirted with him? Of course this polished, well-dressed Southern blade would not be interested in her. Everything about him said money and breeding. "I—I think the butler is about to announce dinner."

"In that case, Miss Summer"—he offered her his arm in a grand gesture—"I'd be proud to escort you; you are indeed the most beautiful thing I have seen in this frozen land of Yankees."

She felt like a silly school girl as she took his arm. Iron Knife was strong, virile and protective, but this gentleman of the South knew how to please a lady. Yet there was something about him that made Summer a trifle uneasy. Beau St. Claire was a bit too smooth.

They went into the big dining room with its ornate mahogany table and crystal chandelier. The table linen was crisply white, and her mother's fine crystal made the table sparkle. Beau seated her across from himself. "I'm so glad you invited me to dinner, suh, I had no idea you had such a lovely daughter."

His accent was as thick and smooth as molasses, and it added to his polished charm.

"I—I have children," she blurted, and then felt foolish because there was no reason to tell him that since he was only here on business.

"I envy that lucky man, then, Miss Summer." Beau

beamed at her and brushed the light curl from his fore-head. "I have never been so lucky to meet a flower like you or I would not now be almost forty and still a bach-elor."

It was fun to flirt with him even though she loved her Cheyenne dog soldier. In the back of her mind, she was a bit peevish and annoyed that she hadn't heard from Iron Knife. "So, Mr. St. Claire, what is a Southerner doing in the north at these times?"

The butler poured the wine, and she sipped hers. *A very good year,* she thought, *Father must be trying to impress Beau St. Claire.*

"Like you, dear lady," Beau drawled, "I'm hoping this sad business will soon end and we can get back to really important things, namely business and making a profit." He savored the wine. "A good year." He nodded appreciatively at Silas.

Father nodded. "I thought you'd appreciate it, Beau. You have the class and breeding to know fine wine and food."

"Fine women, too." Beau held his glass up in a toast and smiled at Summer.

She looked down at her plate, felt the blood rush to her face. "Have—have you been in Boston long, sir?"

He shook his head. "I just came from Washington; before that, I was in Atlanta and Louisville. My sister and I have managed to keep Yankee troops from destroyin' Shannon Place, so we're one of the few plan-tations still turning a profit."

Father leaned back in his chair as Evans began to serve a rare haunch of beef from a heavy silver tray. "Beau, you really are a man of the world. What's hap-pening in Washington these days?"

"I can't see how the war can last more than a few more weeks." Beau smiled at Summer and sipped his wine. His waistcoat fit him to perfection and was of the finest fabric, Summer noted. "I saw several good plays while I was in the capital."

Summer was intrigued as was everyone she knew at the excitement of Washington. "Did you see that handsome John Wilkes Booth? I hear all the ladies just swoon over him."

Beau laughed. He had a charming, easy laugh. "Well, as a matter of fact, I did, ma'am; saw the president, too. He was passin' by in his carriage one day when I was on the street."

"And does his wife really have all those fine clothes people say she does?" Summer asked.

"I reckon. You do know some of her brothers and brothers-in-law are fightin' for the South?"

"We heard that." Silas frowned and cut into his roast beef. "But what can you expect from the wife of a nobody like Lincoln? He ought to go back to being a country lawyer."

"Now, Father," Summer soothed, "he's gotten us through the war all right. Some think he's a great president."

Silas snorted. "Humph!"

Beau regarded him kindly. "Suh, you and I have both profited well from the conflict as smart businessmen always will."

"That's true," Silas said and sipped his wine.

The big grandfather clock in the hall began to boom out the hour. Both men took out their pocket watches and checked them.

"Right on time," Father said.

Summer looked at the ornate gold watch in Beau's hand. "Such a beautiful timepiece, Mr. St. Claire."

"Isn't it, though?" He held it out so she could see the inscription. "My dear sister gave it to me for my birthday." *To Beau St. Claire with all my love, Savannah.*

Father beamed at the Southerner. Obviously he'd

found a man after his own heart. They both put their watches back in their vests. "I do hope you'll come to dinner often when you're in town, Beau. Isn't that right, Summer?"

"Yes, of course." He was interesting and charming, too, Summer thought as she began to eat. Or was it only that this was such a sad, gloomy household that any guest was wonderful?

"I reckon I would hate to impose in this sad time," Beau drawled, "knowing about the missus and all."

Summer realized he was speaking to her. "There isn't anything we can do but wait," she answered softly. Abruptly, the sight of food was making her nauseous.

"I understand, Miss Summer." He paused in eating, and his voice was soft with sympathy. "You're stayin' 'til it's over?"

Summer blinked back the tears and nodded. She was getting more nauseous as she smelled the food.

"I didn't mean to upset you, Miss Summer, I am sorry." Beau's handsome face furrowed with concern.

"Why don't you gentlemen go on with your dinner?" She gulped and attempted to rise. "I—I'm not feeling well."

"Summer?" Father said. She caught the note of command in his voice. How dare she leave the table when he wanted her to stay and entertain his guest?

"Father, I'm suddenly quite ill." She pushed back her chair, and Beau was instantly on his feet to aid her.

"Miss Summer, may I be of service?"

"No, I'll be all right; something I ate, I think."

"Ate?" Father roared, hawklike features crimson. "You haven't taken three bites!"

"Perhaps it was the wine." Before either of the men could say anything else, Summer turned and fled from the dining room, up the stairs to the washbasin in the bathroom. She just barely made it.

Mentally, she began to count up the weeks. Yes, she knew this feeling all too well. She and Iron Knife had made passionate love in late December. This was March. She had to face the fact she had been denying, even to herself. She was pregnant.

* * *

It was a blustery night in late March when Iron Knife slipped through the Denver streets to the newspaper building. In the back office, a single light still burned. He crawled through a window; his moccasins made no more noise than a cougar padding across the floor. A man sat with his back to Iron Knife, reading at a cluttered desk.

"Todd?"

The man started, whirled around, his chair creaking. "Good God, Iron Knife, you scared me out of a year's growth!"

Iron Knife grinned. "Sorry."

Todd gestured. "Come in and sit. I'll get you some coffee." He got up, went over to the potbellied stove, and poured a mug. "It could cost your life to come into town."

Iron Knife sat down, accepted the cup, and warmed his hands around it as he regarded the handsome younger man. "A warrior who does not wish to be seen comes and goes as silent as a ghost."

Todd laughed. "Arrogant and fearless as always." He sipped his own steaming cup. "So just why have you taken such a risk?"

He hesitated, not wanting to admit why he had come all this long way. He looked toward the letter Todd had been reading. "Any—any news from Boston?"

"As a matter of fact, I had just opened this letter from Mother; I seldom hear from her because I don't write back." Todd tipped his chair back and reached for it, frowning.

Iron Knife sipped the hot, savory coffee, watching Todd's hazel eyes. "There's something about Summer Sky?"

"Well, not much; just dull stuff about everyday things in Boston." Todd looked away.

He was hiding something, Iron Knife thought. "I would like to know."

Todd shrugged. "It's just my mother's gossip. She never really liked Summer or her mother; I suppose because they both saw through her."

It was not good manners, but he had to know. Before Todd could react, Iron Knife reached and took the letter from the other's hands. "You try to protect me, my friend?"

Todd frowned. "Don't pay any attention to my mother's opinions; she never knows what she's talking about."

Iron Knife's gaze ran down the letter until he saw Summer's name.

. . . Austin's back on the front with his friend, Custer. Everyone's saying the war should be over in a matter of weeks. I keep hoping Austin can manage to get another leave soon, but I'm not fooling myself; if he does, it will only be because he's still in love with that scandalous Summer. Imagine her coming back bold as brass with three bastard Indian offspring! Her mother's still alive, but just barely. In the meantime, that handsome Beau St. Claire has been seen at that house several times. Officially, he's there to talk business, but he can't fool me! If it were business, he could go to old Silas' office. Silas would probably be thrilled if he could marry Summer off. . . .

Iron Knife felt as if he'd been hit hard in the gut. Very slowly, he laid the letter down on Todd's desk.

"My mother is just a gossipy old biddy," Todd said, grabbing the letter, tearing it up, and tossing it in the wastebasket.

Iron Knife didn't answer. He felt too stunned to move, to think.

"Are you all right?" Todd leaned toward him, looking anxious.

He had been wounded many times in battle. He had survived the Sun Dance, heat, cold and starvation; yet a few words on paper had just destroyed him. In his mind, he saw his woman in the arms of another man, a handsome white man who knew the proper things to say and do to impress a rich, educated girl like Summer. "Do you know this Beau?"

Todd stuck a pencil behind one ear. "I may have met him once or twice when he came to talk business with my father. I think he sold cotton to our fabric mills."

"Is he handsome?"

Todd shrugged. "Some might think so, kind of a dandy, well-dressed and knows the latest dances and gossip among the rich and powerful."

Just the kind of man he was not, Iron Knife thought. He would look like a primitive savage by comparison.

"Summer wouldn't be interested in a man like that." Todd seemed to read his thoughts. "She'd prefer a genuine, sincere type."

Iron Knife looked him in the eye. "She hasn't answered any of my letters or wires."

"Well, no"—Todd shook his head—"but you've got to consider she's dealing with a dying mother and three little children—"

"Maybe back among civilized men, she's decided I'm not the right choice; I always feared this would happen."

"Well, eventually, her mother will die and she'll come back—"

"Will she?" Iron Knife closed his eyes and sighed. "Or will I seem more and more like a distant memory, and she'll decide she should stay in Boston?"

Todd tapped his fingers on his coffee cup. "I don't know what to tell you, friend. I wish I did. Knowing Summer, I figured that with her, love would last a lifetime and that nothing else mattered."

Iron Knife stood up. "I feel that way; I've got to know if she does, too. The longer she's gone, the more likely that she'll never return."

"Life is hard among the Cheyenne," Todd said, "especially with an Indian war going on; you couldn't blame her if she began to think about the luxurious living her father's money could buy. Most women would not be able to resist the temptation to stay back east."

Iron Knife paced the office in an agony of emotion. In his mind, he saw some white man embracing Summer, kissing her. "She said we had a once in a lifetime love."

Todd sighed. "People change, friend, and maybe nothing can be counted on to last a lifetime in this world."

"She could count on me, always. For me, nothing can ever change the way I feel about her."

Todd made a soothing gesture. "There's not much you can do except wait and hope you two can work this thing out if—I mean when—she returns."

"If I were there, I could sway her thoughts by holding her, making love to her; reminding her what we have meant to each other." He went to stare out the window at the cold, dark night. "I will not give her up so easily; I might go to Boston."

"Boston?" Todd stood up so quickly, his chair rattled

on the wooden floor. "Do you know how far it is to Boston?"

"It is another world away"—Iron Knife turned to him—"but I would go anywhere, do anything, rather than lose her without a fight."

Todd ran his hand through his tousled hair. "This is crazy! With all this Indian war, you think a Cheyenne can just get on the nearest train and go off to Boston?"

"I lived among the whites in Texas for five years," Iron Knife said. "I know a little about civilization, and if I had some help—"

"But Boston is a long way! Lots of things could happen or go wrong trying to get there. Even if you made it, there's no guarantee she'd come back with you."

"I'm willing to take the risk." Iron Knife came over to him, blinking as his vision seemed to blur at the thought of losing the woman who was the center of his universe. "I do not know what else to do."

Now it was Todd who paced up and down. "You have no idea what you're taking on trying to get to Boston—"

"I have fought Utes, Pawnees, the U.S. Cavalry, a panther and a bear," Iron Knife said. "I would fight them all again to reclaim Summer Sky."

"A Cheyenne dog soldier on the streets of Boston," Todd said with a shake of his head, "no one will know what to make of it; you might end up arrested or shot by the police or some soldier."

"I would risk that, rather than lose her," he argued stubbornly.

"Silas Van Schuyler would try to have you thrown in jail if he heard you were coming."

"If no one knows, he wouldn't be able to stop me."

"You'd just show up at Summer's house as a surprise?" He paused and frowned. "It is the craziest idea I ever heard and dangerous. Anything could happen to you. No one would be concerned or know if you should disappear, go to jail or be killed by soldiers or the police."

"I only want to see her, have her tell me with her own lips our love was a lie," Iron Knife said. "If you won't help me, I'll do the best I can."

Todd sighed. "If I could get away from the paper right now, I'd go with you; but with the war and the Indian trouble, we have a difficult time now getting the paper out, so I can't leave."

"I am not afraid to try the long trip alone," Iron Knife said.

"I don't imagine anything scares you," Todd said, and put his hand on his friend's shoulder. "Let me give it some thought on the best way to proceed; we'll stay in touch through Cherokee Evans. If you feel you have to go to Boston, you might be able to wear Cherokee's clothes. He's about your size or I'll try to buy some in your size."

"You would dress me like a white man?" The idea of the tight clothing did not appeal to him. "You would tie a bright rag around my neck?"

Todd laughed. "A necktie is a pretty silly thing when I think about it, but yes, we'd have to dress you like a white man. After all, you're halfwhite; if you dressed Western style with boots, maybe no one would notice you."

"Not cut my hair." Iron Knife shook his head.

"No, we could put it up under a Western hat, but you may have to take your earring and bone whistle off for a while. Let's not rush into this drastic step yet. Wait a few more weeks and see if you get a letter, and in the meantime, I'll send Summer a wire myself; see if I can find out anything. I'll send word."

"Thank you, my friend."

They shook hands solemnly, and Iron Knife turned toward the window. "Goodbye for now." Then as noiseless as a whisper, he slipped out the window and into the cold night air.

Chapter Fifteen

So cold for the first week of April. Shawn O'Bannion stood in the Boston train station looking around. He had been back to this city only one time since he had left as a young man many years ago. He had returned once he was rich to reclaim the woman he loved, but he was too late; forever too late. He would not think about that now.

Turning up his coat collar against the raw wind, he hailed a carriage outside the station. The cold rain was turning into sleet and snow as darkness fell, and the raw wind cut right through him. He stood under a street lamp, feeling that he was reliving that long-ago night all over again. The unkempt cabbie reined in, then climbed down to open the carriage door.

"Take me to a flower shop," Shawn ordered.

"A flower shop? You must be jokin'! Shops will be closed at this hour, mister."

"There's a good tip in it for you, my man, should you find me one that's open."

Shawn felt the cabbie assessing his fine clothes and the diamond stickpin in his necktie. "Get in, then; me thinks one run by a pair o' sisters might still be open."

"Good enough." Shawn watched the man as he looked around for luggage. "There isn't any. I plan to leave out again tonight." There was, after all, nothing to stay for. He thought about the letter in his pocket that had been gathering dust for weeks at the small country post office, but the Yankees had just begun releasing their prisoners. With his wounded right hand, Shawn was finished as a soldier; and besides, the war would be ending any day now. He only hoped he wasn't too late on his quest.

Shawn got in and leaned back against the seat with a sigh. It was as cold as an English landlord's heart, he thought, remembering the peasants being thrown off their lands as the potato crops failed. Shawn was lucky; he had made it to America, but millions of others had starved to death.

He looked out the window at familiar sights as the carriage clopped along. Each brought back a memory, and he was almost sorry he had come. Yet if she still breathed, he had to see her one more time; he loved her so. He reached in his coat for the reassuring feel of the pistol. With his crippled and weakened fingers, he couldn't handle a saber, but he might be able to pull a trigger.

The carriage pulled up before a small shop. The driver leaned in the window. "Here 'tis, mister, shall I wait? Looks closed."

"Aye, wait; perhaps they will open for me." He stepped from the carriage. Around him, in the dark chill night, snow was falling again. So cold for early April, he thought. Hadn't it been an unseasonably cold April night that he had waited under a street lamp in vain so many years ago?

Osgoode Sisters' Flowers. The lights of the shop reflected off the frozen puddles of the road. The carriage horse's steamy breath floated on the cold air. Shawn went to the shop door, and it jangled as he started in.

"I'm sorry, we're just closing, sir." A rather prim girl

who might have been in her mid-twenties came out of
the back room shaking her head.

"Oh, please, miss, I'm here to pick up an order." He
saw her hesitate. "I tip well."

"I don't know. . . ." She seemed to assess his fine
coat, then stepped back to let him enter. He sized her up
even as a slightly younger version of her came out of
the back room. Genteel sisters down on their luck and
reduced to working in a shop, he thought. "I need a
bouquet of roses," he said, looking about the shop, "a
big bouquet."

"Impossible," the younger one sniffed. "Now, we
might have a few mums or daisies in the greenhouse."

However, he was already brushing past her toward
two giant bouquets in vases on the counter. "This is
what I had in mind; and just the colors she loved, too,
deep burgundy and pink." He buried his face in the
roses, took a deep breath. Whenever he smelled the fra-
grance of roses, he would always think of the beautiful
young girl he had loved so very long ago.

"Impossible!" the older one said. "The Griswold
coachman is due any moment to pick those bouquets up
for the lady's evening dinner dance."

Shawn pulled out his wallet. "Surely Mrs. Griswold
can get by with a bouquet of roses and one of daisies or
such."

"We can't do that," the younger sister protested.
"She'll think those are too common for such a lavish
party, and that large family's so prominent and good
customers."

He was very weary and heartsick. Shawn threw down
a handful of twenty-dollar gold pieces. "That should
pay for the bouquet many times over."

"Yes, but—"

"I am taking these flowers to a dying sweetheart,"
Shawn said softly, "and I will have them if I have to

take them at gunpoint." He laid the pistol next to the money.

The two looked at him with wide eyes, then at each other. No doubt they thought him crazed, but he was past caring. He didn't even mind if they called the police—as long as the officers didn't get there in time to stop him from seeing Priscilla.

The younger lady wrung her hands. "Sister, for that much money, don't you think we could rearrange Mrs. Griswold's flowers into mixed bouquets so the gentleman could have the roses?"

The other one stared at the pistol. "I—I believe so."

"Good lasses." Shawn breathed a sigh of relief, slipped the gun in his pocket, and watched the older one take the bouquet from its vase, then wrap it in tissue paper. "One thing more; I'd like one yellow rose in the center, if you please."

"One yellow one in a center of pink and burgundy roses? It won't look very artistic—"

"Damn artistic, I said one yellow rose."

Both women looked at him as if they were dealing with a madman. "Y—yes, of course."

He watched them place one yellow rose in the center of the bouquet, then hand it to him. His eyes misted, and he had to blink as he turned to go out in the cold. A yellow rose. It was their secret; a yellow rose for remembrance. He hoped he wasn't arriving in Boston so late he would end up placing it on her grave.

Shawn hunched his shoulders against the cold and went back out to the carriage. To the cabbie, Shawn said, "Do you know the Van Schuyler mansion?"

"Who don't?" The driver shrugged. "Rich one, he is; big house, everything money can buy, he's got."

Including the woman I love, Shawn thought bitterly as he said, "Take me there."

He got in and the carriage pulled away. Shawn felt

for the pistol in his pocket with his crippled hand, buried his face in the roses. The scent reminded him of a warm summer night a long, long time ago. He had made love to her in the garden with the roses dropping their spent petals on their naked skin; so very young and he had been so very poor. He was the Blackledges' gardener, and she was a blue-blooded aristocrat from the best section of Boston. He had loved her more than life itself, but she had not loved him enough.

The snow was falling faster and thicker now, just like that night when they had arranged to meet and run away. Shawn would always remember the cold and how it had bitten into him as he stood under the street lamp outside her father's home, waiting. Waiting. Waiting. . . . He didn't know how many hours he had stood there before he realized she had changed her mind and wasn't coming.

As he had walked away into the darkness, he had vowed that night he would make money, lots of money! He wasn't sure how, but by Saint Patrick, he would do it! Then he would come back all dressed fine and with a good carriage, fling the gold down before her father. *I've come for Priscilla,* he would say. *I'm not just a poor Mick of a gardener anymore.*

It had taken him longer to get rich than he had hoped it would. Shawn had drifted around at first, trying to decide what he could do to gain wealth. Then he'd heard rumors of gold in California. He had land staked and claimed during the big rush to Sutter's Mill. Finally Shawn had gold nuggets piled in several banks. His next task had been to build a castle to bring his princess home to, something more grand than the home of her father. So Shawn had found his way to the bountiful rolling country of Tennessee and built a plantation that was sumptuous beyond his wildest dreams: Shannon Place. Shannon Place on the rolling Mississippi River, so much like the wide Shannon River in Ireland. He had his castle, Shannon Place.

Then he'd been ready to claim his bride. It had been at least ten years. He hadn't wanted to think that she might not have waited. Even though he was a good Catholic, he'd thought that if she had married, he might steal her away and take her with him.

"Here we are, mister." The driver leaned in the window. "Are the Van Schuylers expectin' you?"

"Hmm," Shawn said, and stepped out, still clutching his bouquet. He reached to pay the driver.

"Shall I wait, mister?"

Shawn shook his head. "I—I don't know how long I'll be." *Or even if I'll get in,* he thought.

Shawn stared at the big, imposing mansion with all its lights ablaze as the carriage clopped away into the cold darkness. Aye, he had been here that one time. Even now, it brought him pain. He had come to reclaim the woman he loved, and a servant at the old Blackledge home had taken pity on him, directed him to the new Van Schuyler mansion. It was an unseasonably warm afternoon that time.

He had stood here before this mansion just as he was doing now; except it had been a Sunday. While he stood there that long-ago day staring down the drive, he had seen a fine barouche coming out and had hidden behind some shrubbery to watch. The big iron gates had opened, and a pair of high-stepping grays in a fine black harness studded with silver pulled the red-wheeled open carriage with its plush scarlet seats. The driver wore the best livery and snapped his whip.

Shawn felt his heart skip a beat. There were four passengers, a stern older man with hawklike features, whom he recognized as Silas Van Schuyler, and a beautiful blond woman in a bonnet with roses on the brim. She looked like a garden in her flowered fine dress.

Priscilla. He had to force himself not to run after the carriage, calling her name. Children. There was a little boy and girl about nine or ten years old. Twins maybe, for they looked alike and they were as fair and blue-eyed as his Priscilla.

Children. Somehow, he hadn't thought about children. How could he take their mother away? In his pain, Shawn had come out from behind the shrubbery, staring after the coach.

Silas saw him; he knew that immediately from the expression of hatred on the other man's face. He glared at Shawn until the coach was lost from sight over a hill.

Shawn slumped against the fancy iron gate and shook. He had returned for Priscilla, and she was as beautiful as he remembered, maybe even more so. Now he had money to give her father, a mansion to house his princess, and he could not take her because she had children. Shawn's gold might as well have been pebbles. He had come too late—too late.

That night, Shawn had gotten roaring drunk, gone back to Tennessee and married an elegant, blue-blooded beauty who looked amazingly like Priscilla with her blond hair and blue eyes. But she wasn't Priscilla, and Shawn had to face the fact that Savannah St. Claire had never loved him; she had married him for the same reason Priscilla had married Silas: money. Her aristocratic Southern family had gone through all their holdings and needed money; otherwise, the snooty Savannah would have disdained the common Irish gardener with his new wealth. She told him that once in a terrible quarrel. That was all right, Shawn thought now with a sigh; he didn't love Savannah either, even though they had a young son. He had married her because she was everything Priscilla was; but she was not Priscilla.

The cold wind blew through him again, and Shawn realized he had been standing for some time in front of the big iron gates. Clutching his bouquet of roses, he went through the gate and up the drive to the imposing entrance. He paused on the step before ringing the bell, then felt to make sure he had the pistol. He would see Priscilla one more time even if he had to kill Silas Van Schuyler to do it!

Silas stood staring into the library fireplace. Behind him, he heard Angela twist in her chair and sigh.

"Father, you know she will die tonight, don't you?"

He turned and looked at his pretty child sitting in an overstuffed chair, stroking her black cat. No, she was no longer a child; somehow, the years had gotten away from him. She seemed so strange, or was it the witches on Priscilla's side of the family? "We've been expecting your mother to die for months; what makes you think it will be tonight?"

Angela shrugged and looked at him with eyes as cold and pale blue as his own. "It will happen at almost precisely nine o'clock."

Silas snorted and reached for his glass of port on the mantel. "Then she'd better hurry."

After all these weeks, he was too mentally worn out to go rushing up the stairs where Dr. Morgan and Summer were by his wife's bedside. He listened to the wind rattle the windows as if something dark and unnamed prowled around the mansion like a thief, wanting to get in. Was it coming for Priscilla? She hated cold weather; it killed her damned roses every year.

Roses. He turned and looked at Angela again, remembering. Once he had adored Priscilla; maybe he still did. But soon after the wedding, he had realized she had only married him for his money to rescue her aristocratic parents, who had fallen on hard times. She had let him know he could have her body, but never her heart; that belonged to Shawn O'Bannion.

A damned Mick; an Irish dirt grubber. Shawn O'Bannion. Even now, when he thought of him, a rage came over Silas. The whole damned house was a shrine to him and his damned roses. Silas sipped his port and stared into the flames. Why had he thought that once he married the proud beauty, he could love her enough, give her enough that she would warm toward him and forget that lowly immigrant? It hadn't happened. Silas kept thinking that in time. . . . It hadn't happened. After those first few official marriage couplings, Priscilla had always locked her door against him.

Years passed. Priscilla had produced twins, Summer and David. The Irishman had long ago gone away and been swallowed up by this giant country. Silas dared hope that maybe someday, Priscilla would forget him, and certainly as the decade passed, he breathed easier, thinking Shawn was surely dead or had at least forgotten about her.

Then one unseasonably warm Sunday afternoon, Silas had taken his family for a carriage ride. Leaving the estate grounds, he saw a figure lurking in the shrubbery. He recognized him instantly, even though the man had aged in ten years: Shawn O'Bannion. So he had returned for her!

That night, Silas had been in a rage of jealous frustration and had gotten roaring drunk. More than ten years Priscilla Blackledge had been his wife, and things were no better between them. Now Shawn O'Bannion was in town. Who knew if he would rendezvous with Priscilla, steal her away, make Silas the laughing stock of all Boston society? Already he seemed to hear ladies' delighted giggles behind their fans: . . . *did you hear that rich Silas Van Schuyler's wife ran off with a gardener?*

That night, he had broken down her door and raped

Priscilla most violently out of sheer fury and frustration. Angela had been the result. At least with her belly swollen big, Silas had not worried that his wife would run away with her lover. They had never spoken of that night, but Silas had never again been in his wife's bed. He had put his energy into making money, building a financial empire; Priscilla had lost herself in her rose garden, her laudanum habit and an ocean of sherry.

The big clock out in the hall chimed, and Silas came back to the present as he pulled out his watch. "Eight-thirty," he said to no one in particular, "has run perfectly all these years."

"But it will stop in thirty minutes," Angela said matter-of-factly, "and it will never run again."

He turned and looked at her. "Not likely! That clock has run day in and day out for more than a quarter of a century."

"But it will stop thirty minutes from now." Her cold eyes seemed to be calmly stating a fact.

"You think you can always see the future?"

"Sometimes." She stroked her cat. Such a cold personality and the one most like himself; too bad she was a girl. Angela had that hard streak that would have made her the perfect heir to take over his kingdom.

The snow blew against the windows. Would tonight really be the night Priscilla died? There had been so many false alarms, and Silas was physically drained by all this waiting. Even Dr. Morgan had said she should have been gone a long time ago; she was holding on by sheer force of will. What was it she waited for?

The doorbell rang, and he heard Evans going to answer it. "Ye Gods," he muttered, "who would be out in this weather at this time of night?"

"The one she's been waiting for," Angela said without changing her expression.

A chill ran right up Silas' back. He paused with the drink halfway to his lips and scowled at her. "Who?"

Angela shrugged and stroked the black cat. "I don't know; but you will."

Before he could say anything else, Evans came to the door. "Beg pardon for disturbing you, sir, but there's someone here to see Mrs. Van Schuyler."

Silas glanced toward Angela, who smiled slightly. Who was it? Death? He had a sudden vision of the grim reaper with a grinning skull's face and a long black robe standing in the front hall. "Impossible! Did you explain that my wife is bedridden, dying?"

The butler gestured helplessly. "I tried, sir, but he won't take no for an answer! Shall I send for the police?"

A man was pushing past the butler, a tall, handsome man with gray-streaked black hair and green eyes. Snowflakes clung to the wool of his fine topcoat, and in his arms, he carried a large bouquet of roses. "Aye, you may call the police, but I will see her, Silas, and I'm armed. I will kill whoever stands in my way!"

Shawn O'Bannion. Silas dropped his glass of port. The sound of the glass shattering echoed loud in the silence. A rage began to build in him. He wanted to attack the man with both fists, but the other looked grim and equally determined. "You dare to come into my house with my wife dying upstairs?"

"You've had her all these years; I only want to see her one more time."

The years had treated Shawn kindly, Silas thought; except for the gray in his hair, and the fine lines around his expressive eyes, he was still handsome and lean. Silas smiled in triumph. "You can't take her with you if that's why you came; she's dying."

And now Shawn smiled sadly. "Aye, I know. I feel sorry for you, Silas. Something about you tells me you never possessed her; not really. I feel very, very sorry for you." He turned and left the doorway. Silas heard his footsteps going up the stairs. For the first time since the night he had raped Priscilla, he leaned against the mantel and wept for all the wasted, bitter empty years.

Summer wound the music box and placed it on Priscilla's pillow again, then looked around at Dr. Morgan and Mrs. O'Malley as the tune began to play. "It seems to soothe her somehow."

Dr. Morgan sighed. "It doesn't matter; although I'm not sure she hears it. I think she's in a coma."

"Oh, she hears it," Summer said. "Her expression changes when she hears the music, almost as if she were remembering happier times."

Dr. Morgan took off his stethoscope and shook his head. "I don't know what's keeping her here; sheer willpower, maybe. By all rights, she should have been dead months ago."

Mrs. O'Malley wiped her eyes. "Angela says she's waiting for someone."

The three of them looked at each other. Summer searched her mind. Everyone had been to her bedside to say goodbye, although half the time, her mother didn't seem to recognize them. One more name crossed her mind, and then she bit her lip. Maybe that man had never gotten the letter, or didn't care enough to come. Maybe her mother had even forgotten him—that lost love. It had been a rash act on Summer's part to write him; her father would be furious if he knew.

. . . *'Tis the last rose of summer, left blooming alone, all her lovely companions are faded and gone; I'll not leave you, lone one to pine on your stem, where the lovely are sleeping, go sleep you with them.* . . . It had gradually run down. The silence seemed almost to shout. Summer looked at the music box, then toward the window. It was snowing, such a bad, miserable night for early April. Priscilla had hated cold weather; it killed her flowers.

She heard the slightly ajar door creak and turned as a man came in.

"I followed the music," he said. "I'm—"

"I know who you are," Summer said, and she smiled with relief. "Oh, I knew you from her description. Come in, but don't expect much; she's in a coma."

He came to the bedside, so handsome and tall, snow-flakes still clinging to his coat. The armful of roses scented the room until abruptly it smelled like a summer night in a garden.

Summer stepped away from the bed so he could come closer. He hesitated; then hands trembling, he laid the armful of roses on Priscilla's pillow next to her face, staring down at her. "Priscilla? Priscilla, my love, it's Shawn; can you hear me? I've come back, just like I always said I would. I brought you roses, me darlin', pink and burgundy, but with one yellow rose for remembrance."

He reached over, and Summer noted that his hands trembled as he wound the music box, opened it and it began to play. "Remember, darlin'? I didn't think you'd save my little gift all these years. Remember that summer night in your father's garden?"

Summer could only imagine what had happened that warm night. She blinked rapidly to keep the tears back. This was no time to break down.

As the tune played, Shawn took Priscilla's frail hand between his two big ones and talked earnestly to her in a whisper as if the two were alone. The whole room smelled of roses.

Gradually, Priscilla's eyes opened, and she smiled.

"Priscilla? It's Shawn. Do you know me, love?"

* * *

Priscilla looked around the room. Slowly, things came into focus. Who were all these people? The white-haired man and the plump woman seemed vaguely familiar, and that blond girl standing at the foot of the bed with tears running down her face looked exactly like herself. Maybe she was looking into a mirror.

Roses. She smelled roses; and her favorite tune was playing somewhere. Such memories it brought back. She closed her eyes. Once again she was in her father's garden, lying under the rose bushes with a young man not much older than herself. Petals fell on their faces as they pledged eternal love. However, the time came when she had to make a choice, and she had made the wrong one. She had always hoped she would get a second chance. Oh, all these long, long years she had prayed for it! So many times people made the wrong choice and wanted to go back and do it again, correct that mistake.

A voice seemed to be coming to her from a very great distance. "Priscilla, it's Shawn. Do you know me, love?"

She opened her eyes again and tried to focus her vision on a handsome older man who held her hand and spoke earnestly to her. No, it couldn't be Shawn; although there was a resemblance, so it might be Shawn's father. Her Shawn was young, not more than nineteen or twenty, while this man must be almost fifty with gray streaks in his hair.

"Priscilla?"

No, he couldn't be Shawn, although he certainly sounded like him. Perhaps someone was playing a trick on her. Oh, where had all the years gone? Could a quarter of a century really have slipped away? She turned her head and looked toward the door. Yes, it was there, waiting.

Shawn's voice. "What is she looking for?"

"Her suitcase," the girl who looked like her said. "We don't know why; but she keeps packing up to leave, and no one knows where she thinks she's going."

Of course no one knew; it was a secret between Priscilla and her lover. She smiled and managed to turn her head to look out the window. It was snowing outside, the flakes white against the darkness of the night. Yes, she needed that suitcase; tonight she was running away with Shawn O'Bannion, defying her father, who wanted her to marry that brash Silas Van Schuyler.

She closed her eyes, took a deep breath of the scent of roses and listened to the music. She was ready to go; she had only been lingering to make sure he would be there waiting. For a long moment, she was not sure she could take another breath; it was so difficult.

"Priscilla, I've come; I—I always loved you so." His voice was soft and so familiar, but he sounded as if he were crying. The hand gripping hers felt so comforting. She was scared; she didn't want to go alone into the cold night.

"I knew you would come," she whispered. "I've waited so long."

"What did she say?" the girl who looked like her asked.

No one answered, but Priscilla could hear someone weeping softly. Snowing outside. Her bag was packed. Shawn would be waiting under the street lamp outside her father's house. Tonight they would run away together and never, never be separated again. Once before she had faced this choice and had hesitated; too weak, too scared to pick up that suitcase and go down to him, turn her back on the life she had. As clear as yesterday, she remembered standing at her upstairs bedroom window looking down at the young man under the street lamp. He had stood there for hours, his shadow distorted against the white snow. Finally, he had seemed to realize that she had made her choice; she wasn't coming. Shoulders slumped, her lover had turned and trudged away into the darkness.

She had never told anyone, not even her maid, about the nightmares; why she drank. Almost every night she had a dream where she relived that scene over and over and over. In her tormented sleep, she changed her mind, grabbed her bag and ran down the stairs and out into the cold, crying his name and looking for him. She ran and ran through the snow, the cold wind cutting into her face, but the streets were dark and deserted; he was nowhere to be found, and she was so alone and afraid. She would wake up sobbing, sit up in bed and know she was in Silas Van Schuyler's big home and she had thrown away her chance to have the man she loved.

Tonight was going to be different; she knew it somehow. Tonight that young man from her past would be waiting to welcome her. She had held on, even though it was so very hard, until he could come.

She took a breath, forgot to breath, struggled for another. That hand held on to hers, and Shawn's dear voice whispered, "It's all right, Priscilla; I'm here. You're not alone. You hear me, love, everything's all right now."

Permission. She had permission to leave. The dream began again, just as it always did. It seemed she was picking up her suitcase and staring out at the storm. She was eighteen years old, and she was supposed to marry that older man her father had chosen. She wanted a chance to change that decision she had made.

A poem. Bits and pieces of a favorite poem came to her: . . . *God pity them both and pity us all who vainly*

*the dreams of youth recall, for of all the words of tongue
or pen; the saddest are these: it might have been. . . .*

Oh, no, she was getting a second chance to right
things. Once again she was running down the snowy
street with her suitcase, calling his name, so alone, so
afraid in the deserted darkness as she searched the shadows for him. Oh, surely this time. . . .

The doctor's voice: "I think she's going now."

Going? Of course she was going; how could these
people be so stupid? She wouldn't even attempt to explain. She opened her eyes and saw the plump man with
the stethoscope standing near the foot of her bed. Who
was that man and how had he gotten into her dream?
Women were crying in the background. Priscilla closed
her eyes again, annoyed. How could they be so selfish
and not want her to leave when she had waited so very
long for this moment?

She smelled roses and heard a music box playing.
Roses in the wintertime? Now she was on the sidewalk
again, so alone and afraid. *Shawn . . . where are you?
I've looked and looked. . . .*

"I'm here, Priscilla." Yes, that familiar voice and his
hand on hers. Why did he sound as if he were crying?
Why, joy, of course; sheer joy. All these years and finally the two young lovers were going to be reunited.
Yellow roses for remembrance.

She had waited for this moment all this time, and just
as she had always dreamed, he had come back. She was
out in the darkness searching, but his hand was holding
hers and his dear voice whispered that he loved her.
This dream was going to end differently tonight. Tonight she wouldn't wake up weeping in a big empty bed
because she had searched and searched and couldn't
find him.

Shawn? She whispered his name in her mind because
it took too much effort now to say it. *Shawn?* It seemed

to echo around her as if she were running down the deserted dark street through the snow calling his name. *Shawn? Oh, wait for me, I've changed my mind! Can't we go back a quarter of a century and do this all over again? Shawn?*

And abruptly, he seemed to step out of the shadows of the buildings, and he was twenty years old and he loved her. *Priscilla? I thought at first you weren't coming.*

She was eighteen years old with her whole life ahead of her all new and fresh and not used up. *I love you, Shawn O'Bannion, and I have waited all these years for you.* She flung herself into his arms, and he held her close and kissed her just as all the times he had kissed her in her memory. Oh, she had waited so very long for this reunion. Suddenly it was summer again, and he was kissing her; their music box was playing, and she smelled roses ... roses ... roses. ...

"She's gone." Summer watched Dr. Morgan lean over her mother's frail form, then step back. "I'm sorry."

For a moment, Summer felt nothing at all as the big grandfather clock downstairs began to boom out the hour. She had been watching her mother fighting for breath these last few minutes. Now she felt unusually calm and at peace. After all these weeks, it was finally over. She came to the bedside and saw the slight smile on Priscilla's features. She looked happy for the first time that Summer could remember.

Shawn O'Bannion hid his face against the coverlet, and his shoulders shook. Summer reached out and put her hand on his shoulder. "It was you," she said, "she was waiting for you."

He seemed to pull himself together, stood up very slowly, and crossed himself, looking down at Priscilla's still form. "I wonder what it was she experienced those last few seconds?"

"I suppose we'll never know until we experience it ourselves." Summer was suddenly weary. She didn't feel sadness or loss, only exhaustion and relief that it was finally over. She looked toward the suitcase and wondered why Priscilla had kept it packed? Where did the frail invalid think she might be going? Perhaps that was one mystery they would never solve, and maybe it didn't matter.

She was too numb and too ill herself to feel much of anything. She was vaguely aware that Mrs. O'Malley crossed herself and sobbed as she moved to cover the mirrors in the room.

Dr. Morgan said, "My deepest sympathy; I'll take care of things. Do you want to be the one to tell your father?"

Father. Oh, yes, there were others outside this room. For a few moments, everything else had ceased to exist.

Shawn straightened his shoulders and cleared his throat. "Thank you for contacting me so I could get here in time."

"Thank you for coming," Summer whispered, "and giving her permission to go."

His green eyes welled over again. "You might have been our daughter, if only ... well, those are the two saddest words in any language, aren't they?" He thought a moment. "And the four saddest are: 'it might have been.' "

He had regrets, too, Summer thought. She reached to hand him the music box. "She would want you to have this. I'm so glad you got here in time."

He clutched it to him like a drowning man. "I—I've made a mess of my life, always comparing every woman I met to Priscilla, putting her memory on a pedestal. In my mind, she became the most beautiful, most desirable prize to be won in this whole world." He looked toward the bed and sighed. "Somehow, I expected her to look just as she had all those many years ago."

"Perhaps she thought the same," Summer said, "both of you trying to hang on to a moment frozen for eternity in your past." She put her hand on his arm, felt him trembling.

"Such a damned shame," he murmured again, and she was not sure if he spoke to her or himself, "married a girl just because she looked like Priscilla, then hated her because she wasn't. No other woman could live up to that first love's memory; that once in a lifetime love."

Summer felt tears come to her eyes. A once in a lifetime love. Where was Iron Knife tonight? She felt ill and lonely and sad. If she let herself, she could dissolve into hysterics, and there were things to be done; there were always things to be done when someone died. "Do you need me to see you out?"

Shawn took a long look at her. She might have been his daughter if Priscilla had made a different decision. He shook his head. "No, I—I'll be okay."

A burden seemed to have been lifted off his shoulders. Still clutching the music box, he went down the stairs. *Savannah.* He hadn't done right by his wife; he realized that now. He had not loved the spoiled blond beauty; he had married her because she looked like Priscilla. Maybe they could yet make a fresh start; give the marriage a second chance. Why, he'd even be polite to her brother, Beau, who was such a scheming ne'er-do-well. That rascal had had free rein with Shawn's wealth and plantation these past four years; but he'd overlook that for Savannah's sake. Yes, Shawn was willing to try again if Savannah was. He paused in the hallway and stared at the big grandfather clock. Strange, it had stopped; the pendulum was still.

A young girl who looked like Summer came out of the library carrying a black cat, paused, and stared at him. "She's dead, isn't she?"

Such strange eyes—blue and cold as a glacier—but such a beauty. He tried to think of a way to soften the blow; no words came. Shawn just nodded.

"I knew it"—the girl smiled ever so slightly—"I knew the moment it happened."

"How—how did you know?"

She shrugged. "There was a rush of wind and the flames in the fire flickered. The clock stopped in mid-chime." She glanced up at it. "It won't ever run again."

There was something eerie about this child who seemed to have her mother's looks and her father's hardness. Without thinking, Shawn crossed himself with his free hand. "Tell your father I'm sorry. We will never meet again."

He turned and went to the big front door where the butler waited. Already servants were scurrying through the house covering mirrors, doing whatever needed to be done. Shawn went out the door into the cold. He stood there a long moment before he started down the drive. The wind bit into his face, and the frozen snow crunched beneath his boots. He at least had her music box, but Silas had her children. The man was lucky in more ways than one; Shawn had fully intended to kill Silas tonight as he left the mansion. Now he paused out on the vast lawns, took out his handgun and threw it as hard as he could with his crippled hand, watching with satisfaction as it disappeared into the shrubbery.

Another chance. Maybe, even though they had made such a mess of their lives, he and Savannah and their young son could start over, find a little happiness. Shawn vowed at that moment that he was going to return to Shannon Place and talk to his wife; *really* talk to her. Maybe they could make a fresh start. What a fool he had been to be in love with a dream all these empty years.

He crossed himself and felt at peace for the first time in a long, long time as he turned and walked away from the mansion, hailing a hansom cab to take him to the station.

Chapter Sixteen

They had buried Priscilla at Mount Auburn, the fashionable cemetery that was so innovative because of its ornate monuments and grounds. It was almost like a lovely park, sharp contrast to the former grim church graveyards. The family was in mourning, wearing black and seeing few visitors. However, within a couple of days, Silas had soon returned to his business duties.

Summer had planned to return west now that Priscilla was dead. However, she felt much too ill to travel, and she hadn't heard anything from Iron Knife, despite her letters and wires. Evidently, that part of her life was over. She waited until a couple of days after the funeral while Father sat reading his newspaper after breakfast to decide to tell him about the coming baby.

"Ye Gods, it's about time the war ended." Silas smiled. "Lee has just surrendered! Custer was right in there for the kill! General Sheridan was so pleased, it says he gave Custer the table on which the surrender was written for his wife, Libby." He leaned back in his chair. "Now David and Austin may be coming home. Elizabeth Shaw says Austin is still smitten with you, despite all the half-breed children."

She decided to ignore that. Outside in the cool morning, the laughter of her children playing with Mrs.

O'Malley in attendance drifted through the windows. "It is wonderful it's over, isn't it? No more killing."

Father looked blank a moment, shrugged. "Oh, that, too, I suppose. I was thinking of the increased markets and all the money to be made selling supplies to rebuild the South."

"Father." She took a deep breath for courage, then plunged on, "You—you know I haven't been feeling well lately."

"I was afraid you might have caught something from your mother," he muttered and went back to his newspaper.

"Father, we need to talk."

"Hmm," he grunted and hid himself behind his paper. Silas Van Schuyler never really communicated with his family, she thought, not in all these years. He talked about business; they listened. No conversation went any deeper than that unless he was chiding Priscilla about her drinking.

"Father, there's something I need to tell you." It took real courage to tackle the subject again. *I must tell him I am expecting another child, but he will be furious.* Everyone had always been afraid of Father's wrath.

"Beau St. Claire has asked permission to call on you."

"With Mother just dead, it isn't appropriate."

"Quite so," Silas agreed, and appeared to be thinking aloud. "Austin's almost as soft as David; neither one of them could run my empire. Now Beau might be able to until little Lance grew up and took over."

"My son?" The idea surprised and horrified her.

"Why not?" Silas' cold blue eyes gleamed. "He's smart and he seems to like business. If you gave him the choice, do you think he'd rather be living in a tipi eating half-cooked meat and hunkering over a fire like a savage?"

"He belongs with his family; he's only a little boy."

He seemed to realize he had pushed her too far. "You're right, my dear. I was only pointing out that should you decide to remain in Boston, I can offer your children every advantage."

Hadn't they had this conversation already? "Angela won't like your idea; she hopes to run your empire herself someday."

"She's enough like me to do it, too, except she's a girl and so she can never make her mark in business, no matter how ambitious she is."

More and more, Summer was beginning to feel like her mother, trapped in this house by circumstances she couldn't control. How long could she hide her pregnancy before it was noticed if she couldn't get the courage to tell Father? Yet how could she return to Colorado if she wasn't certain Iron Knife wanted her? She was no longer sure how she felt about him. On the other hand, as poorly as she felt, even if Iron Knife wanted her, she was too ill to make the long trip. What on earth was she to do?

"Father, we must talk," she said again. Her heart began to hammer as it always did when she had to confront him.

"Damn it, you keep saying that, but you don't say anything!" Father roared. "Now, if you're upset because I promised Lance a new pony and fancy red-wheeled cart, I'll have you know, it's my money and I—"

"No, it's not that; I didn't even know about the pony."

"Well, out with it then!" He glowered at her.

Summer took a deep breath for courage. All these years he had bullied Mother, and mostly, no one had stood up to him, demanded he stop. She felt deeply ashamed of that now; Mother was such a pathetic thing who had made such an easy target for his venom.

"Well?"

It was so quiet, she could hear birds chirping outside the window. There was no easy way to do this except blurt it out. "I—I'm expecting another baby."

Silas looked at her a long moment as if he didn't comprehend; then his face became mottled with anger as he stood up. "Ye Gods!" Silas put both hands to his head and paced the floor. "Who is this villain? Austin? Beau St. Claire? To think I trusted both of them—"

"Father, don't be ridiculous; it's Iron Knife."

That put him into a fresh tirade of swearing as he paced. "Oh, isn't this a pretty kettle of fish now? Three bastard children now and another—"

"They are not bastards!" Summer's temper rose, and her voice did, too. Silas might bully her, but she would go toe-to-toe with him for her children. "We were married in a Cheyenne ceremony."

"Wonderful!" He paused and glared at her, his words cold with sarcasm. "When is this blessed event due?"

"September."

"Can't you just see that in the *Boston Sun?* 'Mister Silas Van Schuyler, the eminent financier and social leader, announces his daughter's latest child by a savage who paid many ponies for her!' "

"I don't have to stay and listen to this!" She was raging and brave now that he had dared to attack her man and her children. From outside, she heard the wail of a child and the noise of Lance and Storm arguing. It sounded as if they were fighting over a toy. Lance would try to negotiate and bargain; Storm Gathering would sock his brother in the eye and take it.

"Excuse me, Father, my children need me. We'll talk later." Summer stalked out and went outside to settle the dispute. At least now she no longer had to dread telling him. The next move was up to him.

Silas lit a cigar and poured himself a glass of brandy.

Dr. Morgan had warned him that someday he might have a stroke if he didn't do a better job of controlling his rage. He mulled over Summer's unwelcome news. Ye Gods, now what was he to do? All those plans he'd had for marrying her off to either Austin or Beau were shot to hell. Then again, maybe not. Silas smiled and took a deep puff from the expensive cheroot and savored the taste of the brandy. Obviously, as badly as Summer felt, she wasn't going anywhere for a while, which gave him an even longer time to plot. This new turn might even help his plans for his grandson.

Silas stared out the window at the bare dirt where the rose garden used to be. Immediately after the funeral, he had ordered it destroyed and had had the pleasure of being there to watch it happen. Cold, calculated action, that's what always paid off. Tomorrow, he would force himself to apologize to Summer, be kind and sympathetic. Maybe this latest news wasn't a problem, but an opportunity instead. This new child might be a handsome, white-skinned little grandson like Lance, and that would give Silas two heirs.

Time. Time was on Silas' side. By next autumn, Summer could be interested enough in Beau or Austin to stay, and that savage might be dead or have another woman in his tipi. If Beau was loathe to take on a woman with four children, Silas would give him a partnership, or offer to raise the children—at least the white ones.

Yes, this might work out fine after all. Silas sipped his brandy and willed himself to cool his rage. A smart businessman always figured the angles and how to work them to his own advantage. Now maybe it was time to send that final telegram that would end this relationship between the daughter and that savage. Silas had lost Priscilla, but he damned well didn't intend to lose Summer and her children!

* * *

Summer heard the doorbell ring and leaned over the upstairs bannister, listening to the butler answer it. Who could that be? In mourning as they were, she certainly wasn't expecting any company. Father was at his office and had been very kind to her since that initial blow-up yesterday. In fact, he had even apologized to her this morning before he went to the office. Maybe her mother's death was softening him a little. "Evans, who was that?"

He looked up at her. "A messenger boy, Miss Summer, a telegraph wire for you."

Her heart leaped with hope as she hurried down the stairs. At last! It was bound to be a message from Iron Knife, or at least from Todd Shaw. She took the envelope, stared at it a long moment, then realized Evans was discreetly hovering in the background. "I'll be in my room," Summer said coolly and went up the stairs. She wasn't about to share this with that snooty servant.

As she went down the hall, she could hear the children in the nursery with Mrs. O'Malley. Summer went into her room, sank down on the window seat and stared at the envelope for a long moment. It must be important or Todd would have just written a letter. The more she stared at it, the more unsure she was that she wanted to open it. Suppose Iron Knife had been killed? Suppose—?

Stop it, Summer, you're imagining the worst, she scolded herself. *It's been difficult for messages to get through because of the Indian war or maybe Todd has not been able to connect with Iron Knife and sent a wire because he knew you'd be in a hurry for news.*

She found she was holding her breath, and her hands trembled as she opened it. She read it twice before the words sunk in:

Dear Summer: Stop. Sorry to be the bearer of bad news. Stop. You have been gone so long, Iron Knife has taken a Cheyenne girl as wife. Stop. Perhaps it was never meant to be. Stop. You were not cut out for this rough life. Stop. My best and warmest wishes. Stop. Todd.

She stared at the words for a long moment as if they were written in some foreign language. She felt empty inside, and then the grief came and the anger and the jealousy. With an oath, she tore the paper to bits and collapsed on the window seat in a torrent of sobs. If she had felt pain at the knowledge that he had made love to Gray Dove, this was sheer agony. Summer wept until she had no tears left and her eyes were swollen and red.

What should she do now? Contact Todd for more information? Why? Try to get tickets to return to Colorado Territory? What for? She wasn't in any kind of physical condition to travel west, even if she had been certain of a warm welcome. How like a man! She had been gone about three months, and already her supposed once in a lifetime eternal love had found himself another woman. Summer was too ill to journey a long distance to fight for what was hers right now, or she would be on a train this afternoon. She wasn't one to let another woman take her man without a fight. She found it almost impossible to believe Iron Knife would do this, but here was the evidence in her hands.

She finally forced herself to stop weeping because she began to fear her melancholia might be harming her baby. Late that afternoon, when she finally emerged from her room, she refused to discuss it with the sympathetic Mrs. O'Malley, and the other servants were looking at her swollen eyes with curiosity.

Father came home early and immediately sought her

out in the music room, his voice warm with sympathy. "Summer, are you all right?"

"What are you doing home?" Father never let anything interfere with business.

"Evans sent for me; the whole house is abuzz that something terrible has happened!"

She tried to make an airy gesture, but her voice was ragged. "It—it's nothing. I—I may not be returning to Colorado Territory after all."

He didn't say 'I told you so,' as she had dreaded. In fact, for a long moment, he didn't say anything at all. "I know you won't believe me, Summer, but I really am sorry." He didn't look her in the face; he studied the piano where Priscilla used to sit and play.

"Thank you, Father." She was touched by his concern. Perhaps all these years, she had misjudged him. Perhaps he wasn't as cold and calculating as she had always thought.

He cleared his throat. "Please don't take it so hard, daughter; you know this was an improbable union to begin with—"

"Please, Father"—she held up her hand to shush him—"I'd rather not talk about it."

"All right." His voice was almost gentle. "You and your children have a home here as long as you wish."

"Thank you."

"I know this may seem like the end of the world to you, but you'll get over it in time; they say time heals all wounds."

She didn't want to discuss this. Her soul felt bleeding and raw. Summer didn't want to think about next week, next year, or even tomorrow. Just getting through the rest of the day was all that mattered right now.

Silas said, "Summer, if you don't want to have supper with us, would you like me to have Bridget bring a tray up to your room?"

She thought about having to face Angela's imperti-
nent questions and the servants' stares. "Yes, I—I
would like that. Maybe by tomorrow, I'll feel better."
She turned and fled up the stairs.

Silas watched her go. He was almost ashamed of
himself for having sent the telegram; almost, but not
quite. After all, it was for her own good, and certainly
it was better for the children. Eventually, when Todd
Shaw finally came home for a visit, Summer might figure out what Silas had done; but by then, she might
have forgotten about that damned savage and married
again, so it wouldn't matter. The end justified the
means; every practical person knew that. He smiled
with satisfaction; yes, it was for her own good. Now
that the war had ended, Austin might be coming home,
and certainly Beau would be back in town during next
weekend, and Silas would prevail on Summer to invite
him to share Easter dinner. One way or another, the Van
Schuylers would be rid of that savage half-breed, and
Silas would have Summer's children in his power.

It had been a long, long week since Lee's surrender,
Summer thought. In the several days that had passed
since she had received the telegram from Todd Shaw,
she had pulled herself together but was still not certain
what to do about her life. Well, she certainly had time
to think about that between now and the time the new
baby arrived.

It was Saturday morning, and Summer had just finished breakfasting with Father and Angela. Once Father
had gotten over the shock of her announcement of an
impending child, he had been quite nice and good-
humored toward her; in fact, almost sympathetic over
the fateful telegram. Perhaps she had misjudged him.

Now she sat in the music room planning a festive

Easter dinner for tomorrow. They would go to church. Even Father attended on Easter and Christmas; he said it made a very good impression. Beau was in town again, and Father had insisted they invite him for Easter dinner, since the poor man really had no place to go for the holiday. It was still quite early; the ice man had not yet made his delivery. She'd left Father sitting in the dining room drinking coffee and reading his morning paper.

The front doorbell rang suddenly, over and over as if someone was hitting it in great agitation. "Who on earth can that be—?"

She got up and ran into the hall as Evans hurried to open the door.

Father stuck his head out of the dining room. "Ye Gods, what idiot would be—?"

Portly Robert Shaw burst through the door as the butler opened it, his florid face agitated, his breath coming in gasps. "News just came in over the telegraph! No telling how it will affect the future of our investments!"

"Ye Gods, Robert," Father bellowed, "have you gone daft? What—?"

"The president was shot last night at Ford's Theater by some crazy actor! Lincoln died early this morning!"

The nation had never had a president assassinated before and went prostrate with grief. Newspapers told of how the president and Mrs. Lincoln had gone to the theater on Good Friday evening to see a play called *Our American Cousin.* Because there had been threats on the president's life, he had been urged not to go, but pouty Mary Lincoln had insisted on attending the entertainment. Numerous people had been invited to accompany them, but each had a reason or excuse not to go. The stalwart Major Rathbone and his fiancée, Miss Clara

Harris, daughter of New York's Senator Harris, had finally been persuaded to accompany the president.

The handsome and popular actor, John Wilkes Booth,
had burst into the president's box, shot him in the head,
and stabbed Major Rathbone when he tried to stop the
assassin from fleeing. Booth had jumped from the box
to the stage, and escaped. He was still at large, although
a huge manhunt was now in progress.

Newspapers described in great detail the expensive
walnut casket with silver handles, the cross of lilies at
Lincoln's head, and the anchor of roses at the foot of his
casket during the funeral in the East Room of the White
House. Lincoln and his little son, Willie, who had died
while his father was president, were to be reburied in
Springfield, Illinois. As the funeral train wended its way
back to Springfield, it stopped in many cities along the
way where the body was placed on display for the public to see. It was estimated that seven million people
saw the coffin along its journey.

John Wilkes Booth was cornered in a Virginia barn
and shot to death April 26th by a policeman named
Boston Corbett. Seven other conspirators were arrested,
including a Dr. Mudd, who protested he had done nothing but treat Booth's leg which the actor had broken in
jumping from Lincoln's box to the Ford Theater's stage.

Almost lost in the news was the sinking of the river-
boat *Sultana*. The overloaded craft, carrying more than
two thousand returning Union soldiers, blew up and
sank in the Mississippi River just above Memphis on
the night of April 27th. The loss of life was horrible,
some said more than fifteen hundred dead, but with all
the other news, the boat disaster got small notice by the
newspapers.

In May, to celebrate the end of the war, there was a
huge victory parade in the nation's capital. According to

the papers, young General Custer, sporting a scarlet scarf at his throat, looked dashing on his spirited mount leading his troops. His horse ran away with him along the parade route, creating much publicity and setting ladies' hearts aflutter.

Summer had hoped Austin and David might be coming home soon, but there were still so many wounded to deal with and rebellious Southern soldiers returning home to be controlled by victorious occupation forces.

In late May, Summer attended the wedding of her old friend Maude Peabody, who had survived the sinking of the *Sultana*. Maude and her new husband then moved to his home state, leaving Summer feeling lonelier than before.

Again it was dark and dangerous to go to Denver, but Todd had sent him a message. The Cheyenne had split up. Those who favored peace had gone with Black Kettle to the land south of the Arkansas River; the ones who wanted to fight had joined up with some of the Sioux and were ranging the northern plains. The choices split families, even Iron Knife's. His younger cousin, Two Arrows, took his wives and children and went south with those seeking peace. Lance Bearer, his other cousin who carried the Dog Rope, elected to join up with the warring Sioux and ride the war trail. His old uncle, Clouds Above, was so feeble, he and his wife, Pony Woman, went south with Two Arrows.

However, Iron Knife could only wait near Denver, refusing to leave the area until he heard from Summer. Now Todd had sent a message to come. He slipped into town to Todd's office.

Todd frowned when he turned from his desk at the sound. "I—I got a message, but I wasn't quite sure what

to do about it." Todd opened his desk drawer and took out a piece of paper. "This came by telegraph and—"
Iron Knife jerked it from his hand.

To Todd Shaw, Denver, Colorado Territory. Dear Todd. Stop. Mother still very sick. Stop. May be in Boston for months yet. Stop. I'm also having second thoughts about the Cheyenne. Stop. Not sure I didn't make a terrible mistake. Stop. May not return after all. Stop. If you see him, break it to him gently. Stop. Summer.

Iron Knife reread it three times before he remembered to breath again, and when he did, it came out as a ragged sigh that sounded almost like a sob. "No"—he shook his head—"she wouldn't do this; she wouldn't say our love was a mistake." He wadded the paper and threw it against the wall. For a long moment, only the sound of a wagon passing by in the street out front and the creak of Todd's chair broke the silence.

Todd chewed his lip. "I wish I knew what to tell you. Things change and people change, too, Iron Knife."

Iron Knife shook his head and took a deep breath. The offices smelled of ink and newsprint. "Our love is a forever thing; nothing can change that." He paced the floor. "I must talk to her, find out why she sent this." He whirled on Todd. "I will go to Boston now."

"It's a loco idea."

"I know, but I'll go anyway."

Todd shrugged in defeat. "Okay, you're a stubborn fellow. With a little coaching, you might manage to ride the train to Boston without any trouble."

Iron Knife felt his spirits fall. "I have no money for a ticket or clothes."

"I have plenty of money; my father, you know."

Iron Knife drew himself up proudly. "I'll not take charity."

"Oh, you are an arrogant one." Todd grinned. "All right then, sell me one of your many horses. I could use a good saddle horse and I'll pay top dollar."

Iron Knife brightened and held out his hand. They shook solemnly. "Will you help me; tell me what to say? What to do?"

"You bet! I'm only sorry I can't go with you. I'd give a year of my life to see all the proper aristocratic faces when a Cheyenne dog soldier walks into their parlors in Boston!"

Chapter Seventeen

Iron Knife looked out at the Missouri landscape passing the train windows faster than a horse could run. The reflection staring back at him from the window glass was almost not recognizable with its hat, coat and shirt. The boots that had replaced his soft moccasins seemed heavy and hard on his feet. In the early summer heat, the coach was stifling, and Iron Knife could feel sweat running down his body under the heavy clothes. How he longed to be riding half-naked and free across the prairie, but he would endure anything to see his woman again. He opened the window, and the breeze blew the stink of the engine and a shower of cinders back on him and the other passengers.

He closed his eyes, lulled by the rocking motion of the train, and thought about Summer Sky. In only a couple more days, he would be in Boston. Maybe he should have just accepted Summer's decision that she didn't want him anymore; she hadn't loved him enough to forgive him over Gray Dove. Or was it because the Cheyenne life was just too difficult? A woman who had been reared in civilized luxury would have to love a man a lot to endure such dangers and hardships.

If only he could talk to her, reason with her. Because of that, Iron Knife hadn't let Todd write or wire that he was coming, afraid that maybe she would write back and say she didn't want to see him. At least if he surprised her, he'd get a chance to plead his case. He was desperate enough to try anything.

Summer Sky. In his mind, he saw her riding with him across the prairie, her yellow hair blowing wildly in the wind. They had a favorite little dell where they sometimes rode, he on Spotted Blanket, she on her fine mare, Starfire, which Iron Knife had given her as a gift. They would ride to that private paradise and slide off the horses, laughing and hugging while he swung her up in his arms and kissed her face. She was his whole world, and when he made love to her, everything seemed to stop for both of them but that moment when he held her against him and kissed her tenderly. In his mind, he kissed her lips and remembered the taste of them. Her skin felt so warm against his as he cuddled her in his embrace. His strong arms could break a man's back, but with her, he was always gentle. Sometimes they would roll on the grass, laughing and teasing; but then their gazes would lock, and abruptly they would grow silent.

"Make love to me," she would command.

"You think I am nothing more than a brown stallion to be used to please a female's wants?" he would tease.

"Very well, then, I will make love to you." She would kiss him, her soft lips moving against his until he opened them to her probing tongue. When she pressed her breasts against him, he would forget everything but how much he wanted to possess her body. She had a way of locking her long, slim legs around his hips, pulling him down on her deeper and deeper still until nothing mattered but meshing with her velvet warmth, emptying his seed within her. He could take her every night and still not get enough of her. She had a talent for building a fire in him that centered his very being in a whirlpool of yellow hair and blue eyes.

"Ne-mehotatse," he would murmur, "I love you, Summer Sky. *Hahoo,* thank you for coming into my life. I never knew what love was until I took you from that wrecked stagecoach and made you my captive."

Then, with her kisses, gradually the big dog soldier had become her captive. There was nothing he would not do for her, no distance too far, no danger too great to endure for the white girl who had taken control of him body and soul. He had not meant to mate with the evil Arapaho girl, Gray Dove, but Summer had gone away, and he had thought she would never return when he succumbed to Gray Dove's seductive charms that one brief time. Because of that, he might have lost Summer forever. If she would only give him one chance to prove how much he really loved her; he would spend the rest of his life making it up to her.

He leaned his head back against the seat and dreamed of her holding him close and kissing him, saying she would never love another as she loved him . . . kissing him . . . kissing him. . . .

"Wartonville! Coming into Wartonville! Wartonville, next stop!"

The conductor shouting down the aisle awakened Iron Knife from his fitful slumber. He sat up and looked around at the other passengers as the hissing train snorted and began to slow, pulling into the station. The late afternoon sun threw distorted shadows across a dusty prairie town as the sun retreated into the far horizon.

The conductor paused in the aisle. "We'll be here a couple of hours, I'm afraid, folks; there's trouble with the track between here and St. Louie."

An elderly lady touched his sleeve. "Excuse me, what's the trouble?"

The squat, round-faced man shrugged. "Nothing big, just something with the rails. We'll be here awhile 'til they send word down the line it's fixed; so plan to have a bite to eat, and then maybe we'll be on our way."

Iron Knife was superstitious, so he had brought some of his dog soldier things tucked safely in a carpetbag in the overhead luggage rack. The dream shield had too many taboos attached to its usage to bring along, and his father's massive war bonnet was too delicate. He had brought his raven feather dog soldier headdress, the decorated and beaded Dog Rope, his moccasins, a fine and soft deerskin outfit, and small pots of war paint. His bone whistle and the brass earring were tucked inside, too.

He felt naked without the big knife he always wore, but it had been left behind. Todd had thought Iron Knife might attract too much attention wearing it under his coat, and it certainly wouldn't do him any good in his valise. In fact, he had not brought any weapons at all.

"Wartonville!" sang out the conductor, "coming up!"

Iron Knife pressed his face against the smudged window and stared out at the drab frontier town. It wasn't so big as Denver; but it was more than a village. His belly grumbled with hunger.

"Wartonville!" The conductor passed him, swaying in the aisle.

Iron Knife said, "Can I get something to eat here?"

The conductor nodded. "Stay away from the station food; it's bad, but there's a cafe downtown that's pretty good."

"You think we'll really be here several hours?"

"At least." He pushed his hat back and scratched his round head. "Don't worry about gettin' left; we'll blow the whistle to warn everyone before we pull out. You'll have plenty of time."

The brakes shrieked as the train slowed coming into

the station. Yes, he was hungry. The candy butchers sold
a few things from a basket; but Iron Knife wanted some
hot, hearty fare, and he had money in his pockets that
Todd had given him. Afraid he might lose it, he had
tucked the Van Schuyler's address in his valise. He was
unsure about finding the house in a giant city like Boston, but Todd had instructed him just to give the address
to a cabbie and that driver would take him to the house.
After that, Iron Knife was on his own. Iron Knife did
not want to think about the wire he had gotten from
Summer, saying she had thought it over and was staying
in Boston, her union with him had been a mistake.
Maybe when he faced her, he could convince her to return with him.

He stood up, stretched, and reached for his bag. His
muscles ached from all these hours in that seat, and he
welcomed the chance to walk and exercise his cramped
legs. With the others, he went along the aisle and down
the steps onto the platform. The warm air smelled of
soot and smoke from the train, and a thousand other
scents of the town. How he longed for the crisp, clean
air of the high plains and the mountains.

The wildflowers would be blooming across the wild
country he loved, and the sun would be warm on his
back as he swam in the creeks with his children. In his
mind, he saw little Lance and Storm Gathering diving
like small otters and coming up laughing. Summer
would be sitting on the bank with the plump baby, Garnet, both dangling their feet in the water and laughing as
they watched. Iron Knife swallowed hard. He missed his
family so much. What would he do if she refused to
return?

Iron Knife stood on the platform with his little suitcase in the orange rays of the sun soon to be sliding behind the distant hills. People brushed past him, paying
him no heed. He took his wallet from his jacket and

opened it, brought the green paper out and counted it for reassurance. Strange that white men considered green paper of such value. Todd's name and address were in the wallet, too, in case of any emergency that he couldn't handle.

Iron Knife mingled with the crowd walking into the station. The building was stifling and smelled of stale food and smoke, sweat and dirt. He wrinkled his nose, remembering the conductor's warning and went out the other side to look around. There seemed to be a lot of people in town, buggies, farmers driving wagons.

Saturday. White people always came into town to shop and trade on Saturdays, he remembered. His belly rumbled again as he looked toward the late afternoon sun now beginning to sink like a fireball behind a gray-blue horizon. At least when the sun finally set, it would be cooler; for that he could be grateful. His shirt seemed to stick to his big body, and the boots cramped his feet. He wished he could wear his moccasins.

He started down the street. He'd find that small cafe and eat something, then get back on the train. It might not be leaving for a couple of hours, but he was nervous about missing it. Iron Knife knew so little about all the mazes of track; he was worried about getting on the wrong train and ending up somewhere besides Boston.

Well, the conductor had been right; this town was small enough that one could surely hear the train whistle when it made ready to leave the station. A tall man with a star on his chest sauntered past him, glaring with hostility. The young man was handsome in a cruel way, Iron Knife noted. The deputy wore wicked Spanish spurs with jinglebobs that rang when he walked and a big Colt pistol on his hip.

Some of the white men in these towns didn't like Indians, and Iron Knife's Indian blood was evident, even though he was dressed like a white man. He could break that lawman in half if the white man challenged him to a fight, but Iron Knife didn't want any trouble that would interfere with his getting to Boston and Summer. He'd hurry to eat and return to the security of the train. That way, when it left the station, he wouldn't have to worry about running to catch it. Anyway, there was something about Wartonville that made him uneasy.

Iron Knife found the small cafe, sat down at the counter, placed his bag at his feet, and ordered a steak sandwich and coffee. Even though the weather was hot, the coffee tasted good. The fresh, crusty bread and the fried meat filled his empty belly. Beef was not as good as buffalo or deer, but among whites, they were only beginning to enjoy the taste of buffalo meat. It was just as well, he thought; if the whites ever discovered the succulent buffalo meat or how warm the fur was, they'd begin killing the big beasts, and the Plains tribes depended on buffalo to survive.

He was finishing his food when that lawman sauntered in and sat down at the counter near him. He didn't look up, but he heard the big spurs as the man crossed the floor. Iron Knife felt his stare; decided to ignore it.

The deputy banged on the counter. "Hey, Hank, how about some service here? If you can feed Injuns, looks like a white man could get something to eat."

The atmosphere changed, and people gradually stopped talking. Iron Knife paused, feeling the tension in the air, thinking that he didn't need any trouble if he was going to get to Boston. He sipped his coffee.

The elderly white man rushed from the kitchen, wiping his hands on his dirty apron. "Sure, Jingles, right away; please don't make no trouble with the sheriff out of town and all."

"Trouble!" The deputy sneered, "I can handle it alone if it comes, but I don't want me no trouble. Now, Injuns, they bring trouble."

Iron Knife gripped his cup so hard, he thought it might shatter in his big fist. The young stud was spoiling for a fight in front of the crowd, backed up with his own sense of importance and that big pistol. No doubt he had looked Iron Knife over carefully to make sure he wasn't wearing a holster under his coat. Iron Knife managed to control his temper. What he'd really like to do was put his knuckles in the deputy's arrogant mouth, but he must not pick up the challenge. Getting to Boston was more important than protecting his honor. He threw down some coins to pay for his meal, and they rang loud in the silence.

Everyone was waiting to see if he was going to challenge the lawman; he could sense it in the quiet and the expressions on the other diners' faces. Instead, he picked up his carpetbag, stood, and slowly walked toward the door.

"Well, big as he is, who'd think he was such a yellow coward!" The white man snorted behind him, "Reckon he's got a suitcase full of scalps from women and kids!"

"Don't crowd him, Jingles, you don't have to prove nothin', " the old cook cautioned in a hoarse whisper. "He's dressed pretty well; he might have money or important connections."

Iron Knife didn't pause to hear more; he forced himself to walk outside into the darkness. He was so angry, he was trembling. Someday, some real man would kill that sneering young gunman, but it wouldn't be Iron Knife. The Saturday night street scene was busy, people, wagons and buggies still moving up and down, cowboys riding down the street. In the distance, faint laughter and music drifted from the saloon one street over: . . . *Buffalo gals won't you come out tonight, come out tonight, come out tonight . . . ?*

Through the darkness, he could see the lights of the train station. Night hadn't cooled the Missouri heat much. He felt passersby staring at him either with curiosity or hostility.

Carrying his valise, Iron Knife decided to take a different route back to the station to avoid the Main Street crowd, and just in case the swaggering deputy followed after him to pick a fight. He strode down the wooden sidewalk. Up ahead, he saw the lights go off in a small millinery shop; then a woman came out and paused to lock the door. She walked on down the sidewalk far ahead of him. He couldn't tell much about her because her hat shadowed her face, except that she walked as if she were weary.

His long legs were carrying him closer to the petite woman, and this street lacked the crowds the main street held. In fact, except for a saloon she was passing, most of the shops were darkened and closed now. Iron Knife slowed his pace, afraid that if the woman glanced back and saw him, the fact that he was big or maybe that he was a half-breed might scare her. White women didn't generally go out on the streets alone at night, unless they were poor working women, and then they had to take their chances.

Even as he watched, a man staggered out of the saloon. In the moonlight, Iron Knife saw that he was young and well-dressed. A diamond stickpin reflected the moonlight.

"Hey, honey," the man confronted the girl, "how about having a drink with me?"

She tried to walk past him. "I'm sorry, but I'm on my way home."

The man grabbed her arm. "Hey, don't you know who I am?"

"Of course, everyone knows who you are, Mr. Warton, but—"

"Then you know I'm important; my family owns most of this town."

"Please"—she tried to pull away—"you're drunk. If your father finds out—"

"I'm a grown man. Why does everyone treat me like a kid; think I always have to answer to him?" the drunken rake said. "Come have a drink, honey, get to know me better."

"Please, no." The woman's hat fell off, and the pins from her hair fell so that the yellow strands tumbled around her shoulders. Except for her hair, she was rather plain and somewhere in her thirties. She struggled, but the brash aggressor was pulling her to him, attempting to kiss her.

"Now, honey, you just come along and we'll have a drink. I'll bet you never had a drink of whiskey in your whole life."

"Please. My mother is alone; I need to get home." She sounded desperate now.

Young Warton laughed. "So have a drink with me and then I'll let you go take care of the old lady."

She struggled, but she wasn't very big. "I—I'll scream for help!"

"In this town, no one would cross a Warton." He swayed as he attempted to kiss her while she tried to break his grip.

In the distance, Iron Knife heard the train whistle a warning. He looked toward the station, then toward the couple struggling in the shadows. The woman was petite and slightly built, just like Summer. The rich young rake was now overpowering her, even as she fought him, dragging her toward the saloon.

Iron Knife was a stranger in this hostile town, and he did not even know this woman; he owed her nothing. In that split-second as he listened to the train whistle, he paused, holding his small suitcase, watching her struggle. She wasn't Iron Knife's woman, and he had no stake in this. Yet she was small and defenseless, and a real man always protected the weak. He reacted, running toward them as silent as a shadow. The immature drunk seemed to hear him at the last minute and half turned as Iron Knife hit him with the valise, dropped it, then pulled him away from the girl.

The dapper boy cried out in protest as Iron Knife hit him in the mouth with one big fist while the woman cowered against the wall, her dress torn. In the moonlight, her plain little face looked drained of color.

Iron Knife knocked the drunk over the hitching rail and into the dust of the street. The young dandy stumbled to his feet, blood running from his lip and down his weak chin. He began screaming for help.

"You drunk bastard!" Iron Knife hit him again. "Keep your hands off decent women!"

He could hear people running and shouting now, but he owed this rich young rake a lesson for the terror and humiliation in the shop girl's eyes.

The drunk attempted to defend himself, but he was no match for Iron Knife's steel fists. The half-breed was wiping up the street with him even as a group gathered. In the background, he heard the running jingle of spurs and saw the flash of moonlight on the deputy's badge. He couldn't fight the whole town, but he had to protect himself. Yet as he hit the deputy in the mouth, he heard the train whistle again. He had to be on that train. He must grab his valise and run. He must not miss that train to Boston; Summer was waiting. Summer.

That was his last thought as he saw the reflection off the deputy's pistol barrel coming down toward him. Then lights seemed to explode in his head, and he felt himself falling as somewhere in the distance, the train began to chug out of the station.

* * *

"Stop it!" Serenity shrieked. "Stop it, you'll kill him!"

About that time, a passing buggy reined in. "What's going on here anyway?"

She recognized Hershel Warton, Senior. There was dead silence for a long moment as the stout but still-handsome man climbed down. Everyone looked at each other uneasily. Warton was the richest, most powerful man in town; he owned everything and almost everybody.

"Billy, what's going on here?" He pulled at his mustache.

"Hello, Dad." The young rake smiled sheepishly. "I—I was just on my way home; you didn't need to come lookin' for me."

"Might have known if there was trouble, you'd be in the middle of it. What's going on here, Jingles?"

She could see the sweat on the deputy's face. Like everyone else in town, he owed his job to this man. Jingles doffed his hat. "Well, sir, with the sheriff gone, I was tryin' to keep the peace, and this big half-breed drifted into town."

Warton was no dummy, Serenity thought as his gaze swept over the scene, took in the unconscious man, her torn dress. "What happened to Miss Peterson?"

Before she could answer, Billy blurted, "I was just on my way home, Dad, when I heard the lady scream for help; came to her aid."

"Is that right, Miss Peterson?" His only child, Hershel William Warton, had a bad reputation as a spoiled wastrel.

"Well, I—"

"Of course that's what happened," Jingles interrupted and was rewarded with a grin from Billy. "I heard the racket and had just got here to make an arrest." With that, he leaned over and snapped handcuffs on the unconscious man. "Take him down to the jail, fellas."

"Wait!" Serenity protested.

In the silence, the only sound was the chugging and the puffing of the engine pulling out of town, its lonely whistle echoing across the landscape. All the men turned and stared at her.

In that few seconds, Serenity remembered that Hershel Warton, Senior, owned the building that housed her struggling shop and that his bank held the mortgage on her modest home. His wife was also Serenity's best customer. "I—I—"

"Now, Miss Peterson"—Hershel Warton patted her shoulder kindly, but the threat in his eyes was unmistakable—"you've had a bad scare, and your elderly mother needs you at home; we all know how ill and dependent on you she is. If you want to make a statement, why don't you come in Monday when the sheriff gets back and talk to him?"

She paused, wavering, as she watched the men loading the half-breed in the back of the buggy. Billy was standing close enough that she could see he was cold sober now and nervous. He was afraid of his father, just like everyone else in this town. Young Warton had never earned a dime in his life, and town gossip said he lived in fear of Dad cutting off his money. In her heart, she knew what she ought to do; that stranger had tried to help her. "What—what will they do to him?"

"Oh, nothing at all." Hershel Warton shrugged it off. "When he comes to, they'll probably just turn him loose, tell him to get out of town; ain't that right, Jingles?"

"Whatever you say, Mr. Warton."

"But—" Serenity began.

"Just don't worry about it, Miss Peterson." The older man stroked his mustache and gave her a long, significant look. "This stranger is just passin' through town; the rest of us have to live here, get along. Do you get my drift?"

She felt all eyes upon her. Almost everyone in the little group was beholden in some way to the Warton empire. In the silence, the only noise was the jingle of the deputy's spurs. Handsome young Billy still looked a little unsteady on his feet, but he was smiling as if he knew he'd already won.

"Now you just go on home, Miss Peterson," the father urged. "If you want to file any charges against anyone, you come in Monday morning, before you open that little shop of yours, and see the sheriff."

"If I don't file any charges against anyone, what happens?" All the men were looking at her. They knew who had the power and the wealth in this town.

"Why, nothing at all," Hershel almost crooned. "We just forget this ever happened; right, Jingles?"

"If you say so, sir, I'm sure the sheriff will see it your way."

She knew what was right, but she also was the sole support of an elderly, sick mother. The Wartons had the money and the influence to ruin Serenity's business, run her out of this town. "I—I'll think it over."

"You just do that, Miss Peterson, I'm sure you'll come to the right decision. Why don't you just go on home now? You've had a bad scare."

She was suddenly very tired and disgusted with herself. This stranger had helped her, and she stood here silent, knowing women would always be victimized until they had the courage to speak out against men like Billy Warton. For herself, she would have braved it; but what would she do about her mother if she lost her home and small business? Humiliated and defeated, Serenity watched the Wartons and Jingles get into the buggy carrying the unconscious stranger, slap the horse with the reins and drive down the street to the jail. Serenity was uncertain and afraid with no one to ask for help. She looked around the circle of faces in silent appeal. The men all avoided her eyes, then began to disband and drift away. Perhaps there was nothing to be done until tomorrow.

As she turned to walk away, she stumbled across the valise and paused. If she ran after them, gave it to the deputy, would the stranger ever get it back? Maybe not. This was one favor she could do him; not much in the way of gratitude, but the best she could do at the moment. She picked it up and took it home.

"Serenity, is that you?" She heard her frail mother's voice from the bedroom as she entered.

"Yes, Mama, I'll bring you some soup in a minute." Serenity opened the valise. Maybe there would be a clue as to his identity, something that might help her decide what to do. Puzzled, Serenity stared at the feathered and beaded costume it contained. The only other item she recognized was a scrap of paper with a name and address in Boston. The half-breed didn't appear to be the type who would have connections in Boston, but since he'd been carrying luggage, maybe he had gotten off that train that had pulled in several hours ago.

Serenity opened her reticule, counted what little money she had since she'd just paid her rent and the note on the house; not much, but enough to send a telegram. The telegraph office was at the train station, and it might still be open, although she wasn't sure messages were delivered on Sunday. Maybe this woman in Boston could do something to help the gallant stranger. That made Serenity feel a little less guilty. She put the address in her reticule. "Mama, I've got to go out again; just for a few minutes. I'll be right back and then we'll have supper."

Before Mother could protest, Serenity went out the

door. Sometimes being the sole support of an elderly parent with as few jobs as there were available for women was a heavy burden. She never seemed to have time to meet eligible men, and now, she was past thirty. Anyway, she wasn't pretty. Mother and everyone else had always told her she was as plain as her name.

Well, she had tonight and tomorrow to decide what to do about the attack and whether to file charges. Maybe Hershel Warton was right; it would be so much better for everyone if she filed no charges and the law just turned the stranger loose. She looked at her reflection in the station window as she approached the office. *How can you live with yourself if you let this happen?* She hadn't asked the stranger to step in. If he hadn't shown up and interfered, what was the worst thing that could have happened to her? Billy would have torn her dress a little more, given her a worse scare; but he'd been drunk, and he probably would have let her go if she'd insisted. Maybe it was her fault; maybe she'd done something to encourage the wealthy young rake who had a wild reputation in this town.

When her mother finally died, Serenity intended to leave this place forever, start again somewhere else. At the moment, as Hershel Warton had said, she had to live in this town, and that was the cold reality of it. She would do what little she could to help her rescuer; she would send a telegram.

Over in the jail, Hershel Warton looked down at the handcuffed, unconscious half-breed sprawled on the jail floor and cursed. "Big as he is, Billy, it's a wonder he didn't kill you."

Jingles said, "I came to Billy's aid; remember that, Mr. Warton."

"Aw . . ." Hershel made a dismissing motion and

sneered. "Neither one of you could fight worth a damn if I melted you and poured you on this galoot. Billy, you must have been dead drunk to bother that drab little milliner."

Billy hiccoughed and staggered over to sit down on the corner of the desk. "Now, Daddy, I told you, he was attacking the lady and I was saving her—"

"Don't lie to me!" He struck his son across the face, and the sound seemed to ring out in the silence. "I know you better than that; you haven't a gallant bone in your lazy body!" Hershel watched the deputy searching through the stranger's pockets. "Find anything?"

Jingles grinned and held up a handful of greenbacks and other papers. "Money, a train ticket, and a man's name, Todd Shaw, in Denver."

"Let me see that." Hershel jerked the name from the deputy's hand. "Wonder who this is?"

"Who knows?" The deputy still held the money, looking at him with a question in his eyes.

"Yeah, keep it," Hershel grumbled, "call it a fine."

"What'll I do about the ticket?" He tucked the money in his vest, nodding his thanks.

"Same thing I'm doin' with this name." Hershel tore up the paper and threw it into the air. He turned and glared at his errant offspring again. "Jingles, get some coffee in him and see if you can get him sobered up before I take him home. I don't want his mother to know; she dotes on him."

"Yes sir, Mr. Warton." His spurs rattled as he crossed the weathered floor. He glanced down at Iron Knife. "What do you want I should do with him?"

Hershel sighed and put his fingers to his throbbing eyes and paced up and down. He had spent a lifetime building this empire. Now he had only a wild, worthless son to leave it all to. It was Louise's fault; she had always spoiled their son rotten. "I don't know; we'll talk about it tomorrow. Reckon we'll turn him loose; run him out of town."

Billy took the coffee, sipped it. "You suppose she'll press charges?"

"Oh, now you're worried, are you?" Hershel stopped his pacing and glared at his heir. "Why didn't you think of that before you tried to rip her clothes off right out on the sidewalk?"

"I—I don't know what came over me," Billy mumbled. "She isn't even pretty." He sipped his coffee.

"Skirt crazy, that's what you are." Hershel put his hands to his eyes again. "That drab little hat maker is plain as her name—'ceptin' for her hair. You must have been drunken than a boiled owl."

Jingles grinned and pushed his hat back. "You know what they say, Mr. Warton: I never went to bed with an ugly woman, but I've woke up with a few."

"Very funny!" Hershel snapped and renewed his pacing, pulling at his mustache. "Billy, you just can't paw respectable women; sooner or later, one will have the nerve to press charges. Besides, there's girls in the dance hall and pretty whores over in St. Louie. Sometime when I'm goin' on business, I'll take you along."

Jingles poured himself a cup of coffee. "Could I go too, Mr. Warton?"

"Oh, you're as worthless as he is!" Hershel swore. "Billy, I'll talk to Miss Peterson again tomorrow, use my influence to make sure she sees this as what it was: a boyish prank."

"Stop calling me Billy. I'm not a little boy, Daddy!"

"Then damn it, stop acting like one!" Hershel paced some more. "Next fall, I'm going to send you off to college, or the military; see if they can make a man of you."

"Now, Daddy—"

"Don't 'now, Daddy' me!" Hershel paused and looked

at the prone half-breed. "Anybody got a clue as to who he is besides the name in his pocket?"

They both shook their heads.

Jingles stuck out his chest. "I tried to roust him a little at the cafe, but he turned tail when I insulted him."

Hershel peered at both of them. "I'd say by the bruises on both of you, he got in a few good licks. Judging from his clothes, he might have some influence somewhere."

"Him?" Jingles guffawed. "Naw. Maybe he stole the clothes. He was just drifting through town, maybe."

"Well, throw him in a cell and I'll tell you what to do with him tomorrow. Reckon it would be best just to take him to the county line and throw him out, tell him not to come back. Come on, son, let's get home before your mother starts worrying and then meets us with a bunch of questions. Next time you want a pretty whore, go along with me over to St. Louie; I'll take you to the right places."

"Good night, Mr. Warton; Billy—er, Bill." Jingles touched the brim of his hat respectfully and watched the pair as they went out the door. They only gave him a dismissing nod as they got in the buggy and drove away. Damn rich, uppity Wartons!

Someday, Jingles would have money and power, and he wouldn't have to scrape and bow to anyone. He was damned good with a gun, and Wartonville wasn't big enough to hold him. Someday, maybe he'd be sheriff in some wide-open boom town, and everyone would point him out when he walked down the street with his spurs ringing. *There goes Jingles Johnson,* they would whisper, *he's one tough lawman; when you hear those spurs comin', you'd better mind your manners and step aside.*

He grinned, thinking about it, imagining how pretty women would smile and flutter their eyelashes at him. The big saloons would pay him to keep the peace and not bother their gambling and whores. Yes, someday he'd be more than just a deputy in a hick town.

The man on the floor moaned and stirred. Damned half-breed. Gingerly, Jingles felt his own bruised, swollen face. The girls at the local saloon told him he was handsome, but getting his face beat up wouldn't help. Now, a romantic knife scar down one cheek, that would be impressive for the ladies, but just getting his face swollen and covered with purple and green bruises would only cause laughter.

The man stirred again. "Now it's my turn, you half-breed," Jingles muttered. "Tomorrow I may have to turn you loose, but tonight, I can do anything I want with you!"

Jingles grinned and looked down at his sharp-toed boots with their wicked Spanish spurs. The half-breed lay there with his hands cuffed. Oh, this was gonna be fun! Jingles brought back his foot and kicked the man in the groin, then brought the spur across his chest in the torn shirt. When he got through tonight, this half-breed would remember Deputy Johnson.

Summer sat stark upright in bed, heart pounding. What was it that had awakened her? A bad dream? She looked around, listening, but she heard nothing except her own breathing. The whole house was asleep on this sultry summer night. It was late. No, it hadn't been a bad dream; it had been a terrible sense of danger—of foreboding. For whom? Iron Knife's rugged face came to her mind. Was he in some kind of trouble? Was he dead? Perhaps it was a nightmare after all. Certainly she didn't think she had the uncanny gift of foresight her younger sister had inherited from the Blackledge side of the family.

She got out of bed, lit a lap and tiptoed down the hall

to the nursery. Her three tots lay snuggled in their beds all safe and warm. She looked down at the swell of her belly as her unborn child moved. Something was wrong; what was it?

Turning, she tiptoed back to her room and put out the lamp. She got into bed but couldn't sleep. The feeling persisted that something terrible had happened at the very moment that she had sat bolt upright in bed. She and her lover had been so very close that sometimes she thought she could read his mind. Maybe she needed to go to him. According to the wire from Todd, Iron Knife had taken a Cheyenne girl now, and she had better stay in Boston. Doubts assailed her. She would have bet her life he would never do that. Yet when she pictured him locked in Gray Dove's embrace, she thought that maybe she didn't know him at all.

Besides, she felt much too ill to travel. This pregnancy wasn't going well, or maybe it was only the grief of dealing with her mother's death that had laid her low. Her baby was due in September. Her belly seemed bigger than usual, yet she hadn't been eating that much.

The house was ghostly quiet. The grandfather clock didn't tick or boom out the hour anymore. In fact, the best clocksmiths had been unable to get it to run again. It stood silent in the front hall, its hands stopped at nine o'clock, ever since the night her mother died. Sometimes she pitied her father. Once she had found her mother's bedroom door slightly ajar and peeked in to see him sitting in there among the small pieces of Priscilla's life as if he were visiting a shrine. He had allowed nothing to be changed or removed, but if he had noticed that the music box was gone, he said nothing. Yet in contrast, Silas Van Schuyler had ordered her mother's rose garden ruthlessly plowed up. The first time Summer had looked out at the fresh dirt, it reminded her of nothing so much as new graves.

Priscilla. She had not realized how much she would miss her mother. Summer blinked back a tear and touched the tiny locket she still wore on a gold chain around her neck.

Was she getting more like her mother every day? Would she, too, be trapped in this house by circumstances as her mother had been? Again Summer felt a great sense of loss and despair sweep over her and thought of her half-breed lover. She went back to bed, but she couldn't sleep. Something was very, very wrong at this moment; she only wished she knew what it was.

Chapter Eighteen

The doorbell rang as the Van Schuyler family was getting up from the breakfast table.

Silas frowned. "Ye Gods! On a Sunday morning? Who would be calling at this hour?"

Evans put down the silver coffeepot. "I'll see, sir."

"I'll be in the library," Silas said and took his coffee cup with him. "Join me, Summer?"

She shook her head, looking pale and wan. "The scent of your cigars make me ill. I was thinking of attending church, but I don't feel well. I didn't sleep much last night. Come along, children, maybe we'll play hymns in the music room instead."

Little Lance said, "When this is my house, I will go to the library and sit behind Grandfather's desk."

Silas grinned in spite of himself. The little rascal was a Van Schuyler, all right.

Angela's pretty face turned ugly as she glared at the little boy. "This will never be your house, and when it's mine, I will sit behind that big desk and run things."

It really was too bad Angela wasn't a boy, Silas thought; if she were, she could probably run his empire as well as Lance could. "Oh, stop the fussing! Go on to church or the music room, Angela, and take that damned cat with you. A man needs a little peace and quiet."

His younger daughter looked as if she might argue, then picked up the black cat and followed Summer and the children out of the room.

Peace and quiet. If it hadn't been for Summer's children, now that Priscilla was dead, the house would have been so silent, it echoed. The solitude would be more than he could bear if she ever took her children and returned west. Silas didn't even want to think about that.

Silas took his cup of coffee and went into the library and stared at the shelves of books and his desk. He probably should go to church; he hadn't been since Easter, and it did make such a good impression for a businessman to be seen at services. Image was so important and so were good contacts, but the services bored him, and he wasn't up to it today. He'd send a large contribution this month again instead.

Evans appeared in the doorway. "It was a messenger with a telegram for Miss Summer, sir. They don't usually deliver on Sundays, but since you're so prominent . . . well, here it is. I brought it right to you."

"Good." Silas took it, sat down at his massive walnut desk and leaned closer to the lamp as he read the message. Ye Gods, that savage was on his way here and had ended up in jail in some hick town in Missouri. It went on to explain that the telegram was being sent by a Miss Peterson, whom the half-breed had rescued and who had his valise where she had found this address.

Silas stared at the print. Iron Knife on his way here. What would happen if he got out of the Wartonville jail, showed up here and Summer found out Silas had destroyed all the messages both ways?

"Sir, do you want to send an answer?"

"Let me think about this, Evans." He dismissed the butler, leaned back in his leather chair, sipped his coffee and reached into the humidor for a fine cigar as he re-read the telegram and considered. What to do?

From the music room drifted the faint sound of the piano playing hymns. After a moment, the tempo changed, and Silas heard the high, sweet voices of Summer's children struggling with the English words of "Beautiful Dreamer." Summer had been working hard to teach them English at Silas' urging. After all, he smiled to himself, if he were going to turn them into little civilized Van Schuylers, they had to be able to speak English before their proud grandfather could enroll them in some fine private school.

"... *beautiful dreamer, wake unto me....*"

Stephen Foster. Silas snorted and sipped his coffee. Worthless minstrel show music. Thank God, the drunken composer had finally cut his own throat and died last year. Maybe the interest in his worthless trash would soon die, too, and young people would return to something more classical and worthwhile.

Silas clipped the tip off his cigar, listening to the music, staring at the telegram and thinking. He would not give up his grandchildren without a fight; at least, not the white two. They would be so much better off with him anyway. He read the message once more, then leaned over the lamp chimney, lit his fine cigar, and watched the tip glow as he inhaled the fragrant smoke. After a long moment, Silas held the corner of the message to the glowing tip of his cigar, smiling as it ignited. Holding the paper by the opposite corner, he stood, walked over to the empty fireplace, and tossed the flaming paper into the grate. He enjoyed his cigar as he watched the message burn.

Where in the hell was Wartonville? More importantly, who did Silas know in Missouri who owed him a favor? He needed someone with power. A name came to mind and he smiled. Oh, yes, a judge in St. Louis that he had done a favor for, part of that big, rich Griswold family. Quickly, he scribbled a message, rang for Evans, and handed it over to the man. "See that this goes out right away."

The portly butler made a little bow. "I'll see to it personally, sir."

Good man, Evans. Silas smiled as the servant turned and left. Surely Judge Griswold could deal with a little matter in a nearby hick town. With any luck, that damned savage was about to disappear, whether dead, or into jail, never to be heard from again.

Serenity Peterson hardly slept all night for thinking about the incident of Billy Warton and the gallant stranger. What was she going to do if the deputy didn't turn her rescuer loose? She hoped she didn't have to find out. Serenity fixed breakfast for her frail mother, hardly hearing the querulous complaints anymore. Mother had never been the same since Father had finally died two years ago. In fact, his clothes were still hanging in the closet; Mother wouldn't let her give them away. Sometimes it seemed Serenity had spent her whole life looking after sick, elderly parents with never a life of her own.

They finished breakfast and dressed for church. In a small town like Wartonville, everyone went to Sunday services, whether it was because there wasn't much else to entertain respectable folks or they were all afraid they would get condemned and talked about by the local gossips if they didn't show up. Serenity dreaded attending this morning. News traveled fast in a small town; a lot of people would have heard about last night, and there would be curious stares.

She had never felt as lonely as she did this morning when she and her mother walked slowly to church. It would be nice to own a buggy, but the millinery shop didn't make that big a profit. When her mother finally died, Serenity dreamed of closing her shop and going farther west; yet she sometimes feared she would spend the rest of her drab life making hats for the prosperous matrons of this farming area.

As they settled themselves in their pew and picked up a hymnal, Serenity felt the bold stares of most of the congregation. She decided to ignore the unspoken questions. The church was hoping to build a larger, finer chapel, and of course, Hershel Warton was the biggest donor. The school needed land donated for a new building, and of course, the Wartons owned more land than anyone in the county. In spite of talk about right and wrong, Serenity might not be too popular in this town if she upset the status quo.

Billy and his mother took their places just as the first hymn began. The young rake looked a bit green, his face was swollen and bruised, and he seemed as nervous as a long-tailed cat in a room full of rocking chairs. Perhaps he wondered if Serenity might stand up and denounce him before the whole congregation. Mrs. Warton was wearing the fine new hat she'd just bought from Serenity last week. Hershel Warton was nowhere in sight.

Serenity forced herself to focus her attention on her hymnal. After services, she would go to the jail herself and see if they had turned the prisoner loose. Other than that, she didn't know what she was going to do.

Iron Knife awakened gradually, but he didn't move. Every bone in his body seemed to ache. Where was he and what had happened? He wrinkled his brow, attempting to remember. There had been a woman in trouble, and Iron Knife had tried to help her. He looked at the early morning sun streaming through the tiny eastern window, throwing a pattern of bars across the dirty floor. Already the heat was soaring and the place reeked.

The train. He had missed his train. Even as he struggled and realized his hands were manacled, he heard men talking in the outer room.

"Don't know why," Jingles' voice said, "but I got a telegram a few minutes ago from Judge Griswold in Saint Louie about that Injun."

"Oh?" That older man's voice from last night. "What'd he say?"

"He gave me instructions not to turn him loose; dangerous, he says."

"Lots of dangerous felons loose. Why would a low-down half-breed be someone an important judge would bother to send a telegram about?"

"Who knows, Mr. Warton?" The other man's spurs jingled as he crossed the floor. "Maybe it's just as well that we follow the judge's orders in case Serenity Peterson decides to talk."

"Well, let's do it; get him on his way before services are over. She might come by to see about him."

Iron Knife closed his eyes and pretended to be asleep. With leg chains and handcuffs, he didn't stand a chance unless he took the pair by surprise. Through the barred window, the faint music of morning services drifted on the hot breeze. Spurs jangled as the pair came to the front of the cell. Iron Knife kept his eyes shut.

"Big devil, ain't he? Looks kind of beat up, Jingles. What happened after I left last night?"

The tall deputy laughed cruelly. "I owed him something for messin' up my face; figured after the marks he put on your son, you wouldn't care."

"Jingles, you may get to be a sheriff someday yet," the older man said.

"I'm countin' on it, sir." His keys clattered as he opened the cell.

Iron Knife forced himself to lie still as the two entered. What were they going to do with him?

"Jingles, some of my men are waiting out back. We'll throw him in a wagon under a tarp, do like Griswold said."

What were they planning to do to him? Iron Knife lay coiled like a cat, ready to fight as they approached his bunk. As they hauled him to his feet, he came to life, fighting.

"What the hell—?" Jingles swore.

Even as Iron Knife slammed into Hershel Warton, he felt the deputy's pistol crashing down across his skull and almost blinding pain.

As he fell, he caught the last faint words from the older man. "Wouldn't you fight, too, to keep from being sent to a chain gang?"

The summer sun felt hot as Serenity walked her mother home after services, fixed her dinner and returned to the jail. The cells were empty. Jingles Johnson sat trimming his fingernails with a pocket knife behind the old desk.

"Mornin', Miss Peterson." He hopped up, made an exaggerated bow.

She nodded without speaking, knowing Jingles was sneering at her. "What happened to the man from last night?"

"Him? Why, Mr. Warton told me to turn him loose at dawn, so I did."

Why did she wonder about that? After all, the cells were empty.

"So just like we discussed, Miss Peterson, you're not gonna rock the boat now, are you?"

"I—I suppose not." She turned and left, hating herself for her weakness, yet relieved that she didn't have to make a moral decision that might cost her everything. She had done what she could do by sending that telegram; and after all, she had to live in this town. But that didn't make her feel any better about keeping silent.

One last thought occurred to her as she walked through the dust of the hot afternoon toward her small house: why hadn't the stranger come by to get his valise?

Water drenching him brought Iron Knife back to consciousness, coughing and choking. He came up fighting, heard the clank of chains, felt the irons bite into his ankles. He collapsed on the dirt as men laughed.

"Boy, he's a tough one, ain't he?"

"Don't worry, fourteen hours a day, six days a week buildin' roads in this hot sun will calm him down."

Where was he? Cautiously, he let his eyes flicker open again and looked around. He lay among a bunch of other men on the bare ground near an oversized wagon that might be sleeping quarters. A short, big-bellied man in a uniform was just setting down the water bucket. Keys at his belt rattled as he poked Iron Knife roughly with a rifle barrel. "You finished with your beauty sleep?"

The other men guffawed and chains clattered. Like him, they wore leg irons, and some looked meaner than a pack of wolves. The chain ran through all the leg irons and was secured at the wagon. Convicts; they must be convicts.

"What—what day is it?"

The rough, ugly man chained next to him scratched his beard and yawned. There were lice in his beard, Iron Knife realized with distaste. His long arms looked like his hands would drag the ground if he stood up, even though he was a big brute of a man. "It's Sunday afternoon; otherwise we'd be out on the road with picks and shovels."

The guard laughed and spat on Iron Knife's shoes. "That's right; don't never say our county judge's construction company ain't religious and kind to prisoners and that Farley don't do his duty."

Iron Knife must think, decide what to do. The summer sun beat down on the sweltering land, and sweat ran down his muscular body. He wanted a bath or a swim in a clear creek. He looked at the filthy men around him, the big brute with the lice in his beard. Was all this legal? This county judge must be powerful as well as corrupt.

"What're you starin' at, Injun?" The ugly brute scratched and glared at him. "You want trouble?"

Before he could answer, the guard prodded the bully with his rifle. "Easy, Tanner, you got that much energy to burn, use it on the road tomorrow."

He had to get out of here. Iron Knife searched through his pockets. His money and train ticket were gone. He wondered about his luggage, remembered dropping it in the street after he'd hit the drunk pawing that woman last night. He had nothing but the clothes on his back, and they were torn and stained. "Look," he said to the guard, "I don't belong here; there's been a mistake made."

The men around him laughed, and the guard laughed so hard, the keys on his big belly jangled. "Yeah, and you must have made it, Injun! Judge Griswold told us to take especially good care of you."

Maybe there had been a mistake; Iron Knife didn't know anyone named Griswold. Maybe he was a friend of the rich man from last night. "I've got to get a message to someone."

The guard yawned. "What's in it for me?"

"I don't have any money on me, but if you'll contact a Todd Shaw in Denver, he'll come or send money—"

"Yeah, and folks in hell want cold water, too." The guard grinned. "Forget it, Injun; you ain't goin' nowhere." He walked away.

"But I didn't do anything, except get in a fist fight! I don't belong here!"

Around him, the other chained men laughed and punched each other.

"I tell you I'm innocent!"

"Ain't we all?" said Tanner, picking lice out of his beard, popping them between his fingernails. "That don't make no nevermind. You upset someone very important, or they wouldn't have sent you here to Fatso."

"Who?"

"The guard, Farley; you know, the one with all the keys." Tanner nodded toward the short, squat guard. "We don't call him that to his face."

This was only a bad dream. Any minute, he'd wake up on the train again. "I've got to get to Boston."

Tanner frowned. He looked like the gorillas Iron Knife had once seen in a picture book. "You deaf, Injun? You ain't goin' nowhere; maybe never."

Iron Knife stared at the big chains on his own ankles. His fine boots were gone, and he now wore a pair of cheap, badly fitting shoes. It dawned on him that with no money and no way to reach anyone outside this isolated place, he could spend years like this and Todd or Summer couldn't find him, even if they tried. His head was still throbbing from the blows he'd suffered in

Wartonville. He lay down and closed his eyes, thinking. He'd have to watch and wait; come up with a plan. Otherwise, he might never escape this hellhole!

They chained the prisoners inside the wagon that night and locked the door. It was just like a cage, Iron Knife thought, and there were too many animals. It was sweltering hot, crowded and miserable, men sleeping on the floor wherever they could find a spot with one thin blanket each. In their sleep, men sobbed and swore. Some turned over restlessly, groaned in their sleep or prayed. He barely slept, as wary as a big wolf of danger. No one bothered him—perhaps because of his size—but he had a feeling that in the darkness, the strong were preying on the weak, stealing from them, taking revenge for past wrongs.

He heard a man cry out, then beg for mercy. The moon came from behind a cloud, and Iron Knife saw the scene in silhouette, recognized Tanner, and realized with horror what he was doing to the younger, smaller man. Iron Knife reacted, grabbing the big man, dragging him off the other.

Tanner came up cursing and swinging his powerful arms. Chains rattled as they fought. Around them, men awakened and scrambled to get out of the combatants' way as they struggled and rolled.

Iron Knife tasted blood as Tanner's big fist caught him in the mouth. He grabbed the man's leg chain, yanked him off his feet. When Tanner hit the floor, the whole wagon shook, and he swore under his breath.

"What the hell's going on, you lawless bastards?" a sleepy voice called out.

Immediately, there were lanterns and running feet, grumbling guards.

The prisoners around Iron Knife crouched against the floor and lay without moving.

"Now you've done it, Injun, we'll have Fatso comin'," Tanner snarled. "When you been here awhile, you learn to mind your own business!"

"You sorry—!" Iron Knife's words were cut short as he heard the sound of jangling keys as the fat guard ran, then paused.

"You jailbirds got time to fight? I'll see you get extra work tomorrow!" A bucket of water sloshed through the bars of the wagon, splashing them all. "I don't give a damn what you do to each other, just keep quiet about it!"

No one inside moved or spoke, and maybe Fatso didn't expect anything else. "It's okay," he called to the others, "no one out. Maybe just the usual; you know how long they been without women." He laughed coarsely as he walked away.

"Injun," Tanner whispered, "you'll regret messin' with Deek Tanner! I'm gonna get you sooner or later; I boss this bunch."

"Not anymore," Iron Knife said and lay down again with a sigh. Now not only was he in a hellhole, but he had made a dangerous enemy. Why did he always feel he had to come to the rescue of the weak and defenseless?

Tanner flopped back down. "I warn you, Injun, I'm a survivor and a lucky one, too. You'll regret you tangled with me."

"How long you been here?"

"More than four years," Tanner said. "You won't last that long if you play by the rules."

"We'll see." Four years. Iron Knife cringed at the thought. He wasn't sure he could stand four nights of this hell; much less four years. One thing was certain: he'd better not turn his back on Tanner.

The younger man had crawled over next to him. "Thanks," he whispered.

"How long's that been going on?"

"I—I—" his voice trembled. "I don't want to talk about it."

Iron Knife shuddered. "Stay close to me; you'll be all right."

The others settled back down, and Iron Knife could feel the tension ease a little throughout the wagon. Evidently Tanner had been running roughshod over all the prisoners, and now Iron Knife had challenged him. Sooner or later, he thought, he and Tanner would come to blows again. When he finally dropped off to sleep, he dreamed of Summer Sky running to meet him and him lifting her from the ground and carrying her while she kissed his face. The three children were scampering around their feet like playful puppies. Summer, oh, I love you so! Will I ever see you again? He was going to survive all right; he had to get to Boston!

Iron Knife's head still throbbed painfully as he leaned on his shovel in the sweltering Monday morning heat. It seemed like a million years ago since he had gotten off the train in Wartonville Saturday night, attempted to rescue a woman, gotten thrown in the little jail and woke up somewhere out in the country with this chain gang yesterday.

"All right, Injun, get back to work!" The big-gutted guard jabbed him with the barrel of his rifle. "You can rest when you're dead."

Iron Knife's hands clenched on the shovel handle, and he fought the urge to attack Farley with it. This was not the time or place to try to make his escape. He would have to make plans.

Grimly, he returned to shoveling along the road the other chained men were digging. The sun looked like molten brass in a dull blue sky, and he felt sweat running down his broad back under his soiled shirt. The iron cuff bit into his ankle, and the sweat made the raw skin sting. Leg chains clanked as the men worked without pause.

He glanced up and down the line, wondering what the other men's stories were. Some were young, some were old. Some looked too innocent to be guilty of much of anything, except being at the wrong place at the wrong time. The only one who looked like a vicious convict was Deek Tanner.

Iron Knife licked his dry, cracked lips, and gazed longingly toward the water barrel. "What about some water?" he yelled at the guard.

Fatso glared at him, then grinned. "Thirsty, huh? You got anything to trade?"

"You know I haven't; everything I had was stolen."

He felt the tension among the other men. No one dared to stand up to this short, big-gutted man with all the keys on his belt.

The guard bore down on him, keys rattling, while the others watched. He was going to get a beating; Iron Knife could see the anticipation in Fatso's small, piglike eyes.

Just then, another man in the line groaned and collapsed in a heap. That diverted the guard, who strode over and began to kick the downed man. "Get up, you lazy loafer! Get up!"

Despite the kicks, the man didn't react at all. Iron Knife looked down at the man. "You're wasting your time; he looks like he's dead."

The guard swore as if he'd been cheated. "Okay, Injun, drag him outta the road."

Iron Knife waited while they unchained the dead man, lifted and carried him over under a tree, laid him down very gently, then stood looking at him. The man was thin and might once have been handsome. There was no telling whether he was young or old because of all he'd been through. Flies were now lighting on the dead man's face.

"Okay, we ain't got all day," Fatso yelled. "Go back to work!" He gestured menacingly with his rifle.

Iron Knife looked from him to the dead man. "Are we just going to leave him here?"

Fatso yawned. "You can bury him on your own time after work tonight; otherwise, leave him to the crows."

It didn't seem right somehow, Iron Knife thought. He took off his shirt, spread it over the dead man's face to keep the flies off him, then went back to his place. Even as he began to shovel again, his sinewy muscles rippling, he heard a murmur among the men and looked up. They were all staring at him.

The guard said, "So you've been in worse jails than this! Where'd they beat you like that?"

He had almost forgotten the whip scars on his back. "Texas."

A scene flashed through Iron Knife's mind of that long-ago time in a small Texas town. He had been only a half-grown boy when an army scout named Jake Dallinger had whipped him almost to death.

"And I thought this county was tough on cons." Fatso guffawed. "What about those marks on your chest?"

These white men would never understand about the self-sacrifice of the Sun Dance. "Knife scars."

"You're a tough one, ain't ya? Now get back to work."

"What about the water?" Iron Knife demanded.

Again, he felt the tension as the other men paused. As

cruel as this guard was, most of them would take their
chances on dying from the sun rather than bring Fatso's
wrath down on them.

The guard walked over to the barrel, got himself a
dipperful, sipped from it slowly and deliberately, then
threw the rest of the dipperful on the ground. Every
man's gaze went to that muddy patch of dirt. "There's
your water, Injun."

He must not lose his temper and attack the man; that
was what Fatso was expecting, no, hoping for. It would
give him a chance to beat or shoot a prisoner.

"You'll lose some more men in this heat if they don't
get water," Iron Knife pointed out. "You won't get your
road built."

That seemed to give the guard pause. Obviously he
didn't give a damn about men, but he might have to answer to someone if the convicts didn't finish the road on
time. "All right"—he gestured with his gun—"everyone
can have a drink."

The men rushed the water barrel, Tanner clubbing the
others away with his big fists. The guard seemed
amused by the desperate struggle, and made no move to
bring order to the chaos.

Iron Knife pushed forward. "Take turns," he ordered,
"otherwise, you'll spill it all."

Tanner glared at him. "Who made you boss?"

"No point in wasting the water," Iron Knife said, and
gestured to another man. "You handle the dipper, give
each man some as they come by."

Deek's ugly face contorted in rage; then he seemed to
decide this wasn't the time or place for a showdown.
"Me first!"

He grabbed the dipper from the man's hand, gulped
the water, and grinned with it running down his dirty,
bearded face while the other men licked their lips and
watched.

Next, the man held the dipper out to Iron Knife, but
he shook his head. He had never been as thirsty as he
was at this moment. Memories of his life as a dog soldier flashed before him. A novice riding on his first war
party was always in charge of the water but the last to
drink. There were rituals about eating and drinking for
a brave warrior. Out on a war party, a brave must not
eat or drink that first day until after sundown to show
his strength of character and his body. He had learned
that honor was more important than thirst. "See the others get a drink," he said softly.

The others lined up orderly now, nodding their
thanks. Iron Knife could feel Tanner and the guard
watching him.

"All right"—Fatso scratched his big belly—"don't
take all day about it; we've got a road to build!"

Finally, the last of the men had had a sip of water,
and Iron Knife urged the man who held the dipper to
take a drink. He himself was the very last to dip into the
barrel. The water was warm from the sun's heat and
tasted a little muddy, but he drank it. In his mind, he
saw Summer laughing as she held her small hands
under the icy cold water of a mountain spring and he
drank from her dainty palm, then kissed her fingertips
and embraced her. Her lips were as warm as her fingertips were cold. . . .

"Everybody back to work!" The guard nudged him
with his rifle.

Images of Summer Sky faded, and Iron Knife sighed
as he returned to the dusty roadway. What was he going
to do? He had no money, no way to reach anyone. Even
if Todd Shaw or Summer were looking for him, they
wouldn't know where to search. By now, that train he
had ridden was probably in Boston. He didn't even want
to think about that. Todd would assume Iron Knife had

arrived. As a matter of fact, Iron Knife wasn't sure exactly where he was, except somewhere in Missouri. He wasn't even certain which way it was to the nearest town or the closest railroad track.

Finally at noon, another guard down the line blew a whistle, and the men stacked their tools and sat down in the shade of a tree to have some stale bread and a cup of bad coffee. It didn't seem like enough food, Iron Knife thought, knowing now why the dead man had been so thin. Tanner was sitting close to him, staring at him. "I was raised by Injuns; I know how you think."

"So?"

Tanner lowered his voice. "You plannin' on escapin', I reckon."

Iron Knife shrugged. "Isn't everyone?"

"Naw!" He made a face. "Some of 'em will plug along like tame mules like that one this mornin' until they collapse and die in the road."

Iron Knife said, "Are chain gangs legal in Missouri?"

Tanner laughed and combed a louse out of his beard with his dirty hands, cracked it between his nails. "I don't know; but this is Judge Griswold's county, and he has an interest in this construction project. He pretty much runs things as he sees fit."

"I haven't done anything to attract this judge's notice and I never got a trial," Iron Knife said.

Deek snorted. "So what? I got a trial and you see what it got me? I've been in almost four years; they gave me life."

Life. The thought sent a chill down Iron Knife's back. He saw himself laboring in summer's heat and winter's cold forever. Even four weeks seemed like more than any human could endure.

His eyes must have betrayed that feeling because Tanner grinned. "Deek Tanner's a survivor, Injun, and you'll learn to be one, too, or end up dead as that poor bastard out under that tree." He nodded toward the dead man lying under Iron Knife's shirt in the distance. "I reckon I'm lucky at that; I was supposed to be the scout on that wagon train that became such a disaster."

Iron Knife thought a minute. "You mean the Donner party where the people got stranded in a blizzard and ate their dead to survive?"

"There was a worse one than that," Tanner said, "it just didn't get much notice. Like I said, I'm a survivor. Sooner or later, I'll escape from here."

The guard walked past just then, keys jingling on his fat belly. "You two, back to work."

This must be what hell was like, Iron Knife thought dully as he returned to his shovel, laboring in a red-hot sun from daylight until dark on a few mouthfuls of food. Tanner looked to be in fairly good shape; he must be stealing the other men's bread. There was no telling what lengths the ruthless convict would go to to live.

Iron Knife shoveled and thought about escape. Tanner seemed as cunning as a coyote, and yet he hadn't managed to escape in four long years. The horrible thought occurred to him that he could labor on this prison work force for four months, four years or forever and maybe Todd or Summer would never know what had happened to him.

Deek Tanner was right: somehow, Iron Knife was going to have to be a survivor—think and plan. He leaned over to the boy working next to him. "What did Tanner do to get here?"

"Murder, I hear. He was raised by Injuns: Blackfoot."

Blackfoot. A formidable enemy of the Cheyenne, cunning and dangerous. Yes, Tanner would be a survivor, all right; he'd have to be if he'd been raised by that hostile tribe.

Iron Knife labored and felt the sweat run down his naked, scarred back. He intended to be a survivor, too, so he could finish his journey to Boston. Nothing mattered to him so much as holding his beloved Summer Sky in his arms once more.

Chapter Nineteen

The heat of the summer months seemed almost unbearable for Summer as her pregnancy advanced and her belly swelled. In July, the sentencing of the conspirators in the Lincoln assassination were carried out: three to prison, four hanged, including a Mrs. Mary Surratt, who some weren't convinced was guilty of anything except owning the boardinghouse where the plotters met and made plans.

President Andrew Johnson's moderate stance toward the South enraged Northern firebrands who wanted to punish the Rebels severely. There were mutterings of eventual impeachment.

Summer would not let herself think about the future or about Iron Knife. She concentrated on getting through this pregnancy, which seemed so much more difficult than usual, and nurturing her children. Father had insisted they needed to learn more English, and he was probably right; so she worked with them on that. It seemed to make the time pass, she thought. Only Lance appeared at home in the big mansion. For such a small boy, he was intelligent and took to civilization; he liked going to the office with his grandfather.

Storm Gathering was the one who reminded Summer of Iron Knife. One day, a vicious dog wandered into the yard. In answer to Storm's shouts, she went out to find him striking at the big beast with a stick, protecting his little sister. His father would be so proud, she thought.

Iron Knife. Her heart turned over as she thought of him. She couldn't believe he might have left her for another woman. Sometime soon after this baby was born, she intended to go out to see Todd Shaw, find out what he knew, perhaps arrange a meeting with Iron Knife. She could not, would not believe their life together was over until she heard it from his own lips. Soon the heat would turn slowly into crisp autumn with cool winds and golden leaves swirling around her feet when she went out on the estate's beautiful grounds; but in her heart, it was already as cold and lonely as winter.

So the weeks passed. It was now September, and in Boston, the heat seemed unusually sultry to Summer; or maybe it was only that she was so very pregnant. As near as she could figure, her baby was due late in September. Why was she so large? Perhaps she had misfigured the time. Dr. Morgan had shrugged off her worries, but then, men often treated women like idiots. Besides, he was busy with his usual typhoid and cholera cases that always seemed to hit in warm weather and were just beginning to taper off.

But only a couple of nights later, she was awakened by uncomfortable pangs in her back. Perhaps it was the way she had been sleeping. She got up and went to get herself a glass of water. Maybe it was something she had eaten. She certainly hoped she wasn't going to come down with something; that was always a worry, for who knew if modern medicine would ever figure out the cause of things like the dreaded yellow fever?

She took her lamp and went down the hall to check on her children. The three were sleeping like angels, she thought fondly. If only their father could see them now—no, she must not think of Iron Knife. She had stopped writing finally, when she got that telegram from Todd telling her Iron Knife had taken a Cheyenne girl as his woman.

With the Civil War ended, the government could now send many of its soldiers to fight Indians and drive them back to their reservations or deeper into the mountains and hidden valleys. Summer didn't even want to think what might have happened to her friends among the Cheyenne; she could only hope they were all safe. Her brother, David, was still working with the wounded in that Washington, D.C. hospital, and Austin and Custer's command had been transferred from Louisiana to Texas to keep the peace and deal with sullen Rebels who resented the victorious Yankee troops and carpetbaggers already pouring into the defeated South.

As far as Iron Knife, once this child was born, she would contact him again and tell him about it. Maybe then her man would have a change of heart, and Summer loved him still whether he loved her or not.

The baby moved, and she experienced a pain that radiated from her back around to her belly. It felt like . . . no, Summer shook her head; it wasn't time yet. She patted her belly fondly. Poor little tyke, she had been too worried, too preoccupied with everything that had happened to even think of names. Would it be a boy or a girl? Should she give it an Indian name?

Summer frowned and settled herself in her rocking chair near her bedroom window where she could get a breath of air on this warm night. The pain radiated around again, and she shifted her weight in the chair, trying to find a comfortable position. Maybe it was that fish she had had for supper; it might have been tainted. No one else had complained about indigestion.

Out in the hall, she heard plump Mrs. O'Malley's heavy step, and the woman stuck her head in the door. "Love, are ye feelin' all right?"

Summer shook her head. "I—no, I'm not. Maybe it was something I ate. Are you ill, too?"

The woman shook her head. "I'm fine, love; got up to check on the wee ones." She turned, and Summer heard her slippers padding down the hall.

A pain gripped Summer hard, and now she faced the reality of what it was. She cried out as she felt a hot rush of fluid.

Immediately, Mrs. O'Malley hurried back into the room. "Is it time?"

"Yes!" Summer gasped. "I didn't think—but my water just broke; the baby's coming!"

The maid looked alarmed. "It's not time, is it?"

"I—I thought not, but I'm so very big; maybe I miscalculated. Help me to my bed."

The maid obliged. "Now, don't you worry, lamb, I'll get the doctor, rouse the house."

Summer caught her arm. She didn't really want Father and Angela in her room. "No use waking everyone yet."

Mrs. O'Malley's plump face mirrored concern. "I'll send the coachman for the doctor, and me and little Nancy will handle everything. You just rest, lamb, we'll take care of things!" She rushed from the room.

Summer lay back on her bed and wished her mother were alive to comfort her. Even though there were many people in the house, Summer felt so alone. Iron Knife; she wanted Iron Knife.

Don't be so silly, she told herself, *you've given birth three times already in a tipi on the windswept plains.* She could feel the sweat beading on her face and dampening her hair as the pain started again. She would not think of the pain; she would think of names for this baby. Dr. Morgan would be here soon, and he would have the latest in modern medicine, chloroform, so she wouldn't have to endure all this pain. Wasn't it wonderful what modern medicine could do?

A boy's name. She searched her mind and came up with nothing. Among the Cheyenne, a favorite uncle usually offered a name for the child, but Summer was a long way from the Indians. A girl's name, yes, she had thought of a number of those, finally getting it down to two. Her artistic twin brother, David, had suggested Lark, and Summer liked the association with nature and the song bird. On the other hand, she also like Lacy; that name sounded so feminine. If it was a girl, maybe she would just flip a coin.

Nancy scurried into the room. "Oh, Miss Summer, is it time?"

"I—I didn't think so, but my water broke."

"Well, now, ma'am, you just lay back and rest while I get things ready. Mrs. O'Malley has gone down to send Flannigan for the doctor."

Everything would be all right, Summer thought as she lay back and closed her eyes, conserving her strength. After all, she'd had no trouble with her other three births. A horrifying thought crossed her mind: suppose she died? Who would rear her children? Did she really want them raised in this grim house if she wasn't around to protect them from her father's stern wrath? Besides, he played favorites and doted on and spoiled Lance. The other two, Silas paid very little heed.

Even lying here with her eyes closed, she could hear the house beginning to stir awake. Through the open window, she heard Flannigan driving the buggy out of the carriage house. The cook was stirring around downstairs. Then the plump Irish woman's heavy footsteps started back up the stairs.

Summer could do nothing now but wait, she thought, and think about happier times; no, maybe she didn't want to think of that, either, because she always thought of Iron Knife and that made her incredibly sad. She heard Mrs. O'Malley puff across the room.

"Everything's taken care of, lamb, now you just relax."

The pain started again. "Is—is Dr. Morgan on his way?"

"Aye, lamb, don't worry about anything. Now what do you intend to call this wee babe?"

The maid sounded worried, trying to keep Summer's mind occupied. She thought about names so that she wouldn't feel the pain radiating around from her back. "I—I don't have a boy's name yet. If it's a girl, do you like Lark or Lacy?"

Mrs. O'Malley's gentle hands laid a wet cloth across Summer's sweating face. Oh, it felt so good.

"Well, lamb, they're both pretty; maybe ye could put both names in a hat."

"Maybe," Summer muttered. Right now with this pain grabbing her, it didn't seem important. What was important was surviving this childbirth so her father wouldn't end up controlling her children. After that, Summer would have to decide whether she was going to try to hold her union with Iron Knife together, stay in this gloomy house, or possibly marry Austin or Beau.

When the pain released her, she lay back on the pillow, breathing hard while Mrs. O'Malley mopped her hot face with the cold cloth. Summer closed her eyes and endured. After what seemed like a lifetime, she heard Dr. Morgan's firm step in the hall. Now she could stop worrying; he would have all the latest to make childbirth easier. She looked up at him with his white mustache and sideburns.

He put his hand on her head, very cool and professional. "You just relax, my dear, I've got some chloroform, very latest thing. I'll give you a little of it."

The pain was beginning again. "Hurry, Doctor."

"Here it is."

Summer took a deep whiff on the sweetish scent and immediately felt a bit giddy. She knew she couldn't have a lot of it, but a little just to dull the pain was wonderful. When she opened her eyes again, he was scowling slightly. Something must not be going well.

"I wish I knew more about Cesareans," he muttered to himself, but she heard him, "afraid to risk it, though."

In the background as she faded away under the chloroform, she heard Nancy say, "What about the hospital?"

"Blessed Mary!" Mrs. O'Malley's shocked voice floated to Summer like an echo. "Everyone knows that's where you get infections—die. Miss Summer's better off in her own house!"

"Have to agree with you there," Dr. Morgan said under his breath, "but they're getting better. Maybe she can manage with just some hard labor and some chloroform."

Summer smelled the scent under her nose again, took a deep breath of it so the merciful blackness would make the pain fade.

She seemed to be drifting somewhere, maybe in a pleasant stream or through the clouds. She and Iron Knife were running together, laughing. She looked toward the dazzling sun of her dreams. The face of God. Was He calling to her? She wanted to go so very badly; yet she hesitated because behind her, she heard Iron Knife's voice, and his plea echoed in the deep silence: *Don't go; not without me. I need you so. . . .*

She turned toward him; yet she could feel the blinding light warm her, and it seemed to be more than she could do not to run up the clouds toward God.

"I'm afraid we're losing her." The voice came drifting through the swirls of darkness. Dr. Morgan's voice; what was he doing in her dream? And the sounds of

Mrs. O'Malley saying her rosary amid sobs. The sounds echoed around her as if they drifted over a great distance like waves crashing against the shore.

Even the pain seemed so very far away now, and Summer turned toward the blinding light. Where that light was, there was no pain and unhappiness, and she was so very tired.

A faint cry . . . a baby? Her baby, her baby needed her. Not yet then, she couldn't go yet.

Somewhere far away, she heard a familiar Irish voice saying a rosary, and Dr. Morgan's worried voice: "Her pulse is stronger, but if she makes it, she'll never have another child. Here, Mrs. O'Malley, take the baby, Summer's coming back; she's breathing again! Wait a minute, what have we here?"

Summer forced her eyes to open. Dr. Morgan hovered over her. He looked as unnerved as she had ever seen him. What was he so upset about?

"Stay with us, Summer, dear; stay with us. You're needed here."

A baby was wailing in the background. It was making a lot of noise for one baby.

The blinding light faded completely now, and Summer took a deep breath and surveyed the room, realizing where she was as Dr. Morgan worked feverishly. She was so very, very weak and tired. Her old bedroom. She was in her own bedroom. Disappointment washed over her. She didn't want to wake up in this lonely old house. Why was Dr. Morgan here and why was she so very tired? Then she remembered and craned her head toward the maids in the background. "Girl?"

"Aye." Mrs. O'Malley came to her bedside, plump, kindly face beaming, and she held a bundle in each arm. "Aye, lamb, and you won't have to make a choice of names between Lark and Lacy."

"Why?" Summer looked up as Mrs. O'Malley bent

forward, and Summer saw two perfect small faces with delicate features and just wisps of dark blond hair.

"Twins, love! And aren't the wee lassies beautiful!"

Summer looked at the two tiny bundles Mrs. O'Malley held, and reached out to stroke the soft down of their dark blond hair. It seemed to take all her energy to speak. "Are they all right?"

Dr. Morgan nodded. "Fine, but small. You gave us a bad scare, young lady!" He took off his stethoscope. "Your color is better. Why don't you rest now and let us worry about everything?"

She wanted to tell someone now about how she had seen the face of God and how wonderful it had been. Would they believe her? Was it only something Summer had imagined? She wasn't sure now and maybe it didn't matter. The babies had stopped their wailing as Mrs. O'Malley cuddled them close. Lark and Lacy. Twin girls. How proud Iron Knife would be if he knew . . . or would he? She couldn't think about that now; she would take on that worry when she was strong enough. With a sigh, Summer dropped off into a deep, healing sleep.

As days had turned into weeks and the summer passed, Iron Knife's muscles had grown even harder as he worked with pick and shovel in the hot sun. What kept him going was the memory of his woman and seeing her again. Somehow, he vowed, he would escape and make his way to her, but he was no longer even sure how long he had been here, except that the leaves were beginning to yellow.

Deek Tanner threatened him again after Iron Knife stopped him from stealing another man's bread. "I'm gonna kill you one of these days, Injun, and I'm lookin' forward to it. The Blackfeet know how to keep a man alive while they cut him to little pieces."

"I've killed Blackfeet," Iron Knife sneered, "don't count my scalp yet."

"Stop that talking!" Fatso yelled, and he waved his rifle, making the keys jangle on his belt. Iron Knife looked at those keys and wondered for the thousandth time how to get his hands on those.

As days passed into weeks, yellow leaves turned red and gold and the weather gradually cooled. All the men did with methodical sameness was work on that road. Periodically, the camp was moved as the road progressed, but nothing changed except the faces as men died or served out their sentences. They worked in the rain and in the dry dust. At least the yellow and gold leaves and crisp mornings finally signaled the end of the terrible heat. Iron Knife kept his sanity by planning his escape and dreaming of making love to his beautiful Summer Sky and riding across the prairies, free as the wind.

As he labored, he watched the guards, wondering how and when would come the opportunity. He also kept one eye on Deek Tanner, who seemed ready to challenge him at every chance. Since Iron Knife had arrived and had stood up to the bully, Deek had lost a lot of his prestige and power. The other men were not as afraid of him as they had been in the past, since Iron Knife had shown them uniting and standing up to a bully would protect them.

Chained as the men were, it didn't seem possible to ever escape. How could anyone ever get those keys from Farley's belt when the fat guard was armed? If Tanner had been working on an escape for four years without any luck, could Iron Knife ever come up with a workable plan?

In the meantime, Tanner never missed the chance to trip him or shove him out of line, which always started a fight. In fact, on Saturday night, when the guards had been drinking and were wanting entertainment, they often staged a fight between two prisoners. With their shackles attached to each other on a short chain, the guards would put a pair of men out in the center of the circle and let them fight. The winner got extra food.

One cool autumn night, they put Iron Knife and Tanner on the chains in the firelit circle while the guards drank and made bets.

"All right, you bastards," Fatso growled, "you been fightin' off and on for weeks, now let's see what you can do."

The sturdy chain was not more than ten feet in length, Iron Knife thought as he and Tanner stripped to the waist. Iron Knife knew he was quicker on his feet, but Tanner was as big as he was and had the advantage of long arms and powerful shoulders.

Even the men in the prison wagons were watching as the firelit audience fell silent. Iron Knife and Tanner circled each other warily. Then abruptly, Tanner dived for Iron Knife's legs. They meshed and went down, carried by the heavier weight of the white man. They rolled over and over, chains rattling while the guards goaded them on.

"Sic 'em, Tanner, get that Injun!"

"Hey, Injun, kill 'em and we'll let you eat his liver!"

They rolled in the dirt, each fighting to come up on top. Even though the night was cool, both of them were sweating, and dirt and leaves stuck to their big bodies. Iron Knife could smell Tanner's sweat as they meshed and struggled. Tanner, with his superior weight, was edging Iron Knife toward the fire. He felt the heat of the flames as they twisted and moved. The fire was hot on his arm as they fell again, and Tanner grinned with delight as he slowly forced Iron Knife's arm down toward the flames. The heat seemed unbearable as they struggled, with Tanner grinning and the guards shouting and cheering them on.

Iron Knife felt intense pain as Tanner forced his arm still lower. "Burn, Injun." Deek grinned. "Let's see how much of this you can take!"

Iron Knife gritted his teeth. The pain was pure agony, but a Cheyenne warrior did not cry out and disgrace himself; especially one who had done the Sun Dance, and who carried the *Hotamtsit.* He smelled the scent of burning flesh, and in that split-second, he thought he must scream; but with a superhuman effort, he shifted his weight and tossed the clumsy Tanner to one side, then staggered to his feet. His arm seemed a mass of agony as he faced the grinning Tanner, who came toward Iron Knife like a big animal, clumsy, lumbering. Iron Knife was faster on his feet and sidestepped easily while the guards shouted and cheered them on.

Even as Tanner turned toward him, Iron Knife grabbed the chain, jerked hard. Tanner's feet went out from under him, and he fell heavily. Instantly, Iron Knife was on him, taking him across his knee, bending his back.

Tanner began to scream in craven terror. "Stop him! For God's sake, he'll break my back!"

Iron Knife applied even more pressure while Tanner struggled and begged. The wolfish faces of the guards were alit with pleasure at the excitement, the pain. Tanner was weeping now. "Please. . . ."

"Kill him!" Fatso shouted. "You've got him; now kill him!" The other drunken men urged him on.

Abruptly, Iron Knife wearied of the game. There was no honor in killing a coward who begged like a terrified woman for his life. He stood up, and dumped the weeping, groveling man in the dirt. "Warriors don't stoop to fighting dogs and crying cowards," he sneered.

"By God, why didn't you kill him? I had five dollars

bet on you!" Fatso shouted, evidently angry that Iron
Knife had let him go. In the background, the others argued over who had won what bet.

Iron Knife shrugged. "He isn't worth killing; a Cheyenne boy could handle him."

Tanner struggled to get up. "You'll regret not killing
me tonight," he vowed. "Sooner or later, I'll get you!"

"I sleep lightly; you won't catch me unawares."
Chains rattling, Iron Knife strode over, picked up the
bucket of water, plunged his throbbing arm into it, and
sighed with relief. He wasn't burnt that badly. One thing
he knew: by humiliating Deek Tanner in front of the
other men, Iron Knife had made a mortal enemy. He had
better be doubly careful about turning his back on the
vicious convict ever again.

Only that fight broke the miserable monotony as the
days passed with many dead leaves swirling around
their feet now as the convicts worked on the roadway.
Soon, Iron Knife knew, their common enemy would be
the cold, not the heat. If he was ever going to escape, it
needed to be soon before the hellhole cost him his sanity.

He hadn't reckoned on Tanner's cunning. One afternoon as shadows lengthened, Fatso's crew had gradually
worked their way farther down the road away from the
other crews. Iron Knife shoveled dirt, glad his arm was
almost healed. His thoughts were on Summer Sky.

"Look out!" a man shouted, even as Iron Knife felt
the shadow fall across him. He whirled as fast as a
heartbeat, throwing up his shovel in self-defense even as
Tanner brought his down at Iron Knife's back. Iron
Knife's shovel handle deflected the downward blow,
and steel rang on steel as the two men fought, feinting
and jabbing like two fencers with crude weapons. Tan-

ner had the advantage of longer arms; but Iron Knife had fought all his life with a deadly Cheyenne lance, and he was quicker, smarter.

They battled silently now, each breathing heavily, the other convicts ringing them to watch. The only sound was the clang of razor-sharp steel on steel. Tanner jabbed, and Iron Knife defended himself; but the white man feinted, came in under Iron Knife's arm. He meant to gut him, Iron Knife knew, but again, he deflected the deadly blow and took a glancing cut across the arm.

The pain felt like fire across his dark skin, and Tanner grinned in triumph as he saw the scarlet blood on the steel of his shovel. "And now, Injun, I'm gonna gut you; spill your insides all over this road!" The fading sunlight reflected on the bloody steel as he raised it again.

"What the hell's going on?" Fatso bellowed, lumbering up behind Tanner. Past his opponent's shoulder, Iron Knife saw the fat man's eyes light up with anticipation at the bloody fight, and the guard paused, his rifle lowered.

Cunning as a coyote, Tanner whirled abruptly. Fatso never got out the scream that was caught in his throat as Tanner buried the sharp blade of the shovel in the fat neck. Blood spurted and keys jangled as Fatso fell, his head half-torn away.

Tanner dropped the shovel and grinned as he dived for the guard's rifle. "And now, Injun, you get yours and I escape!"

Even as he brought the gun up, Iron Knife moved faster than a scorpion's sting. He charged in with the shovel, hit Tanner across the forehead. Blood spurted as the big man fell, the rifle under him.

Iron Knife heard his own labored breathing in that split second as he grabbed for the keys and unlocked his leg irons. In the distance, he heard whistles blasting high and shrill as other guards yelled at each other, and came running toward the crew.

He hesitated, caught by the mute appeal in the other prisoners' eyes. Without a word, he tossed the keys to the nearest man. The rifle—he needed the guard's rifle, but it was under Tanner's big body. In the distance, a guard passed and fired; the bullet sang close to his ear. He looked once more toward the rifle under the two bodies, glanced toward the running, shooting guards. It would take precious seconds to get that gun. The guards' bullets were whining around him now, throwing up dust.

Iron Knife stood near dense woods. It was almost sundown. Turning, Iron Knife raced into the thick trees where he had the advantage. How long would it take for the guards to bring in hounds to search for him? A couple of hours? If he was captured this time, he'd be hanged for murder. He'd take his chances in the forest and be killed rather than be captured. He ran easily like the warrior he was, remembering now how he had run in vain, attempting to save the camp at Sand Creek. He ran now until the noise and confusion behind him was lost on the breeze; paused, breathing hard, trying to decide what to do.

It would be fairly easy to steal a horse at some farm house, head back to Colorado where he was safe in the endless Rockies or trackless plains. Yet Summer Sky, his beloved, was in Boston, and he wanted to be with her more than he valued his own life. What to do? He had no money, no weapon, not even a change of clothes, and the ones he wore were recognizable prison garb. No doubt, the guards would blame him for Fatso's death, too. When word got out a prisoner had killed someone and escaped, there would probably be a reward offered, and every scout and farmer in the area would be loading weapons. Even unarmed, a Cheyenne warrior was fierce and dangerous. While the odds were staggering of him getting out of this area alive, he was a carrier of the *Hotamtsit,* one of the bravest of the dog soldiers, and he carried the scars of the Sun Dance on his brawny chest. No, he would not retreat to the safety of Colorado; he was going to Boston, no matter the odds.

He must not leave behind his sacred dog soldier things. Where in Wartonville might they be? Was it possible that woman he had rescued might have picked his valise up or were they at the jail? Many answers lay in that town. Following the stars for directions, Iron Knife set off for Wartonville. He had no idea how far it was or whether he could get out of that hostile place alive, but he had to try. No dog soldier worthy of the name would abandon his ceremonial costume. What he would do or how to proceed when he got to the town, he wasn't sure. One thing was certain, he thought as he ran through the night, he had to go back to Wartonville, no matter if it cost him his life!

It was late when he reached the town. Had word reached here yet about his escape? The town looked asleep, few lights burning. He wished he had time for the luxury of revenge; the temptation was strong. Even as the thought crossed his mind, Iron Knife shook his head. As much as he would like to hunt down that deputy and the Wartons, to do so would be to risk recapture or death. At this moment, not even vengeance was as important as recovering his dog soldier things, if possible, and going on to Boston.

Which house was Serenity Peterson's? He searched his memory for bits of conversation, remembering she had a small house not too far from where he had rescued her. That narrowed it down to half a dozen homes. Some of the houses looked too prosperous; several had children's wagons and toys in the yard, which eliminated them. He peeked in the window of another that had a light on, saw two old men playing checkers. That left one house, a weather-beaten, modest place with faint light coming from a window. Iron Knife peered in. Serenity Peterson sat on a sofa reading a book in the dim light of a kerosene lamp.

Very gently, he rapped on the glass. She started, dropped her book. When she turned her head and saw him, shock and surprise registered on her plain little face. Then she smiled, got up, and gestured toward the door. He went to it and heard her unbolt the lock as she opened it.

"What in the world are you doing here?" she asked.

"Please," he said, "they're looking for me; I might be seen out here."

She stepped back and gestured him inside. While she went to draw the curtains, Iron Knife looked around. The parlor was clean but threadbare. There was no doubt that the woman was living in the most modest circumstances, having a difficult time surviving. "Are you alone?"

She shook her head. "My mother's gone to bed; she isn't well. Serenity smiled and it lit up her plain little face. "I returned to the jail the next day to thank you, see what I could do to help, but Jingles said they had turned you loose."

"He lied, but it doesn't matter. I've just escaped and they're looking for me."

She appeared horrified. "But they told me—"

"It's too complicated to explain"—Iron Knife shrugged —"but they may come ask you some questions."

"Well, I certainly don't intend to help them!" Serenity vowed. "I still feel guilty about not speaking up that night; but I have to live in this town—at least until Mother dies."

"Until women are willing to stand up for themselves, have the courage to speak out," Iron Knife said, "you will always be victims." He looked around. "Did you by any chance pick up my suitcase that night?"

"Yes, I've kept it all this time, uncertain what to do with it." She went to a chest in the corner, opened it, and handed Iron Knife his bag.

He took it, opened it, then breathed a sigh of relief. All his dog soldier things were there. "Thank you."

"No, I should be thanking you for rescuing me."

"Have you had any more trouble from the son?"

Serenity shook her head. "Warton has sent him away to a military academy." She bit her lip, shame-faced. "I want you to know I did try to help you later that night; I sent a telegram to the woman whose name I found in your valise."

"Summer?"

She nodded.

"And?" He was afraid to hear the answer.

"And nothing." Serenity shrugged. "I got no answer of any kind, so I didn't know what to do next. Then the deputy told me they had turned you loose, so I thought I had done all I could."

Iron Knife considered for a long moment. All he could think of was that Summer hadn't been interested enough to even inquire further. He was heartsick at the thought, but not surprised; that only confirmed his own experiences with telegrams and letters. Yet he could not give up until he had faced her, heard from her own lips that their union was over. "I've got to go; the law will be searching everywhere for me."

"Do you need money?" Serenity reached for her small reticule.

He looked around at the frayed furniture, her faded dress. Whatever she gave him would probably be money she had saved back for rent or food. "No"—he shook his head—"I can manage."

"Are you sure?"

"I'll be fine."

Serenity looked at his clothes. "You won't go far in that prison garb. My father's things are still in the back closet, and he was about your size."

"I don't think—"

"I insist. There's even shoes, but maybe not a very good fit."

Iron Knife hesitated, then realized she was right; what he now wore marked him as a convict. "All right." He went into the back room, hurriedly changed, and came out. "Thank you, miss, I must be going."

She reached out and caught his arm, her plain little face looking up at him earnestly. "Let me at least give you some leftover meat and bread." She hurried to the kitchen with him protesting that she needn't bother.

"Serenity, don't bother."

"It'll only take a moment." She was grabbing bread, reaching for a newspaper to wrap food in.

He would be needing food, and it seemed churlish to refuse this gesture of gratitude.

She handed it to him, then hesitated, wiping her hands on her faded apron. "I—I realize I'm older than you, but if things don't work out in Boston, or you should ever be in this area again—"

"Thank you, Serenity." Very gently, he interrupted before she could say words she might regret. "I must be going now and put many miles between me and this town before daylight."

Serenity watched him slip out the door. She stared at the door for a long moment, wanting to run after him shouting, "Take me with you! For a man like you, I would turn my back on everything. Take me with you!"

With a sigh, she went to lock the door and leaned

against it. The house was deathly silent, the only sound that of the clock on the wall ticking . . . ticking . . . ticking. . . . She could only envy the woman he loved, and at this moment, Serenity was painfully aware of her dull, drab lonely life. Somewhere maybe there was a man who would love and appreciate her, a real man like the one who had just walked out her door. Someday, Serenity thought, she would find that man, and now she vowed from this moment on, she would never be a victim again!

Carrying his small valise, Iron Knife ran through the darkness. That dear face came to his mind again, that heart-shaped face with its pale blue eyes and wild yellow mane of hair. *My once in a lifetime love; my Summer Sky.*

Somehow, against impossible odds, he was resuming his journey, and now it would be even more difficult with no money, no ticket and the law searching for him. None of that mattered; all that mattered was that he was on his way. One thing was certain, the whole drama would finally come to a climax when he arrived in Boston and faced Summer Sky!

Chapter Twenty

Even if he had the money for a ticket, Iron Knife would have been too cautious to board the train at Wartonville because he knew the law would certainly check the station. What to do? The easiest thing would be to give up, steal a horse from some isolated farm, and return to Colorado.

Iron Knife had never been one to take the easy route. Although he knew he risked disgrace and death if recaptured, he determined to finish his journey to Boston. It was worth risking his life to see his once in a lifetime love again in hopes that she would return with him to his beloved West.

Iron Knife stayed in the shadows until he was clear of the town, but he kept the distant railroad tracks in sight. The silver tracks gleamed in the moonlight as he ran through the darkness, his strong legs covering many miles.

Finally, he came across a water tower and knew that here the Iron Horse must stop in its journey to take on water. Perhaps he could steal a ride on a boxcar when a train heading east stopped for a few minutes. He hid under some bushes, rested, ate the meat and bread Serenity had given him and waited while the night air blew cool against his body.

It brought back memories, and he smiled, remembering the times on cool nights such as this, when he had lifted Summer to the broad back of his stallion before him. They had galloped through the darkness, his big arms holding her protectively while she leaned against him, her small, soft body fitting with his as if she were created for only that purpose. Her yellow hair was like loose, scented silk as he buried his face in it, kissing the nape of her neck. Finally, they had stopped, and he had slipped his hands under her loose deerskin shift, marveling in the satin of her skin, the heat of her breasts and belly. Just the feel of her against him made his maleness throb with wanting.

He had slipped from the stallion and held his hands up to her wordlessly. *Come, my little one.* Her gaze held his as she slid off into his embrace. Summer Sky was like a small, delicate treasure in his powerful arms as he carried her up to a snug haven in the rocks. There in the moonlight, they made leisurely love throughout the night, their bodies blending together in a rhythm of mutual ecstasy and pleasure over and over and over. . . .

A shrill whistle echoed through the blackness of the night, and he started, torn out of his memories. Somewhere in the distance, a train was approaching from the direction of Wartonville. He could hear it long before he could see its one yellow eye coming down the track. The sound of its whistle and chugging engine were followed by the scent of its burning wood and flying cinders.

Cautiously, Iron Knife waited in the underbrush and watched while the crew refilled from the water tower. In the windows of the coaches, he could see people; most of them asleep, a few looking out at the landscape. He had no way of knowing where this train was going, except that it was headed east. Somewhere east of here was this place called Boston, and that was all he needed to know. He must leave Missouri, where armed posses were even now scouring the landscape for him. Once he was out of this area, then he would worry about how to find the train that would take him to Boston. Iron Knife watched and waited until the train began to pull away from the water tower. He must not be seen by the crew as he got aboard. Carrying his small valise with his precious dog soldier costume, he ran toward the track as the train began to pick up speed, hoping to swing aboard one of the last box cars.

The train picked up speed faster than he had expected. He was running alongside, looking for an open boxcar door. If he didn't get aboard and was outdistanced, the man in the caboose might spot him and alert the rest of the crew. How long would it take for a mounted posse to ride out to the area, hunt him down?

An open boxcar. He kept pace now and threw his valise in. The wheels thundered on the track as he raced along, knowing that if he slipped and fell beneath the rolling train, he would be cut to pieces, or lose an arm or leg. Iron Knife reached, grasped the rough wood of the door, running hard. With no one to help him, it would take tremendous upper body strength to swing up into the moving freight car. The train whistled again as it hit the straight away, picking up speed. Now or never! He gripped harder and swung himself upward. For a split-second, he hung between heaven and earth, the dirt moving beneath his feet at a dizzying speed. For a heart-stopping moment, he wasn't sure he was going to make it. He envisioned himself falling beneath those giant wheels, being crushed to pieces, his scream lost in the thunder of the engine.

Then he seemed to see Summer's beautiful face in his mind. He could not die now, not without seeing her one more time, holding her close again. With a mighty effort, he lifted himself up into the boxcar, then lay there panting. So far, so good! How far was it to Boston? Could he travel there before the posse caught him? He wouldn't think about any of that right now; it was enough just to be aboard and headed east. Iron Knife stretched out in the soft hay of the boxcar and dropped off to sleep.

The whistling and the slowing of the train brought him out his sleep abruptly. What was happening? He peered out the boxcar door into the pre-dawn darkness, saw many buildings and other trains silhouetted against the lights of a big town. They were coming into a major train yard. How long was it until dawn? He knew his chances of being seen and recaptured increased in the daylight. Iron Knife decided he would burrow down in the straw and hope that while the train stopped here, no railroad crew came along checking the cars for the tramps that sometimes rode the cars. With any luck, the train would soon be on its way again.

Hidden in the straw, he could only guess at what was happening as the train gradually ground to a halt. After a few minutes, the car bumped as it moved backward slowly. More bumping and screeching of wheels. He lay very still and waited. The dark of night was turning the deep gray of just before dawn, and the air was cold. He hoped the train would pull out soon, because in the daylight, the so-called railroad bulls might be checking the boxcars, throwing tramps off the trains, beating them up or tossing them in jail. He lay very still while the bumping and noise continued a few more minutes. Then the train whistled again. Iron Knife heaved a sigh of relief. Maybe they were about to be on their way again. He heard the train begin to chug out of the yard. His freight car didn't shudder and creak; it didn't even seem to be moving. He waited a few minutes, afraid to even think what the problem was.

The train whistled again. He could hear it picking up speed. Strange, it sounded far away. He crawled to the door and looked out. From a distance, the engine wailed again. His heart sank. The car he was in was among those that had been uncoupled, left behind. Now what? Prowling around the rail yard in daylight, attempting to hitch a ride on another train, he might be noticed by a crew member or the railroad bulls. Staying in this car was no good; these boxcars might be on this side coupling for weeks.

Clutching his valise, he crept off the train, across the rail yard. There were lots of trains with yellow headlights beaming down the tracks, silent boxcars on sidings, crews moving about. He had no idea what to do next in this bewildering confusion of people and trains. Even if he'd had the money for a ticket, he would have been nervous about drawing attention to himself by walking up to the counter, asking a lot of questions that most white people would surely know. In his cheap, badly fitting clothes, he was certain to stand out. Possibly the law wasn't looking this far away in a big city for an escaped half-breed convict, but how was he to know? Iron Knife had already made a vow that he would fight to the death rather than be recaptured and put in chains or a cage again.

The weather was crisp with a touch of frost in the first gray light of the coming dawn. He was hungry, too. Carrying his small bag, he slipped across the train yard, through the maze of warehouses and empty boxcars sitting on side trestles. Trains huffed in and out of the station, and here and there, men worked loading or unloading boxcars. There was a big water tower near the tracks. In the gray light, he read the lettering: *Saint Louis.*

A big building loomed ahead, and people were thronging up and down the platform in the early morning rush, getting on and off trains. Could he mingle with the crowds and not be noticed? Certainly such a bold move would arouse less suspicion than lurking about the tracks where some crew member might see him and wonder.

He had faced death many times in battle, and he did not fear it; what he feared was disgrace or being caged like an animal again. Could he somehow get a message to Todd Shaw? He wasn't sure what Todd could do to help him at the moment, and he would be leery of hanging around here very long for an answer, uncertain whether the law or the army might trace him that way. Somehow, he must find out which train might be going to Boston, and figure out how to sneak on board.

There was a bewildering number of trains in this rail yard, all pulling out in different directions. Could he somehow mingle with the crowds, listen to the people or loiter near the ticket window, see if he could hear something or read a train schedule that would help him? Taking a deep breath, he walked out onto the station platform, sauntering easily as if he had every right in the world to be there with his valise, as if he, too, were about to catch a train. The scent of bacon frying wafted on the crisp air from the station cafe. His belly rumbled, but he paid it no heed. He had been much hungrier than this any number of times out in the wilderness. His heart beating hard, he tried to appear casual as he walked into the station, then paused. There were crowds of people coming and going from the building, even though it was early morning. Saint Louis must be a big place. Certainly, just from what he could see of it, it must be bigger than Denver. Crowds of people pressing together like rats in a cage made him think of the prison wagon, and he shuddered at the thought.

He loitered near the line at the ticket counter, every sense alert for the possibility that a posse might even now be searching train stations for several hundred miles in any direction. Iron Knife watched the line move, attempting to read the bewildering schedule on the wall behind the counter. A man in a string tie sold tickets. "Next?"

A little old lady asked, "What's the fare to New York?"

The clerk told her and she paid.

Iron Knife was too cautious to approach the clerk. He stood instead and listened.

A young woman with a whining child approached the counter. "Is there a train to Texas?"

The little clerk adjusted his string tie. "Yes, ma'am, but it'll be this afternoon. It makes connections with our train coming in from back east that's arriving in a few minutes."

She nodded and left.

A portly man asked, "When's the train to Boston coming through?"

"Sorry, delayed." The clerk shook his head. "It'll be two or three o'clock this afternoon at least, maybe a little later."

The man frowned and left, grumbling.

Two or three o'clock. That meant he would have to climb on board a boxcar in broad daylight. In this crowded station, that would be difficult. He might do as he had done before, wait at some curve in the track way ahead for a chance to slip on board. How would he know which one of all these it was? In the meantime, with all these hours until the Boston train, what was he to do? Iron Knife wandered out onto the platform, still carrying his small bag.

He watched the comings and goings as orange and brown leaves swirled across the platform with the chilly

winds that blew from the north. October, the month the
Cheyenne called Seine: moon when water begins to
freeze on edge of streams. It had been so many months
since he had seen Summer Sky. Much might have
changed; but one thing would never change, and that
was his love for her.

His belly rumbled again, but he ignored his hunger.
He must wait for that afternoon train, try to figure out
which one it was and hitch a ride in a boxcar again.
What to do in the meantime? Was it safer to find a hiding place in the empty freight cars or stay here, hoping
he looked like any bored passenger waiting? Surely the
law wouldn't look for him in the midst of the crowded
Saint Louis station; maybe they would think he had
headed back west.

Iron Knife sat down on a bench out on the platform,
trying to decide what to do next. Trains pulled in and
out, puffing and whistling, showering the platform with
cinders. People talked and called to each other as they
hurried to catch a train or ran to meet people arriving.
He imagined himself getting off the train in Boston,
Summer running toward him with a glad cry. He shook
his head, thinking again about what Serenity Peterson
had said about sending the message and getting no reply. At the very least, he had to hear from Summer's
own lips that she no longer wanted to be his woman. If
that happened, he wasn't sure whether he could turn and
leave, or would he throw her over his shoulder and
carry her off? She was his woman, and he wouldn't give
her up without a fight.

Now the chill October wind blew the leaves around
his feet as he watched a train from the east puffing into
the station with its dirty smoke and shower of embers.
It screeched like demons from hell as its big iron wheels
slid along the steel tracks.

He watched with casual interest, wondering if that

was the one that would connect with the Texas-bound train? He'd spent a lot of time in Texas; it would be a safer place for him to go, but it was the opposite direction from Boston. The conductor put down the step, and people began alighting from the train: an elderly couple, a drummer in a brightly checked suit, half a dozen soldiers in blue uniforms with shiny brass buttons. He stood up; soldiers made him apprehensive. He thought again about Sand Creek. It had been almost a year; yet he would always grow cautious now at the sight of a uniform or a badge. A long time ago, Texas Rangers had recaptured him and his mother, forced them to return to her white family. That had not been a happy time.

Were the soldiers staring at him? Perhaps he should leave this station. Picking up his suitcase, he began to walk slowly. Because his attention was centered on the blue uniforms, he bumped into a couple who had just alighted from the train. "Excuse me." He brushed past them, hardly noticing as he walked.

"That's all right, partner," the man dismissed him. "Come on, Cimarron, what would you like to do until the train leaves this afternoon?"

Cimarron. Why did that pull at him? He turned and looked at the couple moving away from him as they started down the platform. The man was as tall and dark as he was himself and dressed in an expensive black Spanish short jacket with fine leather boots. Everything about him was a mixture of Spanish aristocracy with perhaps a touch of Indian thrown in.

"I don't know, Trace," the girl answered. "I reckon we could go into town and go shopping; at least, I'd like some breakfast." She was pretty, with dark blond hair, and wearing a green wool traveling dress and a big hat with feathers and veils around the crown. Something

about her caught his eye. It was only because she was
pretty, he told himself, and possibly part Indian herself.

"Aw, darlin'," her companion drawled, "the breakfast
sounds *muy bueno,* but please don't drag me around to
ladies' shops. Leave me in the cafe with a newspaper
and coffee and you buy anything you want."

"Oh, cowboy, you spoil me so!" The girl had her arm
linked through the man's, and she squeezed it while the
man smiled.

"Why not spoil my bride? Besides, Cimarron, you
know I can afford it."

Cimarron. Cimarron. Cimarron. Iron Knife walked
over and caught the beauty's arm. "Excuse me, but—"

The girl recoiled in surprise. "Just who do you
think—?"

"That's my wife, mister, get your hands off her!" The
man called Trace appeared as jealous and volatile as a
volcano, his hand going under his vest as if he carried
a hand gun.

"I mean no harm," Iron Knife said hurriedly. "I—I
thought I knew her; she looks like someone—"

"You don't know her." Trace made a dismissing gesture. "And, *hombre,* I'd advise you not to be grabbing
respectable married ladies."

"Now, Trace, I'm sure it's a case of mistaken identity." Cimarron straightened her sleeve and looked up at
him.

Iron Knife's heart seemed to stop. Did he know her?
She was beautiful with her dark eyes and dark blond
hair. Cimarron—it meant "wild one" in Spanish. Maybe
it was a more common name than he thought, and yet,
there was something about this girl. . . .

"You look like someone I know," he said again,
knowing he might be attracting the attention of the soldiers. Even worse, this big, handsome *vaquero* looked
as protective and hot-tempered as a gun fighter.

Trace scowled. "Mister, I'm warning you; stop annoying my wife. Any man ought to know better than to touch a Texan's woman."

She was looking up at Iron Knife with increasing confusion. "Double damnation," she murmured. "Who—?"

"Come on, darlin'," Trace drawled, "I'll get us a carriage."

Texas. Cimarron. Texas and Cimarron.

She was still looking up at him, too. "Maybe ... Do we—do we know each other?"

Trace looked from one to the other. "Just what is all this? Cimarron, you've never met this *hombre;* don't let him annoy you or I might have to kill him!"

The moody rancher took her arm protectively, and they started walking away from him again. Iron Knife watched her walk. There was something about the shape of her face, the way she tossed her head. Texanna—just like Texanna. He hurried after the pair, his emotions and thoughts in confusion. "Ma'am, I must talk to you."

Trace whirled, his hand reaching under his vest. "I told you—!"

"No, Trace!" She caught his hand, and Iron Knife knew the dark, moody cowboy must be as deadly as he looked. "Mister," she said, "I must insist you leave us alone or I don't know if I can control my husband—"

"Does the name Texanna mean anything to you?" He stared into her eyes. "If it doesn't, I'll leave you alone and—"

"Texanna?" The girl was looking up at him, and she was turning deadly pale. "W-who are you? That was my mother's name!"

Texas. Texanna. Cimarron. He shouted out loud in his excitement. "Cimarron! Do you know me? I'm your brother! Do you know me?"

She was staring at him in bewilderment, and now he was so certain of the family resemblance, his words poured out. "I'm your brother. We left you in Texas; the town of Fandango! Our mother's name was Texanna and our father was War Bonnet!"

For just a moment, he thought she would faint. Her face turned deathly pale, and she swayed so that her husband caught her and held her close. "Darlin', are you all right? What's this all about?"

"My brother! Oh, I barely remember!" She was weeping now as she buried her face in her hands, then threw her arms around Iron Knife. "Trace, this is my big brother, remember what I told you?"

He held her close while her husband looked from one to the other, then finally held out his hand awkwardly. "Well, stranger, I reckon I owe you an apology. And your name is?"

They shook hands. "Once I was called Falling Star, but I am now Iron Knife."

Trace grinned as he tipped back his Western hat. "Well, Iron Knife, why don't you go have breakfast with us and we'll talk?"

Iron Knife was abruptly aware of people around them staring at the noisy reunion. "I—I'd like that."

"Oh"—Cimarron caught his arm—"there's so much I want to know; so much catching up to do!"

"Darlin' "—Trace smiled—"let's not stand out here on the platform; let's buy this man some steak and eggs and you all can talk at leisure. Our train doesn't leave 'til this afternoon."

The beautiful girl talked excitedly as Trace hailed a carriage. "Take us to the best cafe in town," he ordered the driver.

Iron Knife had thrown caution to the winds now, so eager was he to talk to his sister. He would worry about his own problems later.

He hardly said anything, nor did the Spaniard until

they were seated in a fine restaurant. His sister was the one who talked, her lovely face animated.

He watched Trace watch her. Evidently, the wealthy Texan adored her; it shone in his dark eyes. For the first time, he noticed that Cimarron wore expensive jewelry: blood red rubies, and a large diamond and ruby ring.

"All right, partner"—Trace grinned, as the waiter stood by—"you want a sirloin or a T-bone?"

He wasn't certain what to order. "Whatever you're having."

Trace gave the order with a flourish. Evidently he was a man of wealth, used to having the best of everything. Within minutes, Iron Knife wrapped his hands around the warmth of a strong cup of coffee and savored it gratefully.

"Now"—Cimarron sipped hers and leaned forward—"I want to hear everything from the beginning."

"There's so much to tell." Iron Knife drank the coffee and sighed with pleasure. "I don't know how much you remember about the past."

"Not much," she admitted, "I was raised by an old preacher and his wife. When they died, I went to live with Aunt Carolina and her two fat daughters."

Iron Knife frowned. "Yes, I remember Aunt Carolina; she didn't like me."

Cimarron laughed. "She didn't like me, either. In fact, I had to leave Fandango when—well ..." She smiled fondly at Trace. "How I ended up on the Triple D Ranch and became Señora Trace Durango is a long story in itself."

"Tell me," Iron Knife said as a steaming platter of steak, eggs and biscuits was placed before him. He and Trace dug into the food with hearty appetite, but Cimarron ate lightly as she told her brother everything that had happened to her over the past years.

The food was excellent, and Iron Knife tried not to

wolf it down; but he ate with gusto as Cimarron talked. When all the food was gone, he pushed back his plate with a satisfied sigh and sipped his coffee.

"Double damnation," Cimarron said, "I've talked your ears off; now it's your turn."

Iron Knife told her how, as a little boy, he and Texanna had been captured and forced to return to her white family. Texanna had been expecting a baby girl who was born months later. For five miserable years, the three had endured the prejudice of the little Texas town. "It all came to a climax the night Jake Dallinger tried to whip me to death, and about that same time, our father, War Bonnet, rode into town to rescue us."

"Why did I get left behind?"

He shook his head. "There was a mob between us and the preacher's house, so there was nothing to do but escape back to the Cheyenne. Then Texanna died and War Bonnet was killed by the Pawnee warrior, Bear's Eyes."

Cimarron blinked hard, and Trace handed her a hand-kerchief with a gentle gesture. "Are you all right, darlin'?"

She nodded and wiped her eyes. "I didn't know our parents were dead, but I reckon I'm not surprised. If they had been alive, I know they would have returned for me."

Iron Knife patted her shoulder. "They meant to come for you; but they both died within a few months of each other, and I was just a boy. Once I grew up, I didn't know where to look any longer."

"You wouldn't have found me," she comforted him, "I've left Fandango. Trace and I were recently married." Cimarron looked at her husband fondly. "I'm Cimarron Durango now."

"This must be the season for reunions," Trace mused. "Just before we left on this trip, we got a letter from my sister, Dallas. She's been missing throughout the war, and we just found out she's married and on a ranch in Arizona, the Wolf's Den."

"You know what?" Cimarron's eyes lit up for excitement. "Wouldn't it be fun to have a family reunion sometime? We could all meet at our ranch, the Triple D. We're in the Texas hill country near Austin and San Antonio."

Iron Knife's mind had returned to his personal problems. "I would like that," he said. "You've been back east?"

Cimarron nodded. "A honeymoon and business trip."

"You know about trains? Which ones go to what cities?"

"Sí," Trace said, and he looked puzzled by the question.

Iron Knife hesitated. How much should he tell them about his problems and where he was headed?

Cimarron was staring at him. "Brother, now that I think about it, what are you doing in a train station in Saint Louis?"

He hesitated again. He didn't want to cause them any trouble.

Now they both seemed to be studying his cheap, ill-fitting clothing.

Trace said, *"Amigo,* I don't like to pry, but if you're in some kind of trouble, I want to help you."

Cimarron reached out to put her small hand on his arm. "Trust us; what can we do?"

"I am a dog soldier," he said proudly. "I can take care of myself."

"Sí,"—Trace nodded—"but I am half-Cheyenne, also. Does not a brother help a brother?"

He looked into their eyes, knew he could count on them. They would not speak with crooked tongues. With a sigh, he told them everything that had happened.

They listened, concern in their eyes.

"So that's it," Iron Knife finished. "I don't know if the law is looking for me, why this Saint Louis judge, Griswold, would want to jail me. Hershel Warton owns Wartonville, and I'm afraid he might cause trouble for Serenity Peterson."

"Hmm," Trace mused, "the Durangos have money and power, too; maybe there's something I can do."

"And if the train stops in that town"—Cimarron smiled—"I'll buy a bunch of hats from this woman who helped you." Her gaze seemed to look him over.

"Her dead father's things," Iron Knife explained. "I could hardly be seen in prison garb."

"As big as Saint Louis is," Trace said, "I reckon there's plenty of men's stores here."

Cimarron's eyes lit up. "That's right. Trace, let's dress my brother, buy him a ticket, get him on the right train—"

"I couldn't let you do that." Iron Knife shook his head.

"But of course you can," Trace insisted. "It will be my pleasure; you have made my wife very happy this morning."

"You men finish your coffee," Cimarron said. "We've got a lot of shopping and visiting to do before we put Iron Knife on a train to Boston."

He felt his eyes fill up, blinked rapidly. With all he had been through, it seemed almost like an answer to his prayers to cross his sister's path here at the railroad station. Sometimes, maybe God stepped in. "I can't thank you enough."

Trace stood up, and shrugged off his gratitude. "You are my wife's kin, sí? Blood runs thick among the Durangos. It is only fitting that we help you."

* * *

So it was that over the next several hours, they visited and shopped in the best stores in Saint Louis. At first, Iron Knife was nervous about the soldiers, the occasional lawman, but it dawned on him that his sister and brother-in-law looked so prosperous that no one would dare to question them. Besides the lawmen were looking for a lone Indian, not three people on a shopping spree in Saint Louis.

Finally, it was afternoon, and they returned to the railroad station. Iron Knife now wore fine clothes and the most expensive and softest of boots. He had money in his vest and a ticket to Boston.

Trace lit a slender *cigarillo* as they stood waiting for the eastbound train. "*Hombre,* that's a round-trip ticket," he said, "so you can get back from there; there's one for her, too ... if she'll come."

Cimarron's beautiful face clouded. "Oh, brother, is there a chance she won't?"

He shook his head. "I don't know. That's why I'm going—to find out."

He and Trace shook hands solemnly.

Trace said, "Good luck to you, *amigo.* Remember, you and yours are always welcome at our ranch. Just ask anyone in Texas for directions to the Triple D Ranch. Big as it is, anyone can tell you where our spread is."

"Thank you," Iron Knife answered warmly, "I think my sister is very lucky."

"No, I'm the lucky one." He slipped his arm around his wife and hugged her. "Where can we reach you if we ever need to?"

"I have a friend named Todd Shaw who works at the newspaper in Denver, and another friend there in Colorado Territory named Cherokee Evans."

In the background, the train whistled and the conductor called, "All aboard!"

Cimarron made a little cry of dismay. "We can't part yet; we haven't had time to really talk!"

Iron Knife picked up his small valise and looked toward his train. "I'll come visit you sometime."

Cimarron's eyes watered. "Are you sure?"

"I promise."

Trace held out his hand and they shook again. "Iron Knife, remember, our place is yours. You ever want to come see us or need a favor of any kind, just ask."

"I'll remember that . . . friend."

"All aboard!" echoed in the background.

Cimarron threw herself into Iron Knife's arms, hugged him. *"Vaya con Dios,"* she whispered, *go with God.*

He held her close, thinking how much she looked like their mother. All these years, he had vowed he would find her and now she had found him. This had to be more than a coincidence. Iron Knife's heart was at peace except for his own problems with Summer. "Cimarron, I'll bring my family down to Texas sometime, and we'll have a family reunion. I promise."

"All aboard!" The train gave a warning whistle.

Iron Knife paused. There was still so much to say.

Trace cleared his throat awkwardly. "You'd better go, *amigo,*" he whispered. "You'll miss your train."

Cimarron smiled. "I'm so glad I found you after all these years. We'll look into this thing about Warton, I promise, and try to help Serenity Peterson, too."

"Thanks, sister. The great god, Heammawihio, must have made our paths cross each other's today. And thank you, Trace."

The train in the background shuddered, then began to move away from the platform.

Cimarron threw her arms around Iron Knife's neck. "My brother; oh, my brother!"

He hugged her breathless. "We'll see each other again. I promise! *Hahoo naa ne-mehotatse.*"

"What does it mean?" She was crying.

He wiped a tear from her lovely face. "It's Cheyenne: thank you and I love you." His own vision was blurring as he grabbed his small bag and ran for the moving train. Once aboard, he went to a window and waved to the couple on the platform until they were lost from sight.

Now he found a seat and relaxed. With money and fine clothes, he could travel in style, and no one would question him or connect him to an escaped convict in Missouri.

A face came to him, a beautiful heart-shaped face with pale blue eyes and yellow hair. Summer, his woman, his love. He must see her; must go to her. My once in a lifetime love, my Summer Sky. One thing was certain, the whole drama would come to a climax when he arrived in Boston!

Chapter Twenty-one

Outside the fine Van Schuyler mansion, the gold and russet October leaves blew across the expansive lawns. Summer turned from the window, watched her father settle himself in his library chair with his morning coffee. Upstairs, the noise of the children playing reverberated through the big house. The twins were taking their mid-morning nap. "You wanted to talk to me, Father?"

"We've something to discuss." He sipped his coffee and frowned.

She had a feeling this was not going to be a meeting she would enjoy. More and more as he aged, Silas, with his prominent hooked nose and piercing eyes, reminded her of a hawk. She felt abruptly like a field mouse or a rabbit under his withering gaze, so she returned to the window and looked out instead. The early morning sun was just melting the shimmering frost off the trees and rooftops. The last few days of October. In a few days, winter would begin with all its cold and snows. That made her think of those times she and her love had shared their cozy buffalo robes in a tipi on the windswept prairie. Tears came to her eyes. Her once in a lifetime love. She had written him of the twins' birth and had heard nothing in reply. Yes, it must be true that he had found another love. Yet could she give him up without a struggle? A trip to Colorado in bad weather with five children would be difficult, even though she was fast regaining her strength.

Father cleared his throat behind her, and she whirled around. "Summer, I've been quite patient with you as I know the last few months and particularly the last few weeks have been very difficult; but the twins are flourishing now, and it's time to get on with your life."

"Hmm." She thought of her mother's room upstairs. Silas had not allowed one thing to be moved. It was exactly as it had been the night Priscilla died—like a shrine. Silas was not getting on with his life. She dared not say that, of course. She might as well face this unpleasantness head-on. "What is it you want to talk to me about, Father?"

"You know you are very welcome to stay here with me indefinitely," he said.

Summer saw herself trapped like her mother in this eerie house, she and her children under the control of her grim, overbearing parent. She managed not to shudder visibly. "Thank you, Father, I—I haven't really given it much thought."

"Then it's time you did." He put his coffee cup down on the small table next to his chair and looked at her.

"I had some idea of returning to the West."

"To what?" he snapped, and glared at her. "We've discussed this before and I thought you would come to your senses! There doesn't seem to be anything there for you; and certainly no good prep schools for Lance."

"I do have four other children besides Lance," she reminded him pointedly.

He shrugged. "Quite so, but the other boy looks too much like a savage, so he'll have a hard time of it; and after all, what value does the world place on girls unless, of course, they make a good marriage?"

"Your attitude appalls me!"

"And your actions appall me!" he snapped back. "A girl reared with the best of everything and attending the best schools runs away with some savage and lives in sin with him, produces bastard offspring, and causes this family no end of embarrassment—"

"I doubt anyone was embarrassed but you," Summer shot back.

"Be that as it may," he said crisply, "I'm in control of the family holdings and fortune. Remember he who has the gold has the power."

"I don't need your money!" Summer was seething.

"Oh? You can say that, can you, when you have spent most of this past year living in luxury at my fine home, with maids at your beck and call?"

"I can be packed in five minutes," she said. At least in the past few months, some things had changed; Father's angry bluster no longer scared her.

"And pray tell, where would you go with your five little children?" He smiled coldly now, as if he held all the winning cards.

Where would she go? What could she do with no job skills and no money? She took a deep breath and swallowed back her anger. "I'm sure, knowing you, there is a point to all this."

"You do know me pretty well, don't you?" He leaned back in his chair and surveyed her as if he were assessing the value of a property. "I always thought you would marry Austin Shaw, thus merging my empire with theirs."

"You know I visited with Austin when he was in town a few months ago." Summer dismissed that suggestion with an impatient shrug. "He knows I love another."

"Who doesn't seem to love you," Silas said. "What do you think of Beau St. Claire?"

"He's . . . charming," Summer hedged.

"He's more than charming; he seems to be an astute businessman with good connections."

"What is your point, Father?"

"The Shaws have moved their annual costume ball from New Year's Eve this year to Halloween."

"So? We all know that; that's tomorrow night. Mrs. Shaw had said in her note that they hoped Austin would come in on the train for the ball, but he couldn't get leave. Anyway, I've already written Mrs. Shaw a note, declining the invitation."

"Robert Shaw has invited me personally to come and bring my two daughters just like always."

"I know," Summer said, "but I'm sure it was just a gesture of politeness; the Shaws know we are still in mourning and that it wouldn't be proper—"

"Don't you dare use the word 'proper' around me, young lady!" His chair's four legs came down hard on the floor with a resounding bang. "You and I and Angela are going."

"But Father—"

"We won't wear costumes or dance, of course, and will be very subdued and discreet since the whole town knows we're in mourning, but it will give any man there a reminder that you're available."

"I'm not."

"You prefer to live at home the rest of your life?"

Shaking her head, she thought of spending forever as her mother had in this grim house. "I—I'm just not quite sure what I'm going to do yet."

"Then let me offer suggestions," Silas said, rubbing his hands together in his best "take charge" gesture. "Since Austin seems to have withdrawn from the courting, consider Beau St. Claire. You know he hasn't been coming to visit or to dinner just because he's doing business with me."

"Beau?"

"Don't act so shocked," Silas snapped. "You must have known he was serious about you. He's asked me what my reaction would be if he asked you to marry him."

"He could have mentioned it to me first." She was a little angry with Beau that Silas' opinion obviously had priority over hers.

"In proper society"—and he emphasized the word "proper"—"a gentleman makes sure he is acceptable with the lady's family. Besides, you should feel relieved that Beau is willing to take all your children and raise them."

"Not withstanding that he would expect to come into the Van Schuyler money someday for being generous enough to do so."

"I see no point in discussing this further." Silas stood up abruptly. "I merely wanted to tell you our plans for tomorrow night and that Beau will possibly ask you. I thought I'd give you time to think it over. Now I have business to take care of." He strode from the room before she could object to anything.

Summer sank down on a chair before the fire and sighed. What were her alternatives? Not many. While Austin might be willing to marry her, he was too decent, knowing she was in love with Iron Knife. The only choices she could see were two: stay in this gloomy house under her father's control the rest of her life as her mother had done, or marry Beau St. Claire. Obviously the dashing blade of Southern society would be expecting a favorable answer. What other course was open to her? The answer seemed to mock her: none.

The early afternoon sun slanted through the window of the hotel room. Beau St. Claire smiled as he looked into the mirror. He had just awakened after a night of drinking and carousing in a fancy bordello, but the dissipation didn't show. He needed to look good tonight.

Tonight was the big Shaw costume ball. He had already gotten himself a costume; he would go as a dashing pirate, complete with sword and cloak. "How appropriate, suh." He winked at himself while brushing his light-streaked hair back. "I reckon all the ladies will notice you."

He must stop thinking of conquests, Beau thought as he dressed. Probably if he married Summer, her father would expect him to be the proper Boston husband; at least be very discreet about his love affairs. Summer was a choice morsel indeed, although it annoyed Beau that some savage had had her first.

"Be patient," he admonished the handsome rake in the mirror, "old Silas can't live forever, and once you've got his empire, you can do as you damn well please."

Yes, he could do that. Beau combed his hair, smiling with approval at his reflection. Yes, he would enjoy that Summer all right. Besides the fact that she was pretty, with five children, she ought to be experienced enough to make it exciting. He smiled, thinking of the other elegant lady he knew; that Southern matron could give most whores some lessons. No, he didn't intend to give up his married mistress just because he wed the damn Yankee girl. He would have plenty of time to be in Tennessee on business, and if he was careful, he could arrange those trips when her stupid husband wasn't around.

He must go get a shave. Beau put on some cologne, slipped into a fine, handmade shirt, and tied his cravat while he considered his future wife's little sister. That Angela was a pretty morsel, and probably fifteen or sixteen, plenty old enough for what he had in mind. Certainly with black slave wenches, he'd used them starting at about twelve. Angela had smiled at him a time or two. Would she be willing? and if she wasn't, once he'd caught her in the house alone and took her anyway, she'd be afraid to tell anyone. Besides, who would believe her?

His costume lay spread over a chair, and Beau inspected it critically. Yes, he would look suave and dashing in this tonight; all the ladies would be flirting with him. Later in the evening, he would take Summer into the conservatory and propose to her. It didn't appear to him with that whole pack of brats that she had many alternatives. Children. What was he going to do with them? He didn't like children much; they were noisy nuisances. He wouldn't even consider a woman with five brats if she weren't pretty, rich, and if Shawn weren't threatening to kick him off the plantation.

That Irish dirt-grubber didn't even appreciate what Beau and Savannah had gone through to protect Shannon Place from the Yankees. Shawn had called him a traitor and a collaborator. Yes, Beau had better find a rich wife fast, even if she did come with five Injun brats. Maybe old Van Schuyler could be persuaded to keep Summer's children, or if the old man died, Beau could dump them all in good boarding schools far, far away.

That wasn't today's worry. Everything was going good for Beau, and even his mistress understood that he needed to marry to keep up pretenses so her husband wouldn't get suspicious. Although she wouldn't like it, he would tell the Southern lady that it was a marriage in name only. He laughed to himself. Not likely. Beau intended to have that pretty Summer three or four times a day until he tired of her; then he would think about her younger sister. Oh, he'd been lucky, all right; he'd never been caught by his mistress's husband in all these years. Humming with satisfaction, Beau walked jauntily down the hall. First a shave, then to the hotel dining room for a leisurely drink.

Iron Knife took a deep breath for courage as the conductor yelled again, "Boston! Coming into Boston!"

He put his face against the window and looked out at the late afternoon scene. He hadn't realized there were this many people, buildings and carriages in the whole world. How could people live so crowded up? The city looked like an anthill to him. Not realizing it would be such a huge place, he hadn't thought it would be difficult to find Summer. Now he wasn't even sure how he would go about finding the Van Schuylers. Vaguely, he remembered Todd writing down instructions for him, but those were lost along with almost everything else except his dog soldier outfit he carried in the small carpetbag.

The train whistled and began to slow. Around him, travelers were stirring, gathering up their things. He clutched his luggage and stared out the window at the big station looming ahead. Somehow, he would find Summer. This town couldn't be that big.

The train gradually pulled to a stop with creaks and groans of the rails, cindery smoke raining down across the cars. People began pushing to get off. Iron Knife held on to his bag and stepped out into the crisp late afternoon. Crowds of people milled and shoved past him like bleating, mindless sheep. He didn't have the least idea what to do next, and he was wary of approaching strangers. Among white people, how did one know whom to trust?

He stood looking around a long moment, trying to decide where to go and what to do next. The noisy crowd seemed to shove and buffet him along until he stood out near the street, watching people get in carriages and leave. While he stood there uncertainly, he heard a voice behind him: "Iron Knife? Iron Knife? Is it really you?"

He whirled around, ready to defend himself, but the man smiled incredulously and took the pipe from his mouth. "I'm Austin Shaw, remember me?"

For a long moment, Iron Knife stared into the familiar face, remembering the last time he had seen this man—the day Summer had given the big diamond and sapphire engagement ring back to her rich fiancé and ridden away with Iron Knife into the Colorado Rockies. "Austin?" He held out his hand uncertainly, and the other shook it warmly.

"Good to see you! Here, let's get out of this crush." He caught Iron Knife's arm and steered him through the crowds. "I must say I'm surprised to see you here in Boston."

"Your brother helped me get here," Iron Knife explained. "I came to see Summer."

"We'll get a carriage," Austin said, leading him out to the street. "You say Todd helped you? I've been away with the army, don't exchange as many letters with Todd as I'd like, but we're both so busy."

"I came to see Summer," Iron Knife said again, "get some things straightened out."

Austin sucked his pipe, looking troubled. "Hmm. She know you're coming?"

Iron Knife shook his head. "I—I don't know. She was notified, but there was no reply. So now I'm going to surprise her."

"Oh, she'll be surprised, all right." Austin signaled a carriage. He looked as if he knew things he wasn't sure how to share. "You were planning on going there now?"

Iron Knife shrugged. "I did not know what else to do; I wasn't even certain how to find the house."

Austin tapped his pipe against his teeth as the driver climbed down and opened the carriage door for them.

'No one's expecting me, either. I'd told my folks I couldn't get leave, then it came through. I thought I'd surprise my folks in time for this big party they're throwing tonight."

They got into the carriage, and the driver stared at Iron Knife curiously, then looked at Austin. "Where to, mister?"

Austin glanced at Iron Knife. "You have any place to stay?"

Iron Knife hesitated. The only thing on his mind had been making his way to Summer Sky. Ordinary things like food and shelter had been the last items on his mind.

"I thought not," Austin said. "You can share a room with me." He ordered the cabbie, "Take us to the Winslow Arms."

"You were going home," Iron Knife protested, but Austin waved the cabbie to proceed.

"So I'll change my plans and get us a room," Austin said.

Iron Knife sighed and looked out at the passing buggies and bustling crowds as the carriage started away. "I don't know what to do next; will you help me, my friend?"

Austin puffed his pipe, and the sweet scent drifted on the air. "If it hadn't been for you that day in Colorado, my men and I would have been killed. I haven't forgotten that. Yes, I'll help you."

"Thank you, Austin." Iron Knife smiled. "I know you loved her yourself."

"And still do," Austin said with a resigned shake of his head, "but I never had a chance with her after she met you; that once in a lifetime love."

Iron Knife closed his eyes and winced. If she had loved him, why had he not heard from her? "I'm not sure what to expect if I show up on their doorstep."

"Knowing old Van Schuyler like I do, he'll try to keep you from ever seeing her; call the police and have you hustled away."

That made him think of St. Louis. Iron Knife knew Silas was a man of wealth and power. He was also ruthless. Out on the plains, Iron Knife would have an equal footing with any man, but here in the city, he was helpless; they would be playing by white civilization's rules and on Van Schuyler's home ground. There was no telling what he could do to a penniless half-breed, once he found out the law was looking for him on a charge of murder. "What can I do, Austin?"

Austin considered. "As I said before, my folks are having a big Halloween ball tonight, and lots of people in disguise will be coming and going."

He didn't understand. "Halloween? I'm not sure I understand—"

"I'll explain later." Austin smiled. "Old Silas is not going to let you get close to Summer if he can help it. Maybe, just maybe, Summer and her father will attend my parents' party, if only briefly. Suppose we both show up?"

Iron Knife shook his head. "I have no invitation; your parents will call the police."

"Not if you're in disguise and I bring you," Austin said, and from the expression on his handsome face, he was already caught up in the excitement and the drama of the thing. "You might get a chance to talk to Summer without anyone realizing who you are."

Iron Knife hardly dared hope. "Suppose she doesn't come to the party?"

"Then we'll have to make new plans."

The carriage stopped before the hotel, and the driver climbed down and opened the door. "Here you be, sir."

They got out, and Austin paid the driver. "Come on old friend, we'll get a room, rest and wash up."

Iron Knife followed him inside the lobby, looking around, almost in awe, at the ornate trappings. How could he compete for Summer's affections when there were white men who lived like this every day and he had nothing to offer but a buffalo robe in a tipi? He followed Austin to the desk where Austin got a room, paid for it, and took the key.

"Come on, friend."

They went to the room. Iron Knife was eager to see Summer, but he knew Austin was right; if he tried to go to her house, her father would try to stop him. "Did you say a costume ball? I have no costume."

Austin pursed his lips and considered a moment. "I can go to a shop and rent them for both of us, I suppose." His gaze went to the small bag Iron Knife carried. "What's in that?"

In answer, Iron Knife put it on the bed and opened it for display. "Just my dog soldier things. I felt uneasy not taking them with me."

"By George, I've got it!" Austin snapped his fingers, threw back his head and laughed. "We'll have a bite to eat, then I'll go rent a costume. You already have one!"

"What?"

"Do you have war paint, too?"

Iron Knife nodded. "You aren't thinking—?"

"But of course I am!" Austin paced up and down with excitement. "What a joke on everyone concerned! I'll introduce you as an old friend from the West, which of course you are, and with war paint, you won't need a mask. Yes, Iron Knife, I'll take you to my parents' costume ball, and maybe you'll even win the prize. After all, it isn't often a man shows up dressed like an authentic Indian dog soldier!"

"Now I know you are loco, my friend." Iron Knife shook his head. "I'll never get in the door. Your parents will call the police."

"Not if I bring you to the party. Don't you see? The one place old Silas would never expect you to turn up would be my parents' costume ball. Before he can do anything, you will have had a chance to draw her to one side—maybe the conservatory—and talk to her."

"Then what?"

Austin clapped him on the arm. "Then it's up to you. If she doesn't want you anymore, I can't help you."

Did she? "Have you seen Summer since she returned to Boston?"

"Briefly. I've been away fighting a war, you know, but I hear Beau St. Claire. . . ."

"Yes?"

A look crossed Austin's face, and he sighed as he filled his pipe. "Nothing. He's just a fellow who's been visiting the Van Schuylers a lot. I'm sure everything else is just gossip from people with nothing else to do."

Beau. He tried to imagine what this man who might have stolen Summer from him would look like. He didn't know whether he was feeling jealousy, rage, sorrow, or perhaps all three.

Austin acted as if he'd like to escape this questioning. "I'll go get myself a costume and you wash up. Then I'll have some food sent up, okay?"

Iron Knife nodded. The sun was getting low on the horizon. Tonight he would finally see Summer Sky again after all these months. His once in a lifetime love; could she possibly be untrue to him? In his mind, he saw her small, heart-shaped face looking up at him as he kissed her. "Go on," he said, "I'll wait."

When Austin returned, it was dusk outside. "I got myself a cavalier's outfit"—Austin smiled—"and a mask. My parents always give a prize for the best costume."

Prizes held no interest for Iron Knife. "Suppose she doesn't come?"

"We'll worry about that when we get to it. Now, let's have a bite to eat and get ready."

Austin had the hotel send up excellent food, but Iron Knife could hardly eat for thinking about what was yet to come later this evening. However, Austin finished off the succulent roast beef with gusto and wiped his mouth with a linen napkin. Then he leaned back with a good glass of wine and his pipe. "Excellent food! I've been at the front with Custer too long; then down in Louisiana and Texas. The locals didn't offer any of their best to the conquering Yankees."

Iron Knife was not used to sitting with nothing to do. He paced the thick carpet like a cougar, thinking about Summer and the future confrontation. In his mind, he imagined the police coming, attempting to drag him away in chains; the thought of being hanged. "Austin, there's—there's something I haven't told you; I'm wanted for murder."

"Hmm." Austin puffed his pipe thoughtfully. "You do it?"

Iron Knife shook his head. "I didn't mean to. He was trying to kill me. There's a lot more; but who'd believe an Indian? I don't think I'd get a fair trial."

"Then you're taking a big chance staying in civilization. She really means that much to you, doesn't she?"

Iron Knife paused in his pacing, then faced Austin. "I would do anything—risk anything—to see her, hold her once more."

"If the authorities are looking for you, you need to get out of town as fast as possible."

"Not until I at least get to see her, find out if she still loves me. When do we go?"

Austin stood up and knocked the ashes from his pipe. "I thought we'd wait until the party was in full swing before we arrive. That way, it'll be easier for me to get you past my parents without a lot of questions as to your identity. Also, if there's a big crowd, all wearing costumes and disguises, it'll be easier for you to move about unnoticed."

"I hope it works," Iron Knife said, "otherwise. . . ." He let his voice trail off. No, he wouldn't even think of that. One moment in Summer's arms was worth the risk he was taking.

They began to dress. Iron Knife mixed his war paint, then painted his features with black lightning bolts, scarlet streaks, and a dragonfly symbol.

Austin stepped back and surveyed Iron Knife. "How do I look?"

"I don't know," Iron Knife said seriously. "I never saw a cavalier before."

Austin laughed. "Well, you certainly look fierce in your getup; raven feathers, war paint and all. The bead work on that buckskin is beautiful; I wouldn't be surprised if you win a prize for best costume!"

"I don't care about that; I only want a chance to see her—talk to her."

Austin nodded. "We'll get a carriage now."

Iron Knife paused, his excitement mounting. Soon he would see his Summer Sky. Did she still care about him? Had she forgiven him for Gray Dove? He could only hope so. If not, could he stop himself from just throwing her across his shoulder and carrying her off? Yet her happiness meant everything to him.

"How can I repay you for all this?" Iron Knife asked.

"Once you saved my life from a man named Jake Dallinger; I'd call that payment enough. Wonder whatever happened to him?"

"He's dead. It's a long story," Iron Knife said. "Shall we go?"

Austin nodded as he filled his pipe, choosing his

words carefully. "Just don't do anything rash tonight, all right?"

"I'm not armed; Todd was afraid I'd get in trouble if I wore my knife or carried a lance."

"With strength like yours, you don't need weapons to be dangerous; take it easy."

He wasn't sure he understood what Austin meant, but he nodded. The two of them started down the hall in their costumes. Iron Knife didn't intend to count coup and scalp anyone in Boston; he had enough troubles already with the police in Missouri searching for him. On the other hand, he wasn't sure what he would do to anyone who tried to keep him from seeing Summer Sky and his children. If he was wanted for murder, it couldn't be any worse if he had to kill someone else, fight his way out of town. What ever the sacrifice, it would be worth it to hold his beloved once more!

Chapter Twenty-two

Summer did not really want to attend the Shaws' Halloween ball; she was not sure it was socially correct when they were all still wearing mourning. Besides, the twins were less than two months old, and she was still weak—or was it only depression? Father, however, insisted that it was time to make a bold move, begin wearing light mourning and advertise the fact that the Van Schuyler family was getting on with their lives.

So Summer had compromised by wearing a dark dove gray satin dress and decided that, of course, she would not dance. Angela, on the other hand, was on a pout as the family made ready because she could not dress up in some flamboyant costume. "I wanted to go as a witch and carry Coaldust."

"Considering the fact that most of Boston society knows the Blackledge side of the family had an ancestor hanged at Salem for that very reason," Silas said crisply, "that doesn't seem to be a very good idea."

"Father's right," Summer said as she reached for her cloak. "Now remember, you are a little girl and—"

"I'm almost sixteen," Angela snapped back. "Other girls my age are getting married or at least have a sweetheart."

Father rolled his eyes. "What are children coming to

these days?" He glared at her. "You will behave as a young lady who has lost her mother only months ago. I will not have all Boston society gossiping about us ... again." He gave Summer a significant look.

She pretended she didn't see it as she buttoned her cloak. She wasn't looking forward to this. Beau St. Claire would be at the Shaws' party. In truth, he had asked to escort her to the ball, but Summer had declined, saying the family wanted to attend together and she would see him there.

Evans appeared in the doorway. "Flannigan's brought the carriage around, sir."

"Very good. We'll go to the party early, make an appearance, and come home before most of the crowd arrives fashionably late," Silas said. "Tell the staff they may have the evening off, except Mrs. O'Malley, of course; she'll take care of the children."

Summer turned and looked with yearning up the stairs. "I hate to leave my children alone."

Father snorted as they went toward the door. "Ye Gods, they aren't alone! They have servants dancing attendance on them. You're just trying to avoid attending this ball."

That was certainly true.

Angela scowled at Father. "My first real party and you want me to leave early? I'm so looking forward to it."

He glared back at her. They were so very much alike, Summer thought as she looked at her younger sister. Like Silas, Angela was obstinate and determined. Too bad she wasn't a boy; she could match Silas Van Schuyler's ambition and interest in power. However, Angela had grown to be a beautiful young woman. In a short time, Summer thought, all the eligible bachelors in Boston would be courting Angela. She'd even seen

Beau staring at Angela a couple of times as if dazzled by the young, spoiled beauty.

They got in the carriage for the short drive to the Shaw estate. Even as they pulled up before the Georgian mansion, they heard music and laughter already drifting from inside. Lights streamed from every window, and out in the courtyard, carriages and drivers waited in little groups, drinking spiced punch and gossiping among themselves.

The Shaws met them at the door. Elizabeth Shaw was a small, birdlike woman who controlled the men of her family by having "spells" when she didn't get her way. Priscilla had never really liked her distant cousin, Summer remembered now as they greeted each other.

"Why, Summer, we're so glad you decided to come after all. As I remember, the last ball of mine you attended, you announced your engagement to our son."

"Now, Elizabeth," her florid-faced husband blustered, "you needn't have mentioned that."

"Did I say something wrong?" Elizabeth feigned too much innocence as she looked at her husband.

"It's all right," Summer put in quickly, "she's correct, of course." It had been New Year's Eve of 1858, she thought. She had become engaged to Austin that night. So many young men who had attended that New Year's Eve were dead now in the Civil War which had turned out to be as bloody and brutal as her twin, David, had predicted. "That night, Austin brought his friend, George Custer. Who would have believed that Custer would end up a general so soon?"

"Or that Austin would be in the midst of all that action with Custer?" Mrs. Shaw sighed. "We were hoping both our boys would get here for this; now it appears neither will."

"We'll have a good time anyway," Robert Shaw blustered. To Summer, he said, "The young men have been asking me for weeks if you'd be here; especially that Beau St. Claire. We've bought a lot of cotton through him all during the war, you know; had to pay outrageous prices, but it kept our mills running."

"Made excellent profits off that fabric as I recall," Father said. "Too bad so many of those we know invested in that uniform factory of the Huntingtons."

"Oh, Father," Angela groaned, "don't start talking business right here in the front hall."

Mrs. Shaw said, "Quite right, my dear, we're here to enjoy ourselves and celebrate the end of the war. Later on, with everyone wearing masks and as large a crowd as we're expecting, I'm not sure anyone would recognize anyone else."

Angela smirked. "Then I could be the belle of the ball, couldn't I?"

Her father frowned. "Now, Angela, you might dance discreetly with one or two of the young boys who will be here, but remember—"

"I know, I know," Angela said, shrugging him off.

Robert Shaw said, "Angela, my dear, I think there's milk and cookies in the kitchen."

"Milk and cookies?" Angela sneered with disdain. "I was thinking of champagne." She swept into the ballroom, and Summer shrugged helplessly at Elizabeth Shaw. "You must forgive my little sister's rudeness."

"My dear cousin Priscilla must be turning over in her grave at Angela's behavior," Elizabeth sniffed. "On the other hand, I shouldn't speak ill of the dead, but—"

"Then don't." Summer cut her off as she handed over her cloak to the butler.

"My, I had forgotten how outspoken you are." Elizabeth gave Summer her best vinegary smile.

It was time to change the subject before the overbear-

ing lady got any snippier. "Are you certain neithe
Austin nor Todd will be here?" Summer certainly
wanted to talk to Todd and see if he'd heard any more
from Iron Knife.

Robert's face fell. "Not Todd, but Austin had hoped
to get leave. It doesn't appear that he'll make it
though."

Summer looked up to see the butler ushering Beau
into the entry hall. Beau grinned at her. "Why, hello
there. I do hope you'll save me every dance."

Summer looked imploringly at Elizabeth.

Elizabeth said, "Now, Beau, you mustn't monopolize
her. Besides, some of the other ladies have been asking
after you and wondering when you'd arrive."

"Ma'am," he drawled as he bent to kiss Mrs. Shaw's
hand, "I have the two most beautiful women at the ball
right here before me; who could ask for more?"

Elizabeth tittered with delight.

It was going to be a long evening, Summer thought.
The orchestra began to play; servants in fine livery were
passing through the laughing crowds with ornate silver
trays of refreshments. Out of the corner of her eye, she
saw young Angela filch a glass of champagne off a butler's tray and drain it, then stop to flirt with a known
rake old enough to be her father. The rake was leading
Angela over to the refreshment table and getting her another champagne. Summer started to point that out to
Silas, decided her younger sister couldn't get into all
that much trouble right here under her father's nose, and
kept quiet.

The orchestra began a waltz. Beau looked longingly
toward the dance floor. "I suppose it is really not proper
for you to dance, is it?"

For once, Summer was glad she was still in mourning. "I'm afraid not; but there are other ladies here who
would love the chance."

Beau smiled and bent to kiss her hand. "I may do that later, but right now, I'm just happy to be with you. I'll get you some punch."

She watched him walk away.

Father came to stand beside her. "Beau might be planning to ask you to marry him tonight, you know."

"Hmm." She wasn't sure what she was going to say if he did. He was persistent enough to wear any girl down. The thought crossed her mind that it wouldn't be any worse married to Beau than imprisoned in her father's large house with Silas controlling every move she made.

Father drifted over to a nearby group of his friends, and they were already discussing retiring to the billiard room for a smoke and something stronger than champagne. Over in a corner of the ballroom, Summer saw Angela with yet another glass of champagne in her hand. Yes, it was going to be a long evening. She just hoped Angela didn't make a fool of herself. There was already enough gossip about the Van Schuylers with what Summer had done in Boston with people whispering about her behind their hands as she walked past and Summer pretending she didn't see it.

Summer stood on the edge of the dance floor, watching the crowd grow. Most of Boston's wealthiest and most influential people were here, and some who had lost their fortunes but were still important because of their ancestors. There were the two prim Osgoode sisters, Summer's old school mates, dressed like pilgrims and standing forlornly by the refreshment table. They seemed to pretend not to see Summer. Although they had attended her mother's elaborate funeral, the two had not been to call on Summer in the months since she had returned. Obviously running away with an Indian lover was just too scandalous for them.

She nodded to some of her other old schoolmates, but most also seemed to pretend not to see her. Maybe Father was right; she had scandalized this proper, staid city, and she might never again be invited to any social event. Had it been worth it? She closed her eyes and remembered Iron Knife's rugged face. Yes, if she had it to do all over again, she still would do it. In her mind, she remembered the taste of her man's kiss and blinked back tears. She had loved him so.

Father came to her side from the billiard room. "Have you seen Angela?"

"No, but she's probably in the kitchen eating cookies."

"I just checked the kitchen," Silas grumbled. "She's not there; I haven't seen her in a while."

Summer remembered the way Angela had grabbed a glass of champagne off a butler's tray. There was a big pantry in this house where the liquor was kept. Surely her younger sister wouldn't do anything really wild and crazy. On the other hand, she might. Added to that was the fact that Angela was quite innocent and so young. "Father," she soothed, "now you go back to the billiard room and have a smoke. I'll look around for her; I'm sure she can't be very far. Maybe she and some of her friends from Miss Priddy's Academy are sitting in the parlor trading giggles and secrets."

Father looked uncertain but angry. "Maybe you're right. If you find her—"

"Yes, yes, now settle down, I'll find her." Summer was delighted to be able to escape from the ballroom with all the young men looking at her longingly, but their mothers giving her cold glares.

* * *

Beau thought he must be crazy, but Summer's younger sister had flirted with him, and now had led him into the pantry. "I've something to tell you."

"About Summer?" Angela was drunk; he could smell it on her. What had she done, snatched drinks off butler's trays on a dare?

"No." She closed the door behind him and leaned closer. "I've been watching you a long time, Beau St. Claire, and I'm on to you."

He felt a chill go up his back. How had this brat found out about his financial problems and his married mistress? "What—what do you mean?"

She slipped her arms around his neck. "Admit it; you don't love my sister. I've seen the way you look at me sometimes."

Oh, God, she had noticed and probably read his thoughts. He took a good look at her. Everyone thought of Angela as a little girl; but she must be about sixteen, and her curves filled out that plain dark gray mourning dress she wore. He didn't know what to say. She was so drunk, she was unsteady on her feet. What did she expect him to do? "Miss Angela, I beg you not to say anything to your sister."

Angela smiled up at him, and he realized she might be young, but her eyes were sensual. "Not if you'll kiss me."

Beau smiled. The little tart; stealing her sister's man. And Angela was pretty, too. He bent his head and kissed her deeply. In answer, she made a small noise in her throat and rubbed against him. He felt his manhood come up hard and throbbing, and he deepened the kiss, putting his hand on her breast. He could taste the liquor on her lips, and he pressed her back against the row of shelves. He must be crazy, he admonished himself, to be kissing and pawing his future wife's little sister in a pantry at the biggest party of the season. Suppose someone opened the door? Suppose he had misread Angela's intentions and later she yelled rape? Besides, it just wasn't practical to take a woman standing up in a pantry. Yet, for a long moment, his passion and his need overcame his good sense, and he kissed her.

"Want me?" she said in a taunting voice.

"Of course I do!" His voice was shaking now as he tried to push her skirts up. "Where can we go?"

Angela pulled away, laughing. "I knew you didn't really love my sister; you're after my father's money. Suppose I tell him you tried to drag me into the pantry and make love to me?"

He felt himself go pale. "You little vixen! Have you no principles?"

"We're two of a kind, Beau!" she taunted, then pulled away and slipped out the pantry door, weaving slightly on her feet and laughing.

Beau leaned against the wall and cursed. His manhood was so swollen and throbbing that he dared not leave here yet. That cold-blooded little wench had deliberately led him on; then when she got him shaking and ready to beg for it, she had laughed and walked away. He brushed his hair out of his eyes and tried to compose himself. God, he had been a reckless fool, and she was as cunning as he was. He'd get even with that little Jezebel once he married Summer. There'd be plenty of times when the two of them would be alone together. Angela wouldn't dare tell; she'd be too ashamed, and anyway, who would believe her?

Beau grinned as he straightened his costume and peeked around the door. He was in luck, no one in sight. Beau came out of the pantry, taking deep breaths to compose himself. Yes sir, he still had his lady in Tennessee, and he'd soon have both the voluptuous Van

Schuyler sisters. God, he needed a woman! Summer had known passion with some savage, so it wasn't as if she were some teasing virgin like her little sister. He began to wonder if he could end up between her thighs tonight. Where would be a good place to seduce her? What about that wicker chaise in the conservatory? He wouldn't need but a few minutes to overcome her objections. Humming to himself, Beau went to join the men playing billiards and talking.

Summer had been searching frantically; now she spotted Angela walking through the dining room, her clothes slightly mussed. She grabbed her arm. "You brat, have you been drinking?"

Angela looked at her with those eyes as cold as ice flakes and smiled. "I've been doing a lot of things; things that would surprise you—"

"Angela!" Father rounded the corner then and glared at them both. "What have you been up to?" He took a deep breath. "Liquor! Have you been drinking?"

"I'm a bit tipsy, that's all." She stood her ground.

Father caught her arm. "I won't have this, young lady! You hear? I've had one daughter humiliate me, but you won't be the second."

Summer winced. "Father, let me walk her around out in the cool air and—"

"No," Father said, "she's going home!" He led her toward the kitchen door. "I'll have Flannigan take her home in the carriage and come back for me later." He smiled. "I imagine Beau will want to drive you home, Summer."

"I don't want to go home." Angela pouted. "I want to stay here where the fun is!"

Summer pictured herself fighting off Beau's ardent advances in his carriage when they were alone. "Father, I'll ride home with Angela, look after her."

"No," Father snapped, "I accepted this invitation so someone would marry you; so you circulate, look for Beau. He'll be delighted to see you home, I'm sure."

Angela grinned. "I know something about—"

"Be quiet!" Father thundered. "Flannigan will take you home, and no one need ever know what a fool you made of yourself tonight. Tomorrow, we'll talk, young lady."

Angela was still protesting as Father led her out the side door to the family carriage. Summer breathed a sigh of relief that nothing scandalous had happened. When Father returned, she saw him heading for the billiard room to smoke a cigar with Robert Shaw and the other older businessmen.

Well, she had put it off as long as she could; she supposed she'd have to go be charming to Beau and the other young gentlemen. Pasting a weak smile on her lips, she went back to the ballroom and found Beau.

"Summer?" He took her hand, kissed it. She noticed his fingers were sweaty and trembling. "I've been looking for you; where have you been?"

She didn't want to tell him about the trouble with her younger sister. He was holding her hand as if he didn't intend to let it go the rest of the evening. Was he going to ask her to marry him? She hoped not, because Father would be upset if she turned him down.

Iron Knife thought it seemed a long way from the hotel to the Shaws' home. Or maybe it only seemed like that to Iron Knife because he wasn't sure what he was getting into. He had fought many battles, gone through much danger, but this was unfamiliar to him.

Summer. What was he going to do about her? He

didn't know himself how he would react when he saw her. He was still thinking about it as the carriage clopped down the street and halted before the Shaws' mansion. Iron Knife peered out the window in awe. It had more than one story, white pillars out front and lights streaming from many windows. The courtyard was full of fine carriages and drivers; the sound of music and laughter drifted from inside on the cold autumn night. "What a grand house! This belongs to one family?"

Austin nodded. "Mine. The Van Schuylers live next door, and theirs is every bit as fine as this one."

Iron Knife was still marveling over this fact as the two of them went up the steps to the front door. No wonder Summer had changed her mind and decided to stay in Boston. Perhaps it wasn't that she had a new love; perhaps it was only that she had decided she couldn't live in the poor and primitive way the Cheyenne lived.

From inside, music and laughter floated. They stopped at the big front door. Austin looked over at him. "Are you ready?"

Iron Knife took a deep breath. What would happen when a fully costumed Cheyenne warrior walked into this fine home? It might take more courage to face all these strange, rich white people than fighting soldiers or Pawnees. Then he seemed to see his love's sweet smile, and he would have faced anything, crawled through fire, to get to her. He nodded. "I'm ready."

"Courage, my friend," Austin said, "just keep quiet as much as possible and let me do the talking."

Iron Knife's heart pounded hard; whether from the possible danger or the thought that he was about to come face-to-face with his only love, he couldn't be sure. "I'm ready for whatever comes."

"Then here goes!" In the dim glow of the porch lamps, Austin gave him an encouraging smile as he reached to ring the bell.

Chapter Twenty-three

Iron Knife held his breath as the big door swung wide and the old butler looked surprised. "Mr. Austin!"

"Of course!" He clapped the old man on both shoulders. "And I've brought a friend."

About that time, a small, birdlike woman wearing an elaborate costume and mask and an older, florid-faced man who bore a striking resemblance to Austin appeared in the hall. "Son! Why didn't you let us know you were coming!"

Austin hugged them both. "I wanted to surprise you, and look, I've brought a very good friend with me."

They seemed to pause, staring at Iron Knife's costume.

Austin said, "He's dressed as an authentic Indian chief."

Iron Knife gave them his most disarming smile and bowed low.

"How charming and original," the woman said.

Austin's father shook hands with him. "What did you say your name was?"

"Uh," Iron Knife paused, "Iron Knife."

Mrs. Shaw clapped her hands together. "Staying in character; how clever of you! Why, I'll guess you're one of those young blades from Harvard or Yale."

Iron Knife merely smiled. "You'll have to guess who I am, dear lady."

"Oh, so daring and won't the ladies be abuzz!" Mrs. Shaw fluttered her nervous little hands. "Austin, do make sure your handsome, mysterious friend enters the costume competition and meets all the young ladies."

"I'll do that, Mother. Now we'll mingle and have some refreshments. Are the Van Schuylers here?"

His father said, "Yes, arrived a while ago."

Iron Knife nodded to them again, and Austin motioned for him to follow. As the two went into the ballroom, Iron Knife heard Austin's mother say: "He's bound to be some wealthy young officer from one of the best families. It's such a clever costume."

"Wonder where he managed to rent something like that?" Mr. Shaw said.

Iron Knife breathed a sigh of relief as he and Austin walked toward the refreshment table.

"So far, so good," Austin laughed. "Can you waltz?"

"A little; Summer showed me how once. It isn't something I'd have much use for among the Cheyenne." He glanced around, looking for Summer in the crowd. Many women seemed to be staring at him. Would someone see through his disguise and call the police?

Austin got them each a plate, and they went down the buffet line. "All the ladies are smiling at you," he whispered. "I think they're all hoping you'll ask them to dance."

Iron Knife felt panic. "What will I do?"

"Just smile and look mysterious. That will make you even more interesting to them."

They stood there sipping their drinks and looking around. Iron Knife glanced over the dancers, hoping to see Summer. Then he spotted her across the ballroom talking with a handsome man with sun-streaked hair who was dressed as a pirate and wearing a cutlass. He must have started toward her because Austin caught his arm. "Not yet. Be careful."

Austin was right. Summer looked sad and a little bored. Or maybe he was only wishing that she wasn't enjoying the other man's company. How could he possibly get a chance to talk to her? If he walked over, struck up a conversation, she might be so shocked to see him that she would shriek or faint. He didn't want everyone turning to look if she did, and who knew what that man with her might decide to do? Iron Knife decided he would bide his time.

Mr. Shaw walked up before the orchestra and held up his hand as the dance ended. "All right, everyone, this is the time you have been waiting for all evening long; the costume contest. The winner gets fifty dollars in gold and a dance with the lady of his choice."

All the women giggled and looked embarrassed.

"Now, men"—Mr. Shaw gestured—"don't be shy! If you feel your costume is original enough to win, step right up here and we'll see what the ladies think."

Several handsome young men pushed through the crowds to the front. Iron Knife leaned over to Austin. "Why don't you go up?"

Austin shook his head. "It's my parents' party; I don't think it's proper for me to enter."

Iron Knife watched various men hesitate, then go up to stand next to Mr. Shaw and smile at the crowd.

Mr. Shaw gestured toward the pirate standing with Summer. "Now, there's a handsome swashbuckler who looks like he could steal a lady's heart; come up here and compete."

The man swaggered up to stand next to Mr. Shaw, and Summer smiled at him.

Iron Knife felt jealousy wash over him. Summer had not looked his way yet; she was watching the handsome masked pirate who had been with her. He leaned over to Austin. "Who is that man?"

Austin paused. "Can't be sure behind that mask, but it might be Beau St. Claire; my father does some business with him."

Robert Shaw turned and saw Iron Knife. "Oh, I forgot our visitor who's masquerading as an Indian chief. How about you, sir; won't you compete?"

Iron Knife froze, then slowly shook his head. The last thing he needed was to draw attention to himself; but now Mr. Shaw was asking him again, and the crowd was beginning to applaud, urging him on.

"What should I do?" He leaned over to Austin.

Austin looked alarmed. "I wasn't expecting this," he whispered. "You can't get out of this without making a scene, just go up there and stand and don't say anything."

He had a terrible urge to turn and run out the door. The crowd was applauding. He glanced toward Summer, but she was visiting with a lady standing next to her and hadn't even seemed to notice the stranger. Iron Knife took a deep breath for courage and began to push through the people. Austin was right. He would stand up there and smile, not say anything. Then when one of those others were chosen, he could blend back into the crowd until he could get a chance to speak with Summer Sky. It was all he could do to keep from running to her, sweeping her into his arms. He must not give himself away.

"Now"—Mr. Shaw smiled at the big crowd gathered around in the ballroom—"we have a number of handsome contestants. I'll hold my hand over each one's head, and with your applause, you'll pick the winner."

Iron Knife looked over at Austin, who appeared to be nervous and sweating. What kind of mess had he gotten himself into? He imagined himself in the Boston jail.

He considered running out into the crowd, throwing Summer over his shoulder, and disappearing out the door while people gaped and wondered if it were some kind of joke.

Mr. Shaw held his hand over the Revolutionary War soldier's head. Applause. Next he held his hand over Robin Hood's head. Scattered applause. He went down the line. When he held his hand over the pirate's head, there was a lot of applause, more than anyone had gotten so far. The pirate grinned, confident now he had won.

"One more," Mr. Shaw said, "our mysterious Indian chief costume." He held his hand over Iron Knife's head. Iron Knife was amazed and astounded at the loud applause. He watched Summer. She had started out applauding automatically; now confusion crossed her pretty face, and she hesitated, stared hard. She seemed to be trying to decide if what she was seeing could possibly be. . . .

Robert Shaw said, "Well, there's a clear-cut winner. It seems the ladies really like our Indian chief."

Immediately, the pirate turned and glared at Iron Knife, hand on the hilt of his sword. Iron Knife pretended not to notice, instead kept his gaze on Summer. Her face mirrored confusion, and she shook her head as if she must be having second thoughts about her own sanity.

"Now, sir"—Mr. Shaw placed a pouch of gold coins in his hands—"here's the prize; now which lady would you like as a partner?"

Iron Knife looked toward Summer, then pointed as he disguised his voice. "That one."

A murmur ran through the crowd. Summer was staring at him with a strange expression half of disbelief, half of horror.

Mr. Shaw looked embarrassed. "Oh, perhaps you

haven't heard, sir, Miss Van Schuyler is in mourning; it's really not proper. Please choose another. Come closer, all you pretty misses, so our mysterious Indian chief can choose a dance partner."

Iron Knife started to object, but young ladies in elaborate costumes were crowding around him, giggling and fluttering their fans. What to do now? He didn't wish to insult any of the women, but he wanted to get across the room to Summer. The orchestra had started playing again, and the ladies were crowded around him. For a long moment, he was in a panic. If any of them saw how poorly he danced, they would know immediately that he was no wealthy, young aristocrat. He didn't want to get Austin in trouble, and he certainly didn't want to end up in jail, held on a murder charge. "Ladies, you're all so charming, I just can't make up my mind." He gestured Austin over. "Austin, would you dance with all these ladies and decide which one I choose?"

Before Austin could say anything, Iron Knife had him by the arm, handing him over as a sacrifice to the giggling bevy of Boston debutantes. Then Iron Knife pushed through the crowd, looking for Summer.

Summer had stood there staring at the tall man in the Indian costume. Surely that couldn't be—? No, of course not. Even if Iron Knife had somehow managed to get to Boston, what would he be doing at an elegant society ball? She would have to talk to that mysterious man. From this distance, she was certain it was her beloved, but it just wasn't possible. She began to push through the crowd toward him. "Excuse me. Excuse me, please."

The orchestra struck up a waltz, and abruptly, Beau was at her elbow. "Imagine the nerve of that young rake! He must have friends in the audience applauding for him; that's all I've got to say. I presume you're saving this dance for me, Summer?"

She tried to object, but Beau swept her into his embrace. Across the room, the handsome, costumed man was surrounded by admiring ladies. She must get to him—talk to him. Even as she objected, Beau danced her off the floor, took her arm. "We need to talk, my dear."

"Yes, we do, Beau, you see—"

"Not here, dear girl." Even as she tried to explain, he was steering her down the hall to the conservatory.

When Iron Knife pulled clear of the lady admirers and looked around the crowded ballroom, he saw no sign of Summer or that pirate either.

Mr. Shaw stood visiting the two old ladies near the refreshment table. "Excuse me," Iron Knife said, "did you see Summer Van Schuyler?"

"Why, yes," the plump, red-faced man blustered, "I believe I saw her leave the floor with young Beau St. Claire." He gestured.

"Who?"

"You know, the dashing pirate."

"Of course." Beau St. Claire, the man gossip said had been courting Summer. With the music playing, the big crowd and people out on the floor dancing and laughing, they didn't even seem to notice Iron Knife as he turned toward the hall.

Now just where had Summer and that pirate disappeared to? Silent as a stalking panther, he went down the hall of the fine home, glancing in the parlor, the library, the music room, as he passed. Where could they have gone? Had they left the party? He wanted to smash that pirate's grinning face at the thought that even now the other man might be standing in the darkness somewhere kissing Summer.

Iron Knife passed a big glass room that seemed to be

almost a jungle, a steamy room full of plants. He stepped inside, take a deep breath. The scent of flower hung on the air, and it was lit only by the full moon out side and the light from the hallway. He could hear a man's and woman's voice as he crept between the plants.

". . . Beau, I really think we should rejoin the others."

"Now, let's just sit out here on this bench a moment," the man's oily voice said. "We've got so much to talk about."

"Couldn't it wait? I've got to get back. There's a man—"

"No, it can't wait because I want to kiss you."

"No, Beau, I don't think—" and then sounds as if the pirate was kissing her anyway.

His woman. Iron Knife felt his jealous fury flash like gunpowder as he crossed the shadowy greenhouse. Now he could see their outlines, the man kissing and caress ing the woman as she struggled to pull away.

"Don't, Beau, you're drunk and this isn't the time or place!"

"Oh, but we'll be wed soon, so don't be modest with me, Summer."

The slight girl slapped him hard across the face.

"You little wench, don't play indignant with me!" The man grabbed her wrist and yanked her to him, his mouth covering hers.

Iron Knife crossed the distance between them, his heart pounding with fury. He caught the white man's arm, whirled him around, and hit him as hard as he could, putting all his fury into the blow. "Get your hands off her!"

Summer cried out in surprise as Iron Knife stepped out of the darkness and hit Beau hard enough to send him staggering. However, in the ballroom, the music played loudly as the crowd did a folk dance, so she was certain no one could hear the disturbance.

The two men meshed and fought, knocking over potted plants as they did so. In the darkness of the conservatory, all she could do was stay out of their way as the two struggled. Should she go for help? Call the police? She couldn't even tell who was winning except that now and then the moonlight touched them as they meshed and fought, sending pots of flowers crashing. "Stop, you two! Stop this, do you hear me?"

Beau drew his sword with a terrible oath; the moonlight filtering through the conservatory reflected on it. "I'm goin' to geld you like a nigger slave!"

The other man dodged as Beau slashed, then caught Beau's wrist in a powerful grip. Beau screamed out as he dropped the sword.

"We'll see who gets gelded!" The light gleamed on the blade of the big sword as the other grabbed it and held it to Beau's throat.

"Oh, my God!" Summer shrieked. "Don't! Iron Knife, don't kill him!"

He paused, the sword at the other man's throat. "You've made your choice then, Little One; I make you a gift of him!" The big man tossed the sword away with a clatter, picked up the whimpering pirate, and threw him at Summer's feet. Then he turned to stride toward the outside door at the end of the conservatory.

Beau groaned in a heap at her feet, but she stared after the silhouette of the victor. Iron Knife here in Boston and now he was leaving. The angry resignation in his tone, the way he walked, told her that when he went through that door, she would never see him again. She had only a moment to make her decision before he exited her life forever. In that split-second, she thought about his sleeping with Gray Dove and the hardships and dangers of life among the Cheyenne.

She balanced those things against the love she felt for him. Was it worth it? At that moment, Summer seemed to hear her mother's voice: *When you find a once in a lifetime love, run after him, don't look back and damn the consequences!*

"Iron Knife! Wait! For God's sake, stop!" He paused with his hand on the door handle and turned even as Summer hurried toward him. "Iron Knife, don't leave without me, my dearest!"

Once, a long time ago, he had asked the question he asked now: "Who are you?"

There was only one answer; only one. "I am Summer Sky of the Hevataniu Cheyenne, and I am Iron Knife's woman!" She ran into his powerful arms.

He reached out and dragged her to him. He swept her into his embrace, holding her so tightly, she wasn't certain she could breathe as his mouth covered hers, possessively, passionately. She threw her arms around his neck and held him close, her body shaking with emotion and unshed tears as his mouth claimed hers, and they melted together. She didn't try to speak; she let him kiss her in a way she had only dreamed of in all these lonely months. *Iron Knife! Oh, Iron Knife, my love!* She was where she wanted to be, no matter what he had done; no matter the consequences of loving him so!

She had a million questions to ask, but nothing mattered at this moment but that she was in her true love's embrace and he was kissing her as if he would never get enough of her. "Iron Knife," she murmured. "Oh, I'm so glad to see you!"

Nearby, Beau groaned and attempted to get up.

Iron Knife paused, and looked down into her face. His expression told her he had questions, too; but for that moment, they only looked deep into each other's eyes, and he seemed to see what he was looking for there. "Are you going with me?"

"You know I am; did you ever doubt it? Nothing matters to me as much as you do!"

Without another word, he swung her up in his strong arms. "Then come, my once in a lifetime love, let's go get our children."

"Wait, you two!" She heard Austin's voice as he ran into the conservatory.

"Don't try to stop us," Iron Knife threatened.

"Stop you?" Austin laughed. "I'm going to help you. I've got a carriage waiting just outside the conservatory door!"

Summer slipped her arms around her lover's brawny neck and laid her face against his powerful shoulder as the three of them hurried into the cool night and got into the coach. Iron Knife didn't relax his grip and held her close as the carriage went out the gates and down the street to the Van Schuyler estate. She was safe in the warm haven of her love's protective arms, and it felt as good, as secure, as she remembered.

"Thank you, Austin," she murmured.

He shrugged. "Always your best friend, Summer," he said, and he sounded as if he were trying to keep his voice light. "All these years, I was always your best friend; nothing more than that."

"And my good friend, too," Iron Knife said, "thank you, Austin."

"I want Summer to be happy," Austin said, "and I'll do whatever it takes to accomplish that."

"Oh, Austin," she began, but he gestured her into silence.

"It's difficult enough for me," he said softly, "handing you over to another man; don't make it worse. I'm going to try to get you on that late night train before Silas realizes you've left the party and calls the police."

Austin really had changed, she thought; in the past he
would never have done such a scandalous, daring thing.
His mother would be furious, and who knew what Boston society would say?

Iron Knife held her against him as if he would never
let her go, and it was enough, she thought, enough.

They drew up before the ugly Victorian house.

"Go in and get the children," Austin said, "but be
quick about it. I'll wait with the carriage. Hurry now;
we may have Beau, Silas and the whole Boston police
on the way!"

Chapter Twenty-four

Summer and Iron Knife ran from the carriage to the door. She rang the bell again and again, conscious of the precious moments slipping away. Finally she heard Evans coming to answer it. She got one look at the sleepy butler's shocked face as he saw Iron Knife and tried to close the door again, but Iron Knife kicked it open and pushed him aside. "Out of our way, or I may slit your throat!"

With a frightened cry, Evans turned and fled.

Summer laughed. "That's the only time I've seen him lose his composure in all these years. We have to hurry." They ran up the stairs. Summer awakened Mrs. O'Malley and quickly explained.

"Ah, lamb, are ye sure you're doin' the right thing now?"

"I'm following my heart; that's all I know," Summer answered.

The plump widow smiled. " 'Tis a shame your dear mother didn't. I'll help you."

"We've got to hurry," Summer said. "Any moment, I expect Father to show up."

"And you're afraid of him, lass?"

Summer paused. Without thinking, she reached to touch the little gold locket around her neck under the

mourning dress. Like her mother, all her life, Summer
had cowered before Silas and his angry bluster. He had
kept the whole family in line with his fury, and only
rarely did any of them dare confront him. It wasn't too
late. "I will stand up to him if need be," Summer said
with conviction. "I'm going with my man!"

Mrs. O'Malley brought out Priscilla's little suitcase. "She would like you to use it for this, lamb, I'm
sure."

"I suppose it's poetic justice," Summer answered.
They packed only a few things. "Where I'm going,"
Summer said, "I lead a simple life; I won't need
much."

As she started down the hall toward the nursery,
Angela stuck her head out of her door, looking sleepy
and rumpled. "What's the confusion about?"

Summer paused. "Angela, I'm leaving; returning to
Colorado."

Had she expected dismay or sadness from her sister?
Angela actually grinned. "Good! I'm sick of competing
with your children for Father's attention."

"Angela," Mrs. O'Malley scolded, "that's not nice!"

"I am tired of being 'nice,' being shuttled aside while
Father makes plans to hand over everything to Lance. I
want it all."

Summer smiled sadly at her. "I pity you, little sister,
you'll have it all, all right. I hope you don't end up like
King Midas."

Leaving Angela staring after them, Summer and Iron
Knife went to the nursery, where she introduced him to
his two new daughters. The babies were asleep, but Iron
Knife gently touched their soft cheeks, his dark eyes
filled with tenderness and awe. Then he gathered his
three sleepy children around him and held them close.

"My children," Iron Knife murmured in Cheyenne.
"I've come to take you home."

Storm said, "I thought you wouldn't come for us."

"Never!" Iron Knife said. "Nothing could separate
me from my family."

Garnet had her arms around his neck, squealing in
Cheyenne, "Daddy! Daddy!"

Even Lance appeared delighted as Summer and the
plump maid dressed the children quickly.

Summer took a sleeping baby and grasped Lance's
hand. Mrs. O'Malley carried the other twin and took
Storm's hand. Iron Knife picked up Garnet and took one
of the suitcases. "Have we got everything? Let's go,
then, before Silas gets here!"

"Too late!" Mrs. O'Malley gasped. "Me thinks I just
heard a carriage crossing the cobblestones out front!"

Iron Knife looked at Summer, and when their eyes
met, she knew he was asking if she had the nerve to
defy her father for the sake of love.

"Let's go!" Summer said. The three of them and the
children hurried down the stairs. Just as they reached
the front hall, the door burst open, and Silas stood there,
red-faced and angry.

"Not so fast, young lady!"

Summer took a deep breath. "Father, don't waste
your time. I'm going to do now what I should have
done last spring; I'm going back west!"

The butler came into the hall just then, and Silas gestured to him. "Quick, Evans, go for the police!"

"Yes sir!" Before anyone could stop him, the man
was out the front door.

Silas smiled. "Now, while we wait, let's be reason-
able, shall we, and discuss this?"

Iron Knife shook his head. "I love Summer and I'm
taking her back with me."

"And what can you offer her?" Father's face was distorted with sarcastic scorn.

"Love," Iron Knife said simply, "only love."

"Love!" Silas' lip curled, and his eyes grew colder. "Sentimental twaddle; that's all." He shook his finger in Summer's face. "I haven't gone to this much trouble to keep you here all these months so you can throw it all away for silly claptrap!"

Summer took a deep breath. "Father, get out of our way or we'll miss our train."

"The police will be here any minute," Silas said. "Don't do something foolish that you'll regret, Summer, don't throw it all away for this—this savage."

Iron Knife's face darkened with anger. "If you were a younger man and not the honored father of my woman, I'd kill you for that insult."

"Neither of you appreciate what I can do for the children," Silas shouted. "Why do you think I went to all that trouble with the fake telegrams? Someone in this family had to do something to separate you two. I want my grandchildren raised as Van Schuylers!"

Summer looked at him a long moment, then at Iron Knife. Their eyes met, and she saw the sudden realization there of what the old man had done. "You are despicable, Father. I don't know how you can live with yourself with your plots and lies!"

"Oh, you're so high and mighty, just like your mother!" Silas roared like a wounded lion. "She thought love meant everything and look what it got her!"

"And where did your money get you?" Summer asked.

He reacted as if she had struck him hard, and his shoulders slumped. Suddenly, she felt very sorry for him. "Goodbye, Father."

She wanted to reach out to him, leave him on some sympathetic note, but he only glared at her. She was free of his fury, of his bullying tactics, she realized now. "Goodbye, Mrs. O'Malley, and Godspeed. Come on,

Iron Knife, let's get out of here before Evans returns with the police."

The Irish maid hugged her and dabbed at her eyes as she handed over her little charges. Gathering up the children, they brushed past Silas and went out the door into the night.

Austin rushed to help them into the carriage and shouted orders to the driver. As the carriage raced down the drive, Summer said, "Austin, we'll have to hurry; Evans has gone for the police."

"Has he now?" Even in the moonlight, she could see him smile as he lit his pipe. "Actually, Silas only *thinks* he's gone for the law. In reality, I gave that pompous rascal a good whack on the head and laid him behind the shrubbery."

"What?" Iron Knife said.

Austin chuckled, obviously quite pleased with himself. "By the time Silas finds him and they do send for the police, I expect to have you on that train. It leaves in about fifteen minutes. By the way, while you were in my conservatory, I ran up to my room and got a few clothes for you, Iron Knife. I'm sure you will want to change on the train so you won't be so conspicuous."

Summer leaned back against the seat and sighed with relief, holding the sleeping twins close. "Austin, you amaze me."

He smiled and smoked his pipe. "I'm just being a good friend; that's all."

The children were cuddled down around them, all half-asleep as the carriage raced toward the station in the chill night. They caught the train just as it was about to pull out. Summer hugged Austin. "Thank you, I can never repay you."

"I did it for friendship and love," Austin said gruffly. Then he blinked as if to clear his eyes of a mist, waved, turned and disappeared into the darkness, walking rapidly.

As they boarded the train, Iron Knife said, "He loved you; he was good to help me."

"I know." She sank down on the seat as the train whistled and chugged out of the station. She didn't look back at the lights of the city as they pulled away.

Back at the house, Silas stood staring into his library fire, wondering what was keeping Evans and the police. If they hurried, they could still take her off that train. Summer wasn't legally married to that savage. Silas would have her placed in a mental hospital and that savage in jail.

He heard the door behind him creak. Summer. She had reconsidered and come back. With a great sense of relief, he turned. "I wondered if you'd—"

It was Angela. She stood in the doorway in her nightgown holding her cat. "They're gone?"

He didn't like the smug satisfaction in her voice. "They're gone; and after everything I did for them."

"You still have me. In fact, I'm all you've got left, Father."

"I had such plans," he muttered.

"I do, too. You underestimate me."

He only grunted and returned to staring into the fire. The big house seemed so very empty. The wind had picked up and rattled the shingles and whistled through the eaves. It almost sounded like a woman's mocking laughter. Priscilla. She had won after all. He had everything and he had nothing. *What is a man profited if he gain the whole world and lose his own soul?*

He had forgotten that there was anyone else in the room until the cat meowed. "Go to bed!" he bellowed.

Angela watched his stooped shoulders a long moment. He really was getting old and weak. It was only a matter of time before his anger pushed him into a stroke or heart attack. By then, Angela would be grown up, and she would push him aside, take over the helm of the Van Schuyler empire. She would show him what ruthless ambition was; she was more of a Van Schuyler than any of them. "Good night, Father." She paused in the doorway and smirked. "Oh, by the way, Evans never went for the police. I think he's out front someplace in the shrubbery."

"How do you know—?" He knew better than ask that. Silas watched his youngest leave the room and heard her go up the stairs. Once again, he remembered the history of the Blackledge family and shuddered with apprehension. Perhaps he had underestimated Angela; perhaps Priscilla would finally have her revenge after all.

Summer settled herself in the train seat next to Iron Knife. The babies were asleep, but the other three were chattering with excitement as they pressed small faces against the glass and stared out at the passing darkness. "Happy, my love?"

He hugged her against him and kissed her. "Happier than you'll ever know!"

She thought about Gray Dove one more time, then closed her mind on that forever. While it might hurt to think of Iron Knife making love to the Arapaho girl, she understood now and she had almost wrecked what she had. *Love and relationships are very fragile*, Summer thought, *like roses, they need tender care; they don't just grow and flourish on their own.* She loved him, and because of that, she would forgive and forget everything but that he loved her, too. The train whistled and began to pick up speed as it hurtled into the night.

"Little One, what are you thinking?"

There were times when truth was not the best thing for a relationship, Summer thought. "Nothing; nothing except how happy I am to be with you again. I—I think I should tell you Dr. Morgan says I can never have another child."

He leaned over and kissed the tip of her nose. "What would we do with more than five, Little One? As it is now, I'll have to be the Cheyennes' best hunter to feed them all." He looked around at his sturdy brood, pride on his handsome features.

"You are the Cheyennes' best hunter," she reminded him, "and now we won't have to worry about making love."

He grinned. "Don't you think I haven't thought of that?"

"You rascal!" She reached to kiss him. "Somehow, I think our five will help write the history of the West."

He nodded agreement. "Lance, Storm, Garnet, Lark and Lacy. If only we could look into the future and see what excitement and adventure awaits them."

She reached to pull the blanket over the sleeping twins. "The West is changing, whether we like it or not, and who knows what will be happening fifteen or twenty years from now?"

His face saddened only a moment. "Perhaps things will not improve for the Indian people."

Summer considered a long moment. "We can't help that, my dearest. I only know that we have strong children and that they will adjust, survive and maybe prosper as the West tames down."

He held her close. "We won't worry about that now," he whispered. "It is enough that we are all together again. I only regret I never got to marry you in the white man's way," he whispered.

"Does it mean so much to you?" she asked. "We've done the Cheyenne ceremony."

"I would like to know that you care enough about me to stand up before the whites and say you belong to me forever and always," he said.

"Hmm." Summer leaned back against the seat and began to think.

The trip with five noisy children was difficult, but every time she looked up and saw her beloved, she was so glad to be on her way back to Colorado. They discussed all the wires and letters, shocked at what Silas had done attempting to destroy their union. At one station along the way, Summer slipped away and sent a wire to Todd in Denver.

When Iron Knife and Summer Sky finally reached the end of the track, they took a stagecoach the rest of the way, but evidence of rail building and track laying was everywhere.

Summer said, "You know, some of my father's friends are involved with that railroad; they say it will be across the whole country in a couple more years."

Iron Knife frowned as the stage rocked along. "That means that the time of the Indian grows short. Soon there will be trains all across our buffalo plains, and the wild free days will be gone forever."

Little Lance looked up at him solemnly with his bright blue eyes. "Then I shall become governor or maybe a senator, like Grandfather Van Schuyler says, and do good things for my people."

She started to smile, then realized her handsome but solemn little boy was serious. "I'm sure you will, Lance."

Storm Gathering scowled. "And I will kill and scalp many white men and become a great warrior."

Iron Knife smiled and looked from the two little boys to their three girls. "I think our five children will play a big role in the West's history. By the way, Little One, I know it has bothered you to have me riding with war parties."

"It has," she admitted.

"Black Kettle and his band have headed south and are going to try again to live at peace with the white men; I thought we'd join them. No more war parties for me."

She threw her arms around his neck and hugged him. "I love you," she whispered, "and I've got a surprise for you."

"What?"

She winked at him. "You'll just have to wait until we get there; that's all."

"Maybe I'll kiss you 'til you tell me," he wheedled.

"Try me!" she challenged; but about that time, one of the twins woke up hungry, and she was too busy shushing her to be kissed.

"Just wait, Little One," Iron Knife said, "just wait until I finally get you alone."

She smiled at the memory of his lovemaking. "Oh, we have so much time to make up for."

"By the way," he hesitated, "I forgot to tell you that on my trip up to Boston, I accidentally met my sister."

"Cimarron? Where?"

"She got off the train in St. Louis. There's a lot to tell, Little One; you have no idea what I've been through getting to you. I've been in jail, on a chain gang; it's a long story."

"Oh, my poor dearest, I want to hear all of it," Summer said, "but tell me first about your sister. Is she all right? Did she know you? Is she married?"

"Wait! Wait!" He held up his hands and smiled. "One thing at a time! Cimarron is married to a handsome half-breed named Trace Durango who owns a big ranch in Texas. She's invited us to come down and bring the children."

Summer laid her face against her shoulder. "I'm glad you found her; I'll be eager to meet her."

A troubled look crossed his rugged face as if he were remembering the circumstances of their meeting. Abruptly, he hugged Summer to him. "Have I told you I love you?"

"About a million times since I got on this train, but I like to hear it again."

When they finally got off the stage in Denver, Todd, Silver and Cherokee were waiting for them. Summer hugged her friend. "I'm so glad to see you."

Little Wannie pressed forward. "I got a new dress for the wedding—"

"Wannie!" Keso scolded. "Dumb little kid, tellin' the secret."

"What secret?" Iron Knife asked.

Cherokee grinned and pushed his hat back. "Well, now, I reckon it isn't. The womenfolk have been plotting by telegraph."

Todd smiled and reached out to shake his hand. "You don't know it, Iron Knife, but you're getting married today."

"What?" He looked at Summer as they stood next to the buggy.

Summer held a baby in each arm. "Are you turning me down? You said someday you wanted me to stand up before white people and say I loved you enough to take you in a white man's ceremony."

She saw tears come to his eyes, and he blinked and cleared his throat. "Oh, Summer!"

"Now, stop it, or you'll have me in tears," she said.

They began getting in the buggy, Keso driving.

Silver chimed in, "After Todd got Summer's wire, he contacted me and I got busy, hunted up the preacher who married us to do yours. We've even got a wedding cake."

Keso picked up the reins. He glanced back, his dark eyes alight. "Good! I love cake."

Little Wannie clambered up on the seat beside him. "And Silvery says I get to dress up and be a bridesmaid with a new dress and jewelry."

"Humph! Women!" Keso snorted. "Here, Lance, climb up here by me."

Wannie pushed Lance to one side. "I sit be Keso, you sit by me, Lance."

Summer smiled. "Do we have a romance going here?"

Keso blushed crimson. "Wannie? Why, she's just a dumb little girl! Tell you what, kids, Lance, you sit on one side, Wannie, you sit on the other, and I'll sit in the middle." He turned to the amused adults. "Dad, will you put the rest of those babies in the back with you?"

Cherokee nodded. "Sure, Keso."

However, Storm Gathering retorted, "Me no baby!"

Iron Knife chuckled and put his son in his lap while Summer and Silver each took a twin. They drove out to the Evans' cabin high in the Rockies where the old preacher waited. The groom wore buckskins; the bride, her finest white doeskin ceremonial dress with much fringe, beadwork and elks' teeth—the legendary One Thousand dress.

The minister cleared his throat. "Now, if someone will keep those two little boys from chasing each other around the table, and Keso, you see if you can keep those twins quiet, we'll begin." He looked at all the little ones, awestruck. "Are these all yours?" he asked Summer.

"No, only five of them."

"Then it's high time you did this, young lady." The old man again cleared his throat. "Dearly beloved, we are gathered together today before God and these witnesses. . . ."

Summer reached out and took Iron Knife's hand. Her heart was so full, she felt it would burst. Tears rose to her eyes, and she blinked them away. *You never appreciate love until you almost lose it,* she thought. *True love may sometimes have a rocky road; but it lasts. It endures against all odds. That's how you know when you've found the real thing.*

She looked up at him and smiled. Iron Knife looked into her eyes, clutching her hand as if he would never let it go.

". . . and do you, Summer Priscilla Van Schuyler, take this man to be your lawful wedded husband, from this day forward, forsaking all others as long as you both shall live?"

"Excuse me," she corrected him, "I am Summer Sky of the Hevataniu band of Cheyenne."

"All right, do you take him as your husband?"

She looked deep into her love's eyes. "I do."

"And do you, Iron Knife, take Summer Sky to be your lawfully wedded wife, forsaking all others as long as you both shall live?"

"I do."

"Then, by the power vested in me by God and the Territory of Colorado, I now pronounce you husband and wife. You may kiss your bride."

He took both her hands in his and looked down at her. For a long moment, no one else existed in the whole world but the two of them. *"Ne-mehotatse,"* he whispered.

"Ne-mehotatse, my once in a lifetime love."

They went into each other's arms, and he kissed her, holding her close against his heart. If she had him, she didn't need gold or power. No, she thought, she was already rich.

In the background, the children were fidgeting and punching each other. "Cake! Let's have cake!"

The adults all laughed. "All right, cake it is!"

Iron Knife leaned over and kissed her again. "Happy, my Little One?"

"Happy!" She nodded, eyes shining. Tomorrow after their honeymoon night in the Evans' cabin, they would ride south and rejoin the Cheyenne, but for tonight, they were just another newly married couple.

Silver took over dealing with the children for a few precious hours, and Summer and Iron Knife could at last retire behind their closed bedroom door.

"I didn't think the house would ever get quiet." She sighed.

"I know." He kissed her bare shoulder as he pulled her dress low. He was kissing along her collarbone in a way that sent chills up and down Summer's back. "Are you cold?"

"No, you do that to me"—she smiled—"the way you kiss me."

"I intend to kiss every inch of you," he said, "and see if you still taste the way you always did."

"Right now, it's enough to just hold you." She sighed, and they held each other close so that she could hear his heart beating against her. How could she ever have thought she could live without him?

She lay back on the pillow and looked down at his black hair and his dark skin against her white breast. His hot, greedy mouth fastened on her nipple, and she watched his big, hard hand kneading her other breast. Heat began to radiate through her body as he caressed her bare skin. "Tell me how much you love me."

"I'd rather show you," he whispered, and his breath was warm against her skin as he stroked her, his hand moving lower until he caressed her dewy velvet place.

"Women like to be told," she said.

"You yellow-haired vixen, isn't it enough that I traveled over a thousand miles against all sorts of odds to reclaim you, and now you want me to grovel and beg for your favors?"

"Did you fight any dragons along the way getting there?"

He hesitated a long moment. "Oh, Little One, if you only knew what all I have been through to get to you." There was anguish in his voice. Someday there were things he would tell her—things he had suffered along the way—but tonight, all that was important was that they had each other and their love. Whatever had happened in the past didn't matter; all that mattered was being together; all that mattered were their fine, strong children. Summer took a deep breath and stroked his hair. "Do you love me?"

He looked up at her, caught her hand, and kissed her fingertips. "More than anything in this world, and I would have crawled through hell to get to you!"

In stroking his hair, she found a scar that had not been there before and wondered how he had come by it, but she did not ask. Someday he would tell her of his adventures getting to Boston, but not tonight. "If you love me, dearest, I don't care about anything else."

"Hahoo naa ne-mehotatse," he whispered, *thank you and I love you.* He looked relieved as he reached to kiss her. "You make love to me, too."

She needed no urging. She knew every nerve in his body, every response after all these years. Summer ran her fingertips over his nipples, and he moaned aloud and kissed the tips of her fingers. "You like that, do you?" She smiled.

"I love it; don't stop!"

So they touched and stroked and kissed; exploring every inch of skin, every nerve ending, every kiss as if it were for the very first time; reveling in each other's bodies, each other's love. And finally he took her gently, holding her safe and secure in his love and devotion as he entered her and brought her the gift of his passion.

She answered his need with her own, swift and sure and surging as she took him deep inside her. Even as the embrace deepened, she locked her arms and thighs around him and felt his mouth cover and claim hers. He caressed the inside of her mouth, teasing and tantalizing with his tongue deep inside her throat as her body took his deep into her very core, wanting more than just seed, wanting an affirmation of his love and caring.

"Give me everything you've got," she demanded in a hoarse whisper.

"You blond vixen, I haven't got any more to give," he whispered, and then he thrust into her hard one more time and surrendered to his ecstasy. His passion ignited hers, and they locked onto each other's bodies and drifted away into sweet splendor. Finally they drifted back off to sleep, naked and fulfilled, wrapped in each other's arms and with her head in the hollow of his broad shoulder. For the first time in almost a year, she slept soundly, satisfied and well-loved in her Cheyenne warrior's embrace. Where he was, there she would always be, safe in the arms of love.

To My Readers

CHEYENNE SPLENDOR is the long-awaited sequel to my first best-seller, *CHEYENNE CAPTIVE,* the Zebra novel that won the 1987 Best Indian Romance by a New Author Award from *Romantic Times* magazine. Yes, *CHEYENNE CAPTIVE* has been reprinted and is available at this time from Zebra Books, and eventually, I will do novels about all five of Summer's children.

The novel you have just read is #12 of my Panorama of the Old West series. Iron Knife's sister, Cimarron, had her own Zebra romance called *CHEYENNE PRINCESS.* The Van Schuylers' red-haired Irish servant, Sassy Malone, became the heroine of her own novel, *HALF-BREED'S BRIDE.* Silver and Cherokee Evans also had their own book, *QUICKSILVER PASSION.* Someday, I'll also tell the story of Wannie and Keso when they grow up and get caught in Colorado's Ute Indian war. We also haven't seen the last of the Van Schuylers, the O'Bannions, St. Claires, and some of the others.

By the way, there is no town in Missouri named Wartonville; it is strictly fictional.

Someday I'll tell you the story of the worst wagon train tragedy in the history of the California-Oregon Trail, the one Deek Tanner mentioned. Some of you may think I'm speaking of the ill-fated Donner party that became stranded in the Sierra Nevadas and resorted to cannibalism to survive. You're wrong. Believe it or not, there was a worse disaster than that; one very few people know about.

The year 1864 was the third bloodiest year in the Indian wars for the whites: 357 whites killed. The worst year was 1862, the year of the bloody Sioux uprising in Minnesota when 630 whites died. We can only guess at the number of Indian fatalities, but they must have been high; nor do historians agree on the number of casualties at Sand Creek. For more information on that time, you might enjoy a research book called *THE INDIAN WAR OF 1864,* by Eugene F. Ware.

I have been in Julesburg, Colorado, for research and walked that area where the battle was fought. I have also walked the ground at Sand Creek and talked with the rancher who owns the land. There's not much to see except barren, windswept prairie, but if you're curious, the site is about fifteen miles northeast of the city of Lamar.

In the ensuing outcry and investigation over the Sand Creek Massacre, the public forgot Chivington's service as a minister of the gospel, his stance as an abolitionist, and the fact that he was the hero of Glorietta Pass. His career destroyed, he spent the rest of his life trying to justify his actions that November dawn. He died of cancer in 1894 and is buried in Denver's Fairmont Cemetery. You may not know that John Evans, Colorado Territorial Governor in 1864, who encouraged action against the hostile Indians, was first offered the governorship of Washington Territory, or that he was one of the founders of Northwestern University, or that the city of Evanston, Illinois, is named for him. Of the men who rode with Chivington that day, Lieutenant George L.

Shoup became Territorial Governor of Idaho, and Major Jacob Downing became a Colorado millionaire.

Some historians have suggested that the South may have possibly fomented and encouraged Indian trouble to keep Union troops busy. The Indian war spread over hundreds of miles into Kansas and Nebraska because the old chiefs could not always control hot-headed young warriors.

Black Kettle wrote to S.G. Colley, the Indian agent, in a letter dated August 29th, 1964:

> ... *We heard that you have some prisoners in Denver; we have seven prisoners of yours which we are willing to give up, providing you give up yours. There are three war parties out yet, and two of Araphahos; they have been out sometime and expected in soon....*

Unfortunately, one of those prisoners, a Mrs. Snyder, committed suicide before she could be returned.

Later, scientists would dig up many of the Indian dead and send the bones to the Smithsonian Institute in Washington, D.C. as curiosities. In the summer of 1993, attempting to finally bring justice to the slain, the Smithsonian turned these bones over to three Cheyenne elders, who brought them back to my home state, Oklahoma, to be reburied with proper ceremonies near tribal headquarters in the town of Concho.

There have been a number of books written about the Cheyenne and Sand Creek, one of them by an Oklahoma college professor friend of mine, Stan Hoig, published by University of Oklahoma Press, *THE SAND CREEK MASSACRE*. For the opposing viewpoint, you might be interested in reading *I STAND BY SAND CREEK,* by Lieutenant Colonel William R. Dunn, published by Old Army Press. For further reading, I recommend *THE FIGHTING CHEYENNES* by George B. Grinnell, published by the University of Oklahoma Press, and *BURY MY HEART AT WOUNDED KNEE: AN INDIAN HISTORY OF THE AMERICAN WEST,* by Dee Brown, published by Dell.

George Armstrong Custer was the youngest general of the Civil War, and while he might have been reckless and foolhardy, no one ever questioned his bravery. General Sheridan admired the young officer and his wife so much that he gave Custer the table on which the surrender was written as a souvenir for Custer's wife, Libby. Today, that table is in the Smithsonian Museum in Washington, D.C. The marble-topped table on which the surrender was actually signed was presented to General Ord and is today owned by the Chicago Historical Society.

The Lincoln assassination left even further tragedies yet to unfold. When John Wilkes Booth stabbed Major Rathbone as the brave officer attempted to disarm the actor, Rathbone's blood splashed Miss Harris' lovely satin dress. The major survived and later married Clara Harris, but Rathbone could not rid himself of guilt because he had not saved the president. Nor could his wife bring herself to either destroy or clean and wear that dress again. She finally had it walled up in a closet. Over the years, the self-tormented major began to go insane.

Christmas Eve morning of 1883, Rathbone shot his wife to death and attempted to commit suicide with a knife. He survived and was sent to an insane asylum where he lived another twenty-eight years. The year before his death, the couple's son broke through the walled-up closet to retrieve the dress that had been hanging there forty-five years. He burned it as "cursed." That son, Henry Riggs Rathbone, became a U.S. congressman and was instrumental in urging the government to restore Ford's Theater as an important historical site.

You have heard, of course, that Mary Todd Lincoln gradually lost her mind and became such an embarrassment to her only living son, Robert, that he had her temporarily committed to an asylum in 1875.

Another player who ended up in an insane asylum was Boston Corbett, the police officer credited with killing John Wilkes Booth. In his later years, Corbett went berserk and tried to wipe out the Kansas legislature with two pistols.

Doctor Mudd, who was guilty of nothing but treating John Wilkes Booth's broken leg, was eventually released from prison because he had helped battle an epidemic of yellow fever in jail. However, the dour prediction, "Your name is Mudd," has become part of our folklore for the unlucky.

While it is ironic, John Wilkes Booth was actually standing close enough to Lincoln to have killed him during the inauguration. Because he was a celebrity, a legislator's daughter had given Booth tickets to the ceremony.

American Indians fought for both sides in the Civil War; however, only in one battle were American Indians fighting on both sides and against each other; the Battle of Honey Springs in eastern Indian Territory during 1863, won by the Union. This was also one of the first battles using African-American soldiers, the 1st Kansas Infantry. In case you are interested, the very last Confederate general to surrender several months after the war officially ended was a Cherokee, General Stand Watie, in Indian Territory (Oklahoma).

I am always glad to hear from readers. You may write me c/o Zebra Books, and they will forward your letter. I'll send a newsletter and an autographed book mark to those who include a stamped, self-addressed #10 envelope. For those of you in foreign countries, please remember the U.S. government will not allow me to use your foreign postage, so please buy postal vouchers at your post office that I can exchange for American stamps.

What story am I going to tell next? One of the saddest and most heroic chapters of America's Indian past is that of the Nez Percé tribe. Native to the great Northwest and known for their fine Appaloosa horses, they had always lived at peace with the whites—until settlers began to want their land. Trouble escalated when gold was discovered in the area. Then greedy whites clamored to move the Nez Percé to reservations, and the valiant warriors refused. What happened next is one of the most gallant and heartbreaking stories of American history as a handful of Nez Percé held the whole United States Army at bay during four months of 1877. Led by Chief Joseph, they decided to fight their way across fifteen hundred miles of the Pacific Northwest to cross the border into the safety of Canada. They hoped they could link up with Sitting Bull's Lakota (Sioux) who had retreated north after Custer was wiped out at the Little Big Horn the previous year.

Some of you may recall Springtime, the tempestuous Indian girl who was murdered in *HALF-BREED'S BRIDE.* The heroine of my next book is a mixed-blood cousin of Springtime's. Our heroine's been raised back east and returns to the West to work as a teacher among the Nez Percé.

Remember that Iron Knife owns a fine Appaloosa stallion, Spotted Blanket, given to him by a grateful Nez Percé chief for saving his young son's life many years before? That son is all grown up now, tall, darkly handsome, and a warrior riding with Chief Joseph. He's too savage and untamed for our civilized teacher, and he resents her bringing her white ways to his people. Both of them are about to be swept up in a great adventure as the Nez Percé fight their way across the untamed frontier, attempting to reach Canada.

I promise you a three-hankie love story as we ride with this warrior and his love, as free as the wild north wind blowing from the vast reaches of the Canadian wilderness. Look for this #13 novel of my Panorama of the Old West series, a Zebra Super Release, tentatively titled *WARRIOR'S SONG* and set for early summer of 1995.

Hahoo naa ne-mehotatse,

Georgina Gentry

Taylor—made Romance From Zebra Books

WHAT'S LOVE GOT TO DO WITH IT?

Everything . . . Just ask Kathleen Drymon . . . and Zebra Books

CASTAWAY ANGEL	*(3569-1, $4.50/$5.50)*
GENTLE SAVAGE	*(3888-7, $4.50/$5.50)*
MIDNIGHT BRIDE	*(3265-X, $4.50/$5.50)*
VELVET SAVAGE	*(3886-0, $4.50/$5.50)*
TEXAS BLOSSOM	*(3887-9, $4.50/$5.50)*
WARRIOR OF THE SUN	*(3924-7, $4.99/$5.99)*